To

Enjoy!

EVERA DARK

FIRST CUT

S.L. Reid

S.L. Reid

Evera Dark

Copyright © 2016 by S.L. Reid

This book is a work of fiction. The characters, incidents and places are drawn from the author's imagination and not to be construed as real. Any resemblance to actual events or persons, living or dead, is entirely coincidental.

Initial cover design by C. Brennan and S.L. Reid.
Flowers, petals and blood drop by Shutterstock.
Final cover design and all photography by A.D. Jobs.

No part of this publication may be reproduced, distributed, or transmitted in any form or by any means, including photocopying, recording, or other electronic or mechanical methods, without the prior written permission of the author, except in the case of brief quotations embodied in critical reviews and certain other non-commercial uses permitted by copyright law.

Tellwell Talent
www.tellwell.ca

ISBN
978-1-77302-209-3 (Hardcover)
978-1-77302-207-9 (Paperback)
978-1-77302-208-6 (eBook)

*For A.J., my sister, sounding board,
confidante, and best friend.*

*And to J.C. (aka Evera),
for loving my story as much as me.*

"You are the knife I turn inside myself; that is love."

Franz Kafka,
from Letters to Milena

EVERA DARK
FIRST CUT

PROLOGUE

Waiting

She waited with bated breath as his footsteps slowly retreated. He paused and her body stiffened, waiting to see if he had changed his mind and would return. Though whether it would be to help her or finish her off she was uncertain. But his steps quickened, fading into the distance.

With burning lungs, she finally felt safe enough to move and take a breath. She fought the urge to gasp and pull in mouthfuls of crisp, sweet air. Movement would be her biggest enemy. Remaining still would slow the blood flowing between her cold fingers. There was no warmth coming from the morning sun; a blanket of clouds shadowed it, keeping the cold grass frozen. Watching, she saw steam rise beside her body as the heat of her blood spilled onto the icy ground. She shivered.

For a moment, the gravity of what had just transpired tried to make itself known. She struggled to drive it back, terrified of her mind letting it in. The knowledge of what she just lost would be infinitely more devastating than the bullets themselves. Too much violence and lies and betrayal, and so much of it her own design.

Despair washed over her, as the reality of her situation sunk in. She would die here, alone, in this field. Even now, she could sense the cold fingers of death reaching for her.

What would be waiting for her on the other side, she dreaded to imagine. For a second, all of her victims' faces flashed before her. A kaleidoscope of eyes and lips, melted together into a single, grotesque collage. Pushing aside the horrifying image, she concentrated instead on the sound of her heart, counting the beats as the pointless seconds passed. To her ears, the sound was strong and vital. Deep down, under the layers of sadness and pain, she wasn't ready for it all to be over. This surprised her. She had always thought when the time came she would be accepting, relieved to let go of a life overflowing with defects and tragedy.

But surrender had never been a part of who she was. She would continue to hang on, regardless of the outcome. Stay still and silent, anticipating a means to an end, for strength or rescue or death. Her face pressed against the freezing ground, she drank in the living scent of grass and dirt. At that moment, a shard of blue sky pierced the oppressing clouds, allowing some heat to touch her cold cheeks. She closed her eyes against the brilliant sunlight and settled in. And waited.

CHAPTER 1
Nine Days Earlier

Evera Grant closed her eyes and leaned back against the first class airplane seat, reveling in the extra elbow room. She had her earbuds in, but, unlike the other passengers, she wasn't listening to the screen in front of her. A peaceful score composition from *The Painted Veil* by Alexandre Desplat, one of her favorite composers, was playing, a welcome distraction from the ambient noises in the plane. Once they were in the air and leveled off, she could concentrate on the file loaded onto her phone; the bio of her next victim.

She stretched out, trying to relax as the plane gained speed down the runway. The sudden, stomach dropping feel of leaving the ground made her hands sweat. She hated flying, especially commercially. The private plane she had arrived on from West Virginia to New York had been a less nail biting trip; it had been short and turbulence free. Just herself, the pilot and the co-pilot. Unlike this sealed vessel with its claustrophobic crush of hundreds of bodies, each with an uncomfortable array of emotions to plague her.

Regardless of the circumstances, she hated flying in general. The idea of giving over trust and control to strangers was difficult for most people, but for someone with her issues it was akin to torture. Trusting in the competence of every person who touched the plane was an impossibility. Keeping herself occupied was the best way to ward off destructive thoughts of crashing and burning. As the plane leveled off, her anxiety lessened and her fingers released their death grip on the armrest.

Trying to relax her tense position, she stretched her bare, tan legs and waited impatiently for the ping of the seat belt sign. Once it sounded, she rushed to undo her seat belt and reached under the seat in front of her, grabbing her purse. She rifled through it and found her phone. Out of the corner of her eye she spied the stranger in the adjoining seat staring at her. Although, she didn't need to face him to know what he was thinking, as he quickly looked down her top. She felt his lustful thoughts brush uncomfortably against her skin. He tried to glance inconspicuously at her legs as she straightened up, phone in hand, but she caught him. Her emerald, green eyes flashing cold fire. He looked quickly away, back to his closed computer waiting on his lap, and cleared his throat noisily.

She pulled her long auburn hair over her shoulder, hoping to block herself from his view. Looking down distastefully at the mass of reddish brown hair resting on her shoulder, she longed to see her true color for a change. Her natural tone was a deep, rich brown, the color of mink. She had to admit that this was still preferable to blonde, which she detested. Not that she disliked any of the colors in particular, it was just the constant process of coloring her hair to match her assumed identity. Going blonde always destroyed her hair.

Ignoring the man beside her and his irritating desire, still pulsing against her bare arm, she focused on the bio and her mission.

Byron Mensen. Even his name was an unfortunate circumstance, she thought as she perused the file on her small phone screen. He was in his late thirties, although his haphazard appearance gave him the look of a much older man. His bio picture was black and white and just a close-up of his face. His hair was thinning but he kept it long, trying to cover up the patches of shiny scalp showing through. His face was thin in the extreme and he wore glasses that were too large for his face. And most importantly, he liked redheads.

As usual, the Section had included everything pertinent to her mission. Once she felt confident she had gleaned everything she needed to complete her task, she wiped the file from her phone with the Section's extensive cleaning app.

The flight attendant interrupted her train of thought, asking if he could get either herself or the man beside her anything to eat or drink.

The man asked for a bourbon and an extra pillow. Evera requested a bottle of water, purposely ignoring the fact that the man had swayed closer to her during the communal conversation.

The flight attendant was back within moments and handed over the pillow. When the man reached behind himself to adjust the cushion, he intentionally brushed his elbow against Evera's arm.

She felt immediately repulsed. Contact always made the sense of emotions stronger and his feelings for her were just as prevalent as they were an hour ago.

The male attendant turned his attention to her as he grabbed her bottle of water from the assistant hovering behind him. He eyed her appreciatively as he asked if he could get her anything else.

"No thanks," she said, smiling politely, while carefully moving her arm close to her side and farther from the man by the window.

The attendant reached across Evera to hand the man his drink and she held her breath. She was grateful for the extra space between the seats in first class versus coach. Most of the time, she could sit comfortably without legs or arms touching. Unfortunately, she could still smell the oakey-sweet of the man's bourbon beside her. The scent turned her stomach, a violent memory threatening to break free; forcing it back, she mentally glared at the man, hating him even more.

She spent the next couple of hours going over the layout of the resort on the sheet of paper perched on her lap. The entrances and exits, access points to the ocean, etc. Also planning an escape route, as well as alternate scenarios if something went wrong. Sipping from the bottle of water while alternatively wishing it was a scalding cup of coffee, she wrote several notes. If at all possible she avoided drinking from anything open, like a cup or a mug, on any flights. The thought of what could be lining the inside of the container from the touch of a dirty finger or the spray from a cough made her shudder.

As she ate a couple of granola bars that she had brought with her, she finished going through the hotel map one last time. Satisfied that she had missed nothing of importance and had a virtually flawless plan, she sighed, relaxing back against the seat. There was an hour left on the flight and she hoped to catch a short nap before arriving in Cozumel.

As was her usual nervous routine, she reached subconsciously towards her neck to fidget with the locket that wouldn't be there. Relieved as always that she had left it behind, she started to fiddle with her bracelet instead. The familiar feel of the cold steel always comforted her, gave her focus. This was the moment she left who she was behind, like her locket, and became Jezebel, her operative name within the Judith Program. As Jezebel, she would take on an anonymous identity and do what she needed to get close to her mark.

For the next two days she would be Karen Greene, an accounting executive from Columbus, Ohio, travelling alone and looking to unwind. She had red hair, brown eyes and lived in a two bedroom condo downtown. She would put her tinted contact lenses in when she was settled in her hotel room.

Her passport said that she was thirty, five foot nine and wore glasses. She was thankful for the nonprescription glasses. Her real age was twenty-seven and even though she spent all her spare time soaking up the sun, she still looked younger than her age; the glasses would help distract from her flawless skin. And she certainly didn't feel thirty, or even twenty-seven, for that matter. She felt much, much older.

Karen Greene—it would be a running mantra in the back of her mind while she finished out the flight. Such a simple common name, easy to remember and just as easy to forget. Unlike her name. Although *Evera* was by no means unique, it was rare. She often wondered if the choice had been pure laziness or an act of retaliation on her parents' part. They had been expecting, and hoping, that their child would come out as *Everett* and have a penis, so she was sure in their dismay they just shortened the name to *Ever* and added the token female 'a'.

Sighing in defeat of sleep, she tried to relax and at least rest before landing. Tension seemed to be a constant presence in her life lately, not just during a mission but always there, pulsing in the background. No amount of deep cleansing breaths or exercise seemed to rid her body and mind of it. Most of the time she had no idea what the cause was. A shitty past life perhaps, but lots of people survived hardships and moved beyond them. It seemed to be more than just that.

Today she could pinpoint it though…it was Adam. As the plane shifted and made its slow decent towards land, she couldn't help but ruminate on their last conversation, or argument to be more precise.

Adam was the best thing that had ever happened to her in her pathetic excuse for a life. He'd saved her, that very first day they'd met, and had watched over her ever since. For her, he was everything anyone could possibly be for another human being. But Adam didn't share her feelings. He wanted more from her, which was the reason for their continuous arguing. And it was the 'more' that had her worried for their future. Because she was almost certain she couldn't give him what he wanted.

She'd been with Adam at the Section for a decade and it had become the one place she felt truly safe, as if she belonged. But ever since she had accepted to be part of the Judith Program three years ago, there had been heightened tension between them. The 'more' and her job were, unfortunately, related.

Adam's angry words were still resonating in her head as the pilot announced they would be touching down in ten minutes. They hadn't spoken for two days, which was unusual for them. But after their fight Adam left on assignment and hadn't returned by the time she left this morning.

The plane touched down in Cozumel around 4:30 p.m., the heat still a blistering one hundred and six degrees. The tarmac reflected the heat back on the passengers departing the plane so that it was nearly blinding. She hated to admit it, but going towards the departure gate at yet another airport, Adam was right, she needed to take a break. Cut down on the back-to-back assignments before she started screwing up. Even spend some time alone with Adam, although the complexity of dealing with a situation like that made her cringe.

She flagged down a cab, paying attention to every detail along the road as they drove in silence towards the resort. The cab pulled into the parking lot at about 6:00 p.m., as she exited she noticed a black BMW in the space closest to the entrance.

She knew from Byron's profile that it was his car and where his bodyguards would be waiting.

She checked in and followed the valet to her room. It was comical watching a rather large, burly man carrying a single white backpack and nothing else. She smiled as she stepped close behind him, her eyes constantly watching, cataloguing the layout of her surroundings. The main lobby was the only entrance and exit to the resort, with fencing on either side of the building. The resort itself had a subtle security fence enclosing three sides of the resort with one side open to access the white sand beach. Directly behind the main desk were the rooms, which formed a rotunda pattern all facing outwards on two levels so that each room had a spectacular view. All the rooms had two entrances, a front door and a set of sliding glass doors at the opposite end of the room, leading to the courtyard below. The valet stopped at her room and turned to face her. He took his first real look, a head-to-toe glance that left him blushing in his less than discreet examination. Thanking him, she pressed a tip into his hand and closed the door.

The room itself was small but brightly decorated with travertine floors and a palette of white with splashes of color throughout. She walked through the room to the back where sliding doors opened onto her own private balcony looking down onto the pool and bar area below. Beyond that, the courtyard opened onto a sugary white beach, encased on either side with wire fencing. She could access the courtyard directly from the set of stairs on her balcony.

Satisfied with the setup of the hotel grounds and her room, she grabbed her backpack and headed to the bathroom. Stripping off her clothes she glanced at herself in the mirror. The mirror spanned the width of the double vanity, easily allowing her to scrutinize her body from her neck down to the top of her thighs. Appraising herself critically, she felt satisfied but indifferent at what she saw reflected back. She was tall and willowy. Her limbs long and slim with small hips and a flat stomach. Her breasts sat high on her chest, a bit larger than proportionate to her body. Striking facial features with a small straight nose, high cheek bones and full lips. Her eyes were emerald green and slightly turned up at the corners. Mysterious. Still, she couldn't help but feel, as she always did, that her beauty was the cause of so much of the tragedy in her life.

She pulled her hair on top of her head to keep it from getting wet, although she wondered why she bothered as the humidity had all but drenched her through. The hot, soothing water rinsed away the stale air from the plane and the sour smell of the cab. Aware of staying on schedule, she got out and toweled off, taking her hair down and shaking it out. Knowing Byron's file and that he preferred red hair, she also kept in mind that he liked his women plain and demure. He was easily intimidated by aggression of any kind, especially considering the dangerous situation he was in now. She dressed simply in a short, dark green dress and left her hair down. Putting in her brown contact lenses she added a touch of lip gloss and no other makeup, her complexion creamy and tan. Her hair was long and slightly wavy from the humidity. Just the right look for Byron, unassuming and with her hair soft and close to her face she looked almost shy and fragile. Definitely not someone he should fear or suspect. The finishing touch was the glasses, which polished off her look.

Tonight would be first contact only as Byron was paranoid, and would usually drag out his interludes at least a day or two. He had chosen this particular resort for two reasons, security and sex. The resort was well known for wealthy and high-profile people hooking up, with the added bonus of a safe and secure location.

Clipping her bracelet to her wrist she was ready. She reminded herself of who she was again, accounting executive Karen Greene from Ohio, as she reached down to slip on her black sandals. All she needed now was the paperback she'd brought, *The Making of Modern Economics*, first edition, as her segue for conversation. She reached into her white backpack and rummaged around not finding it. Perplexed, she dumped the contents onto the bed, the book nowhere to be seen. *Shit!* She checked her purse next and sure enough it was there. She stood staring at the book. She had packed meticulously, so she thought, and was positive she had put it in her backpack and not her purse. She was surprised at herself, it was such a small thing but it bothered her...Jezebel didn't make mistakes.

Shaking off the negative feeling, she put the book back in her purse and rechecked its contents. Lip gloss, condoms, phone and keycard, along with the book. Walking through the sliding doors, she carefully closed them behind her. Making certain the lock clicked, she headed down the flight of stairs to the courtyard below.

Crossing the perfectly manicured lawn to the hostess station, she shivered, wishing she had brought a sweater. Cozumel nights were chilly and she was grateful when the hostess led her to a table for two, situated under a heat torch. She asked the girl for a glass of the house white and picked up her menu. She gave it a cursory glance, already knowing what she would order and then set it down, taking her book out of her purse so she would be ready when Byron arrived.

It was 8:00 and she knew that Byron's reservation was for 8:15, which gave her some time to relax with her wine and get into character. For her, relaxing and getting into character meant turning off her tendency to obsess, and become more aware of the feelings surrounding her. She watched the entrance to the restaurant for Byron and tried not to think about how much she missed Adam.

A silver-haired, male waiter arrived with her wine, placing it in front of her with a smile. As he leaned in she could feel a spider web of emotions wrap around her. Usually, she tried to dull her abilities, shelter herself from the bombardment of people's feelings. But she needed it now, it was what made her so good at what she did.

She couldn't remember a time when she didn't have her unusual skill, able to sense the feelings of others when they were close to her—an emotional Empath on steroids. Most sensitive, intuitive people could do the same thing, like sensing when someone close-by was agitated or angry. Her abilities were to the extreme, however, and she could feel their emotions as they were experiencing them: love, hate, fear, desire. They came off of each person differently based on the depth of emotion and her proximity to them. It gave her the edge she needed, being able to predict when her prey might turn on her.

It was why she had lasted longer than any other operatives in her position. Jonas, her boss, and the man who was in charge of the Section, considered it an invaluable gift. He often told her it was what made her so effective, even special. Although she appreciated his praise, reveled in it actually, she had mixed feelings about her abilities. At times, like when she was close to Adam and could feel his love for her, it felt like a blessing. But sometimes, when she was being bombarded by dark, rancid emotions, it felt like a curse.

She took a quick glance at the clock on her phone—8:15 on the nose. True to his predictable character, there was Byron, checking in at the hostess station right on schedule. It was his usual routine to give himself and his constant bodyguard a few seconds to scope out the patrons and the exits. He followed slowly behind the hostess, his eyes moving nervously from person to person seated in the dining area. He glanced quickly behind himself, checking for his security team and satisfied that they were being discreet but staying close, he sat down. Evera noticed a substantial looking man in a plain black suit wearing an earpiece, situate himself on the outskirts of the dining area.

Flipping her long red hair to catch Byron's attention, she picked up her book and at the same moment she looked towards his table. Their eyes met momentarily and she looked away quickly, feigning shyness.

Keeping her face studiously buried in the book she reached to take a sip of wine from her glass and twisted her hair. She had read the book previously from cover to cover so she paid little attention to the words in front of her and instead tried to gauge Byron's interest level. The waiter arrived with a glass of wine for Byron and she glanced up, catching his eye again. This time he smiled back and raised his glass in salutation. She smiled wide in return, encouraging him.

He looked pointedly down at the book she was holding and got up, approaching her table.

"I couldn't help but notice your book," he commented, trying to sound confident behind his nervous smile.

She turned the book facedown, grateful that he had taken the bait so quickly. "This?" she asked. "I suppose it seems like incredibly boring material to most people." She folded her arms on the table, revealing more of her cleavage.

"Yes, I suppose it would to someone who isn't familiar with it," he replied, his tone superior, as he glanced, not so discreetly, down the front of her dress.

"Oh," said Evera, sounding pleasantly surprised as she adjusted her glasses. "You've read it then? I thought I was the only person here who would consider this interesting reading on a holiday," she replied, gazing at him with interest.

"Not at all," he said, looking more closely at the book. "Is that a first edition?" he asked, his tone excited and impressed. Evera nodded, giving him a smug smile. He gestured at the empty chair across from her. "May I join you for a bit? That is if you aren't expecting anyone," he asked, hopefully.

Just then the waiter arrived to take Byron's order when he noticed he was standing behind the empty seat at Evera's table. "Will you be dining together this evening?" asked the waiter speculatively.

"Please," she gestured to the seat. Byron smiled, pleased, and pulled out the chair. The waiter grabbed the wine glass from Byron's table and set it beside his hand.

He didn't give the waiter his order but continued to look searchingly at her, a confident smile on his lips. "Byron," he said, offering her his hand. "Byron Smith", he added, faltering over the obviously false last name.

She pretended not to notice his stutter and stretched out her hand. "Karen Greene," she replied, smoothly. He grabbed her hand, his palm sweaty and his skin soft. He gripped her hand too hard and too long. She imagined he was trying to impress her with his firm grip, but it was uncomfortable and it took everything she had not to squeeze his hand back hard enough to break his slimy fingers.

When he finally released her hand she put it discreetly under the table and wiped his sweat off on her dress. He was still smiling; however, his attempt at looking seductive came across as leering. He reached up to his balding head, nervously, and smoothed his thin hair back from his forehead. Evera sighed inwardly.

"Thank you for allowing me to join you this evening. I wasn't looking forward to dining alone," he said. He was wearing a V-neck T-shirt under his suit jacket; Evera couldn't help but notice his thin collar bones poking through his pale skin. As a rule, she made it a point to never pay attention to any particular qualities about a mark. Whether or not they were attractive, had a good body or were intelligent, made no difference to her. She was always mildly repulsed by them regardless. Byron, however, seemed to epitomize every unpleasant physical characteristic possible. The one good thing he had going for him was that he was harmless. There were no evil or repugnant feelings coming from him, a welcome change from her usual clientele.

Taking the initiative to keep him interested, she started asking him about the book, her questions keeping him chatting through dinner and into dessert. They were both surprised and pleased to find out that not only did they share the same taste in books but the same profession as well. By the end of the meal, sipping expensive cognac, they were discussing their clients. Or more succinctly, Byron was pontificating about his wealthy client list. Evera felt pity for him on top of being annoyed; she knew all too well that his impressive client list no longer existed. Now it consisted of just one man. And that one man was the reason she was sitting across from Byron tonight.

He drained the last of his liqueur and leaned back, looking content and satisfied. The air around him started to change as he looked her over. She could feel the mood shift from idle conversation to something more sexual. His feelings of lust were building, tingling against her skin in an uncomfortable way.

"I can't remember the last time I've had such an engaging conversation. Thank you." He smiled greedily at her now, the alcohol and intimacy of the conversation making him bolder. He grabbed her hand in his soft limp fingers and brought it up to his lips, his motive obvious as he ogled her.

"I couldn't agree more," she replied, leaving her lips parted. She had planned on this being their first contact, but Byron seemed about to break with his usual routine and move faster than expected. Perhaps his fear for his life made him feel like leaving nothing to chance.

This was the part of her job she liked the least, but it was necessary to get what the Section needed. It was the quickest and most effective way to move close to a mark and get what she wanted without being detected. Her solace would come if and when she got to take down her mark. Unfortunately for Byron, the information he had was invaluable to more than just the Section. Evera wouldn't know for sure when Byron would need to be taken out, though. It would all depend on the intel she could get from him.

Regardless, he was a dead man. Whether it was by her, his boss's enemies, or his boss himself, Byron wouldn't live beyond the end of the week. She hoped, for many reasons, that he would meet his demise with her. Aside from that moment being her favorite part of her job, she took comfort for him in the fact that her way would be quick, whereas his alternatives would most certainly be drawn out and painful.

"Perhaps we could continue our conversation back in my room?" he hinted, his eyebrow raised suggestively at her.

"I'd like that," she replied, trying to sound breathless and wanting.

Rising from his seat, he turned and gave his bodyguard sitting in the shadows a subtle nod. He kept her hand in his as she grabbed her purse and her book. Walking quickly with her out of the courtyard he made his way up a flight of stairs that ended just three rooms down from hers. Swiping his card down the scanner, he slid the glass door open. She watched surreptitiously as the bodyguard made his way around the far side of the rooms and headed towards the lobby.

Byron led her into his room, the door sliding closed behind him and the latch locking. "Can I get you anything? I have some red wine breathing."

"If you're having some, then I'd love to join you for a glass." She set her book and purse on the small table in front of her and sat down on the couch beside the king-size bed. She leaned back and crossed her long, tan legs so that her skirt rode up to the top of her thighs. Byron noticed, his gaze traveling up the outside of her thigh to where her skirt just barely covered what was hidden beneath. He tore his eyes away from her and proceeded to grab the open bottle of wine from the counter and take the paper coverings off of two wine glasses. She wouldn't allow herself to think about the cleanliness of those glasses.

"This is a lovely Pinot noir from West Germany," he boasted. "I brought it with me as I can barely stomach the American crap they serve at the bar," he commented, pouring a generous amount of the wine into each glass.

Evera noticed a movement as someone passed the front of the room, casting a shadow on the window. The bodyguard had repositioned himself at the front door. It had taken him almost two minutes to make his way from the middle of the courtyard, circle to the outside of the building and back to Byron's room.

"Here you go," he said, handing her the wine as he sat close beside her, their legs touching. "To very pleasant and unexpected company," he offered, raising his glass to her in a toast.

She touched her glass to his and left it there. "To what has turned out to be a very pleasant evening...so far," she hinted.

"Yes...so far," he agreed, and drained his glass in one long drink. Wasting no time, he removed his jacket and reached to slither his hand up her thigh. She took a quick sip of wine and set her glass down, holding close her perception and ready to concentrate with a clear head on the task at hand.

Her job was seduction, information retrieval and disposal. Nothing more. And she was very good at her job. She had learned to look at sex as a means to an end and completely detach from the act. She needed him to be satisfied enough to fall asleep, and familiar enough with her to trust her to spend the night in his room. Thankfully, tonight she wouldn't have to pull out all the stops, simple sex would be enough for a man like Byron. She got to work immediately.

She uncrossed her legs and leaned into him so that his hand slipped farther up her thigh. He continued, falling into her trap and moved his hand even higher until it was under the hem of her skirt. His face uncomfortably close, he removed his glasses and closed the distance between them as his lips pressed down on hers.

His kiss was sloppy, all tongue and teeth. Repulsed, she quickly moved her lips away from his, giving him access to her neck instead. It was the kissing she hated more than anything. It disgusted her. It was too intimate, too familiar. Sex on the other hand, allowed her to remain on the periphery of what was happening. Most men looking for one-night stands didn't seem interested in kissing as a means of pleasure anyways.

His mouth was slowly making its way down her neck to the cleavage at the neckline of her dress. But she wanted him in the bed. There was a better chance of him falling asleep afterwards if he was more comfortable. She leaned back against the couch, putting distance between her skin and his probing mouth.

"Do you have anything?" she asked coyly.

"What?" he asked tersely, obviously pissed that she had interrupted his travelling mouth before it had reached its desired destination. "Oh yes...of course" he replied, more politely, remembering that she was there as well and not just her body. He got up and moved around the king-size bed to the bedside table where he emptied his pockets and placed his wallet and phone on top. She took the opportunity to move to the bed and remove her glasses. Sitting on the edge, she slid herself to the middle, never taking her eyes off of Byron. He looked pleased at the obvious turn of events and quickly tossed a foil packet on the bed and climbed up beside her.

"Shall we pick up where we left off?" she murmured. He moved over top of her, his soft hands gripping her upper arms and pushing her down on the bed.

"I intend to," he said, his mouth coming down between her breasts and his hands moving under the hem of her dress to grope at her. The lustful feelings coming off of him were smothering her. She tried to block it out and just concentrate on going through the motions. As his hands moved to take off her dress, she mimicked him, reaching to pull his shirt over his head, and then moving to the zipper on his pants. Roughly, he yanked off her dress, eager to take what he wanted from her. He removed the last of her clothing, throwing her bra off the bed as she pulled off his underwear and tossed them aside. He stared down at her naked body, looking awed and slightly impressed with himself, as though he had just won a prize.

He moved his mouth back to her body and she matched her breathing to his panting, making sure she moaned and writhed at all the right moments as his mouth traveled across her breasts. She started to detach mentally, imagining herself somewhere quiet and serene, lying on her back and seeing nothing but blue sky above. His awkwardness as a lover was distracting though and she couldn't seem to remain focused on her escape. She had had enough of his fumbling...she grabbed the foil packet and proceeded to slide the condom on him. Wrapping her hand around him hard, she pulled him inside her.

He groaned and she bit her lip in mock pleasure, all the while trying to get back to her blue sky. She floated mentally away again as he moved back and forth over her, grunting out a rhythm. The pace of his thrusts increased quickly and suddenly. Then he cried out, his body tensing for several seconds. She arched her back at the same time and moaned as he collapsed on top of her. Breathing heavily along with him, she pretended to be spent.

Byron's breathing returned slowly to normal. He rolled out and off of her with a loud groan. He lay on his back with his arm slung across his forehead, still recovering. She lay quiet beside him, still enjoying the blue sky in her mind.

"That was the perfect end to a perfect evening," he said, his self-satisfaction the only emotion left drifting towards her.

"That was so good," she agreed, sounding sleepy and satisfied. "Now I'm just going to want more," she added, planting the seed in the hopes he'd let her stay.

"There's more where that came from," he replied, sure of himself now. "Just give me a little time to recover," he replied, already sounding half-asleep. He took his arm off his forehead and patted her hand twice, yawned, and then pulled the condom off and tossed it in the trash beside the bed.

Evera reached down and grabbed the sheets, pulling them up over both of them. Tucking her arm under her head, she closed her eyes, giving a sigh of contentment and smiling sweetly facing him. She could feel his sleepy satisfaction and smugness radiating off of him. Concentrating on making her breathing slow and even, she listened for any sounds that would allude to him getting up to use the bathroom or passing out. His breathing sounded slow and deep but she didn't dare peek in case he was still awake and watching her. Her patience was rewarded by a quiet snoring beside her.

After a few more minutes she quietly rose from the bed, turning out all of the lights that were still on. She walked carefully up to the front door and listened to see if she could hear any sign of the bodyguard. He was speaking quietly on his phone, and his voice was clear despite the door between them.

"Yah, the lights just went out so I guess they're done for the evening. You know Byron, five minutes of fucking and he's worn out for the rest of the night." There was a pause as he listened to the reply and chuckled quietly. "You got that right...right, see you at 1:00." He shuffled and gave a tired sigh. She heard him lean quietly against the door and then nothing else.

Shift change was at 1:00 a.m. She looked at the clock beside the sleeping Byron and saw that it was only 11:45. Plenty of time to accomplish what she needed to before any outside disturbances might wake him.

She padded quietly over to the bedside table and Byron's waiting cell phone. She picked it up and grabbed her purse off the table in front of the couch. She walked over to the sliding glass doors and undid the latch, pulling the door ajar...just enough for her small frame to squeeze through. This was just a precaution in case she needed to make a quick exit. If Byron caught her doing anything incriminating she could easily escape out the sliding doors and through the courtyard, eluding the bodyguard at the front door.

She walked back to Byron and peered over his shoulder, confident that he was deeply asleep, she retreated to the bathroom. Inside, she quietly shut and locked the door, not turning on the light in case the glow escaping from the bottom of the door were to wake him. She walked over to the toilet, put a towel down on the seat and sat while opening her purse. Pulling out her cell phone, she took out a small data tag that was in the port. She plugged the tag into the port on Byron's phone, never turning it on, and waited while it copied everything from his phone.

It was an ingenious piece of software. It required no instructions from the phone itself. She never had to turn it on, it simply copied all the data from whatever it was plugged into. It also left a tracer, a thin plastic sheath that was undetectable and good for satellite tracking almost anywhere in the world.

Adam had designed it and, like him, it was brilliant. There was very little about him she didn't love and admire. She was thinking of Adam again and berated herself for the distraction.

Once the retrieval was complete, she unplugged the data tag from Byron's phone and loaded it into hers. While she was sending the data through to the Section, she listened. Still nothing but silence beyond the door. Finished, she unplugged the data tag, crushing it in her fingers and destroying any way of retrieving further information off of it.

The process had taken only thirteen minutes, leaving her plenty of time to wipe the phone clean, as well as anything else she had touched, and possibly still take a quick look through his wallet. Although she expected to find nothing of import; Byron was smart and paranoid, and would not be so foolish as to leave anything of interest in something as unsecure as a wallet. She put her phone and the crushed tag back in her purse.

Unlocking the bathroom door she quietly made her way back to the bedside table. Grabbing her microfiber cloth from her purse she wiped the phone clean. Taking care to place it in precisely the same spot as before. She carefully picked up his wallet and opened it. It was just a small billfold so there wasn't much room for anything, and as she'd expected there was nothing that was of any interest to her.

She went back around to the other side of the bed and carefully climbed in, shifting her arm under her head to get comfortable enough to wait but not drift off. She was surprised Byron could sleep so well with an axe hanging over his head. Whether it was confidence in his security team or perhaps denial, she found most people could keep themselves quite happy if they lied to themselves about the inevitable.

Byron worked for a very powerful man named Santos. Originally a dealer of anything illegal, illicit and profitable, Santos had become very successful, his business practices simple and direct. Unchained brutality and indiscretion. He had started trading in sensitive information about a year ago and the Section wanted him. Ultimately, they wanted his fortune and him dead, but as per protocol they would extract whatever information they could before disposing of him.

It was three months ago that Jonas called Evera for assignment on Santos. He needed her to go in as Jezebel and retrieve whatever information she could. She was meticulous and relentless. She had never failed at a job and although the Section didn't always get all the information they wanted from her marks, she herself had a flawless record.

Jonas wanted her to travel to Curacao and try and hook up with Santos on a two-day stopover before he continued on to Columbia for a meeting. She took the job with the knowledge that he would be used to retrieve information and then, likely left untouched to continue to Columbia. Unfortunately, after a night of demeaning sex, drugs that she pretended to take, and finally tracing his phone, the Section had gotten very little in the way of useful intel. The one thing they did discover was a possibility that Santos was working under more than one alias. The name White was mentioned several times in some encrypted e-mails. White and Santos, along with a few other names, were at the top of the Section's hot list for takedowns.

And now, she was lying next to Santos' money man. She couldn't help but feel a bit of sympathy for Byron. He was incredibly intelligent. His portfolio was such that he had been considered one of the most sought after Financial Planners in New York City. He had very high profile clients, mostly CEOs of large corporations and a few extremely profitable movie directors. All people who wanted to secure some of their fortune in less than legitimate ways. He had amassed a large fortune along with a very successful company. That was a year ago.

Because one of the clients who sought him out was Santos. Once Byron climbed into bed with him there was no getting out. Santos monopolized Byron's time and threatened him to the point that within the year Byron's sole remaining client was Santos. Byron had had no choice but to play nice and now he would be rewarded with a death sentence.

Santos's enemies had grown bolder and tired of him monopolizing the information market. They wanted him dead. He knew this and was wasting no time preparing. He had Byron moving his money around, liquidating assets, and making cash available to him at specific locales. Byron knew where all of Santos's assets were. But Santos was not the smartest of men, relying solely on Byron to keep track of his finances. With Byron out of the picture, Santos would be handcuffed financially and have to rely on his cash assets stashed throughout South America. His enemies knew this as did the Section, but no one knew exactly where the cash was; which is where Evera came in.

Evera's job, or rather Jezebel's, was to get any useful last minute information back to the Section, at which time she would likely dispose of Byron. Santos's competition would love to get a hold of Byron and torture the information out of him. Santos would never allow that to happen and would most likely try and get rid of Byron himself before his enemies could intercept him.

Evera lay watching him, the feelings emanating from him were benign and faint. She let her mind wander, back to the Section, back to Adam. She missed him as she always did whenever they were apart. She missed sleeping with him. His warm, strong arms kept the nightmares at bay, and his love for her wrapped her like a blanket. Usually she disliked her sixth sense, people's emotions could overwhelm her when they were too close. Sometimes she would feel pummeled by crowds, their feelings spanning such and array of happy, sad, love, hate, fear, anger. It was too much to experience all at once and several times she had been physically ill. That was why she preferred her life at the Section headquarters with people hustling about but plenty of room to keep her distance. So many people coming and going on different missions that the numbers were comfortable inside the vast and secretive facility. But she liked having Adam close. Contact made sensations even stronger and holding Adam's hand was one of the few times she was grateful for such an ability. There was no deceiving or hiding true emotions from her with touch, and his feelings for her were undeniable.

Byron stirred beside her, bringing her mind back to the hotel room. His legs moved restlessly. Facing him, she pretended sleep. She could feel him waking and sitting up with a sigh. He shifted his legs out from under the sheets, and she listened as his footsteps took him to the bathroom. She heard the door close, the flick of the light and then the sound of him relieving himself. A few seconds later there was the sound of water running in the sink, followed by the door opening and the quiet slapping of his feet as he made his way across the room. She heard him stop mid-step and opened her eyes a crack to see why.

"What the fuck!" he said, louder than expected in the silence of the dark room. She followed his line of sight and saw why. *Shit! Shit! Shit!* The sliding doors were still open. She had forgotten to close them before climbing back into bed.

Deciding evasive action, she sat up quickly, hoping she looked confused. "What's wrong Byron? Come back to bed." She smiled sleepily at him, while freaking out on the inside.

"Why the fuck is this door open?" he thundered, fear in his eyes. "Did you open it?" he continued, slamming the glass door shut and locking it.

She continued with the upset and confused facade. "I opened it right after we made love...it was stuffy in here. Why? What's the problem?"

He looked even more flustered. "Get your clothes on and get out!" he yelled, picking her dress up from the floor and tossing it in her direction. He came closer, handing over her glasses in a not so gentle way, tension and fear heaving off him.

"Byron, I don't understand. Did I do something wrong?" she asked, her voice on the verge of tears.

"You need to leave, now!" he ordered, his voice getting higher. She caught his fear and uncertainty but there was no anger. It was his paranoia making him overreact. She searched for some way to salvage the situation, getting out of the bed as he started turning on the lights.

"I don't know what's going on Byron, please talk to me," she pleaded, moving towards him. She was still naked and hoped her body would be enough to distract him and change his mind.

He stopped, his mouth open as though he was about to say something and was momentarily tongue tied by her bare skin. Suddenly there was a sharp knock at the door.

"Boss!" shouted the bodyguard. "Everything okay in there?" he questioned, alerted by the lights and raised voices.

He shook his head, his fear overshadowing anything he could want from her. "It's fine Rocco, Karen is just leaving," he shouted back, glaring. "Just go," he commanded, turning his back on her.

Dammit! She quickly pulled her dress over her head, carrying her underwear in her hand and grabbed her purse, leaving the book behind.

She searched for some parting words that might bring him back around.

"I had such an amazing time, Byron" she stammered. "I have no idea what's going on, but if you change your mind please call my room. I'm here for another two days and, just...I don't understand," she finished, turning away from him quickly to hide her nonexistent tears.

Bursting through the front door, she ran into the guard and hoped that her sobs sounded real. She ran down the walkway and straight to her room.

Arriving out of breath and pissed off, she removed her keycard from her purse and once inside, slammed the door.

What the hell! How could she have been so careless? This was so unlike her. She paced back and forth, running her hands through her hair and thinking through any other angles.

She became aware of the dampness between her thighs and decided to take a long hot shower to wash Byron and the angst from her body and mind before constructing a backup plan.

She went into the bathroom and started the shower. She stripped off her dress, popped out her brown contacts and grabbed some fresh towels. Climbing in, she let the heat and water wash her clean. She breathed in deeply, relaxing, clearing her mind so she could start with a clean slate. But after ten minutes in the pulsing water she was no closer to a solution.

As she dried off, the exhausted feeling from earlier in the day came back and she felt a pull towards the bed; her contingency plan would have to wait. She set the alarm on her phone for 6:00 a.m.

She slept naked except for her bracelet. Adam had it made for her and she liked the feel of it against her skin. It somehow made her feel as if he was close, protecting her even now. Longing for the feel of his arms around her, she turned over and drifted off to sleep.

CHAPTER 2

Jezebel

Evera woke from a restless sleep to the beeping sound of her phone alarm. Rolling over with a groan, she swung her long legs off the side of the bed to sit up. Reaching for her phone, she shut off the persistent noise, contemplating throwing it across the room. She was agitated and unrested. Sleep had been piecey at best and peppered with images she preferred not to remember, which was why she hated sleeping alone. Adam's arms seemed to be the only thing that could keep the nightmares from seeping into her subconscious.

But her calculating mind had continued working through her troubled sleep and she had come up with several options to complete her assignment. She had purposely left her book in Byron's room last night, hoping that it would serve as a reminder of her. If he didn't call, she could use it as an excuse to go back to his room. Failing that and as an undesirable last resort, she would have to take out his guard and break in. She would have to wait until tomorrow night and the darkness but that would give her more than 24 hours to prepare. The last alternative though, was the one that concerned her the most. Byron's late night bodyguard was a massive brute of a man, and unless she could take him down quickly she risked serious injury. Not to mention drawing attention to the second bodyguard posted just outside the resort in the black car. And he was just as threatening looking as his counterpart. This was, of course, all contingent upon the Section having deciphered the information they needed from Byron.

She went into the bathroom to get ready, brushing her teeth and splashing cold water on her face. She grabbed a close fitting pair of shorts from her backpack, along with a sports bra, tucking her phone in her pocket.

Running always cleared her head and rejuvenated her, so she was grateful that she had to jog this morning to plan her escape route. If she was able to dispose of Byron by tomorrow night, she would need to make a quick exit before his bodyguards caught on. Her resort didn't allow cabs to sit outside waiting, but the hotel a mile down the road had several. She wanted to run the distance and make sure she knew exactly how long it would take her to get there.

Making her way towards the stairs, she tried to be as discreet as possible as she passed Byron's door and started down. There were no bodyguards posted outside this morning.

Passing through the parking lot she was aware of the black BMW parked right beside the entrance. Without openly looking, she noticed there were two dark shadows inside the vehicle. She couldn't help but notice how much of the front seat their shadows took up.

Once she cleared the parking lot and rounded the shade of trees, she picked up her pace. Five minutes in her phone rang, echoing down the empty road. She answered with silence and waited.

"Jezebel?" asked a quiet, sexy voice.

"Adam," she breathed, slowing to a walk.

"Are you alone?" he asked quickly.

"Yes."

"We got your intel last night, good work," he said tersely. Bitter tension was a constant whenever Adam was in charge of her assignment.

"Thanks," she replied warmly, pretending not to hear the edge in his words.

"Anyways," he continued, "Byron left an urgent voicemail message with Santos early this morning in regards to some of the money we've been hoping to get a lead on. He's trying to convince him to move it and soon."

"Okay," she said, waiting for more.

"Santos called Byron back a few minutes ago and agreed. He had Byron move a sizeable amount of money to a bank in Panama. If Byron dies today then Santos will have only one location to access his money. We have a team headed there now," he informed her. "Byron made another call right after to a private airline. He's booked on a flight departing at 10:30 tonight. He can't get on that plane," Adam insisted.

Dammit! She was hoping for one more day for him to cool down and her to get all her plans in order.

"Alright, Adam," she agreed. "I'll take care of it. He won't leave."

"That's all I needed to hear," he replied, sounding confident in her answer. He may not like what she did, but even he couldn't deny her skills. "Santos's competition is planning a welcome home reception for Byron at the airport. They'll definitely torture the location of the money out of him." He sounded bothered by the idea, but Evera knew it wasn't because he was sympathetic to Byron. Adam hated to fail at taking down a mark as much as she did.

"Consider it done," she said, biting her lip and trying to figure out exactly how she could speed up her plans, and still pull this off clean and untouched.

"Good. I have to go...be careful," he added, his voice tender.

"I will," she promised. There was a click and then the phone went silent.

*****

She completed the rest of her plans after the call, stopping at the hotel to make sure there would be an abundance of cabs hanging around tonight. Then she started the long run back to her resort. Even though her plans had to be accelerated, she was still happier than when she had left this morning. Happier because she had spoken to Adam.

She loved him. Loved his body, his mind, his face, his personality, even his quirks and flaws, which were few and far between. But it was a love with a limit. She loved to touch his face but not to kiss him, to hold his hand and hug him, but not to run her hands along his body. It had nothing to do with Adam, he was sexy and beautiful to an impossible degree, and she was fully aware of the line of women aching to take her place. Her convoluted view of sex and love stemmed from a past she had long since tried to forget.

Slowing her pace, she cooled down as she approached the resort. Just before she reached the shade from the entrance her phone vibrated. It was a text.

'I miss you, dinner tomorrow night, A,' she smiled to herself. Her tension about the task to come subsided just knowing her and Adam were still okay.

She put the phone back in her pocket and walked towards the stairs. As she did she glanced up to her left and saw one of Byron's bodyguards leaving his room with a suitcase.

Anxiety was back. He was already preparing to leave. She would have to make her move sooner rather than later. Byron was a nervous man; she could see him jumping the gun and leaving before the plane even crossed into Mexico.

All she needed was the dark. She had a better chance of escape and evasion if she could melt into the night.

And again, the size of the bodyguards made her nervous. She had to accomplish her kill without getting them involved. Walking quickly past the stairs, she avoided the guard and climbed the set farther down, pausing in front of her room to reflect.

She stood in the blazing sun, her sweaty clothes warming in the heat. The parking lot visible from her vantage point, as was the black BMW parked by the entrance. A few mistakes and now she was facing a scenario she had never encountered before. Could she really pull this off?

Fear bit into her, and for just a second she thought about calling Adam. Admitting to him that she had screwed up and that it may be difficult for her to get out unscathed unless she had help.

She shook off that alternative and pulled out her keycard. Of course she could get through this, she thought as she closed the door behind herself. Never before had she asked for assistance and she wasn't about to start now. She was Jezebel, after all.

Pulling off her clothes, she tossed them on the bed and headed to the bathroom, looking forward to a long, cool shower.

She smiled in self-satisfaction. A shower and a flawless new plan.

*****

The clock read 5:47 p.m. as she watched the last of the sun dip behind the ocean. She had been pacing impatiently and waiting for darkness for the last half hour.

Evera had spent a long day indoors, avoiding Byron, and working out every possible angle as well as contingencies if the plan went awry.

Her bracelet was the only weapon she had and she knew how to use it well. It was made of three strands of intertwined titanium. Slender but strong, it wrapped her wrist like a second skin. For her, it was the ultimate weapon.

The female operatives from the Judith Program before her preferred to use a gun. She imagined that to most assassins, as a method of disposal, it was the most logical choice. In most cases a gun was quick and easy, just point and shoot. Even if you were only a fair shot, if you were close enough, nine times out of ten you could hit your mark, but it was that one out of ten that had been her predecessor's demise. And guns required concealment. In her line of work her outfits left little to the imagination let alone room to hide something as obvious as a firearm. You also had to deal with the sound of the gun. Even with a silencer there was bound to be some noise, especially if you missed a kill shot and ended up maiming your victim. Or, worse still, if your target managed to get the gun away from you.

No, she preferred her silent means of annihilation. It was inconspicuous and unexpected. She could be completely naked and still wear her weapon, her victims completely unaware. She didn't even mind the proximity complication that would make most assassins nervous. In fact, she liked having to be close. So close that she could feel their surprise and anger when she wrapped them in a fatal embrace.

Unclasping her bracelet with one deft flick of her fingers, she grasped the two halves and twisted the hinge, stringing out the wire. It moved smooth and silent, retracting just as quickly. Confident that she was ready, she reattached it.

Having packed everything she had into her backpack and purse, she glanced quickly at herself in the mirror. She was wearing a robe and sturdy sandals which were strong enough to withstand a long run and give her traction. Under her robe she was wearing nothing but a black French lace bra and panties. She was hoping to have enough time to grab her backpack and throw on some clothes before bolting for the exit.

Opening the sliding doors as quietly as possible, she stepped out, her pack and her purse slung over her shoulder. She glanced over at the restaurant, thankful that it was still relatively quiet. Delicately walking down the stairs, she discreetly hung her purse and backpack on the post at the bottom of the stair railing. She looked up and saw Byron's room curtains were still drawn but a trickle of light was visible through the glass doors. Still, hopefully, occupied. Walking softly back up to her room and through the sliding doors, she decided to leave them open as another means of escape. Just in case.

Tying the belt on her robe more loosely so that her cleavage was on display and her long legs were barely concealed, she rearranged her features into heartbreak and her lips into a pout. But there would be no tears. She could fake many things; interest, emotions, even orgasms, but never tears. Swallowing down her anxiety, she opened the front door.

It was quiet outside, the sounds from the courtyard barely a lull from this side of the resort. The lights lining the road to the airport turned on at just that moment, her own personal beacon. Glancing to her right as she exited, she spotted the bodyguard standing outside Byron's room. He turned at the sound of her approach but she kept her eyes downcast, watching him carefully through her lashes.

"Oh," she uttered, faking surprise at his presence. The closer she got the more she had to look up at him. She pegged him at about six foot five and guessed he was pushing three hundred pounds. His neck was massive, there was almost no difference between it and the width of his face.

"Can I help you?" he asked, trying to sound harsh while checking her out.

"Yes, well, I left my book here last night. When I left I was so upset that I forgot it," she bit her lip. "I was just heading to bed because I have an early flight and realized it was missing."

He was close enough that she could feel his emotions. No suspicion, just annoyance. Taking advantage, she moved closer, letting the hand that had been holding her robe closed drop.

"I just want my book back," she pouted, looking down and trying to sound dejected. "And to say good-bye to Byron."

"Look lady," he said, trying to hide the fact that he was looking down the front of her robe, "Byron is packing to leave and doesn't have time for company right now," he glowered.

"Fine," she said, crossing her arms in defiance. "Then I'll just take my book and be on my way." She looked up at him hoping he got the impression that she would not leave until she got what she came for.

"I'll go in and get it for you while you wait out here," he replied, belligerently.

Shit! Looking up she met his glare. She needed to go in alone. She mentally moved on to Plan B. She would have to take the guard out and do it now, as soon as he turned towards the door. Once Byron opened the door, she could push the bodyguard into the room on top of him. If he was pinned beneath this man there was no way he'd be able to escape before she got to work on him. Quick and easy, or so she hoped.

He turned away from her abruptly and knocked on the door. "Boss, it's me, just need to come in for a sec," he said.

She reached for her bracelet as he turned his back and she tried to open the clasp. The clasp opened partway and then stopped, caught in the sleeve of her robe. *Fuck!* She jerked at it as inconspicuously as possible, but Byron was already unlocking the door.

She let the clasp go and pulled her sleeve down to hide the partly open bracelet. She took a deep breath, squared her shoulders and resigned herself to the fact that she would have to improvise.

As Byron opened the door, the bodyguard went to move in front of her, but she pushed past him. He grabbed her hard by the shoulder just as Byron recognized her standing in her robe.

"Ouch!" she said loudly.

Byron's eyes grew wide as he took her in. "Let her go," he demanded harshly. The guard removed his hand from her shoulder but continued to try and block her path into the room with his body.

"She's only here for her book," the bodyguard explained, glaring down at her.

"Byron," she said, quickly. "I came for my book, but I'm leaving tomorrow and I wanted to see you again." She returned the guard's glare.

Byron hesitated and then looked at her open robe. "Of course," he said, "please come in."

"But Boss," he droned, she could feel he was pissed as she pushed past him. "We're leaving in a little over an hour."

"Thank you, Garth," said Byron coldly. "I can tell time and I'm well aware of when we need to leave," he finished, pulling her into the room and shutting the door in Garth's angry face, the automatic lock clicking in place.

This had worked out even better than she had hoped. She was alone with Byron and there was now a locked door between her and literally her biggest obstacle.

Byron turned to look at her, his eyes greedy. The belt of her robe had come undone as he pulled her towards the bed. It was now wide open down the front.

"I, um, must apologize for my behavior last night," he explained, coming closer and grabbing her hands. "I have to leave shortly, but perhaps you could stay a while and I could make it up to you," he questioned, rubbing her hands with his soft thumbs. "I have your book here as well," he said, gesturing to the table where it still lay. "I had some rather pressing things going on last night and was overwhelmed."

She was aware that she needed to take her robe off, not only for freer movement but also because she didn't want to risk catching her bracelet on the sleeve again. He was looking at her, waiting for her to comment on his behavior. She took advantage.

She pulled her hands out of his and in one quick movement dropped her robe. She stood before him in nothing but her barely-there bra and panties. His eyes widened in excitement.

He reached for her, his hands already grabbing at her body.

"I see you've already forgiven me for my bad manners last night," he said, as his dry lips started making their way down her neck.

"Of course, Byron," she said, hitching her breath. "I'm just so glad I forgot my book so I could see you again."

He paused and smiled at her. "Ah yes, the book. Look, I haven't got much time, but I have enough for us to part ways on much better terms." He inclined his head towards the bed.

"I was hoping you'd feel that way," she agreed. "I'll just put my book with my robe so I don't forget it again," she added.

He followed behind her, as she picked her book up and then intentionally dropped it. "Here," he said, as he reached down to get it. In one quick movement she undid the latch on her bracelet, springing it open and grabbed it with both hands. Swiftly she strung out the wire, the thin, strong filament of stainless steel made the smallest of sounds as the spools unwound, leaving a stretch of three feet of wire between her hands. Without any hesitation, just as Byron was standing with her book, she embraced him with the garrote, wrapping it around his neck and crossing her hands. And then she pulled.

Instantly, Evera could feel the metal slip through the top layer of skin. Byron realized too late what was happening. He struggled to stand up, while trying to pull at the wire biting into his neck. She could never understand people's reaction to the garrote; the wire was digging into their flesh with no way to get ahold of it and still they clawed at their neck. Going for her hands or trying to incapacitate her was their only hope of escape. But Byron did what every other victim under her hands had done, and so she pulled his back tight against her chest.

"It's alright, Byron," she whispered seductively in his ear. She could feel the terror coming off of him in pulsating waves. "Just know that this is far kinder than what was waiting for you at the end of your flight."

He continued to struggle, pushing against her and reaching around to try and grab her leg, but it was too late. She had him firmly cradled against her, the most intimate moment of their interlude, holding him close before his final heartbeat.

"It's time to go," she whispered, her lips brushing against his ear and then she jerked back hard with her hands one last time. She could feel the wire cutting through cartilage, slicing through his trachea and ending his breath. And lastly, she could feel Byron's final moment; acceptance, as his struggles abated and his brain shut down from lack of oxygen. Could feel from him the calm after the storm, and then…silence.

His body slumped limp against her as she held him, tipping him so that he would fall forward. Blood was flowing, dripping freely from his neck wound and pooling on the white tile floor in front of him. She folded him over and let the weight of his body slide him across the floor, obscuring most of the blood.

"Boss!" came Garth's voice through the door, punctuating his sentence with a sharp knock. "We gotta go. Rocco just called, the plane's early."

Shit! She thought about calling out a reply but decided against it.

"Boss!" the guard banged on the door insistently this time. "We have to go, now, the plane is only here for half an hour."

Evera leaned over Byron's still body and unwrapped the garrote, the bloody wire automatically retracting up into the bands of the bracelet. She clipped it back together and onto her wrist.

"Byron!" Garth bellowed, his tone suspicious. "What's going on?"

Evera jumped up from the floor and started towards the sliding glass doors. Her leg was inadvertently tangled with Byron's arm and as she tried to wrench it free she stepped in the pool of his blood. The tile floor mixed with the blood was slick as ice. She lost her footing and slipped, going down hard and smashing her head on the travertine.

"Open this door now or I'm coming in!" roared the guard.

Evera lay still for a heartbeat, shocked by her unexpected fall. She tried to lift her aching head, her thoughts reeling. *Move!* She shouted to herself, but her actions felt slow, her vision blurry. She knew she needed to run for the back doors and escape but her legs were too shaky. Making her way around to the other side of the bed where she had dropped her robe, she leaned down quickly to pick it up. Her head spun sickeningly with the movement but she ignored it. Shoving her arms through the sleeves, she scrambled for her next move, desperate for a way to slow down time. Quickly, she adjusted her robe, hoping it hid most of the blood that was streaked across her body, and on weak legs headed around the end of the bed to the sliding doors.

Suddenly there was a loud bang, followed by an appalling crunch of wood breaking as Garth burst through the front door.

Fuck! Offensive action, she thought, might buy her a few more seconds. Hopefully, enough time for her vision to return to normal.

"Thank God," she breathed, running to grab onto him. For once the anxiety in her voice was real. "Byron collapsed! I don't know what happened. He was fine one second and then he was on the floor." She reached for her bracelet discreetly and opened the clasp, gripping it in one hand as she waited for Garth's reaction.

"What?" he demanded, confused and stunned from smashing through the door. "Where is he?" he asked, searching the room.

"He's on the other side of the bed," she answered, pointing.

She followed behind him as he stumbled his way around the bed to see Byron lying face down.

He bent quickly. "Boss?" he hissed, as he shook him. And then he raised his head to stare at the small streak of blood from where she'd slipped. They both moved at the same time. She assumed he was reaching for his gun as she leaned quickly and silently over him to wrap the garrote around his neck. His hand came up towards his ear and as she pulled back on the bracelet handles, the wire cutting into his neck stopped and he screamed.

It wasn't so much a scream as a gurgling yell, the sound altered by the fact that she had managed to dig the wire into the right side of his neck. The wire on the left side of his neck was impeded by his fingers, which were caught in the way. Something clattered to the ground from his hand as Evera pulled harder, straining the wire taut.

She looked down and saw a cell phone. He hadn't been reaching for his gun.

"Hello?" yelled a voice coming from the phone. "Garth, is that you?"

She realized he must have pressed a button on his phone as she circled the garrote around his hand.

"Dammit!" she swore under her breath as she tried to pull the garrote tighter, hoping to cut through his fingers so she could sever his airway.

"Arrrrrrr!" was the only sound Garth could make, but she was certain the bodyguard on the other end of the phone could hear it. She needed to finish him. She estimated that it would take less than two minutes for the man sitting in the black sedan in the parking lot to rush through the lobby and up the stairs to the room.

Suddenly Garth pushed back, shoving her against the bed so hard it moved halfway across the room and hit the wall. She scrambled to get a grip on him, wrapping her legs around his massive torso and gripping her hands even tighter on the handles of the bracelet. She leaned her body hard to the left, the garrote slicing deeper into the right side of his neck.

He started chocking on his own blood but he was still fighting her and trying to stand up. She guessed she was down to about thirty seconds before the next bodyguard came through the door and made it a threesome.

Garth managed to get to his feet with her clinging to his back. He whipped around in a move so fast it made her dizzy. He ran awkwardly backwards and slammed her hard into the wall. She cried out, the air knocked from her lungs, his weight crushing her.

Fighting uselessly to pull in a breath she thought fast. She needed to get his fingers out from under the garrote or this would take too long. She deftly twisted to the side and wrenched one of her knees in between his back and her chest. She had an idea, one she didn't like, but if she could pull it off she would be able to escape. If she couldn't, she was certain he would crush her to death with his bare hands.

She could hear a voice shouting from the outside, still far enough away to buy her a few more seconds. Pulling in what breath she could, she lightly released the pressure from the garrote. He fell for the ruse, using the slack to try and turn around, his hand no longer in the way. She pushed hard with her knee shoving him forward with all her might, while she hauled back on the wire.

The force of it was instantaneous. The wire slipped through the flesh and tendons of his neck easily, nicking his jugular and spraying blood over both of them. He dropped immediately to the floor. She fell forward, collapsing on top of him and gasping for air, the pain in her rib cage making it hard to breathe.

There was a clattering outside as someone came running up the metal stairs. She grabbed the garrote and dropped her blood-soaked robe, forcing herself to stand and make her way to the sliding glass doors at the back of the room.

She reached them just as the second guard appeared in the doorway, his eyes bulging in horror as he took in the scene before him.

He raised his arm, already holding a gun and fired at her. She ducked a second before the bullet struck her and it hit the glass door behind her instead. Glass shards splintered around her and flew across the room. The bodyguard brought his hands up to protect his face from the flying glass. She took advantage and threw herself through what was left of the glass door.

She hit the railing and, without missing a beat, sprinted down the stairs two at a time. Grabbing her waiting purse and backpack from the post, she started running. As she cleared the courtyard she could hear the shouts and gasps behind her. Evera could only imagine the scene she was leaving behind as she streaked past the crowded outdoor restaurant. She kept going amidst the shouts and made her way straight to the ocean. It would be darker there and she couldn't risk running down the beach. She quickly glanced behind her to see if she was being followed or if there was a gun trained on her from the room. She saw nothing from Byron's room but the broken glass door. She slung on her backpack and pulled her purse over her neck as she dove into the water. Thankful for the calm waters, she started putting distance between herself and the shore. After several strokes she glanced back and watched as several people started running down the beach.

Swimming parallel with the shoreline, she tried to put as much distance as possible between herself and the resort. The salty ocean felt good, it was cool and washed all the sticky blood from her body. Her ribs ached but her head felt clearer in the water, as she continued her breast stroke a bit farther before making her way towards the water's edge.

As she came close enough to the shore to stand, she quickly scanned up and down the beach. Satisfied that there was no one waiting for her, she emerged from the water, thankful that there were no lights along this stretch of beach. She ran quickly, keeping low, towards a clump of bushes where she dropped her water-soaked purse and backpack. She spent the next couple minutes wringing out her belongings and putting on her drenched clothes, grateful that her passport and ID's were damp but legible. Slinging everything back on, she started her run towards the hotel. But after only a few strides her head started to ache unbearably. In vain, she tried to ignore it and push herself. As her head continued its pounding, she suddenly faltered and her stomach churned. Turning her head quickly so as not to vomit on herself, she folded herself in half and gave into the nausea. After a few seconds she filled her lungs and set her sights on the road, her legs rubbery and moving slower than she would have liked.

The sound of police sirens were quickly making their way towards her, so she ducked under the canopy of branches just off the road. She waited only seconds after they passed and emerged from the trees, just yards from the hotel. Just then she saw a taxi circling the hotel parking lot and heading for the exit. She moved at an all-out sprint, lungs burning, head and ribs aching. She ran up beside the cab just as it was about to pull onto the main road.

Banging on the passenger window with her fist, she watched as the cab driver whipped his head towards her. Startled, he rolled down the window.

"Hi, can I get a ride to the airport," she asked, resisting the urge to bend over and catch her breath.

"Sure," he answered, taking in her wet hair and one small backpack.

He opened the back door for her to get in. "Good thing these seats are vinyl," he commented unhappily, watching the water drip from her clothes.

"I was just at the beach getting in one last swim and didn't realize the tide had come in and covered all my things," she explained, smiling sweetly at him. She ran her hand across her forehead and along her damp hair. He softened and smiled back.

The ride to the airport was only twenty minutes and she listened to the cab driver's companionable chatter, keeping an eye on the traffic both ahead and behind them. She saw nothing alarming as they pulled into the small airport terminal.

Disentangling herself as she exited the cab, she handed him a small stack of damp bills which he accepted graciously.

Exhausted and shaky, she headed through the doors of the airport. The cool, air conditioned wave hitting her pleasantly as she made her way to her departure gate. When she arrived her ticket was waiting for her with forty minutes to spare before her flight.

Making her way through customs took record time. Only when she was on the plane, taxiing towards the runway, did she finally take a deep breath. She had made it. Barely, and with many errors to contend with, but she had made it out alive. She breathed a shaky sigh of relief as the plane lifted off, taking her back to New York and the Section.

CHAPTER 3

The Section

Evera touched down in West Virginia at 1:30 p.m. the next day. She had slept most of the short one hour flight from New York in the Section's private plane, her body nearing exhaustion. Previous to that she had spent a restless five hours on the plane from Cozumel to LaGuardia Airport, attempting to sleep in her uncomfortable seat in coach.

There was always a sense of relief touching down. Not like coming home, as most people perhaps felt when they arrived, but relief at the familiar. She looked out the small private plane's window to the sparse, brown landscape of the West Virginia countryside.

Stretching in her leather seat, she unbuckled her seat belt as the plane taxied up to the small hangar in the middle of nowhere. She grabbed her backpack and purse and made her way to the exit door.

She walked off the small steps of the plane to the car waiting thirty feet away. The driver, Stan, got out and opened the back passenger door for her. Climbing in, she thanked him warmly as he closed the door behind her.

The air inside the car was balmy and soothing, quiet jazz playing on the stereo. The weather outside was wintry and she felt chilled despite the warm jacket and pants that had been waiting for her on the plane, compliments of Adam, she was certain.

She was suddenly uplifted despite the disastrous turn of events her assignment had taken. She would see Adam in less than an hour.

The ride was quiet. Stan, like her, wasn't much for small talk. Leaning her head back against the seat, she relaxed while the soft music played in the background. She let her mind wander again back to Adam and the last conversation they'd had before she left.

He wanted her to stop, to give up being Jezebel. She knew his request was mostly concern for her as she had been doing this for three years. She had to admit that she was tired as well but the truth was, she was good at it, really good, and she couldn't imagine another path right now.

Secretly, for her, it was more than just a job. Being Jezebel made her feel strong and in control. It had become an outlet, an opportunity to unleash her darkest side. Exacting vengeance under the guise of intent and purpose. Every time she strung out her garrote and took down evil, she felt empowered, as if she had somehow gained back a small part of the innocence that had been ripped from her younger self.

Adam's other reason for her to quit, she knew, was personal; he wanted things to move forward between them. She bit her lip at the prospect of something more intimate. She knew she couldn't keep putting him off indefinitely, although he had assured her he could wait. Lately, though, she could feel his patience receding despite his words.

And she knew about the other women. Knew about them and hated them. Hated them for being able to do for him what she couldn't. But she didn't blame him. How long could he keep lying beside her, chaste, only holding her in comfort? She'd known for years that he entertained other women when she was gone. The guilt coming off of him every time it happened always gave him away. Regardless, her jealousy seethed in silence.

Even now at twenty-seven, after ten years of trying to forget, she couldn't make the connection between sex and love. And she was sure she loved Adam, as much as she was capable of loving anyone. Because of that, and not despite it, she had never slept with him. She didn't want to see him the way she viewed every other man.

The sex with her victims was simply a means to an end. She felt nothing, no pleasure; she did what she needed to do and then it was over. The idea of seeing Adam in that light terrified her and she worried their relationship would never recover. She needed him in her life. Her sanity had survived only because of him.

The car pulled off the main road and took a secluded, paved trail deeper into the forest. The woods suddenly stopped and a large flat field opened up and in the middle was a large industrial looking building. It was two stories high and had a sign out front that said, 'United States Government Facility, Private Property'. Its appearance was unassuming and if anyone came upon it by mistake they would think it nothing more than a warehouse. In fact, the top two floors of the corrugated metal facility were exactly that. A warehouse housing old copiers, computers, large boxes of ancient paperwork of no consequence, complete with a front desk manned by a security guard.

The Section was government owned in name, but it operated independent of any official interference. Jonas ran a tight ship but no one tried to pretend that the Section wasn't exempt from the regular rules of warfare. Jonas' background was as enigmatic as hers. He'd been some kind of high-ranking official in the CIA or the army when he'd been selected to head the Section's programs despite all the competition.

Evera understood exactly why they'd choose someone like Jonas. She was intimately knowledgeable of his emotional state and it was rock solid. He rarely wavered from a passive condition even though he often came across as angry or aggressive. It was the reason Evera didn't mind being close to him. Most people's constantly changing moods were overwhelming and confusing. It was exhausting to always be sorting through the bullshit of a feeling in order to get to the reason behind it.

And Jonas never implied that the Section was anything but a killing machine that made the government money. Even this hit on Santos, at its core, was about money. The government let the Section know which of the dirt bags it wanted a hit on and then it was Jonas's job to setup a team to carry out the orders.

Once someone was captured, the Section was responsible for interrogation and disposal. That way the only hands that were dirtied belonged to the Section, an unsanctioned facet of the government that officials could deny knowledge of if need be. Any money collected was split equally between the Section and the CIA.

Most of the recruits were salvaged from the CIA program; students who had failed psych tests or had tempers too uncertain to control. These kind of people were the perfect fit at the Section. No upstanding, patriotic recruit would be able to justify the acts carried out by the Section, let alone complete them.

Evera, like most of the people around her loyal to the Section, tried not to think about the politics of their job. In her eyes, she was helping rid the world of worthless filth and if someone else made money off it, it was irrelevant to her. Some small part of her understood that the only way she could rationalize her abhorrent behavior was because she was so messed up herself.

Stan pulled right up to the entrance and the short set of cement stairs leading up to the front door. He opened the back passenger door and she climbed out, grabbing her backpack and purse as she went. She thanked him and walked through the grey metal door.

"Hi Evera," said the tall, blond man at the front desk, tipping his security hat at her in a teasing gesture.

"Hi Steven," she answered, following his lead. "How are the wife and kids?"

"Just super," he chuckled, both of them knowing full well he had no kids, and his wife and only family was the Section. She took off her bracelet and checked it in with him where it would be cleaned, locked in the armory, and then returned to her before her next assignment.

"How was your trip?" he asked, as he traded her keycard for her room with her fake passports and ID. He was always curious to hear about the exotic locales she visited. He once told her he liked to live vicariously through her.

"Quick!" she said, sharper than she intended. "I'm sure Cozumel is quite beautiful when one has time to explore it," she finished, smiling and hoping to take the sting out of her first reaction.

"You okay, Evera?" he asked, with concern.

"Not really," she confessed. "Things did not go according to plan." She leaned in closer over the desk. "Have you heard anything about my mission?" she asked, hoping to get a feel for things before making her way downstairs and facing her screw up. "Did Jonas say anything?" Living in such close quarters below there were seldom any secrets that didn't get passed around.

"No," he replied, looking surprised. "As a matter of fact, he was in an unusually great mood this morning when I arrived and checked in."

"Really?" she questioned, also surprised, certain he would have caught wind by now of the mess she had left behind in Cozumel, either by the media, the backup team or Adam himself. Although she hadn't spoken directly to anyone since she left Cozumel, Adam would have done his due diligence to make sure the mission was completed, and to make sure she had made it out safely. She was certain the scene she had made, not to mention the two dead bodies, would have made their way into the news by now.

"Really!" he answered, smiling. "Maybe you should go down now and take advantage of his good mood while it lasts."

"Great idea," she said, pushing off the counter and making her way to the elevator in the back corner. "See you tomorrow," she said, turning back and smiling.

"Won't I see you later at supper?" he asked, curious.

"Nope," she replied, as the elevator door opened. "Dinner out tonight," she answered, as she walked into the elevator.

"Have a good night," he yelled back.

She pressed the button marked 'basement' and waited the few seconds it took for the elevator doors to close. The Section itself was entirely below ground. There was the basement level, which housed the residence quarters as well as the Section's main tracking hub. Below that was the sub-basement where the training facility, dining room and offices were located.

The doors opened and she turned right, heading to the hub, even though she would have preferred to go the opposite direction towards her apartment and a hot shower. As she walked closer to the entrance the din coming from the room got louder. Inside, it was a hive of activity. The room itself was enclosed completely in glass panels so anyone outside could clearly see all the computer screens and activity occurring within. The main door was usually closed to keep the noise level down so she was surprised to see it ajar.

Kent, one of the computer techs and drone controllers, brushed quickly by, a burst of excitement coming off him, not noticing who she was until he was several paces past her.

"Evera," he said, sounding surprised and excited. "I didn't realize you were back already." He was grinning and still walking away from her, pushing up his glasses at the same time.

"Congrats," he said, still rushing off towards the main corridor and the elevator. "Thanks to you, we got him!" he finished, as he turned around.

Her reply, as well as several questions, hung on her lips as he quickly passed from her view. She turned back towards the room and the massive screen on the far wall, which seemed to be the main source of interest.

One of the drones that Kent was in charge of must have taken pictures of something of extreme importance to cause this much excitement.

The room itself was about fifty feet by fifty feet, and although the screen was massive and she could see it just fine, she still had no idea what she was looking at. The pictures were just playing over and over again, shots of what looked like a small building and several men with guns surrounding it. She looked over to the side of the room where several people were gathered and saw Jonas in the middle of the huddle.

Jonas Clayton stood six foot two and ramrod straight, his formidable presence gave him the impression of being even taller than he was. His demeanor and designer suit and tie, along with his perfectly trimmed salt and pepper hair, left no question as to who was in charge. And even though Evera would place him somewhere in his late fifties, his body was trim with a "don't fuck with me" strength emanating from him. He rarely showed any emotion so she was surprised to see a ghost of a smile on his face. Steven was right. She decided to take advantage of this fortunate turn of events and greet him while he was happy and surrounded by other people.

She walked towards the back of the room by the big screen where Jonas was standing, and waited.

"And Kate," he said, barking orders at a pretty, diminutive blonde who looked slightly terrified. "Don't forget to call ahead and get me a car this time," he demanded, staring her down with a bit less ferocity than usual. "I don't want to end up riding in a disgusting Columbian cab again."

"Yes, sir," she replied, and was instantly scurrying away to follow his orders and escape.

He watched Kate bustling away and caught site of Evera, standing beside the remaining group of eager employees waiting to do his bidding.

"Well, well," he said loudly, turning towards her. "What an unexpected surprise. Back already?" She noticed that he did not use a single positive adjective when addressing her. He appraised her, his grey eyes cool and remote.

"Jonas," she simply replied.

"Congratulations," he said, repeating Kent's greeting, all other eyes in the room now focused on her.

The faces looking at her all seemed grateful and expectant, waiting for Jonas' reaction.

"Jezebel," he said, pausing, still referring to her operative name. "Thank you," he replied, with a smirk of gratitude, although Evera had known him long enough to know there was an undercurrent to his comment. "If it weren't for you we wouldn't have been able to capture our target, and his fortune," he said while addressing his audience. "Santos is in custody and on his way to Langley for cataloguing and then to Arlington for debriefing," he finished, his smile not reaching his eyes.

With that she was suddenly greeted with congratulations and thanks from all of the people in the room. She was instantly uncomfortable, too many close bodies, their emotions swirling around her, some as sincere as their words, and some not so much. This was why she chose the field and not the office; she couldn't sort out her own thoughts and feelings from those around her when they were this close.

"Thanks," she responded to the crowd, wanting nothing more than to escape.

She looked to Jonas, hoping he would rescue her and invite her to his office to start berating her, which she would now welcome just to avoid her present circumstance.

"Alright everyone," his voice boomed over the chatter, "back to work." He looked to her and gestured with a tilt of his head that she was to follow.

"I'll be in my office for the next hour or so, continue getting all the details ready for tomorrow," he finished, as he started heading out of the room.

He waited politely for her to leave through the door and then stayed close behind her, but not too close. Jonas always kept a safe distance from her, being one of only a handful of people privy to her ability. And she appreciated it, having no inclination to know her boss's every intimate emotion.

Although, he had become much more than just her boss over the years. He had been with her right from her volatile start at the Section and through all of her training. He was integral in grooming her to become the Judith Program's most elusive weapon. And, most importantly, he kept her ability a secret.

He accompanied her to the elevators and pushed the down button. The doors opened immediately, as if they too felt the need to obey his every command. They remained silent, standing slightly apart during the short decent to the sub-basement. When the elevator doors opened he waited politely for her to leave ahead of him, continuing the silence as they walked towards his office at the end of the hallway.

She waited in front of the door that was always locked while he pulled out his card, swiped it and punched in his code. As he grabbed the door handle his arm brushed close to hers and she caught a drift of tension coming off of him.

She made her way straight to the chair in front of the giant alder wood desk, waiting impatiently as he made his way to his chair. Jonas sat down heavily, leaning his arms on his desk, his hands clasped together and then his eyes met hers.

"What the hell happened, Evera?" he asked, directly.

She bit her lip, not having planned exactly how to explain herself, and not quite sure herself what had happened to cause such a fuckup.

"I screwed up," she answered, looking him in the eyes. She was pissed off at herself for the mistake, as well as for being put on the spot like this.

"You screwed up?" he retorted with anger, his eyebrows pushed together. "It's quite obvious you screwed up Evera, but that's simply a statement of fact, not a viable fucking explanation." He sat up straighter, staring her down and waited for her to continue, to give him something he could either use against her or let her off the hook with.

She searched her mind for the simplest reason without deviating too far from the truth. She couldn't tell him it had all started with her misplacing the book, which had thrown her off. Or that she had forgotten to close the sliding doors in Byron's room, been caught and because of that had to scramble to change her plans. Even in her mind it sounded like more than just a simple mistake, so she went to the crux of the matter, leaving everything else out.

"I slipped and fell on some of the target's blood after finishing him off," she replied. He continued watching her, waiting for more.

"I hit my head on the floor when I fell and I guess it was pretty hard because it took me a while before I could get up and focus," she finished, downplaying the fall as best as possible. She remembered the sound of the crack as her skull hit and the sickening, spinning feeling long afterwards.

He leaned forward, his arms on the desk. "And?" he asked impatiently, although there was also concern in his eyes.

"And then the bodyguard outside started yelling and banging on the door," she continued. "He only waited a few seconds and then busted through so I had no choice but to take him out as well." She ended there, hoping that was enough.

Jonas raised his eyebrows, refusing to allow her to be finished. "What about the second bodyguard, the gun shots, running half-naked and covered in blood through an entire restaurant full of witnesses?" he asked, his voice getting louder with each passing question.

"I made one mistake and then everything sort of snowballed from there," she explained, trying to defend herself.

"Jezebel doesn't make mistakes, Evera," he said, locking eyes with her.

She could feel his doubt and uncertainty from across the desk. She wanted so badly to say something to wipe that feeling from him.

"Nothing that I'm aware of anyways, and certainly not something so indiscreet and public," he stated.

"What's been released?" she asked, trying to divert his train of thought and aware from his words that her mistake had obviously made its way into the media.

"The story released from the Mexican news stations has varied over the last several hours, but the bottom line is a woman known as Karen Greene was seen fleeing the scene and that there were two deaths involved," he answered, looking at her in disappointment.

"We've had several staff call the police posing as reporters and so far they have been very generous in offering up details in order to diffuse the situation as quickly as possible."

She waited, impatient for those details, hoping that her screwup could be swept under the proverbial carpet.

"It's being spun as a drug deal gone bad. The second bodyguard fled and they've yet to locate him. As for Karen Greene, they're still looking into her, and not that hard, I might add. Adam managed to mess with some of the airports passenger manifests and they're still not sure if she died in the water or made it on the plane. Of course, once the police chalk it up to drug involvement, no one else tends to care that much." He allowed an almost smile, obviously feeling good about the end result.

Evera leaned back looking for holes in the story, something that could turn around and bite her in the ass later, but could find none. As far as the Cozumel police were concerned, she was just a victim in the wrong place at the wrong time. Likely, a dead victim. The only person who would be interested in her was Santos and the Section had him in their custody.

Jonas was still leaning towards her, his eyes ambivalent. "The question I have to face now, Evera," he said kindly, "is what do I do about you?"

She wanted to take evasive action, to try and talk him into overlooking what had happened, one mistake in three years. But something about the way he was scrutinizing her told her to hold her tongue and let him speak first.

"If it was anyone else, Evera, anyone but you, they would be finished right here and now," he admitted, still holding her gaze and his words dared her to hope. "But it isn't just anyone," he stated, looking at her with kindness. "And we both know there is no one else like you." He rarely spoke words of praise or care to anyone and so she took it to heart. He valued her; the idea warmed her to the core. She vowed right then and there that she would never disappoint him again.

"Let's continue on," he insisted, straightening up, smiling in reassurance.

"Thank you, Jonas," she said, unable to keep the feeling of gratitude out of her voice. She stood to leave as Jonas was already busy rifling through the mountain of paperwork on his desk.

"Oh, and by the way," he said, lifting his face from the task. "I'll be leaving in the morning for Columbia and then heading back to Arlington to interrogate Santos. I'm putting Garrison in charge during my absence."

"Garrison?" she questioned, confused. "What about Adam?" She hated Garrison. He was an arrogant dick who was only interested in kissing Jonas' ass and making his way up the Section's ranks. He had no appreciation for the employees or the tasks they had to complete, having spent little to no time in the field.

Jonas looked at her with an exasperated expression. "Look, Evera," he said, "I'm not oblivious to your distaste for Garrison, but the fact of the matter is that he's eager to learn and he gets the job done. And he doesn't question every little detail of every decision I make. He knows his place, which is more than I can say for some of the people working here."

She could feel his low, simmering anger as he finished his small speech. She was sure his last two comments were about more than her. He was talking about Adam. Over the last few months Adam and Jonas had butted heads continuously. Sometimes it was in regards to her assignments, which both she and Jonas knew were a direct reaction to how Adam felt about her, but it seemed to be more than that lately. She'd asked Adam about it a couple of times but he brushed it off citing a difference of opinion.

She rose from the chair and turned to leave but he stopped her once more. "And Evera," he said, still sounding stern, "don't forget to see Stella and get that bump on your head checked out.

That's an order!" he finished, his eyes leaving hers to look back down at the papers on his desk.

Leaving, she made her way quickly to the elevators and back up a level, anxious for a shower to wash away the flight as well as the anxiety of the last few hours. Whenever she came back from a trip she couldn't help but marvel at the walk to her apartment. The corridor was so different than the rest of the facility. It was like walking down a posh hotel hallway, with plush carpet, soft lighting and pale cream walls. She had to admit the Section had done a terrific job in making each member feel welcome.

There were ten apartments lining each side, which were almost always occupied. Some housed training staff who would stay anywhere from one month to two years. Others housed permanent residents, like her and Adam, whose stays were close to a decade.

Walking up to the door of her apartment, she pulled her keycard from her back pocket and punched in her code. Before she opened her door, she couldn't stop herself from glancing quickly at Adam's apartment, which was beside hers and the last one at the end of the hall. She had hoped to run into him in the hub but he wasn't there, which most likely meant he was training today. Although Adam was brilliant and loved deciphering intel and coordinating the missions, he was also a trained lethal weapon.

She walked into her small foyer, tossing her bag on the cream couch nearest the door. She was always content to come back to the Section and her tidy one bedroom apartment. It was her small sanctuary from the emotions and noise of the outside world.

She walked past the living room and kitchen area, tastefully decorated in pale shades of cream and grey, to the small bathroom at the far end of the apartment. She reached into the shower and turned the pressure on full blast, cranking up the heat. Walking up to her mirror, she affectionately ran her fingers across the delicate heart locket, hanging in its usual spot on a small hook on the wall beside the sink. She undressed and grabbed two towels from the large square wicker basket under the sink, placing them on the towel rack beside the shower door. The strong clarifying shampoo, along with the scalding heat of the shower, removed the remainder of the red, semi-permanent dye from her hair as well as some of the tension from the last twenty-four hours. She would stay in until the water ran cold and then grudgingly go and face her appointment with Stella. After that she would finally get to see Adam.

•

CHAPTER 4

Masks and Faces

Evera quickly ran a brush through her wet, tangled hair and then blow dried it just enough so that it wasn't dripping down her back. She usually let it air dry while she unpacked and tidied up around the apartment, but she was certain that Jonas would have informed Stella of her imminent visit and she wanted to get it over with as soon as possible. Her routine would have to wait.

Grabbing a fitted T-shirt, she threw it on over her bra followed by jeans and flip flops. Lastly she grabbed her locket from the hook in the bathroom, pulled it over her head and headed out the door. Her necklace always helped her switch back from Jezebel to Evera. It held significant sentimental value and was one of the few things that had come with her on the day she had arrived at the Section.

She walked towards the elevators, as always dreading her visit with Stella. She had nothing against Stella personally, as a matter of fact she was one of the few females within the Section that Evera cared about. It was Stella's position in the Section that made Evera resent her required visit.

Stella was the Section's on staff medical physician and psych advisor. When Evera had agreed to take on the role of Jezebel she also had to agree to a physical exam and counseling after each mission. She understood why the Section found it necessary for their covert operatives to be thoroughly examined as well as feel they could discuss their missions privately. Most of the missions involved violence, often murder, and in her case giving herself over physically. Although, to Evera, her missions were of little consequence as far as her wellbeing. Nothing compared to the horrors of her past.

She got into the elevator, thankful to ride down alone. She fidgeted with her locket, anticipating a more in-depth visit if Jonas had alerted Stella to her possible head injury. The doors opened and she turned left, going all the way to the end, opposite Jonas' office, to a door marked Medical Lab. She took a deep breath before tapping gently to announce her arrival.

"Come in," welcomed a pleasant voice. The room was small and cozy, a waiting area setup like a living room. It had no desk but two comfortable plush chairs and a TV with a small coffee station. Stella peeked her head out of one of the three other doors down the short hall.

"Just finishing up with a call," she said smiling, as she covered the mouthpiece. "Won't be two minutes," and she pulled her head back into her office. The other two rooms were labeled Medical Exam and Counseling. Even after ten years she still dreaded the counseling room. During her first few months at the Section she had spent time in that room almost every day. Luckily, after things settled, she managed to avoid it for most of her career. The one exception had been after her first mission as Jezebel. That experience had been particularly brutal and she would most likely have died if it weren't for Adam.

While she made herself comfortable in a chair, she flipped briefly through the magazines on the coffee table. Bored after two minutes she toyed with the remote control before setting it down and opting for silence. She fidgeted with her locket again. She wondered sometimes if she didn't prefer being Jezebel. It was so much easier to put on the Jezebel mask and leave who she was behind. Jezebel was strong, confident and ruthless. So much of Evera was still trapped in that room in the old farmhouse; a scared little girl, alone and weak.

From the other room she could hear Stella laugh and say goodbye as she hung up the phone.

Stella walked out of her office wearing a lab coat over a tailored navy dress. As always, she looked polished and put together, no blonde hair out of place and a welcoming smile on her lips.

"Afternoon Evera, sorry to keep you waiting," she said, as she took a seat in the chair beside her. "Just the usual bureaucratic bullshit to deal with," she said, and rolled her eyes still smiling. Evera knew the contradiction to her words. She might complain but despite all the red tape she had to deal with, she truly loved her job. And Stella didn't just treat her like a patient, she genuinely cared about her. Although Evera didn't have a sibling, if she could have ever had a big sister she would have wished for her to be just like Stella.

Evera met her kind gaze and smiled back. "That's why I'm here, isn't it?" she asked. "More bullshit."

Stella laughed. "Yes, well then let's get it over with, shall we?" she asked, as she stood up.

Evera stood confidently but with an expression of chagrin as she followed Stella dutifully to the exam room.

The exam was brief and thankfully, after Stella asked her several probing questions in regards to her head injury, she was cleared of any chance of a concussion. She was concerned though, about the beating her body had taken, and asked her to take it easy for the next couple of days. She iced Evera's sore ribs to minimize bruising and applied Arnica cream to help even further. Evera accepted her diagnosis but made no promises to lay low if she was needed.

Stella snapped off her blue sterile gloves, throwing them into the trash at the foot of the exam table. "I know I say this often," she began, "but I'm always here if you want to talk. About anything," she finished, giving her a kind smile. Evera could feel Stella's concern for her; it was stronger and more intense than usual.

"Thanks, but I'm good," she replied with her standard answer. This was the part that always made her uncomfortable, turning down Stella, yet again, in regards to discussing her emotions.

"I'm not just talking about your past or your missions, Evera. I mean, sure, the medical side of me can't help but kick in and want to help fix things for you, but I'd like to think that after all these years you'd consider me a friend too," she waited, with hope in her voice.

"Really, Stella, I'm fine. And you know me, I'm not really the hash-it-out type." More like the bury-it-and-never-speak-of-it-again type.

"Opening up, even a little, might not be as bad as you think," she insisted. "You should talk to Adam about it. He seems to think our time together is helpful. I mean, am I really that scary?" she teased.

But Evera's stomach dropped at her words. "It's not you I'm afraid of," she said, in barely more than a whisper.

Stella's face changed back to concern and she rubbed her hand on Evera's shoulder. The warmth and sadness coming through her touch left Evera uneasy, and she wished she hadn't said anything.

Suddenly the room seemed too small, like the walls were closing in and there wasn't enough air for both of them to breathe. Horrible images started biting into her mind, making the claustrophobia worse.

"I have to go," she said, louder than necessary. She quickly jumped off the exam table, wriggling out from under Stella's hand.

"Okay," said Stella, surprised at Evera's sudden outburst. She was still close enough that Evera could tell she hadn't fooled her. Why did she have to be so kind and caring? It would be so much easier to shake her off if she wasn't so fond of her.

Evera managed a sincere smile but said nothing as Stella left, her throat too tight to speak.

She dressed in record time, anxious to flee the small room and get some air. She passed her office and glanced in quickly. Stella waved as she walked by, already on the phone. Despite her fondness for Stella, she was grateful for her preoccupation so that she could rush to the exit and her escape.

*****

Evera quickly walked down the hallway, after nearly slamming the door of the Medical Lab. She felt a sense of relief as she passed the elevators, as if the proximity from the site of the conversation watered down the potency of it.

She switched her focus and had Adam on her mind just as she passed the elevators and almost ran into Steven.

"Evera," he said, surprised. "Hey, how did things go with Jonas?"

"Not as bad as I expected," she answered, sincerely. "And you were right, he was much less cranky than usual," she couldn't help but grin.

"You must be heading to the gym?" he questioned.

"I was just thinking about it. Is Adam there?" she asked hopefully.

"I just left a few minutes ago and he wasn't there yet, but he should be by now. There were a bunch of people headed down there to watch him do a training session," said Steven.

"Great, then I'd better hurry so I can get a good seat," she said, and turned to leave, his answer making her quicken her pace.

"Catch you later," he said, his words trailing off.

A bunch of people headed down to watch Adam perform a training session, she was certain, was not an entirely succinct statement. She knew from past experience it would be a bunch of women headed down to watch him; the thought made her want to run.

She walked quickly through the large entrance to the gym and scanned the room looking for Adam. He was in the middle of the training square surrounded by six other men, talking and using a lot of hand gestures, giving them direction before sparring. Evera would have to wait to greet him until after he was finished.

Standing along the opposite edge of the square were several men in army uniforms, men who would be critiquing the new blood. Evera couldn't help but feel sorry for the new recruits. It didn't matter how well trained they were, they would be no match against Adam.

Evera made her way to the three small rows of bleacher-like seats that were setup alongside the square. As she walked past all the gym equipment she noticed that the first two rows were already filled, mostly with new female recruits. Not wanting to sit next to any strangers, she climbed to the top row.

As she sat, she scooted to the far left where there was no one in front of her, and no distracting emotions closing in. Most of the women were considerably intelligent and eager to learn; but she also knew that Adam was the real reason for the draw.

She couldn't blame them as she watched him. He was the only man still wearing a shirt, but even through the thin fabric his physique was unmistakable. His face model perfect, he exuded a quiet confidence that was sexy and attractive. Adam was also intelligent, focused and direct. Evera often teased him about having no social skills and no filter for his mouth; if he thought it, he said it. Deep down she admired how genuine he was.

But here, in the square, he was a weapon. At thirty-one, with ten years of the Section's hard core training, his body was honed to perfection. Evera often likened his fighting style to watching an impeccably choreographed dance. He was fluid and flawless, taking on many competitors at once and always the victor, the most dangerous. He was the epitome of brilliant and beautiful.

To her, the only visible stain Adam had to mar his body's sublime canvas was a certain tattoo. He had a few but it was the one on the inside of his forearm that she always tried to avoid looking at. Although she actually liked body art in general, it was this particular symbol that she found offensive. It was a small, black cross that he added permanently to his skin after he gave up drinking and signed up for the army. One more difference of opinion to add to their growing pile of contention.

She watched him wistfully, wishing things could be different between them. She was certain he knew how much she loved him, though she had never told him in so many words. Loved him, yet couldn't find it in herself to be with him.

Adam stood in the middle of the square, three of the six trainees forming a large triangle around him. He stood with his arms slightly raised, his demeanor calm and ready. His dark sleeveless shirt still without sweat and his bare feet planted firm and apart. He was the only one without shoes, the other men opting for the protection of their runners.

He beckoned once with his hand, inviting them to take him on and then the battle began. All three of the would-be attackers hit him at once. Adam turned sideways and ducked at the last second, missing the man trying to grab him, punching the other hard in the chest and kicking the last man in the thigh with his bare foot, taking him down hard. He landed on the mat on his back, heaved himself up to standing and finished the man who had missed grabbing him by sweeping his legs out from under him and pinning him to the ground, his hands a chokehold around his neck.

The audience clapped, impressed, and the men that Adam had put on the ground came over to shake his hand and speak to him briefly about strategy. It was a quick conversation and then Adam yelled, "Next group," needing no time to catch his breath. He paused just long enough to pull off his shirt, throwing it out of the square.

There was a communal sigh of longing from the women in the seats below. Out of the corner of her eye, Evera saw one of the young female trainees in the front row grab the arm of her friend. She didn't need her gift to know what the girl was feeling for Adam. She bit her lip in jealousy as she watched the attractive blonde eye him hungrily.

She couldn't deny, though, that he certainly was something to see. His chest a perfectly sculpted masterpiece, his long arms muscled and beautiful. He was moving on the other three men, taking them down one at a time. As he turned, those on the bleachers caught sight of the muscles rippling in his back, strong and sexy.

He finished them all off and stood in the middle of the square, facing the audience, alone and still. He resembled a statue, legs apart, his perfect chest rising and falling, showing little sign of exertion. Finally, the warrior relaxed his pose and he reached to help up his victims amidst the cheers from the crowd.

He had a brief conversation with the three remaining trainees and then headed to the side of the square where his shirt and a fresh towel were waiting. Several of the female observers had sprinted their way to where Adam was standing, and Evera swore she could see the lust dripping from their faces from across the gym.

Paying no attention to the remaining women, she made her way down the rows of seats towards the square. Feeling surprisingly uncertain, she wondered if she should wait for the crowd to disperse or just head over boldly, through the throng of women and men.

She paused at the edge of the mats, trying to search out his face, hoping to gauge his reaction. Their conversation before she left for Cozumel had ended on a sour note, with both of them angry at the other. It had been a tense parting, to say the least. Even though his text said that he missed her, she was still unsure of how he would feel at seeing her.

As if sensing her, he suddenly looked in her direction, trapping her gaze. The look on his face was one of joy and relief. He stopped talking midsentence and excused himself, already pushing past the women in the crowd and moving towards her. His eyes never leaving hers, holding her captive as if there was no one but the two of them in the room.

He strode across the mat, a step away from her, searching her face, her eyes, and then a moment later she was folded into his strong embrace. He held her tightly, his bare arms a warm caress against hers. "You're here," he said breathlessly. "I didn't know you'd arrived yet," pulling back to see her face but keeping her close.

"Hey," she added, smiling. She couldn't manage anything more articulate. The relief at his unchanged feelings flooded her throat making it impossible to speak.

"Hey yourself, beautiful," he murmured, returning her smile.

"When did you get in?" he asked. "Have you seen Stella yet?"

She felt uncomfortable at the mention of Stella but shook off the feeling. "I've been and gone," she replied, smiling wider. "A clean bill of health as usual," she pretended, abashed at not being completely honest with him.

"Really?" he questioned, his warm hand reaching up to cup her face and sweetly brush her hair back. "Jonas said you took quite a beating. I've been worried sick since I talked to him this afternoon," his tone filled with concern.

"Are you sure you're alright?" He didn't sound convinced.

"Honestly, I'm fine," she replied, exasperated. "Nothing's broken, no concussion. Jonas is just pissed I screwed up and frankly, so am I. So I'd rather not talk about it, if you don't mind."

"Alright," he acquiesced. "I'll let it go for now, but maybe you could fill me in over dinner?" He raised an eyebrow mischievously and grabbed her hand, walking them towards the door and out of the gym.

"Dinner sounds great." She was famished. "But don't you need to finish up with the trainees?" she realized.

"I'll walk you to the elevators and then go back and finish up," he said leading her down the hall. "I won't be long. Let's meet in an hour at the surface. I'll be in charge of transportation for the night," he finished, as they reached the elevator.

"I'll see you then," she said, as he pushed the elevator button for her. The doors opened and he leaned against them until she was in, and only then did he release her hand.

She smiled at him and shook her head in fascination as he moved back and the doors started to close. His light, ice blue eyes watched her until the last moment. He was so extraordinary; she had never in all her travels encountered anyone quite like Adam. She often marveled at how someone could be so brutal and vicious in the field, and yet still be the sweetest and most caring man she'd ever met. It was hard to imagine how all the different sides of him could coexist in such harmony.

The doors opened and she made her way down the hall to her apartment, feeling envious of Adam. He had managed to reconcile his past long ago and accept who he was, while she was still lost.

She went to her bedroom closet looking for just the right outfit for the evening. It was her ten year anniversary at the Section and Adam was taking her out. They made a date like this every year around this time. Always going to the same Chinese restaurant about a forty-five minute drive from the Section headquarters. It was small but the food was always fantastic. It was run by the same elderly couple who had opened it almost twenty years ago. Over the last ten years she and Adam had gotten to know the couple well and sometimes they even let Adam cook something special in their kitchen.

He'd been busy training today so she was curious what would be on the menu tonight. His grin at the elevators had hinted at something special though and she was anxious to find out what surprise he had concocted for the evening.

She searched her well stocked closet, unsure of what she should wear. This was the most difficult part of her life, figuring out who she really was. Looking at the entire selection before her, she had no idea what to wear or who she should be this evening. Adam got to see the biggest part of who she really was but even he didn't get to see her true self, most likely because she didn't even know who that was. There didn't seem to be any situation where she didn't combine her two identities, both Evera and Jezebel.

How many different faces she had worn over the years? Making herself into what everyone else wanted. The face of Jezebel the seductress, in order to capture her prey. The face of the model employee at the Section, trying to impress Jonas. And the face of Evera, somehow combining parts of herself with parts of the others. Never just singular, one dimensional. She often wondered what it would take to just be herself. To live without the mask of the others to hide behind.

She reached for a sexy black halter dress, then paused and thought better of it. Instead she grabbed a deep blue wrap dress, plain but pretty, not wanting to give the wrong impression tonight and complicate things between them further. She kept her makeup simple, with just some black mascara and a hint of lip gloss. And then she went in search of her favorite pair of Jimmy Choo shoes. She found them hiding behind her extensive collection of handbags at the bottom of her closet. Misty grey with a square heel and a strap that laced at the back. Deciding her hair would have to do as it was, just hanging in waves down her back, she grabbed a purse and headed out.

As she reached the elevator doors she paused, anticipation and fear at war inside her. Ten years and she had been doing the same routine with Adam, the same place every year and the same argument. A decade of the same. She had an unsettling premonition, as the elevator doors closed, that a change was coming…a change that would come whether she liked it or not.

CHAPTER 5
A Night Out

The elevator doors opened to the main floor and a cool blast of wind hit her as she exited. Steven was standing at the main door holding it open and speaking to someone outside. She started walking towards the door when he must have heard the click of her heels as she approached him. He stopped talking and turned to look at her.

He let out a low whistle. "Wow," he said, looking her up and down appreciatively. "What I wouldn't give to trade places with Adam tonight," he said, still holding the door and grinning at her.

"Behave," she scolded, but then she saw the car sitting at the curb and realized he was most likely speaking about the attraction outside as opposed to her.

Adam was beside the open passenger door of a jet-black Ferrari 599. Wow, indeed. It was a sleek, sexy machine and looked fast just standing still. He was leaning against the car, his tousled brown hair still damp from his recent shower and she was hard pressed to decide what was more beautiful, the car or him.

Adam was dressed in a tailored black suit, a stark white shirt and a pale blue tie that complimented the color of his eyes. She was surprised and a bit apprehensive, as she had never seen him dressed in anything more formal than a pair of pants and a sport coat.

He came to take her hand and help her into the sleek car. "I thought that ten years deserved something a little extra special," he said hesitantly. "I hope it's not too much."

She smiled to reassure him. "It's just right," she said. "And it would only be too much if you weren't still wearing your glasses," she teased, as she folded her long tan legs into the car. Adam was notorious for wearing his glasses and only grudgingly gave them up for his contacts when he had no choice.

"Yes," he said, rolling his eyes and laughing, "me without my glasses would definitely be over the top."

He closed the car door and made his way around to the driver's side. Adam settled his long, lean frame into the seat beside her and switched out his regular glasses for a pair of Ray Ban aviators. He started the car and it purred; he grinned at the sound. Revving the engine before shifting it into gear, he pulled away fast, the power and torque breaking the tires free and leaving black patches on the pavement.

He spun the steering wheel quickly, the car whipping around and facing the long driveway leading out. He shifted into second gear, gunned the engine and let out the clutch. The car leaped forward so fast that her head slammed back against the seat and they were instantly speeding dangerously fast down the long winding drive.

She peered over at Adam. He had a cocky, confident smile playing up one side of his full lips. He looked sleek and sexy himself sitting there, his window open, the wind blowing his hair into a tempting mess. He looked engineered to drive the vehicle, and he steered it with a skill that made him seem one with the car, his hands running caressingly along the leather clad steering wheel.

He pulled down hard on the shifter with his hand and quickly geared down as they came to the end of the drive and the beginning of the highway.

His face turned towards her, taking her in. "You look amazing by the way," he breathed, his eyes travelling over her from her hair, down her body and ending at her long legs.

"I was about to say the same thing to you," she commented and laughed, hoping to keep the evening as lighthearted as possible. She didn't mind him checking her out, his desire tempered by the love she could feel gathered around him.

"The car is fantastic," she replied, checking out the interior, the tack wrapping around Adam like the cockpit of a plane.

"Yours?" she asked jokingly.

"I wish," he answered, the longing apparent in his voice. "Think we can make the forty-five minute drive in twenty?"

"Let's try," she said, settling comfortably into the butter soft leather seat.

"Stolen?" she continued, teasing.

He laughed as he shifted to first and gunned the engine, the car pulling them fast and smooth onto the highway. "Borrowed," he winked, as he shifted to second, let out the clutch and floored it.

*****

They arrived at the familiar little restaurant around 7:30, the drive taking them only thirty minutes. They had spent most of the drive in relaxing silence, both their windows open enjoying the crisp air and sunshine.

As soon as they pulled up to the entrance Adam parked the car and made his way around to her door. He opened it, helping her out and tucking her arm in his as he shut her door and locked the car. Walking close, they traveled the few steps to the front door where Adam led her into the dark, quiet restaurant.

The owner, Sim, greeted them as they entered the small waiting area.

"Your table is ready," he said smiling politely, not bothering with menus. He led them through the empty restaurant to a table for two in the center of the dining room. "The restaurant is all yours tonight," he admitted excitedly.

Adam pulled her chair out for her and then stood behind her not taking his seat.

"I'll join you in a minute," he said, as she looked up at him to see a smug smile on his lips. "I just need to check on dinner." And then he turned and disappeared through the swinging kitchen doors at the back of the dining room.

She turned back around and saw Sim's wife, May, coming towards the table holding a bottle of wine.

"Good evening," she said in her slightly broken English. She gestured with the wine bottle towards Evera's glass.

"Yes, thank you, May," she said warmly. She enjoyed when May was close, her feelings were that of a kind and thoughtful person; Evera always felt soothed by her presence.

"Adam was here all morning cooking and bossing Sim around you know," she whispered conspiratorially.

"Oh no, poor Sim," she whispered back.

"No, no, don't worry. Sim don't mind," she said. "He likes it much better than when I boss him around," she admitted, and patted Evera gently on the shoulder, laughing quietly.

Evera laughed softly with her and watched as May slipped back into the kitchen.

Minutes later, the kitchen doors swung open and Adam came through, weaving his way past the other tables to join her. He sat facing her, his arms on the table, leaning close.

"How do you like the wine?" he asked, looking to see that she had tried it.

"It's delicious," she said. "Exactly what I would have picked if I could have found it at any store in the state," she said, taking another drink of the fragrant Beaujolais.

"I'm glad you like it," he said, reaching for the bottle and pouring some of the red wine into his glass.

She leaned into him. "So, what's with all the secrecy going on in the kitchen?" she asked, raising her eyebrows. "May said you were in this morning cooking up a storm and giving Sim a hard time."

Adam laughed. "Giving Sim a hard time. Is that what she said?" he asked while reaching for his glass. "I think it was May busting both of our chops. She threatened to skewer Sim if he blew up her kitchen trying to use the pressure cooker."

"So, do I get a hint as to what you're serving tonight?" she asked, appreciating the surprise but still hoping to finagle a small morsel of what was to come.

Adam lifted his chin taking a deep breath. "Can't you smell it?" he asked. "Smells pretty amazing if I do say so myself," he reached for another sip of his wine.

Evera breathed in, the aroma making her mouth water. She placed it right away—Peking duck, one of her favorite meals. She had discovered over the years that Adam was a fantastic cook, and although he had cooked several times for her in his small apartment she knew he longed for a chef's kitchen with all of the state of the art gadgets. This kitchen was a dream for Adam to cook in, he'd even bought several pieces to contribute under the guise of being able to take over the kitchen on occasion.

"So," he began, "are you going to give me a quick rundown on what happened in Cozumel or will I have to wait and sneak an unauthorized peek at the report when you're finished?" he wondered, as he smiled patiently at her.

"What's there to tell?" she replied, bitterly. "I screwed up and it ended up splashed all over the news. I'm just thankful no one got a picture of my face and that the Mexican police there are so inept."

He leaned towards her. "Look, no one likes to admit to making a mistake, and certainly in ten years at the Section you're entitled to one," he continued, looking intently at her. "But seriously, you could have been killed," he finished, nothing but concern in his voice. "This wasn't a simple mistake like leaving a fingerprint behind, or a drop of blood or even being caught on camera and your face splashed all over the news," he said, throwing her own words back at her, his tone agitated. "You are very lucky to be alive."

Her anger ramped up in reaction to his. "But I am alive, aren't I?" she flung back. She regretted it instantly as she could feel his anger turn to fear. Fear that he could have lost her.

"Adam, honestly," she explained softly. "I slipped on some blood, cracked my head on the tile floor and almost knocked myself out," she sighed. "That really is all that happened," she concluded.

Adam looked unconvinced and opened his mouth to speak but she quickly interrupted him. "That's all that happened as far as my mistake. The rest was just a domino effect of my slip up. Things never would have gotten out of hand the way they did had I not fallen in the first place."

He gave the appearance of being satisfied but she could feel his skepticism. Could see it in his eyes.

"I understand how one simple error can cause things to get out of control," he sympathized, "but maybe you should take this as a sign, Evera." Here they were, back to the same conversation/argument they were battling over before her latest mission. She had hoped, in vain, that he would have let it go.

"And what sign would that be, Adam?" her tone sour, bracing for the fight to begin.

"You know full well, Evera." He looked down, frustrated and shook his head. "I fucking hate having this same conversation," he said angrily.

"Then stop having it!" she argued, pissed off, her voice sounding loud in the empty restaurant.

They were both leaning towards each other now, Adam emanating frustration and anger that she could feel tingling unpleasantly against her skin.

Suddenly the doors to the kitchen opened and Sim and May came through, each balancing trays of steaming food.

They instantly relaxed their tense inclination and sat back more amiably in their seats, neither one wanting to make Sim or May as uncomfortable as they both were.

"Happy ten-year anniversary, Evera," said Sim, both him and May beaming with congratulations.

"Thank you," Evera exclaimed appreciatively. "It smells delicious. I can't wait to dig in..." she hesitated, remembering who had initiated the entire meal.

She flashed Adam the hint of a smile, unwilling to let go of her side of the argument but grateful. Maybe they could skip past their last words and steer back to where they were five minutes ago.

They chatted pleasantly with May and Sim as they served dinner, and then they left the still half full platters on the table next to theirs as they left.

She faced Adam, the awkward silence between them stretching out with neither one willing to break it. Evera was stubborn, unmovable. If they were ever going to speak again, Adam would have to make the first move.

His full lips parted as she waited for him to say something, but he just sighed dejectedly and, looking at her, picked up his fork and started to eat. She followed suit as they ate their meal, both of them pretending to ignore the dead air. The only solace in the uncomfortable situation was that the food was delicious. She sipped her wine throughout the meal and had all but drained her glass when Adam grabbed the bottle and refilled it.

She bit the inside of her cheek. Quietly and without looking at him, she managed a grudging "thank you."

He chuckled softly. She looked up at him, miffed, wondering what he could possibly find so funny in this uncomfortable moment.

"Alright, you win," he granted, smiling teasingly at her.

"I win what? What is it you find so funny?" she demanded, trying to keep the annoyance in her voice to a minimum.

"I mean, you win this battle. I concede and will break the silence or we may spend the rest of our lives never saying another word to each other," he answered, still smiling at her. "I should know better anyways, you are so stubborn. It must have been painful, just then, to say thank you. You looked like you were choking on something."

She smirked back at him, unable to help herself. He knew her so well, sometimes she felt he knew her better than she knew herself.

What was the matter with her, she wondered as she looked at him? His eyes, so light blue they looked almost silver, were mischievous and warm. His high cheekbones and chiseled jaw dusted with a dark beard made him look unbelievably rugged and sexy. His lips, full and sensuous, were still smiling at her. He ran his fingers through his tousled brown hair, the gesture alluring, as he leaned back. Even his glasses couldn't detract from the perfection of his face. She stared at him, willing herself to cross that line in her mind and body, to want him as more than just her companion. To love his body like she already loved him.

He noticed her scrutinizing him. "What are you looking at so intensely? Do I have food on my face or something?" he asked, raising his napkin and wiping his lips.

"No," she laughed to hide her sadness. "There's no food on your face," she murmured, still searching her heart. Nothing on his face, and nothing going on inside her either. No desire, no need. She'd always said jokingly that she was dead inside whenever someone asked her how she could do her job; she feared there might be more truth in her words than even she thought possible.

He raised an eyebrow inquisitively, waiting for her to say more, but she just reached for her wine glass and took a long drink.

"The food was delicious, Adam," she said, changing course. "You definitely outdid yourself this time."

"I'm glad you enjoyed it," he said, and started chatting about where he had it flown in from and how he prepared it, picking up on the fact that whatever was on her mind she was unwilling to talk about it.

They chatted amiably about the food and work. Adam told her that he would have to head to Arlington in the next day or two, following Jonas to help with debriefing Santos.

Evera felt the food in her stomach churn as she thought of Santos. What she wouldn't give to be involved in his 'debriefing,' as they liked to call it. How she'd love to be there to watch him squirm and hopefully scream in agony. He was still alive because, when they'd captured him, the Section had decoded his cell phone and found several interesting texts and emails. All alluding to a contact named White.

White was a ghost in the underworld. There was little known about him, no official name, first or last. No idea where he was from or where he was presently located. He was known for coordinating several bombings throughout Europe, and selling volatile chemicals to certain guerilla groups in Africa which resulted in hundreds of deaths. Highly sensitive and destructive information was passed through him, but he was careful to never be directly involved. He always remained on the periphery of each devastation, passing along supplies and information but never directly getting his hands dirty.

Because of this, no one knew what he looked like or how to capture him, as he was never at the scene of any crime. But he always left a sign that he had caused the damage, as if a part of him couldn't resist taking credit for the destruction. He always left behind a textured, white business card, blank on the front and back.

The Section had been tracking intel on him for years now. And even after all the whispers of his alias passed throughout the world and certainty of his involvement, they were no closer to catching him or discovering his true identity.

Evera knew that Jonas was hoping Santos would have some information on White. Or possibly, as far-fetched as it might seem, that Santos himself was White.

Adam vehemently disagreed with Jonas' speculation. He couldn't believe that someone as primitive and lacking in intellect as Santos could possibly be someone as shrewd and competent as White. After spending time in Santos' bed and presence in general, Evera couldn't agree more. Santos was an animal. He had no sense and, without Byron and his bodyguards, was alive strictly by luck. He didn't have the brains or the patience to pull off any of the jobs White was involved in. And Santos craved the spotlight. If he had been involved in any of the devastation that White was linked to, if he was in fact White, Evera was certain he would shout it from the rooftops.

She agreed with Adam, and believed that Santos was no more than a hopeful source of information. There were a few far more intelligent and probable suspects on the Section's radar.

"You wouldn't, perhaps, be willing to sneak me in and let me watch his execution when the time comes, would you?" she asked hopefully.

"I'd let you pull the trigger if I could, Evera," he said sympathetically, his hand reaching to hold hers in comfort.

She tried to brush off the intensity of his feelings. "Pull the trigger? Please. I'd want to get up close and personal. Wrap my bracelet around his neck, our faces inches apart, and pull the garrote tight. Watch as the realization of his own death sparked in his eyes," she deliberated, unable to hide the elation she'd feel in watching him die by her own hands.

"Remind me never to get on your bad side," he replied, attempting to bring some levity back to the conversation. She could feel his concern at the bitterness and anger of her words, his thumb stroking the top of her hand in an attempt to soothe her.

At that moment Adam looked past her towards the kitchen doors. She turned in the direction he was looking and saw Sim peeking his head out.

"Excuse me for just a minute," he said, rising and making his way to Sim. Adam spoke quietly with him and then went into the kitchen.

Ten years, she could hardly believe it herself, she thought as she sat alone in the dining room. Ten years since that horrific day when she had shown up outside the Army Ops headquarters, just outside Quantico and about two hours from the Section's operations facility she lived in now. She flashed back momentarily to that first moment when she had arrived.

She'd shown up outside the headquarters in a rust covered jeep, driving erratically and slamming into the fence surrounding the building. She'd been approached immediately by several men in army gear with guns at their sides. As they moved closer to the vehicle and got a clear look at her, she remembered four of the five men pulling their guns from their holsters.

To this day she felt fortunate they'd all kept a level head and decided not to shoot at the sight of her. As she grabbed her bag and scrambled out of the jeep, her clothes drenched in blood, she gripped a large kitchen knife, brandishing it as if she intended to use it. She was sobbing, disoriented and terrified.

Moving towards the men, she held the knife in front of her for protection. They all closed in, their guns trained on her, but she could tell from the emotions coming off of them that they were neither angry nor afraid. Just confused. A skinny, quivering girl taking on several men with an entourage of guns seemed to them, incomprehensible.

The man closest to her looked with curiosity between her and the jeep. He raised his hand and lowered the gun. "Wait," he yelled.

"She must be Les Grant's daughter. I recognize the vehicle," he announced, and motioned for the others to lower their weapons.

"Adam," he questioned, gesturing to the only man whose hands were empty, "is that Grant's jeep?"

The younger man without the firearm moved forward, cautiously approaching her. She noticed his kind eyes and beautiful face as soon as he moved in, and even though he was tall and muscular she didn't feel afraid of him.

Regardless, she held firm to the knife, her knuckles turning white, and prepared to use it if necessary.

He came closer still, his hands up. "I'm not going to hurt you, I promise," he spoke softly, stopping two feet from her and just inches from the point of the blade.

"Are you alright?" he asked. "Are you hurt?" he continued in his soft voice, never breaking eye contact with her. She noticed his eyes were a piercing silver blue.

"It's not my blood," she replied, barely above a whisper, her hand starting to shake. "Don't come any closer," she sobbed.

"My name's Adam," he said calmly. "I just want to help you." He reached his raised hand towards her in an offering for her to surrender the knife. She could sense no contradiction to his words, only concern and kindness radiating off of him.

"Evera," she said, still unsure of what to do. "My...my name's Evera Grant," she stammered, her voice shaking as her whole body started to vibrate.

The last thing she remembered as the tears blurred her vision, was the cold ground coming for her. She had expected to hit the hard earth, but instead a pair of strong arms caught her. She felt her body being lifted as the arms cradled her. Managing to open her eyes a sliver, she looked up to see the young man with the light blue eyes carrying her.

He looked down at the same moment, their eyes meeting. "Don't worry," he said, his voice sounding far away as the dark tried to take her. "You're safe now," he reassured, smiling kindly. Before she was consumed by the darkness she felt his warm arms tighten around her and for some unexplained reason, she believed him.

*****

She was catapulted back to the present by a ruckus coming from the kitchen. She shivered, wanting to stay in that memory and run from it at the same time.

She looked behind her and saw Adam, Sim and May coming through the kitchen doors, Adam in the front carrying a tray with a single shallow bowl on it and a flame flickering.

May suddenly moved ahead of Adam, coming over to their table and quickly clearing Evera's empty plate away. Adam walked over slowly so as not to extinguish the flame and placed the tray in front of her. Crème brûlée with a single candle poked into the caramel encrusted top and two empty champagne glasses on either side.

Adam reached over to the empty table beside theirs and grabbed two empty wine glasses, handing one each to Sim and May. Sim produced a bottle of champagne from behind his back and Adam popped the cork and filled Sim and May's glasses as the liquid overflowed from the bottle.

He then filled the two on the tray in front of Evera and handed a glass to her.

"Happy decade, Evera," he said, touching his glass to hers, holding her eyes. She sensed he wanted to say more but they were both aware of the audience.

"Blow out your candle and make a wish," said May, pointing.

She closed her eyes searching her heart and mind for a wish and finding only one she knew she truly wanted. An impossible one. She blew out the candle anyway and said the wish silently in vain.

Each of them tipped back their glass and drank the crisp dry champagne. May clapped her hands and patted Evera gently on the shoulder.

"Come on Sim, let's go clean up," she commanded, gesturing for him to clear the neighboring table and then ushering him out of the dining room.

"Thank you both," Evera said to their backs, as they hurried through the kitchen doors. May gave a backwards wave, not bothering to turn around and yelled, "Good night" as the doors swung shut.

Both Evera and Adam laughed quietly at the quick exit by the discreet and thoughtful restauranteurs.

"So, what was your wish, Evera?" he asked. "Or is it against the rules to tell," he asked lightly, leaning his arms across the table and closer to her. In the kitchen he had removed his jacket and rolled his sleeves up, his strong, bare forearms a few inches from hers.

"You know the whole 'I can't tell or it won't come true' nonsense," he mused, waiting for her answer.

"It doesn't matter whether I tell or not," she confessed, sadness in her voice. "It's not a wish that can come true. It was a foolish thought, that's all." She bit her lip, wanting so badly to tell him but afraid of his reaction.

His hand reached automatically for hers. "You can tell me," he smiled in encouragement.

She looked at him and saw everything she could ever want. Her safety, her comfort and her best friend. But never a lover. The one thing she couldn't reconcile to be for him would end up tearing them apart. She could feel it in her bones, it would be their undoing.

"I wished that we could stay like this, indefinitely in this moment. Just you and I together, neither of us needing more from the other." She watched him as she said the words, saw the pain and sadness flash across his face. Felt it wick from his hand and into her.

He lifted his free hand and ran his fingers through his hair in a frustrating gesture. Sighing loudly, he fixed his gaze to the empty space on the table in front of him.

"Why can't you just try, Evera?" he wondered, finally looking up, his eyes pleading with her.

"Why can't this just be enough?" she pitted back. She wondered how many times they could ask each other for the same thing over and over before one of them decided it was too much. Either too much to give or too much to give up. Maybe this was it, his threshold; ten years of waiting for something that would never happen.

He leaned as far across the table as the space would allow, the hand holding hers suddenly gripping her fingers tighter.

"I know in my heart that things could be different, if you'd just let Jezebel go. You'd feel different about the physical side of us. You have no idea what it's like for me when you go away to be her," he said, the intensity of his gaze attempting to brand her insides. But she didn't need to look at him to know. She could feel the anguish of his words in his tight hold of her fingers, flowing into her, so strong it was making the guilt bubble up into her throat and threaten to choke her.

She leaned back suddenly and pulled her hand away from his fingers and his suffering. She couldn't take this; she didn't want to keep feeling his pain and know that she was the cause of it.

"Not wanting to hear or feel it doesn't make it any less real, Evera," he said, guessing her cowardly intentions. "Not for me it doesn't."

"This is my job, Adam," she said defensively. "A job I'm damn good at. I know the circumstances are not what a normal job entails but neither are yours," she reminded him. "Don't you think I worry just as much as you every time you lead an op," she said, trying to draw a parallel between their situations. "Every time you leave to take on the scum of the earth I wonder if that will be the last time I see you!"

He shook his head and suddenly rose from his chair, pacing back and forth in front of his side of the table. "It's not the same thing, Evera," he insisted, astonished that she could possibly compare their two situations. He stopped his pacing and leaned his hands on the table, facing her. "I don't leave on my missions with the sole purpose of fucking the bad guy," he spat.

"You don't know what it's like," he continued angrily. "To know the body you love is with someone else's. Their hands and lips touching you in ways I never have and you doing the same to them. Them inside you," he said hoarsely, his hands gripping the sides of the table hard enough to make it shake. "You have no idea what it's like for me to know that every time you go away you'll end up fucking someone besides me," he finished, love and anger blasting off of him.

She leaned back fuming, watching him. "Oh, I don't know about me having no idea," she countered, equally as pissed. "I imagine it's much like when I go away and know you'll wind up screwing one of your trainees," she hissed, folding her arms and watching his face for a reaction.

He stared, the anger dropping from his body instantly, replaced with a guilt so strong she could feel it from across the table. He sat back down in his chair heavily, holding his face in his hands and hiding his eyes from her.

"I was sure you knew," he said, raising his face to hers, the anguish back. "I kept hoping you'd say something to me, confront me, something," he implored, pained.

"And what could I possibly say to you, Adam," she relented, still angry at the images of him with those women. "Give you shit for cheating on me?" She shook her head. Whether it was a need or subconscious revenge or both, she couldn't fault him. She hated it, but she had no right.

"It's not what you think, Evera," he said, defensively.

"I'm sorry," she said, unable to keep the sarcasm from her voice. "So, it's not what I think, is it? Because I was under the impression you were having sex with these girls, so if what I'm thinking is wrong please enlighten me? Playing cards were you?" She hated that he was trying to manipulate her.

"No, I mean it's not what you think, as in it's not about the sex." She opened her mouth to make a snide remark but he interrupted her. "What I'm trying to say, so inarticulately, is that it's not about sex with them, the women. It's not just about the need, Evera, I have a hand," he said, looking smugly at her. She waited patiently for him to keep talking but he stopped and just continued to search her face.

"Go on," she urged gently.

"I'm worried that if I explain myself you'll be angry or repulsed or think that I'm seriously deranged," he said honestly.

"Ha," she couldn't help but laugh at his comment. "Adam, there is no one in this room more sexually or mentally screwed up than me and we both know it."

He smirked at her. "I don't believe that at all, but we can argue about it another time." He took a deep breath and started talking. "When I choose a woman to be with, I'm not randomly selecting someone. I'm looking for specific attributes." He kept his eyes honestly on hers but it took everything she had not to look away. It was bad enough she knew, she didn't want to have to live with the details.

"It's never a blonde or a redhead," he continued. She couldn't help but take some small pleasure in knowing the attractive blonde who was eyeing him in the arena that afternoon was out of luck. "It's always someone with long, dark brown hair." He looked at her purposefully, at her long, dark brown hair. "Sometimes it's other things as well," he said, looking below her chin. "The familiar curve of her neck, maybe the shape of her lips or the slight upturn of her eyes." He was choosing characteristics that mirrored hers. She couldn't decide if she felt uncomfortable or flattered. "That way when I'm with them, I can concentrate on the things that remind me of you," he sighed. "I know it's not you, but since I can't have you, I've had to play make believe."

She had to admit she was relieved that his actions were in relation to her. Not needing or being interested in sex other than when it pertained to her job, she couldn't understand how you could love someone and still want to be sexual with someone else.

"So you see," he said, leaning towards her and grabbing her hand again. "It isn't about them. It isn't even about me," he searched her eyes. "It's about you. Since the day we met, my life has been about you. I love you, Evera."

He watched her face, waiting. She knew what he wanted, but she wasn't willing to give it to him. His actions still hurt too much, and saying 'I love you' was just not part of her vocabulary. She was selfish and possessive when it came to Adam, and even though she knew she couldn't be with him she didn't want anyone else to have him either. It made her a bitch but she couldn't help it.

He was still waiting for her to say something. The intensity of his emotions and their conversation were making her uncomfortable again. She couldn't handle highly emotional situations and he knew it. It felt like a test, and she did not do vulnerable.

"I can't talk about this anymore, Adam," she burst out. "Can we please move onto something else?" she asked, looking away from his hopeful eyes.

"What!" He sounded shocked. "I tell you how all I want is you. That for the last ten years everything, including the other women in my life, have been about you. That I love you, and all you can say is you want to talk about something else?" He looked so wounded, his pain and incredulity at her dismissive words plain on his face and in his hand holding hers. He pulled his fingers free and sat straighter in his chair. Something flickered across his face. Resolve?

"Fine, if that's what you want then let's talk about something else." She could feel the air around him cool instantly. It seemed to travel across the table and make her shiver.

He continued looking at her, daring her to say something. She scrambled for a safe topic, something lighter, but she knew the evening was ruined and nothing would put it back together.

She opened her mouth unsure of what she would say but he quickly interrupted her.

"It's getting late and I have an early morning, we should just call it a night," he determined, already getting up from the table before she could respond.

As he headed to the kitchen she watched him helplessly. "I have to turn off the lights in the back and grab my coat," he said, not bothering to turn around while speaking to her.

And just like that their evening was over. *Fuck!* She screamed in her head. What had she done? She could feel the wall he'd built from here. She couldn't keep doing this to him. This wasn't love or friendship, this was her dragging him into her screwed up little world so she wouldn't have to be alone. It was cruel. And even though she knew that was how the world was, even contributed to it herself, she didn't want to keep being cruel to Adam. He'd let go of his past, tried to move on, now it was just her selfishly holding him back.

She got up from the table and made her way to the front door, hoping the cool, autumn air would help clear her head. Looking up at the sky she saw the moon was just a crescent of light, the air still and calm. She imagined what it would be like to escape up there; silent, dark and easy.

Adam closed the heavy front door to the restaurant and she heard the dead bolt click into place. She didn't turn around, afraid of what she would see on his face. Or worse yet, what he would feel for her.

His hands were suddenly brushing her shoulders. "Here," he said, draping his coat around her.

She turned to look at him. "Thanks," she said, and she was right. She didn't want to see the look in his eyes, or feel the sadness surrounding him.

He didn't smile in response but averted his eyes. He walked over to the beautiful car, its blackness blending into the night, and hit the button to unlock the doors. As he opened her door she moved close, wanting badly to find a way to apologize.

Turning to face him, she reached up to lightly touch his cheek with her finger tips. Pleading for forgiveness with her eyes in a way she never could with her words.

He quickly grasped her hand, but instead of holding it he pulled her fingers away from his face. He waited, not looking at her, while she climbed into the car, and then he slammed the door.

CHAPTER 6

A Night In

They made the drive in stone silence. Adam pushed the car just as fast on the way back, despite the darkness. The silence though, unlike the drive down, was thick and uncomfortable.

Evera felt more and more anxious the closer they got to the Section. She was scrambling in her mind to find some words that would fix the damage, but for the first time in their relationship she felt like the situation may be irreparable. She was still clueless for a solution as they pulled off the highway and onto the driveway.

Adam sped so fast through the winding turns that she gripped the door handle for support. It took only seconds, it seemed, and he was pulling up at the front door and she was out of time.

He quickly made his way around to her door, wrenched it open, and waited for her to get out, keeping his eyes away from her. She got out quickly, passing close, the anger coming off of him palpable. He slammed the door again and walked beside her, never touching her, as they made their way to the front door. He opened it and let her walk in before him, the warm air a welcome change from the chill of the night and Adam himself.

"Evening," said the night guard. Adam nodded in his direction and Evera was thankful that Steven hadn't been there to witness the complete switch in mood from before dinner.

He walked with her to the elevator, got in and punched buttons for both the basement and the sub-basement. She felt panic rise in her throat...he wasn't going to get out with her.

The ride was quick and as the doors opened for her floor she paused, her legs not moving her through the door. The doors started to close but Adam threw his hand in between to stop them.

"Evera?" was all he said, questioningly. She looked at him one last time before she got out, hoping for some change in his mood. But his eyes were flat and empty, just as they had been when they left the restaurant. She quickly looked away and left the elevator, listening to the sound of the doors closing behind her as she made her way slowly down the long hall.

She reached her door and couldn't help but look one door down to Adam's empty apartment. She pulled her keycard from her clutch, swiped it and then punched in her code.

She opened her door and went in, leaning against it, defeated. Her legs felt weak as she slowly slid down to the floor, feeling a panic attack coming on. She concentrated on breathing, knowing from previous attacks that her weakness and lightheadedness were from holding her breath.

Her head cleared within a few seconds but she still felt weak. Maybe not weak but heavy. Heavy in her heart and her body. It was the sorrow she felt weighing her down. She longed to cry, willing the tears to come and give her body a release, but they wouldn't. She hadn't shed a single tear since the day she arrived here, ten years ago today. The irony of it made her want to scream.

After half an hour or so, she thought she heard something beyond the door. It was the muffled movement of feet down the hallway. The sound stopped in front of her apartment. Holding her breath, she waited for the knock. But Adam didn't knock and she heard the sound of his feet continuing down the hall to his room. Frustrated, she picked herself up and headed to her bedroom. The achy feeling of a headache was starting behind her eyes. She didn't know if it was from the crack her skull had taken or the tension of the evening, but she needed relief before she forced herself to bed.

She stripped off her dress, pulled on a tank top and panties, and headed to the kitchen and some ibuprofen. She grabbed her robe off the kitchen chair, where she'd left it earlier, and walked to the cupboard by the fridge. She poured two tablets from the bottle and opened the fridge to find some orange juice to chase them down with.

She stopped when she leaned in and saw what was in the fridge. A massive crystal bowl of water filled with floating irises. More than two dozen perfect blue flowers with a single white iris alone in the center. A card was leaning up against the bowl with her name printed on it. She reached for it and put it on the counter. She carefully lifted the bowl from the fridge and placed it in the middle of her kitchen table.

Admiring the beautiful flowers, she drew in their subtle fragrance. The bowl itself was stunning, made from Swarovski crystal. She turned quickly towards the counter, remembering the card.

She stared at it, afraid to open it in case it was more of what they had talked about tonight. He would have had to put the gift in the fridge this morning before she arrived. She hadn't opened the fridge since coming back and he never brought it up at dinner.

She picked up the envelope and opened it. The card was a creamy white with lilac lettering that said simply, 'thinking of you.' She didn't want to read it. She couldn't take anymore guilt. She contemplated throwing it in the garbage and never mentioning it. Instead, she sighed and opened it. There were only two words written on the page, 'Yours, Always.' Just two words, but somehow those two words ripped into her. And then she went through the evening in her mind, all the little things he had done for her. That he always did for her. And even though she didn't deserve him, she couldn't stand to lose him.

She was suddenly running to her bathroom, trying not to think about what she was about to do, and grabbed Adam's favorite bottle of perfume off the counter. She looked down at her robe and thought about switching it out for something sexier but then decided against it. It was Adam, not some mark, and she clung to that thought as she left her room.

She walked the few steps to Adam's apartment and tapped on the door. She heard nothing at first and wondered if maybe he was sleeping. Then she heard steps coming towards the door and waited, biting her lip.

He heaved the door open, a look of rage on his handsome face. Then his expression changed to one of surprise. "Evera, what are you doing here?" he asked, looking concerned, the anger draining away. "Is everything alright?" he asked, opening the door wide to invite her in. He led her in, his hand on the small of her back, walking her to the couch. Nothing but concern and care radiating off him. She wondered about the murderous look on his face when he had initially answered the door. Who else would be knocking on his door at midnight?

Realization dawned and she knew he had expected it to be another woman. At first she felt angry and then she realized that his hateful glare would have been for whoever was knocking. She took comfort in that, making her even more certain of what she was about to do.

"Everything's fine, Adam," she soothed, sitting nervously on the couch. "Well, everything's fine in the sense that there's no emergency. I'm sorry about stopping by so late. I know you have an early morning," she said apologetically, closing her mouth so she wouldn't ramble.

As he sat down close beside her she noticed he must have been getting ready for bed. His shirt was untucked and unbuttoned down the front. She could see his perfect chest through the parted fabric and when he moved to adjust himself on the couch, she saw his hard stomach muscles ripple.

She waited for something, some wanton feeling, a craving to touch him. She was certain, as she looked him over, that something would spark. Any other woman in the room with him like he was now—beautiful, sexy, bare chest showing—would have to have him. But inside her, still nothing. No urge, no need. She couldn't dwell on her lack of passion any longer. Maybe her feelings would come after she started seducing him. Maybe in the middle of it something would click and she would want him.

"Don't worry about the time, Evera," he said looking at her, his face sad. "I wouldn't have been able to sleep anyways," he said honestly.

She could see that he was waiting for her to add something, but as usual the idea of talking about her feelings stunted her tongue. She decided to take offensive action and let him know what was on her mind in a different way.

She leaned into him, watching to gauge his reaction, as she reached to remove his glasses, setting them on the coffee table. He stared back, questioningly. She put her hand on his knee and started running her fingers slowly up and down his thigh, shifting closer. He grabbed her hand suddenly and stopped her, his face confused but his body affected.

"What are you doing, Evera?" he asked, his feelings torn. "I thought you came here to talk."

"Who said anything about talking," she whispered, and then the Jezebel in her kicked in and she knew she could do this.

Moving her free hand to his bare chest, she ran her fingers down slowly to his stomach and then to the top of his pants. Her lips found his neck and she started kissing him, her mouth moving lower as her fingers moved to undo his button.

"Evera, stop," he said breathlessly, although his tone was weak and unconvincing. His hands gripped her upper arms but instead of pushing her away he held her still.

Her lips slipped down his chest, her tongue trailing a path to his taut stomach. She deftly undid his zipper at the same moment and dipped her fingers just below the waistband of his Calvin Klein's. Her fingers ran softly back and forth as his muscles flexed and he sucked in a sharp breath.

His grip on her arms suddenly tightened and he lifted her up against him, his elation smoking its way around her. He stood and she wrapped her legs around his waist as his lips started to come down on hers. She moved her face at the last second and gave him access to her neck as he started walking them to his bedroom. She roughly grabbed a handful of his hair, holding on, as she moved her free hand across his shoulder and under his shirt. He tugged at her robe, pulling it off at the same time she pulled his shirt free from his body. Nothing separating the hot flesh of his chest from hers but her thin tank top.

As he neared his bedroom his lips travelled back up to her mouth. Pulling on his hair, she tried to move his lips down towards her chest. His arms still wrapped around her, he stopped moving and lifted his face to look in her eyes. She looked back at him, feeling the desire pulsing through his body, his eyes burning into hers. Watching her intently, he tried to bring his mouth back to hers. But she couldn't seem to stop herself from closing her lips and turning her head, so he ended up kissing her cheek.

He pulled his face away from hers, confused, and suddenly his hands were on her hips, tugging her from his body as he stood her in front of him.

"Don't stop, Adam," she hushed, trying to push herself against him. But he held her at arm's length, his passion and confusion sifting away as anger took its place.

"Kiss me, Evera," he stared her down, challenging her.

Shit! She screamed to herself. She looked up at him, his face so chiseled and beautiful. His lips so full and close. She just needed to lean in, touch her mouth to his and everything would continue. She started to move closer to his face and then paused, uncomfortable. It was too much. Sex and all of its unbearable closeness, she could handle; she could always distance herself mentally, play her role and get through it. It was the kiss that she couldn't reconcile. Not even with Adam.

She was taking too long. She could feel his anger growing, boiling over.

She pulled back, looking at him apologetically. Loosening her grip on the back of his hair she moved her hands to his broad shoulders, unwilling to break their contact.

"Can't do it, can you?" he asked rhetorically, his face grim.

She opened her mouth to say she was sorry but, as usual, her apology stuck in her throat.

"So you're alright to fuck me as long as you don't have to kiss me? Does that sound about right?" he demanded, furious.

He pulled away from her, dropping his hands from her waist. She felt suddenly cold after the heat of his body.

"It's just me, Adam. It's how I'm made," she explained. "It's just too intense and overwhelming for me. It has nothing to do with you."

"Oh, I think it has something to do with me," he answered bitterly. "It's my lips you won't kiss—it's me you won't let get close to you."

She racked her mind for a way through to him and decided to change tactics.

"Can't we just try?" she offered, grabbing his hips, hoping that her hands and her pleading tone would win him over. "You asked me earlier this evening to try," she reminded. "Well, this is me trying for you, Adam," she waited.

"So everything and anything but kissing?" he asked calmly, but she sensed something seething in his question.

"For now," she answered honestly, squeezing her hands tighter on his waist in a wordless apology.

"So who am I really getting tonight?" his eyes darkened and his voice flared. "Sounds to me like I'm getting Jezebel. And believe me, I have no desire to fuck with her," he spat.

She was so shocked by his words that she dropped her hands from his hips and took a step back.

"I'm not one of your marks, Evera!" he yelled in her face. She stood where she was, unable to move even though his anger was painful to take.

He raised his hands to his head. "Arrggghh!" he yelled in frustration, pacing away from her and up to the wall beside his bedroom door. His fist suddenly shot out hard and fast, punching a hole through the wall so far his entire hand disappeared. He stood there not moving, his muscular back a tense rigid line, his breath coming fast.

"No, Adam!" she professed, cringing for his pain. "I don't see you that way," but she was lying to herself and to him. Turning loose the Jezebel inside her to get through the night; and he had seen right through her. "I mean, you're not just some random guy I'm sleeping with because I have an agenda," she amended. "I want to be with you, Adam," she promised. "I just don't know how to do that without feeling like I'm giving myself up."

She watched his sculpted back as his breathing returned to normal. He pulled his fist from the wall, drywall and dust falling to the floor by his feet, his hand a powdery white. He shook most of it off as he turned to face her, his eyes ambivalent.

"You are not a mark to me, Adam," she claimed his gaze. "You are so much more than that. And it's me, Evera, you get. You're the only man who will ever get this side of me."

His eyes holding hers, he walked towards her as his lips parted. "Prove it," he rasped.

"How?" she asked bewildered, as he came closer still.

"By giving me the one thing you won't give to anyone else." He was so close, their bodies almost touching.

"What is that?" she asked, confused.

He shook his head, not relenting. "You know what," he answered passionately. His hands were suddenly gripping her face as his fingers twisted in her hair. His mouth came down hard on hers, his naked chest pressed tight against her, his desire for her burning her skin. His lips and tongue tried to force her mouth open, willing her to kiss him back.

Her head was spinning, he was too close, too demanding, she couldn't breathe. And then she tasted it. Tasted the strong bite of whiskey on his lips, could smell it on his breath. It triggered something inside her, a dark memory. She struggled against it as it tried to claw its way to the surface, her blood simmering.

She shoved him away hard, her hand lashing out as she slapped his face. They stood facing each other, both of them stunned, both of them breathing hard.

"Evera, I—" he began, but she wouldn't let him finish.

"You're drunk!" her voice shrilled. She felt momentarily disgusted by him and tried to shrug it off.

He sighed heavily, the fire in his gaze cooling until it was gone. She felt suddenly horrible about the red mark on his cheek.

"I had 'A' drink, Evera," he defended, walking towards the living room. She looked over at the kitchen table and saw the bottle of Jack Daniel's and a glass with melting ice. "Under the circumstances, I didn't think one drink would be out of line.

Honestly, I wanted to down the entire bottle," he confessed, as he sank wearily onto the couch.

Moving to sit next to him, she leaned her elbows on her knees and stared straight ahead at the wall.

"Jesus Christ, Adam, do you finally see?" she insisted, sitting back and looking again at the table holding the bottle. He was drinking because of her. "I'm unhealthy for you and we both know it." The truth pierced through her and she found herself wishing she could take back her words along with the realization.

"No, you're not, Evera," he disagreed.

She laughed without humor and confronted him. "I am seriously and permanently screwed up."

"That's not true" he argued, shaking his head. "You're just broken inside. It's not something that can't be mended, believe me I know," he insisted, smiling gently and reaching to hold her hand.

She shook her head in disagreement. She knew his life had been just as hard, if not harder, than hers and he had managed to put himself back together. But she was different than him. Weaker.

"I'm not just broken, Adam," she began. "It's like I'm looking out from a mirror that's been cracked a thousand times. Every piece of me gripping the back with all my might because it's the only thing holding me together," she said, her voice full of sadness. "If I open up and let go, I'll shatter into a million pieces. You can't fix shattered." Another truth, she was irreparable.

"That's not what you are, Evera," he looked at her intensely. "You're stronger than you think."

She smiled sadly at him and looked down at her hands. He gave her too much credit. Her appearance of strength was just that, an appearance. It was the facade she needed to keep herself together.

"What now?" she asked, not looking at him.

"Now I guess we both just try and get some rest," he said, rising from the couch and pulling her up with him.

"You're right, I should go and let you get some sleep," she said, unable to hide the sadness in her voice.

"I mean 'we' should get some rest. You can stay, Evera. I want you to," he added, smiling gently.

She wanted so badly to stay, but she didn't want to push him any further tonight.

"I don't think that's such a good idea considering…well, you know, just considering." She felt suddenly unsure with him.

He ran his hand up and down her arm in a soothing gesture. "I think 'considering' everything that just happened between us, that it's the perfect idea." He leaned in and kissed her forehead. "You go ahead and use the bathroom first," he offered thoughtfully.

"Thanks." She looked back at him and smiled without feeling as she made her way down the hall to the bathroom. When she got there she closed the door and sat down on the edge of the bathtub, contemplating everything that had just gone wrong. She couldn't help but wonder how, despite how badly things had turned out, she still managed to end up spending the night with Adam.

She grabbed her toothbrush from under the sink and started her bedtime routine. When she was finished, she wiped down the sink and mirror. She looked at her reflection for a moment. Still no wrinkles despite the constant time in the sun. She looked around her eyes and mouth. Still no laugh lines either. What she wouldn't give for a few of those. To know she'd had enough happiness in her life to have earned some.

She ran into Adam as she was exiting the bathroom. "I'm going to take a quick shower before bed," he said, carrying a towel. "You go ahead and crawl in."

As she slipped between his sheets alone, she couldn't help but wonder what tomorrow would bring. She went over their last conversation in her mind. He knew what it was like to be broken. But unlike her, he'd worked on fixing himself, letting go and moving forward.

She remembered sitting in a coffee shop with him five years ago as he told her the story of the worst day of his life. The point when everything changed and his life became just another story of death and tragedy.

*****

Adam had been four years old and yet his clarity flashing back to that moment in time was perfect. He couldn't remember faces or images but he remembered exactly how he'd felt.

He described the day he'd had with his older brother Ben. Their tyrant of a father had left early that Saturday to go to work and he and Ben had spent the entire summer day outside. Their mother was sleeping off a hangover from the night before and he and Ben broke the rules and went down to the pond two miles behind their small two bedroom house.

Ben was only eleven but he had assumed the role of primary caregiver for Adam. Adam adored Ben; he was his best friend and the only person in his family who didn't frighten him. Ben had packed sandwiches, juice boxes and fishing rods into an old satchel he'd found under the porch. They'd spent the day fishing, swimming, catching frogs and napping lazily by the water. He remembered feeling truly happy. But that was the last time he remembered having that feeling before his life crumbled.

When the sun began to set, Ben packed up their things and called it a day. They still had a two mile walk home and Ben didn't want them walking past nightfall because he knew how much Adam hated the dark.

And the darker it got, the more afraid Adam became. Ben, seeing Adam's discomfort, grabbed his hand and held it tight.

Adam remembered Ben looking down and smiling at him. "It's okay, buddy," he said kindly, "we're almost there." Ben's soothing words comforted him and made him less frightened. To Adam, Ben was his superhero, his protector.

When they arrived home the sun had almost set and it was close to 8:30. Their mother was in the living room watching TV and gave them crap for being out so late. Ben ignored her, as he so often did, and told Adam to go brush his teeth and get ready for bed. Adam said he would after he grabbed a glass of water.

A voice boomed in the background. "You boys better fucking listen to your mother when she's talking to you!" It was their father. He was home and angry drunk.

His loud voice startled Adam so badly that he dropped his water glass, scattering glass all over the kitchen floor.

"Why you klutzy, little asshole," his father yelled. His long hair and matted beard were as wild and fierce as the look in his eyes. He started weaving towards the kitchen and Adam, whose feet were frozen to the floor in terror.

But Ben stepped between them, blocking their father's path. His father stopped, but only so he could swear at Ben, his face turning red from rage. And then he started hurting Ben, his fists raining down on his head, over and over, until Adam started screaming for him to stop. His mother finally managed to stumble over and grabbed uselessly at his swinging arms.

"Stop!" she screamed. "Please stop! You're killing him!" By this time Ben was on the floor not moving and his father started kicking at him like a dog.

"Enough already," begged his mother, sobbing. "That's enough. Just let it go, John," she cried.

Adam saw Ben on the floor beaten and still and something in him snapped. He charged at his father, but for as drunk as he was he saw him coming, and backhanded him across the face, hard. He went sailing through the air, hitting his head against the kitchen counter and crashing to the floor. He saw black spots before his eyes and felt vomit rise in his throat.

He'd landed facing Ben. Ben's eyes were partially closed, blood was trickling from his mouth, his body lifeless.

"Ben," Adam pleaded in a whisper, and then he blacked out.

When Adam came to later that night, in the double bed he and Ben shared, he was alone. He walked down the hall to his parents' room and peeked his head in to see only his mother, sitting up watching a movie and drinking beer.

He was afraid to ask but couldn't help himself. "Where's Ben?" he asked, unable to keep his words from coming out in a sob.

His mother looked at him, trying hard to focus, her eyes bloodshot from tears and booze.

"Ben's gone," she said flatly, a single tear escaping down her face. Then she turned back to her movie without saying another word.

Adam cried himself to sleep that night.

Two days later his father showed up at the house. Adam stayed in his room and listened at the door. His father said he was just stopping by to grab his clothes. He was accepted on a tour in the army for Baghdad and was leaving tomorrow. Adam could just imagine the horrible things he promised to do in order for them to take him back.

"Where did you..." his mother tried to ask, choking on her words. "Where did you put my baby?"

"I took care of it, that's all you need to know," his voice flat and grim. Adam peeked his head out. His father was almost ten feet away but Adam was sure he could see the dirt under his fingernails.

He turned, without looking in Adam's direction, and left. Adam never saw him again.

Six months later they received a knock at their door. An army official stopped by to say that his father had died in the line of duty. His mother received a small sum of money as compensation but drank it away in little more than a month.

After that, Adam's mother moved from place to place and man to man. Most of the men were similar to Adam's father, drunks prone to violence. Adam did everything he could to stay small and unnoticed, and the abuse was always much less if he was submissive. Unfortunately, three of the men took more than a little interest in Adam.

When Adam was sixteen he'd had enough and ran away, ending up in a group home with kids whose pasts were every bit as horrifying as his. He spent his days working whatever jobs he could get, and his nights at the local gym boxing. And drinking.

He was really good with his fists and when he turned eighteen one of the trainers at the gym suggested he check out the army. The last thing he wanted was to follow in his father's footsteps but he'd been told he'd get free food, free training and a free education. He couldn't pass it up and so he enlisted as soon as he sobered. He had to take an IQ test to get in and when his results came back that he was genius level, doors started opening for him. He cleaned himself up, stopped drinking and started moving up the ranks.

He used his security clearance to look into his father's history and it was then that he learned about the experimental drugs his father had been on.

The army had selected several men in their early twenties to participate in a genetics/violence program. The men they selected were men who would have been dishonorably discharged because of their behavior, men who were already prone to violence. They were offered this program, knowing that they would be guinea pigs but told they would be allowed to stay in the army if they agreed.

The experiment was a disaster. The recruits were given two pills a day, one to enhance their anger and the other to try and control it. They wanted to create a mental switch that allowed the men to control their rage. But also, so that when they wanted to unleash it, it would be without emotion or pity; an obedient, remorseless killer.

It failed miserably. The recruits became more violent but still lacked any self-control. Most were honorably discharged within the year, despite the agreement the army had made with them.

After Adam discovered the truth about his father he ended up doing extensive genetic research on himself. He was frightened that somehow the drugs may have altered his father genetically, and passed on his violent traits to Adam. He found nothing of concern in his genetic coding.

He was also disappointed to find out that his father had already been a vicious, violent man before he'd participated in the program. Some part of him had always hoped that his father's behavior wasn't his fault. That he couldn't help being who he was.

The Section ended up being where Adam wanted to settle. He knew about all the special ops training and education offered there, and when Jonas had approached him to come and join his team, he jumped at the opportunity.

He was twenty-one when Evera met him for the first time; the day she drove up in her rusty Jeep and he rescued her.

She learned from Adam that her father had been part of the same experimental drug program as Adam's father. She worried too that somehow some of his evil may have been passed down to her. Maybe her gift for being able to feel people's emotions was a side-effect of the program. But Adam assured her that the violence gene was not something that had been altered or passed down to her genetically. Her special abilities, however, he couldn't be sure of.

It had always surprised her how completely Adam had been able to let go of his past. He willingly saw Stella for counseling, unafraid of confronting the horrors in his life before the Section.

Evera asked him once if he ever thought of finding his mother and he'd easily said no, explaining that he had no desire to ever see her again.

The sound of the bathroom door opening broke through her reverie. Adam came walking quietly into the dark room. She could just make out the snug black boxer briefs he always wore from the light shining under the bathroom door.

He climbed in beside her. "You still awake?" he whispered.

She turned over to face him. He was bare chested, his hair damp and his face clean shaven. She inhaled the delicious scent of his aftershave; masculine, clean and so comfortingly familiar.

"Just waiting for you," she said sleepily. The clock on his bedside table said 1:00 a.m., and with all the emotional stress of the day she was exhausted.

"Come here," he said, as he opened his arms, inviting her.

She scooted close, leaning her head against his hard chest as he wrapped his arms around her. She had felt chilled but he was so warm, she curled against him sinking into the heat from his body. They lay like that, silently together, for several minutes. Adam's love wrapping around her like a cocoon. It had its own feel and taste, a sweetness that settled into her bones.

But then his feelings started to change. His body's need for her a slow burn. She could feel him hard and hot against her hipbone.

"Sorry," he whispered softly, and turned over, pushing his back against her, staying close.

She snuggled up tight against his strong back, drinking in the smell of his skin. This ritual happened almost every time they slept together, but tonight it had a strange edge, almost bittersweet. She didn't want to think anymore, she just wanted to sleep in the comfort of Adam's arms and dream.

CHAPTER 7

Waking Up

Evera awoke to the sound of water running. She felt groggy, like it was still the middle of the night. When she turned over and looked at Adam's alarm clock she saw the bright green 3:30 a.m., definitely still the middle of the night. Adam wasn't beside her and at first she thought he was just using the bathroom but then she heard him brushing his teeth.

She rolled over and groaned. *What now?* She hoped that whatever had Adam up didn't pertain to her. She was beyond exhausted and the bed felt extra cozy and warm.

Adam came out of the bathroom already dressed, turning off the switch quickly so as not to wake her. Too late. He walked stealthily into the room and then saw her laying on her side, her elbow propping her up.

"Hey beautiful, sorry to wake you," he said, leaning across the bed and kissing her hair. "Duty calls," he explained, smiling.

"What's happening that you have to get up now? I thought you weren't leaving for another day or two?" she asked, yawning.

"Jonas texted me about twenty minutes ago. He's leaving on a flight at 5:00 a.m. and he wants me to go with him to Columbia now instead of meeting him in Arlington," Adam answered, sitting on the bed and pulling on his socks. "I had my phone on vibrate and was surprised I heard it. We could have been woken up by Jonas bursting in on us. Talk about the ultimate wake up call," he said, laughing.

Evera cringed at the thought of Jonas walking in on them in bed together. She was aware that most people at the Section knew of their close relationship, but there was much speculation as to whether they were just friends or lovers. Laying here in Adam's bed, she wasn't sure herself.

His socks on, he headed to his closet, grabbing T-shirts and pants and laying them in his black duffel bag. He walked over to his dresser and pulled his designer black underwear from the drawer, along with extra socks, stuffing them in the side compartment of his bag.

He stood by the bed, looking around to see if he had forgotten anything. She noticed he was wearing a black T-shirt that hugged the muscles along his chest and torso, along with weathered jeans. He turned around to grab his watch from on top of his dresser and again Evera couldn't help but appreciate his undeniable sex appeal.

He noticed her looking him over as he was fastening his watch.

"What?" he asked, his lips in a cocky grin. "Taking a good look? Not bad, huh?"

She couldn't help but smile back, even though she felt an ache at the thought of him leaving. This was the moment she always dreaded the most. That moment of panic that something could go wrong and she would never see him again.

"Puleeze," she said, rolling her eyes. "Just be careful," she couldn't keep the worry from her voice.

"Don't worry, it's just interrogation," he rationalized, leaning across the bed and holding her face with his warm hand. He kept his hand there longer than usual, staring into her eyes. She could feel his love but there was sadness mixed in, something that was never present in their previous good-byes. How she wished she could read his thoughts and not just his emotions.

"I'll be back in a couple of days," he released her face to stand, slinging his bag onto his shoulder. He winked as he walked out the bedroom door. A few seconds later she heard the front door open and close, and the lock click into place. And then he was gone.

*****

Evera spent the early morning hours back at her apartment, doing the meticulous cleaning she had missed the day before. She scrubbed down her small bathroom until it was shining. She tackled the laundry that was piling up and set aside some dresses to send away for dry-cleaning before getting ready for the day.

Pulling on her favorite worn jeans she slipped on a white T-shirt over her bra and padded barefoot to the kitchen. She contemplated heading to the dining room for a full, hot breakfast, but the idea of having to be sociable this early when she was so wiped was unappealing.

Picking through the small selection in her fridge she found nothing interesting and gave up. Hoping to find something more appetizing in the freezer she dug to the back until she found some frozen waffles. She didn't keep her fridge very well stocked, as it was pointless since she was often called away last minute. She popped two buckwheat waffles in the toaster and went to make herself a pot of coffee. Only a few lonely grounds remained at the bottom of the tin, just enough for one small cup.

She leaned against the counter waiting for the coffee to brew and the toaster to pop. She liked her small kitchen, unlike Adam, as she didn't cook much. She poured steaming coffee into her mug full of cream and sugar and chucked her waffles onto her plate on the table. Adding a ton of syrup, she leisurely ate her breakfast while admiring the bowl of irises.

As beautiful as they were, she couldn't help but feel as if they were a bittersweet reminder of last night. She wondered what would happen between them when Adam returned and she quickly flashed back to the sadness in their parting this morning. If only she could magically change for him, find some way to crossover from friends to lovers and not feel like she was giving something up. Finally allow herself to be vulnerable enough to fall in love physically and not just mentally. She cringed in fear at the idea of giving herself over so completely.

She drained the last of her coffee and started clearing her dishes from the table. She would have to contemplate the situation with Adam some other time. She still had to get down to the hub and file her official report from her last trip before 9:00 a.m. and it was already 7:15 a.m. Jonas tended to cut her a little slack on deadlines because of their many years together, but she knew from experience that Garrison would not.

She went down the hall to the bathroom to brush her teeth and put on her locket. Just as she was finishing up she heard a sharp knock on her door. She rushed down the short hall and opened the door, coming face-to-face with the last person she expected to see this early in the morning.

"Good morning, Evera." It was Garrison. His lean frame filled her doorway, his suit so angularly cut that it screamed pretention. He somehow managed to sound terse even when he was delivering a greeting. He was close enough that she could feel him; edgy. "I need to speak to you about an assignment, ASAP," he said, in his usual clipped and matter-of-fact tone. The man had the personality of a plastic bag.

"Alright, but I'll need at least an hour" she replied, trying to keep the distaste in her voice to a minimum. "I have to write up my report from my last assignment and, as I recall, you require it to be submitted by 9:00 a.m. sharp. No exceptions," she added.

"Yes, well, today I'm willing to make an exception," he replied. "Meet me down the hall in room fifty-seven in five minutes," he insisted, as he turned and left without waiting for her reply. She had sensed the reigned in tension in his body, so unlike his usual blasé emotional state. Not to mention, Garrison never made exceptions.

She put on her flip flops and grabbed her purse, taking a perfunctory glance at the wall clock. Likely only a minute had passed and she was sure she would fare much better in a room alone with Garrison if she had another cup of coffee to occupy her hands. She headed straight for the elevator and the sub-basement level, hoping upon hope that a few drops of java had survived the breakfast rush.

She rounded the corner and went through the doorway into the almost empty dining room. There were only two seats occupied, both by new recruits, one of them the blonde who was eyeing Adam the day before. They had their backs to her and she was grateful that the coffee urn was still on the serving table behind them so that they wouldn't notice her.

She could hear them going over questions from the training manual, their heads close together as they shared the book.

She started preparing her to-go cup when she heard the blonde laugh loudly from behind her.

"I know, they were all so hot, but seriously," she said, longing in her voice. "It's Adam I can't stop thinking about. I just want to sink my teeth into him. That man is sex-on-a-stick," she finished huskily. It took all of Evera's training in self-control not to crush the coffee cup she was holding and rip the girl's hair out by the roots.

She turned and stepped quickly from the dining room, not bothering to look and see if they had noticed her. She sped towards the elevator and by the time she was in and travelling back up, her anger had melted into despair.

What did she expect? At some point Adam would have enough of her turning him down and there would be no shortage of girls waiting, begging, to take her place. She felt defeated as she made her way down the hallway to room fifty-seven.

She knocked sharply, waiting for an invitation to enter.

"Come in," said the monotone voice behind the door. Evera entered the nearly empty room and walked straight to the vacant chair in front of the desk. The desk held a container of pens, a letter opener and pencils along with a stack of papers and a phone.

"Thank you for being so prompt," Garrison said, although his tone did not suggest any gratitude whatsoever. "I see you stopped and got yourself a coffee," he commented. It seemed he couldn't say anything nice without following it up with something derogatory.

"You said five minutes and I do believe that I arrived here with time to spare," she battled, letting in the sarcasm.

"Regardless," he continued, shuffling through some papers on his desk and pulling out a thin file. "Do you know anything about this man?"

She reached for the file, the cover blank, and flipped it open. Inside was a bio sheet with very little information. In the top right-hand corner was a grainy black and white photograph of a man with dark hair wearing sunglasses. She looked through the bio sheet at the last name, Unknown; first name, Cort; age, Between 35 and 40; and location, Unknown. It continued like that throughout the page, half of the information filled in with 'Unknown' and the other half with speculations.

"I know something of him," she said, trying to recall the few times they had picked him up on the radar screen. "He's an information trader, he likes to play both sides against each other to increase his profit margins and then sells to the highest bidder."

"Precisely," said Garrison, seeming almost excited for the first time since she had met him close to a year ago. He ran his fingers quickly through his sandy brown hair, messing it up in his happy agitated state.

"He does all his dealings behind the scenes from a remote location, never interacting with any of the trades. He sends out an e-mail along with a blue flash drive containing encrypted information. Then the winning bid receives a red flash drive with the encryption breakdown. He never shows his face to his clients so there's no one who can identify him," he said, reaching towards Evera to retrieve the file. As he flipped through it Evera couldn't help but notice how much better Garrison looked when he put some animation into his face. He was actually quite attractive. He was in his early thirties but his demeanor always came across as that of a grumpy old man.

"If you flip to the back of the file you can see that we tracked him on his way to a meeting in Hawaii two years back. We sent a Judith operative to try and get some information out of him but she was unsuccessful. He was in a relationship at the time and so he refused all of her advances," he said, shaking his head. "Who says there isn't honor among thieves?" he commented in disbelief.

"Anyways," he continued, "the meeting back then was exclusive and highly guarded. Each of the guests was required to show up in disguise. We didn't know it at the time but there were several of our most wanted players attending the meeting. Not to mention it was the only time we've ever heard of Cort making an appearance at an underground meeting."

Evera was listening intensely now, intrigued but anxiously awaiting the punch line.

"We just picked up some intel that one of his pilots, who works solely for him, was in a car accident. We were keeping tabs on him and he made a call to another pilot asking him to cover his upcoming flight. He offered to split the pay because he didn't want to miss out on the payoff; apparently Cort pays generously. The flight was this morning to Maui, same hotel as his last visit to Hawaii two years ago," he said, his voice raising up an octave and bordering on excitement.

Evera could see where this was going and she felt exhausted just thinking about it. The flight alone would be eight hours, not to mention stop overs, and Stella had told her to take it easy for the next couple of days. She could still feel the ache in her ribs and her head, and the lack of sleep was seriously pulling her down.

"I want you there, Evera," he said vehemently. "I want you on a plane leaving from the operations airport to New York in ninety minutes."

She opened her mouth to say something but he was already continuing, not waiting for her response. "His plane arrives in Maui at 3:00 their time, so the meeting won't be until tomorrow at least. That should give you plenty of time to arrive tonight and get the lay of the hotel. We don't know if he's in a relationship but regardless, he may not take the bait so to speak. It doesn't matter, if you're there then we'll have an extra set of eyes. And if you do happen to get to him, any data you get—names, even a photograph of him—would be invaluable. He's only a soft target, as he's worth more to us alive. It's been three years since we first picked him up on our radar and still we have almost nothing. This is our chance to finally get something." Garrison was smiling, not bothering to wonder whether she would take the assignment.

She felt so tired at the thought of another assignment so soon, and wondered if she would actually turn down a mission for the first time in her career.

"What do Jonas and Adam say about this?" she countered. "I just got back yesterday from my last assignment, I haven't even filled out my report yet and I've barely unpacked," she complained, frustrated at the position he was putting her in.

His face turned suddenly stoic, his smile shut down. "Adam has no say, nor do I answer to him. And as for Jonas, he left me in charge, which means it's up to me, and me alone, to make decisions for the Section."

"Look," she said, knowing he was right but still hoping for a way around this, "I just think that—"

"Think!" he interrupted sharply, leaning across the desk, his anger drifting into her. "We don't pay you to think. Your job is to fuck and to kill, nothing more," he announced, bitingly. "So I suggest you go and do your job," he finished, sitting back slowly in his chair.

She glared blackly at him, too angry to speak, and rose quickly to leave. The need to escape before she did something stupid was a pulse in her head. She grabbed her purse from the back of the chair, all the while fighting the urge to jam the letter opener down his throat.

"And Evera," he said, stopping her just before she reached the door, "get me something on this bastard," and he threw the file towards her. His face showing gratitude now that he'd put her in her place.

She left, clutching the file hard in her hands and resisted the urge to slam the door. She paced down the hall to her room, fuming and choking over all the crude and vicious names she had wanted to scream at him.

At her apartment, she unlocked the door and went in, slamming her door instead and hurled the file across the room. She paced back and forth in the small space trying to calm herself and focus on what it was she had to do next. She was certain she was going, not really having been given a choice.

She ran her fingers through her hair in frustration and then went to retrieve the file from the floor. After a quick perusal, she attempted to deduce the kind of woman that would appeal to Cort so that she could decide how to pack.

Unfortunately, there was nothing to glean from the information they had on him. No descriptions of his previous or existing girlfriends, nothing to note other than that he didn't tend towards one-night stands. Given the position she needed to put him in, literally, that last bit didn't leave her with much hope of achieving anything. She removed the information stick attached to the back of the file and loaded the more complete, comprehensive profile onto her phone.

She went to her bedroom and grabbed her white backpack from its usual spot on the top shelf of her closet as well as a small carry-on suitcase. She picked out a little bit of everything: short skirts, dresses both sweet and sexy, a couple of bathing suits and underwear. She rifled through one of her dresser drawers looking for some sweaters for the chilly nights and some shorts and T-shirts. Her toiletry bag was already prepacked with the usual essentials so she stuffed it on top of the pile in her suitcase. Looking at her small book shelf in the corner, she decided to grab a book or two as well. She chose her favorite, *Jane Eyre* with its worn pages, the only book she had brought with her the day she arrived at the Section. She also grabbed a book on the different wine regions throughout Tuscany. Imagining that she would spend most of her time observing Cort come and go, she knew she would appreciate the reading material to break up the monotony.

Checking the back of the file, which had an envelope and her itinerary, she realized she needed to leave the apartment within ten minutes. There would be a car waiting outside to take her on the forty-five minute drive to the small airport and the Section's private plane. Looking around, she couldn't help but feel like she was forgetting something. Leaving in a panic like this made her feel disorganized.

Grabbing her purse, her overflowing backpack, and pulling her suitcase she headed to the door and turned for one last glimpse of the irises on the table. She felt sad that she wouldn't get to enjoy them; they would most likely be dead by the time she returned.

The hallway quiet, she arrived at the elevator doors alone and punched the 'Up' button.

Just as she was exiting she spied Steven at the main desk waiting expectantly for her. She hit the heel of her hand on her forehead as she realized she had forgotten her kit of colored contacts.

"Is the car here yet?" she asked, hoping for five more minutes to run back to her apartment. She felt too exposed going in character with her natural hair and eye color.

"Just pulled up. You have great timing," he said, bringing over his clipboard as she passed over her keycard. Steven stashed it in a filing cabinet beside the entrance desk and then had her sign that she'd checked it in. He gave her a thick envelope containing her new identity: passport, driver's license and credit cards. Lastly, he handed over her cleaned bracelet. She put it on and instantly felt the switch to Jezebel.

"How was the dinner last night?" asked Steven.

"It was great," she said, not wanting to be reminded of the last bitter scene in the restaurant. "Peking duck to die for," she added, and smiled as she headed out the front doors.

"Good to hear," he said, following behind and walking her out to the car. Stan was waiting by the back passenger door, holding it open. She walked over, handed him her backpack and suitcase and climbed in. He closed the door and then placed her luggage in the already open trunk, slamming it shut.

Stan climbed into the driver's seat, making himself comfortable behind the steering wheel before shutting his door.

He turned around to look at her. "What's it going to be today, Evera? A music score or some of the classics?" he asked.

"You chose, Stan," she offered. The car was warm and quiet and she felt as though she could finally sleep. "I might just try and rest during the drive," she said, stifling a yawn.

"Nocturnes it is," he decided, searching through his playlist on the cars dashboard. The soft sounds of violins and cellos filled the car, soothing her instantly. She leaned her head back against the seat as her eyelids drifted closed.

CHAPTER 8

The First Time

The commercial plane was angling towards Hawaii's main airport, touching down in another thirty minutes. The flight to New York had been quicker than usual because of the help from a tailwind. During the flight she thoroughly scoured Cort's file on her phone. The last sentence on the bio had been the most intriguing, the speculation that Cort was also White. He was shrewd, discreet and in three years the only photo was a bad black and white taken by a Judith operative, unable to lure him close enough for anything more. Getting Garrison any amount of information was sure to be next to impossible. It was obvious this man trusted no one, which was probably why he was still alive.

As she waited impatiently for a glimpse of the lush ground below, she absentmindedly reached towards her neck and the locket that wouldn't be there. She sucked in a startled breath. Her fingers touched the delicate metal hanging from the slender chain. *Shit!* That was what had been plaguing the back of her mind; she had forgotten to leave it behind.

Never in the three years of being on Jezebel missions had she ever worn her necklace. Once she put on her deadly bracelet and walked out of the Section for a mission she switched over and became Jezebel; the locket was a piece of Evera.

Panic set in. How could she have forgotten this, of all things? The bracelet and locket represented the two different sides of her, she never wore them together. And what if she lost it? It meant more to her than anything else she owned. To anyone else it would seem worthless, a trinket. It was just a heart shaped locket with a crisscross design running across the face of it, and a single row of crystals. But to her it was priceless.

She fidgeted with it gently. It was too late to worry now, but she knew it would pick at her for the whole trip.

She tried to let it go as the seat belt sign went on and the cabin tilted forward. The green of the island was more noticeable. She could make out individual trees and cars. She had never been to Hawaii before and was looking forward to seeing it. Her hope was that Cort would be untouchable and she could spend most of her time just keeping track of his comings and goings.

A part of her couldn't help but wonder if she would be encountering White for the first time. She lost a little of her hope that she would be lounging carelessly by the pool, realizing if Cort was White, this would be a dangerous mission.

Nothing, she was certain, would ever compare to her first mission though. She had come closer to death that day than she ever had before or since. If it weren't for Adam she would have ended up just like the Judith operative before her…an abandoned corpse, rotting away in some back alley.

Her first Jezebel mission had been almost three years ago. And still, the memories from that encounter and the horrifying outcome she had narrowly escaped made her cringe. She couldn't seem to stop herself from reliving the incident as the plane edged closer to her destination.

*****

His name was Daniel Craft. He wasn't just a mark that the Section wanted to retrieve information from, Jonas wanted revenge.

Daniel Craft had been a lawyer for many of the criminals the CIA tried to convict. He was high profile in Europe and always in the public eye. The CIA wanted him out of the picture but didn't want to get their hands or their reputation dirty.

That's when they called in the Section. Their assignment was to retrieve whatever they could on Daniel's clients through either his phone or the laptop that seemed chained to his hand.

Evera was still in training for the Judith Program at the time, so it was her predecessor who was in line for the mission.

Daniel was going to be attending an event in Italy where the current lead operative was to seduce him, and gather any intel she could get her hands on. She had to be extra careful when interacting with Daniel as he had a strange, violent fetish; he liked to strangle some of the women he slept with. That was of no concern to the CIA or the Section, though. They just wanted Daniel.

It had been of no concern, that is, until the Section's operative had ended up dead.

She'd been found in an alley ten blocks from the hotel, shot with her own gun. Of course they had no way of knowing exactly what had gone wrong, but Jonas and Adam shared the same suspicion. They were both sure that Daniel had been tipped off about the Judith Program. Jonas was worried it was White and Adam thought it was a leak in the CIA. Regardless, Jonas wanted retribution. He couldn't do anything about White or the CIA, but he could get to Daniel.

They still needed to get a hold of some intel to get the CIA off their backs and remind them of the Section's effectiveness, but Jonas' main agenda was to eliminate Daniel.

He approached Evera about taking over as the Judith Program's point operative. Jonas felt she was more than prepared. She accepted enthusiastically, eager to impress him.

Adam had been furious with both her and Jonas. He was insistent she wasn't properly trained yet and would need at least another six months to a year before she would be ready to handle a job like this on her own.

But Evera knew the real reason behind his reluctance to accept her in this new position, and she suspected Jonas knew as well.

Jonas brushed off Adam's concerns and lined up her assignment immediately. Daniel Craft would be attending an art gala at the Louvre in Paris in one week. Jonas personally helped Evera prepare for the mission, going over strategies, contingencies and Daniel's itinerary. And it was Jonas who chose her operative name for her—Jezebel.

Adam wanted to go along and watch out for her but Jonas refused. He reminded Adam of the liability factor of too many people involved. It would be Jezebel's mission and all of the decisions would be up to her. One job, one operative, minimal risk.

When it was time for Evera to board her plane, Adam had been nowhere to be found. It had been excruciating for her to leave without seeing him. She knew he was suffering somewhere alone. Her feelings of guilt for inflicting that much pain on him almost caused her to back out at the last second. But she got on the plane, without her good-bye, and pushed aside the fallout with Adam.

Evera remembered how nervous she was making the nine hour flight alone, just her and the pilot. Her nerves were a mix of anticipation and fear. Not fear of the danger inherent, but of what she would have to do to get close to Daniel.

Evera knew the operative who Daniel had shot. Her name was Sharon and she had helped Evera out in the early stages of her training. As angry as she was over Sharon, it was also all the other women he'd killed that made her want to take on this job. He'd strangled countless women just to satisfy his sick, sexual perversion. She wanted to be the one to make him pay.

She barely remembered her journey through downtown Paris to get to her hotel. Beautiful, romantic Paris with its multitude of timeless architecture and history passed her by in a blur while consumed with her assignment and the evening ahead.

Her preparation before she left had been meticulous. Jonas coached her through every detail right down to hair color and dress. She started getting ready the moment she arrived in her suite. Before she had left, she had dyed her rich brown hair a honey blonde. Daniel preferred blondes. She needed to fit in and stand out at the same time. The typical long, blonde, wavy tresses would help her blend in. Her dress would be the stand out.

It was vintage Versace, red lace and mermaid cut, accentuating her silhouette. The slit up the front was center cut and ended just above her knees, revealing her long, willowy legs. She pulled back both sides of her hair into a jeweled clip, adorned with rubies and diamonds. The earrings and bracelet she had been supplied with matched the hairpiece. She didn't even want to think about the price of her jewelry. It was borrowed, as was her outfit, and would need to be returned after her assignment.

Jonas never messed around with replicas. He knew that the people she would encounter could spot a fake from a mile away. They lived and breathed money and power. The crowd Daniel surrounded himself with tonight, like any other night, would all know each other. She would be an outsider. Her and Jonas' hope was that her anonymity would work to her advantage.

Her ensemble complete, with scarlet lips to match her dress, she headed to the event.

It was unfortunate, the location of the party. Here she was in the Louvre moving among historical artifacts and priceless paintings and yet she barely had cause to notice them. Daniel was the main attraction tonight.

She was surprised at how easy it was to get close to him. He picked her out right away at the gala. A fresh face and a new conquest, his curiosity about her immediate. He convinced her to join him back at his room only two hours into the party.

Things started to heat up as soon as he closed the door to his hotel room. The kiss was easy enough to avoid; he was as uninterested in it as she was. But his hands and the roughness contained in them made her uncomfortable the second he started touching her.

Her breath was quickening, bordering on panic. Fortunately, her reaction could easily pass for excitement so Daniel never noticed. But she needed an escape, some way to remain a physical participant but allow her mind to extricate itself from what was happening to her body. She pulled for the one thing she remembered had worked a long time ago. A crystalline, blue sky appeared in her mind. Clouds of different shapes and sizes floated past her while a warm, imaginary breeze followed behind them. The effect calmed her instantly. Keeping her breathing accelerated, she forced her hands to join his in their exploration.

She sensed his annoyance at her movements as their interlude continued. It wasn't just his patience but also his pleasure that was declining. She was inexperienced and guessing. If she didn't come up with a way to prove otherwise this encounter would be over before it even began. They were on the bed, wrestling about to remove her dress when she had an epiphany. A revelation that she was capable of giving him exactly what he desired.

Keeping her mind in her blue-sky sanctuary, she let her hands, her lips and her tongue take over. As she paid attention to his every emotion—what he liked, what his body wanted—the atmosphere on the bed suddenly changed. And she felt Daniel unwittingly give up his control to her.

After that first night together she could feel a shift in his attitude towards her. Her ability to read his wants and desires left him vulnerable to her. Not entirely, but enough that he trusted her alone in the penthouse. She spent most of the next two days with him and managed to copy information off of his phone and his computer. And he lavished money on her, taking her to the best restaurants and clothing stores in Paris.

The morning of day number three, Evera received the text she had been impatiently waiting for. The information she had sent back to the Section had been deciphered and they had managed to gather several important bits of intel. It was time to go ahead and complete her mission.

Daniel was at a breakfast meeting in the hotel's dining room when she received the go ahead to proceed. She had paced the massive penthouse, checking and rechecking her bracelet, waiting for Daniel's return, going over her plan repeatedly.

There were two men directly outside of the door guarding the room and at least one waiting in a car in the hotel parking lot. She was sure there were at least two more cars periodically circling the hotel, keeping an eye out. Her plan was to take out Daniel on the far side of the bed so the body would be hidden temporarily if someone came in the room. She would then run the shower and close the bathroom door. As she left, she would tell the bodyguards she was heading back to her hotel for a change of clothes while Daniel took a shower. It would hopefully be at least a half an hour before the guards suspected anything. In that time she would already be at the airport and boarding her private flight back to New York.

Two minutes later she heard Daniel's voice in the hallway. He was speaking to the bodyguards in a hushed tone so she couldn't make out any of the words. She was perched on the far side of the bed and lay down, grabbing the remote and pretending to watch TV.

As she waited her pulse increased, her heart pounding. She had taken lives before but never quite like this. Shooting someone from a distance was a cold and removed experience. This encounter, however, would be up close and personal.

The door opened and in walked Daniel in a grey suit and tie, carrying his laptop bag. "Hey," he said, giving her an arrogant smile. He was undeniably attractive, with strong features, brown eyes and fair hair. But these attributes only made her hate him more. She'd never come upon a person who's emotional state was so completely arrogant and self-centered.

Even in bed he'd been selfish and harsh. Evera wasn't surprised, having felt the depth of the kind of repulsive human being he was. She couldn't wait to finish the job.

As he turned to shut the door he reached up to flip the safety bar on the door, something she hadn't seen him do before. His action made her feel uneasy. Why would he barricade himself in with her and leave his bodyguards no way to access the room?

Her stomach dropped. He wasn't keeping them out, she realized, he was trapping her inside. Her first thought was that her cover was blown. That seemed impossible though, as the only two people who knew she was here were Adam and Jonas.

She pasted a calm smile on her face as he came around to her side of the bed to greet her. She turned her face so he kissed her cheek hello.

"Sorry, my meeting ran longer than I expected," he apologized, looking her up and down solicitously as she lounged on the bed. There was an excitement coming off of him, potent and dark. He reached to brush the hair from her neck, his emotions ratcheting up a notch. He smiled provocatively at her but she saw something in his eyes that hinted at evil.

And then she understood. Her cover wasn't compromised after all. Daniel's excitement and intent to keep her captive was because he was going to strangle her...she was sure of it. She felt relief and then red, hot anger. It was time for Daniel to get a taste of his own medicine. Anticipation spread through her limbs making her feel stronger, vengeful.

She watched him surreptitiously as he undid his tie and removed his watch, putting them on the dresser, his back to her. He turned towards her, his face expectant and walked slowly over.

She stood suddenly, not wanting to end up lying on the bed and trapped beneath his body. She walked to meet him, a coy smile on her lips. She could feel no suspicion coming from him as she got closer, only excitement.

"You kept me waiting," she said, as she wound her arms around his neck and silently twisted the hinge on her bracelet. "Now you're going to have to pay," she whispered seductively in his ear.

Then, without a moment's hesitation, she pulled the garrote around his neck. She wrapped it around twice so she was holding the bracelet handles and facing him, staring him in the eyes.

He seemed so shocked by the action that, for a second, he could do nothing but stare back at her in surprise.

Then he opened his mouth to scream, but it was too late. She tightened her grip, cutting off his silent call for help. He choked and struggled against her while attempting to dig the garrote from his neck. She jerked down quickly, bringing him to his knees in front of her. He grabbed onto her hands, pulling reflexively, desperate to stop her, but his action only made the wire bite deeper into his neck.

He stared up at her, his face red with pain and anger, no arrogance left. She stared back unwaveringly into his eyes.

"You're going to die now, Daniel," her voice was calm and sweet. "And I want you to know that this is for all the women you put in this very position. All the women who looked up at you, pleading with their eyes while you killed them," she finished, smiling. His hands were still gripping hers only now he was struggling to keep her hands near him to slacken the wire.

She brought her face close to his, so close their lips were almost touching. She could feel the shift in his emotions from anger to fear. She felt a smug satisfaction at how she had turned the tables on him and now it was his eyes staring at her, begging for mercy.

She smiled at him again, devoid of compassion. This time her lips were cruel and triumphant. "Good-bye, Daniel," she whispered, letting her warm breath caress his lips as she yanked hard on the garrote. There was a sickening, abrading sound as the wire sliced sinew and cartilage, tearing through his throat. Daniel fell backwards on the carpet as blood ran from his neck. He lay there, his empty eyes looking up at the ceiling, his body lifeless.

Evera didn't realize she had stopped breathing until she pulled in a shaky breath. She stared down at Daniel's still body, waiting to feel something, pity or remorse, something to mark that she had taken a life in the most intimate of ways. She did feel something, but it wasn't what she had been expecting, she felt victorious.

As she carefully unwrapped the garrote from his neck she looked into his lifeless eyes one last time and smiled. She had done it. Her first official kill as Jezebel completed with no mistakes. Silent and thorough, just as planned. She slackened the handles of her garrote and watched as the blood covered wire retracted obscurely into the bracelet. Amazing. She could leave the scene of any crime with the murder weapon in full view and no one the wiser.

Suddenly, Daniel's corpse started ringing, breaking through her moment of self-satisfaction. The sound of his phone made her body start to take action and her mind refocus.

She grabbed her purse and ran to the bathroom, turning on the shower and shutting the door. Walking towards the hotel room door she saw the safety bar across it. She had forgotten that.

Pausing for a second, she wondered if the bodyguards outside knew what Daniel's plan had been. If so, the only person they would be expecting to leave this room would be Daniel.

She heard a light tap at the door, the sound making her jump. *Shit*! It must have been one of the guards who'd called to see if Daniel was finished with her.

Her mind jumbled and panicked, she tried to sort through her choices. This is what she'd trained for, improvisation. Her best chance was following her original plan; telling the bodyguards she was leaving to change while Daniel was in the shower. And then she'd have to run like hell.

She slung her purse across her body and leaned against the wall, taking deep breaths, preparing her heart and lungs for the chase to come. Without meaning to, her thoughts raced ahead to what would happen if they caught her. It wouldn't be enough for them to kill her for what she'd done. She knew how these men operated, they would take her and torture her in ways she didn't even want to imagine.

Her mental state on the verge of collapsing as she readied herself, she took hold of the one image she could draw strength from, Adam. Without hesitation she grabbed her phone from her purse and quickly texted. "In trouble, sorry," she typed. She wanted to add 'I love you,' but her fingers hesitated, and then Daniel's phone was ringing again and she was out of time. She hit send, disappointed with what could be her last words to Adam.

Reaching for the doorknob, she planted a calm smile on her face and pushed open the door.

She almost ran straight into the two bodyguards huddled around the door, their heads together in deep conversation, which halted the second they saw her. They were both staring, speechless, and not bothering to hide their surprise at seeing her walk out of Daniel's room.

"I'm just heading out to change while Daniel's in the shower." She gave them a wide smile with her explanation and closed the door. As she started walking down the long hallway, her attention turned to focus on the door at the end of hall. On the other side of it was a staircase and her only means of escape.

"Wait!" yelled one of the guards, but she ignored him and picked up her pace. "What the fuck's going on?" she could hear them arguing, followed by the click as they used their card to open Daniel's door.

"Stop her!" one of them screamed, and then she was running all out, her hand already reaching for the door.

Just as her fingers touched the handle she heard the shouts and the stampede of heavy feet coming for her. She slammed into the door and flung it open in one swift movement. As she cleared the corner and started running down the stairs, she heard a soft popping and then the sound of shattering wood. They were shooting at her!

Staying close to the wall, she ran, jumping down the last few steps at each landing. She knew she could easily outrun the two men, not only did she have a head start but their bulk made them slow and awkward. Evera was fast and agile.

Just three more flights and she'd be out. There would be a metal set of stairs once she exited and then a back alley to her left. The alley would be her safest bet with many places to hide if they tried to chase her down or shoot.

She could see the light coming from the exit door's window below. *Almost there*, she thought and could hear the bodyguards' angry voices and clumsy footsteps still several floors above.

Jumping the last few steps to the ground floor, she felt a wave of relief wash over her as she realized she was going to make it. She threw herself against the exit door, sucking in the cool air.

From out of nowhere, vice-like hands grabbed her roughly and threw her up against the door, slamming it shut and knocking the wind out of her.

She was face-to-face with the twisted features of a dark-haired, brute of a man. His huge fingers closed around her neck, pinning her hard against the door, his death grip on her throat crushing her airway.

As she tried to struggle against him he sneered at her, his face close.

"Well, well, little girl," he taunted, his sour breath laced with the smell of stale cigarette smoke. "Sounds like you've been naughty. I like naughty. I'm going to take you home with me and play. We'll get to know each other real well, you and I." The air around him was so saturated with evil that terror coursed through her, making her forget that she couldn't breathe.

There was a sudden flash of movement over the man's left shoulder.

"Let her go," commanded a quiet, deadly voice. "Now!"

Faster than Evera would have thought possible, the man pulled her in front of him, his grip still circling her neck. He pressed a gun muzzle hard against her temple.

She stared straight ahead into the most beautiful, familiar blue eyes she had ever seen.

Adam's.

She chocked in a small breath of relief against the hand wrapped around her neck. The man was holding her close to him, his back pressed against the exit door where she could hear the other two bodyguards yelling.

Adam's hand holding the gun moved left, the barrel trained on the window of the door. The other guards couldn't get out anyway, not without the man holding her moving. And Evera knew from past experience that Adam was cobra fast with his gun.

Adam met her eyes calmly, she could see unwavering determination in them. "I said, let her go," he repeated, his voice harsh and loud. He walked several paces closer to the base of the stairs, moving the gun back to the man holding Evera. With his deep brown hair and dressed all in black, the sun came up behind Adam outlining him so he was just a dark shadow. There was only three steps and a landing separating them.

The man behind her chuckled, his large stomach moving up and down against her back. His foul, hot breath grazed her ear as he spoke. "It seems to me you're the one at a disadvantage here. Once I snap her neck, it'll be three against one," he said, sure of himself. "But if you lower your gun and leave, I might just forget that you pissed me off and not come after you." The man waited for Adam's reply.

Adam looked at the man, his smile malicious. "No thanks," he retorted, his voice polite. "I suggest you shove your offer up your ass and I'll repeat my original request. Let her go. If you don't, in thirty seconds you'll be dead." He punctuated his request by raising his arm higher and coming one step closer.

Evera could feel confusion and uncertainty coming off of the man. "Do you actually want to risk your life for this?" he asked, shaking her. He pushed the gun barrel harder against her temple, making her wince.

Adam's jaw clenched in anger and Evera saw his finger twitch on the trigger, his eyes dark and fierce as he glared back at the man. "If you think how I feel about her gives you any kind of power over me you're mistaken. I would willingly die for her. I'm sure you can't say the same for the two men behind that door?" he questioned, tilting his head and waiting for the man to reply.

Just as the huge man took a breath to speak, Adam interrupted. "Time's up," and he fired his gun.

Evera heard a deafening crack and the grunt from behind her as the man loosened his grip from around her neck, dragging her to the ground with him. Adam continued shooting, aiming at the window in the door behind her, until the clip was empty. Before the dead man's body could slide down on top of her, she was thrown to the side by the two bodyguards bursting past her.

But Adam was already there, waiting for them. He hit the first man through hard in the stomach, grabbing his arm as he tried to swing his gun around to shoot. He wrestled the gun free, just as the second man tried to push his way past and towards Adam.

The guard tried to maneuver around his friend and get his gun up high enough to get a shot, but Adam shoved the first man back into his friend and the gun went off, the bullet punching a hole in the building next door. The man dropped his gun not three feet from Evera.

Still pinned behind the open door, she struggled to get low enough to reach around and grab the waiting gun. The man Adam was holding onto kicked it in his attempt to get free. Evera watched as it tumbled down the stairs and out of reach.

Then there was repeated gunfire as all three men wrestled for the last weapon. Evera wrapped her arms around her head, trying to protect herself from the flying bullets and the noise.

She heard a loud scream and looked up through the window, just in time to see the bodyguard in the back of the melee start to fall, his chest soaked in blood. Adam was still fighting with the last man still standing. Evera was relieved to see Adam seemed unharmed as he slammed the guard in the face with the back of his elbow. The man was momentarily dazed and Adam took advantage, shooting him in the head with his own gun, ending the battle. Without taking a second to recover, he started pulling the door aside, shoving the lifeless pile of bodies out of the way to free her.

"Let's go," he urged, holding his hand out for her. She grabbed it in relief as they started running.

"Car's around the corner. Get in the back and stay down," he commanded, as they rounded the side of the building. He pushed her towards the back door of a silver BMW. She wrenched the door open and climbed in as fast as she could. Daniel's security team would have been circling on standby, and she was sure they would have heard the gun fire.

Adam was peeling away from the hotel, tires screeching, just as she managed to shut the door.

"Fuck!" he yelled, and slammed on the brakes so hard she hit the backside of the driver's seat. "Hold on," he said, as he fishtailed around and started gunning the car down the back alley. Evera lifted her head just high enough to peer out the back window and see a dark sedan chasing after them.

Their car was small and quick and Adam seemed to know every street and avenue, making turns at the last second. The sedan was large and cumbersome, built for comfort not speed, as it tried to keep up with them along the narrow roads of Paris.

The black car was falling farther and farther behind them as Adam sped dangerously fast through the near empty streets. He took a hard right at the last second, mounting the curb and driving partway on the sidewalk before he straightened out. He veered left suddenly and took another fast right towards the back of an office building. He turned into an underground parkade, barely waiting for the barricade arm to lift enough to drive through. He moved quickly around the circular drive, going down a level, before pulling into a spot beside another parked car.

Shutting the car off, he climbed out, holding the door open and listening. Evera watched his face as he strained to hear the sounds of any approaching vehicles.

She watched him in wonder, her constant rescuer, until after several minutes he unclenched his jaw. He turned swiftly towards the back door, opened it and climbed in beside her. His hands were immediately touching her face, caressing her hair.

"Are you alright?" he asked, his voice hoarse with fear and emotion. "Did they hurt you?"

She stared back into his searching eyes in awe. How many times and in how many different ways could one person save another? She could live ten lifetimes and still not repay him for everything he'd done for her. She reached up, covering his hand with hers and held it tight against her face.

"I'm fine, Adam." The fear subsiding, her eyes stayed locked on him. "Thank you," she choked out, lacing her fingers with his.

"You don't ever have to thank me," he said, smiling at her in relief. "I have no choice…I couldn't live without you."

She believed him. She could see it in his eyes and feel it coming off of him. How very much he loved her. The full impact of what had just transpired and what he'd saved her from started to sink in fully. She shuddered involuntarily.

"Are you cold?" he asked, already removing his coat to drape it around her.

"A little. I think it's the shock of—" she stopped, her voice breaking at the end.

He pulled his coat tight around her. It was still warm from his body heat and smelled like him. He rubbed her back, his face close, comforting her.

"You're safe now," he promised, trying to soothe away her fear with his words. But she couldn't seem to shake the feeling of dread despite his rescue. The thought of what could be happening to her right now if he hadn't shown up in time had her stomach churning.

Adam held her face gently between his strong, warm hands, kissing her sweetly on the forehead.

"If you hadn't come when you did, Adam, they would have taken me away and done God knows what to me," she said, her voice barely a whisper.

He pulled back and focused on her. "I would have come for you. No matter where they would have taken you, I wouldn't stop until I found you. Never doubt that," he insisted, his thumb caressing her cheek. "I will always come for you, Evera. Always," he said, fervently, his blue eyes piercing hers with their intensity.

She stared back, her heart filled with gratitude and love for him. But then the atmosphere in the backseat of the car started to change. His feelings of relief and love became charged with passion, thickening the air and making it harder to breathe. Suddenly, his hands tightened their grip. Adam's beautiful face was so close she could feel the heat coming from his lips. She was desperate to let this happen. For their lips to meet and for her to show him how much he meant to her. But something inside her couldn't let go and she cringed internally, her lips tightening reflexively.

Adam felt her hesitation and stopped, their mouths a hair's width apart, neither of them breathing. He tore his gaze from hers but not before she saw the look of defeat and frustration in his eyes. He pulled in a shaky breath and touched his forehead to hers, still not looking at her.

She struggled for words, something she could say to salvage the moment. "Adam, I'm..." but she couldn't choke out the apology. Nor could she say 'I love you.' It felt as if her brain and tongue were trying to sabotage her.

"Shhhhh," Adam soothed. "It's alright, just give me a second." Evera could feel him struggle to rein in his passion and frustration. He filled his lungs one more time and then moved back to look her in the eyes. He gave her a small, sad smile. "All that matters is that you're safe. Now let's get the hell out of here," he rasped, releasing her face.

He started to climb out of the backseat, but his emotions were so charged she could still feel him after he moved towards the door. Pain and love and anger all mixed up into one suffocating concoction. She couldn't help but feel relief at the space between them, as he shut her door and didn't look back.

CHAPTER 9

Introductions

The plane touched down on the island of Maui at 10:10 p.m. Hawaiian time, their landing smooth and uneventful. Evera had spent the last thirty minutes replaying everything that had happened in Paris. And what followed between her and Adam after the encounter in the back of the car.

Adam had been so sure that her first mission would have been her last as Jezebel, but that had not been the case. When she'd arrived back at the Section, Jonas had been waiting for her; his praise and happiness lit a fire under her. From then on, her relationship with Adam changed...there was a constant undercurrent of tension between them.

She let the memories go and headed out of the plane and into the aromatic Hawaiian air.

Because she only had her carry-on luggage, she was able to by-pass baggage claim and be one of the first people from the flight flagging down a cab. As a car pulled over to pick her up she noticed the warm rain coming down. The lush, sweet smell was cleansing to her lungs after the stuffy recycled air in the plane. She wished she could walk and drink in the clean air instead of trading it for what she knew would be stale and musty inside the cab. She reluctantly got in and gave the driver the name of the resort. Her destination wasn't far, only a short twenty minute drive along a road filled on either side with tropical plants and trees illuminated by streetlights. The rain continued softly and despite the late hour she longed to check into her room and go for a run.

The driver pulled up in front of a large, white stucco resort, gated and fenced on all sides. The security guard at the gate waved the cab through and the driver took her right up to the main entrance. She thanked the driver, handed him the fifty dollar bill she'd been holding and climbed out into the slowing rain. A doorman greeted her holding an umbrella, although she would have preferred to let the rain wash over her. It had almost stopped by the time she walked up the staircase and into the lobby.

She couldn't help but appreciate the beauty of the resort. Everything was Carrara marble: floors, pillars, even the check-in desk. The desk was in the middle of the vast lobby and surrounded by couches and fireplaces. Behind the desk was an open doorway leading to the courtyard which was lit by torches, a large fire pit in its center and an outdoor dance bar. Beyond the courtyard was the beach and the ocean, its black waves crashing in the background. It was beautiful and though Evera couldn't see a pool from her vantage point, she knew from her itinerary that there were two.

The clerk at the desk handed her an envelope containing the keycard for her room along with several brochures listing all of the amenities the resort offered. She took it and followed the valet as he led her to her room. He walked through the courtyard and she looked up and saw five stories of rooms lining one side of the courtyard. Close to the beach was the first pool filled with several people using both the pool and the hot tub. She knew her room would be on the other side facing away from the water and closer to the parking lot. He took her around to the other side where the rooms were lined up in front of the second pool, the lap pool. Evera surmised that Cort would want his room here, in the back, for quick access to the parking lot where she imagined he would have a car and at least a couple of security guards waiting.

After climbing the stairs to the second floor, she thanked the valet and handed him a tip as she entered her room. Sitting on the edge of the bed, she pulled out her phone to text the Section's main number confirming her arrival and saw a message waiting for her. It read, "tomorrow morning at 10:00." Meaning Cort would be leaving early if he was attending a meeting on another island at 10:00 a.m. Good, hopefully she could figure out who he was first thing in the morning and then spend the rest of the day reading by the pool. She was suddenly looking forward to the fact that maybe, on this mission, she wouldn't have to dish out sex and murder. It would be a first.

The rain had almost stopped but the air would still carry the smell and feel of it. Deciding on a run before bed, she changed quickly, tucking her phone and keycard into a small pocket in her shorts. She looked down around her neck and wondered what she should do with her locket. She couldn't risk the chance that if she left it behind it could be stolen, so she tucked it down the front of her sports bra and headed out.

As she was winding her way down the stairs she heard voices. Drunken male voices, laughing raucously just on the other side of the pool. There were two of them, facing the shrubs beside the pool and focused on something in the grass. She had intended to walk past them and out to the parking lot, but caught sight of what had their interest, sitting in the grass. It was a squirrel, trapped between the two men who looked to be in their mid to late twenties, unsteady on their feet and holding beer bottles. They were kicking at the animal between them as it scurried back and forth.

Evera felt instantly pissed as she watched them laugh at the helpless animal. Her feet, without her even thinking of it, veered off and carried her towards the intoxicated pair.

"Hey," she said, coming up behind them, trying to keep her tone light.

They both turned towards her at the same time. The taller, blonder of the two men looking her up and down, a leering smile on his face.

"Hey yourself," he said, now diverted and moving towards her just enough for the animal to escape.

"Cam, you fucking idiot," said his friend, pissed that his amusement had made its getaway.

"Shut up, Elliot," said Cam under his breath, too stupidly drunk to realize he was plenty loud enough for Evera to hear. "How can I help you?" asked the leering Cam, taking a step closer to her. "And I do mean literally, if there is any way I can help you out, you just let me know."

"Maybe she can help us out instead?" said Elliot, taking his first real look at Evera and moving closer.

Rolling her eyes, she stood her ground. Obviously looking for some other form of amusement in their drunken state, they somehow found entertainment in picking on something helpless. If they included her in that category they would be painfully mistaken.

"Just how, exactly, would you like me to help you out?" she asked acerbically.

"Anyway you like," said Cam, bolder, moving into her personal space.

"Didn't look like the two of you needed any help a second ago," her words surly.

"I didn't mean help in kicking around a stupid animal," he slurred.

"How would you like it if someone kicked you around just for the hell of it?" she asked, unable to stop her voice from sounding threatening.

"Sweetheart, if it was you, I wouldn't mind at all," added Cam, his sick, unwanted emotions channeling into her.

Lightning fast, she slammed his arm back with her fist and grabbed a hold of his crotch. He sucked in a quick breath, both surprised and in pain, dropping his beer bottle.

"Is this what you had in mind?" she asked, flexing her fingers tighter.

He yelped once in pain, all the playful lust gone, and his anger building.

"Is everything okay here? Can I help you, Miss?" It was a man's voice, appealing and with an accent, the sound coming from several feet behind her. She could hear footsteps getting closer. From the corner of her eye she saw Elliot turn to look past her shoulder.

Fuck, that's all she needed, one more asshole asking her for help.

Unwilling to risk her advantage of having both men in her sights, she answered without turning her head. "No thanks, I can handle it myself," she smiled sweetly at Cam, twisting her fingers once quickly, before releasing his crotch. He went down hard on the grass, falling on his side, whimpering and holding his hands between his legs.

The man behind her chuckled softly. "Yes, I can see that," he replied.

She made sure both Cam and Elliot were staying put, neither of them about to retaliate, and finally turned to see the man behind her. He was in the shadows, his back towards her, already walking away.

She turned back to the two men in front of her, Cam suddenly turned to the side and vomited in the grass. Elliot was looking at her, his hands up in a surrendering gesture.

"Good night, gentleman," she said, glowering as she walked quickly past them and towards her room. Her planned late night run completely forgotten.

Once inside, she headed straight for the shower, all the while castigating herself for her impulsive behavior, but fortunate that her audience numbered only three. She hoped that, in their drunken state, Cam and Elliot wouldn't be able to identify her if they saw her again. As for the mystery man, she hadn't seen his face so she assumed he wouldn't recognize her either.

Cleansed from the leftover heat of the day, she grabbed her phone and lay down on the bed. She checked for messages but had none.

Putting her phone and her locket on the bedside table, she crawled under the covers, missing Adam more than usual. As exhaustion took her, she let herself drift, anticipating tomorrow and the chance for some peace.

*****

Evera was certain she was dreaming. She recognized the scratchy feel of her old patchwork quilt and the musty smell that was always present in the old farmhouse. She didn't want to be here. She struggled to wake up and scream, but it was caught in her throat. She tried to run but, like so often in a nightmare, she was paralyzed...trapped, unable to move beneath her quilt.

Something else was bothering her, something she had forgotten. She couldn't reach for what it was but she knew it was important. Her mind felt foggy in the dream, blocking something. Something that was supposed to happen next.

And then she heard it. The sound of heavy boots making their way up the stairs, echoing through the house. The steps were louder as they came closer to her door. Impossibly loud. She tried to move again even though she knew it was useless. And then she remembered what was so important...remembered just as her bedroom doorknob started to turn. She had forgotten to lock her door.

A flash of light from the hallway burst into her room and then she was screaming herself awake.

She awoke disoriented and frightened by her unfamiliar surroundings. She was panting, close to hyperventilating, when she realized she was not in the farmhouse or her room at the Section, but in a bed in a hotel.

Desperate to shake off the frightful vision still lingering, she climbed out of bed and went straight to the bathroom to splash cold water on her face. She quickly brushed her teeth and pulled her chaotic hair back in a ponytail, checking herself over in the mirror. Now that she was coming down off her terror high she realized how hungry she was.

Grabbing her phone she checked the time, almost 7:00 a.m. No time for breakfast just yet. If she hoped to catch a glimpse of Cort before he left Maui for his 10:00 a.m. meeting, she had to move fast. She threw on some workout clothes so that she could wander around inconspicuously. From the lousy black and white picture with the sunglasses that she had studied in his file, she remembered the shape of his nose as well as his strong chin and jaw. She hoped it would be enough to recognize him. Grabbing what she needed, she chugged a bottle of water to fend off hunger before heading out the door.

The bright sunlight that greeted her cleared her mind and burned off the last of the nightmare. As she grabbed on to the railing to stretch before she ran around the resort, she caught a glimpse of the lap pool below.

Someone was out for an early swim. She took a hard look and saw that it was a man with dark hair. A woman was sitting in one of the lounge chairs at the far end of the pool. Even from this distance Evera could tell she was striking. Honey blonde, probably early thirties and intensely watching the man in the pool. Her swim suit was almost nonexistent; white fabric running in a V-shape from around her neck to below her navel. Evera would bet a month's salary that the suit was strictly for show and wouldn't survive a plunge in the chlorine filled pool.

The woman got out of her lounge chair and walked over to the benches along the shrubs that held stacks of clean towels. She grabbed one and took it back to her seat, all the while keeping her gaze possessively on the man in the pool. Evera assumed they were together because at this time in the morning it was too early for sunbathing.

Evera watched the man swim to the far side of the pool and back again. His hair looked almost black in the water, the color she was hoping for, but he was doing a breast stroke and still hadn't raised his face enough for her to get a good look. She couldn't positively identify him from this distance but she didn't want to draw attention to herself by going in the pool. And then there was the blonde in the lounger. Although Evera loved a challenge, she wasn't sure she could compete with this woman's polished, sucked and tucked perfection.

Waiting patiently against the second floor railing, she pretended to stretch. She couldn't help but be impressed by the man's stamina. He must have made ten laps in the last three minutes and showed no sign of slowing down. From where she was standing to straight down where he was swimming was only about twenty feet. She took a better look at him as he swam by underneath her. His skin looked tanned, his body long and lean.

Six feet plus in height. She could see the muscles ripple in his back and shoulders as he swam beneath her.

He reached the end of the pool, closest to her and opposite where the blonde was watching, and flipped over into a back stroke as he pushed off the edge. He looked up in her direction, and for a moment their eyes met. She looked away quickly, reaching down to tie her perfectly laced runners. She peeked at him from between the railing as he slowly swam his way to the other end. He did another length past her and back again to where the lounge chairs and the woman with the towel were waiting.

The glance between them had been too quick and too far for her to notice his eye color. Still, even though the picture she'd had of him had been less than clear, she was ninety percent certain it was Cort. The shape of his face, his chin and jaw were all similar to the picture, but she would need a closer look to be absolutely sure.

She watched discreetly as he swam over to the ladder and started climbing out. His bio predicted he was somewhere between thirty-five and forty, but his form refuted that. His arms looked strong as he pulled himself up, revealing more of his body as he came out of the water. She'd already seen how muscular his shoulders and back were and her eyes followed down to his swim trunks, black and fitted. His long legs started climbing the steps and then he paused.

She looked past him to see the striking blonde blocking his path and offering him a towel. She said something to him but Evera was too far away to hear their conversation. Her body language was suggestively clear, even from where Evera was standing, and she seemed to be waiting for a response. He took the towel from her and Evera watched the women as he replied. Her perfect face fell and then the man turned to walk past her waving in thanks, and left, wrapping the towel around his waist.

He walked around the pool towards the first floor rooms, giving Evera her first real look at him from the front. Water was running in thin rivers from his hair and over his perfectly muscled chest. He was looking down while walking so Evera couldn't see the shape of his eyes but in the picture he had been wearing sunglasses anyways. From this close though, she was certain it was him. He continued to his room on the first floor and she heard the door click shut below her.

As Evera watched the defeated blonde beat a hasty retreat away from the pool, she concluded that Cort was likely here alone. She wasn't hopeful of actually getting anywhere, what with him turning down the perfect blonde, but maybe she could get something: a name, a location, anything that could prove useful. If she couldn't get near him she would just continue keeping track of him while swimming and relaxing. He was here for work and Cort might just be the type of man who never mixed business with pleasure. Or maybe he was gay? She chuckled out loud as she let herself back in her room. She was sure that was what the blonde was telling herself right now to assuage her ego.

She sat on the bed and wrote a quick synopsis of his description and, after checking the resort map, the room number he was staying in. She sent it off to Garrison and then checked her texts. Still nothing from Adam.

Her stomach growled noisily, reminding her that she hadn't eaten since the plane last night. She got up and changed into some beach clothes before heading poolside for the day. She put on a tank top and cotton skirt over her bikini. Grabbing her oversized handbag with her books, she headed for breakfast and lots of coffee.

When she arrived in the courtyard it was almost 8:00, the dining tables slowly filling up. She grabbed a table with an umbrella, close to the edge of the courtyard and the start of the beach. It was a bit windier, but she liked the smell and feel of the breeze coming off the water.

A waiter came to her table almost immediately. Barely glancing at the menu she ordered a stack of French toast, a side of bacon and coffee to help her stay awake. She settled in to eat her breakfast and continue where she left off in *Jane Eyre*.

When she was finished eating, she put her novel back in her bag and switched to her large picture book on Italian vineyards. She fidgeted with her locket with one hand and flipped open her book with the other, but the breeze started to pick up and she had to use both her hands to hold the pages open.

"I believe this is yours," said a pleasant, familiar voice.

She looked up from her book to see a tall, dark-haired man with piercing navy blue eyes standing beside her and holding a bookmark. Her bookmark.

She was momentarily tongue-tied. It was the same man from the pool earlier. It was also the same voice of the stranger from last night, walking away in the shadows before she could see his face—Cort.

He was looking at her and waiting. She needed to say something.

"Um, yes, thank you," she said, not sure where to look. She needed to try and figure out how to buy herself some time to recover from the ambush. "It's mine, I guess the wind picked it up...I didn't notice." Shit, as if the mumbling wasn't bad enough, she was sure she was also blushing.

She reached to take the bookmark, their fingers grazing, and she could feel pleasant sensations of warmth and interest.

"Glad to be of help, again," he said with a smile. His voice was attractive with a light accent. If she had to guess she would say South African.

She smiled in return at the 'again' in his words.

"Although, I must admit to my services being unnecessary last night," he said teasingly, waiting for her to continue the conversation.

She didn't want to dwell on the incident from last night and her bold behavior so she skipped over it. "Well, I'm very grateful for them this morning," she continued. "I've had this bookmark a long time and I would hate to have lost it."

The personal confession made her uncomfortable. Her bookmark was in her copy of *Jane Eyre* on the day she showed up at the Section.

"I'm glad I could rescue it then," he replied. He seemed reluctant to leave and looked down at her book curiously.

"I see you're interested in the vineyards of Tuscany. It's such a beautiful, unspoiled landscape…like travelling back in time, don't you think?" The strange turn of events had knocked her momentarily off her game but she needed to get a grip. Her mark was offering himself up on a silver platter and she was sitting here like an imbecile. She let the idea of a quiet day by the pool go and took advantage of the situation.

"I'm sure it's beautiful in real life; unfortunately, I haven't been lucky enough to travel there yet." She hoped her words would invite him to say more.

"It is," he smiled and then looked instantly contrite, "Of course, there's beauty everywhere when you travel, sometimes in the most unlikely of places. You just have to pay attention to it, like now," he said looking at her. And then he put his head down, his cheeks warming. "I mean, like here," he corrected, seeming a bit tongue-tied himself. "In Hawaii." He looked back at her, meeting her eyes and she could sense his embarrassment.

"There's this charming little market, about thirty minutes east of here," he continued, seeming to want to keep talking and distract from his last comment. How strange that he was embarrassed by his words; most of her marks would consider it clever that they had snuck in a suggestive comment like that.

"It's very rustic, filled mostly with locals but you can get the most beautiful items there," he said. "The Island itself is really something too. I was fortunate to be able to tour some of it the last time I was here," he finished. She could tell he was waiting for her to interject something, so she decided to use her book.

"Have you been to this particular region of Italy?" she asked, pointing to the open page in her book.

"Yes, actually." He leaned down close to look at the page and she noticed the smell of his aftershave. A subtle blend of musk and spice, not too strong with just a hint coming off him mixed with the heat from his skin. Together it was an intoxicating scent.

"May I?" he asked, gesturing towards the empty chair beside her.

"Please do," she said, and smiled welcomingly. He was wearing a white, short sleeve shirt and shorts. His shirt was unbuttoned partway down; enough that she could see the start of the hard contours of his chest.

He started talking about the look and smell of the countryside in her picture. He had such a soothing, pleasant voice. His words were so descriptive that she felt as though she had been transported to the scene in the book. As she listened and watched him, a wave of déjà vu washed over her. His face seemed familiar and for a moment she wondered if they had met somewhere before.

And then it clicked, why she thought she recognized him. He looked just like a character from her favorite Disney movie, *The Little Mermaid*. He was the living version of the prince, Eric, right down to the piercing, dark blue of his eyes and the cleft in his chin. She fought the smile that was twitching at the corner of her lips...every little girl's fairytale prince come to life, sitting right in front of her.

He met her eyes often as he spoke and they made their way through the book together. Her fascination with him tempering as she reminded herself that he was the farthest thing possible from a prince. A ruthless murderer, arms dealer, information thief and god knows what else. The strange levity of the moment having passed, her mind separated fact from fiction and she started to plan. She would have to be extra cautious with him. He wasn't her typical rich, arrogant mark. He was shrewd and observant and didn't seem to like being pursued.

"I'm monopolizing the conversation, my apologies," he said, after turning to the last page of the book.

"No, don't be sorry" she said, and she meant it. For a change she had a mark who was interesting, polite even. And she was happy to have a first-hand conversation in regards to Italy, as it was a childhood dream of hers to someday move there and own a vineyard. "Really," she continued, "I find it fascinating to learn more about something I've been so interested in. You can gain a much clearer perspective from a person's experience than from just words in a book."

"I appreciate you letting me talk your ear off then," he said, smiling. His face really was quite beautiful. Not in a pretty, perfect way, like Adam's, but in a weathered, masculine way. His teeth were pearly white against his tanned, olive skin. He had dark stubble on his face, which accentuated his jawline and strong cheekbones. She imagined that he must smile often as the skin around his eyes was lightly crinkled, but it didn't detract from his face. On the contrary, it only added to his appeal. As did a thin scar at his temple.

She smiled back and reached for her coffee cup, hoping to buy herself a few more seconds to figure out her next step. Any other time she would have been well prepared for her mark. She would have been dressed for the part, prepared a playful dialogue based on their bio, even orchestrated the first contact. But this was so unexpected. He was supposed to be in a plane on his way to a meeting on another island.

She put down her cup and looked up, meeting his eyes. She was about to ask him about his plans for the day when he extended his hand.

"My name's Kevin Summerhill, by the way," he said, his eyes still locked with hers.

She clasped her fingers with his and felt the warmth travel up her arm. "Jane Dark," she returned. Until this moment she hadn't realized how obviously fabricated her name sounded. Although, his wasn't much better. His sounded like a rip off from an ex-boy-band member turned superstar.

"Jane Dark?" he repeated skeptically, raising an eyebrow. She was very aware that he hadn't let go of her hand. "I would think that even if you didn't want to give me your real name you could have come up with something better than that."

His blunt, observant words surprised her. But he was smiling teasingly and the feelings from him were still warm and curious.

She smiled, chagrinned, and looked down at the table, unsure how to handle being caught in her little white lie.

"Yes," she acquiesced. "I suppose I should have tried for something more original," she admitted with a laugh. "I guess I could have tried copying a popstar's name, Justin, I mean Kevin Summerhill was it?" she retorted, hoping he'd catch that she was just teasing him back.

"Touché" he replied, chuckling and finally releasing her hand.

"Why don't we try this again," he suggested. "I'm Cort." He'd used his real name! Evera struggled to suppress the shock from showing on her face.

"Cort...Summerhill," he grinned again.

She thought about the best way to handle this; she needed a name she would remember without practice if it were called out five minutes from now, but she was drawing a blank. "Evera." *Dammit!* She bit her lip to hide the reaction to her reveal.

"Evera Dark," she continued, following his lead.

"Well, Evera Dark, I'm pleased to meet you," he said sincerely, just as the waiter showed up and asked if either of them would like anything else.

"No, I have to leave shortly, but thank you," again, polite and refined.

He must be heading to his meeting after all. Maybe Garrison's intel was wrong about the time.

"If you have somewhere to be, please don't let me hold you up," said Evera, anxious to get away from him and let Garrison know of the change in plans.

"Unfortunately, I do," he admitted. "But I'm hoping to be back this evening."

She waited, sensing he wanted to say more.

He looked deep into her eyes again. "Would you have dinner with me tonight? That is, if you don't have any other plans?" he questioned expectantly.

"I don't have any other plans." She couldn't believe her fortunate turn of events. "And yes, dinner sounds great."

"How is 9:00?" he asked.

"That works fine," she answered.

He reached his hand out once again. "Until tonight, Evera Dark." He clasped her fingers and she noticed his were strong and rough, the feel of a man who used his hands for a living. The warmth coming from him travelled up her arm again.

"Tonight," she said in return. His eyes locked intensely with hers for a moment, then he rose from his seat and walked away.

*****

She sat at the table after he left trying to sort through the strange turn of events. Suspicion had been her initial reaction but his feelings had claimed attraction and interest, nothing more.

Evera got up from the table feeling excited and a little smug as she headed out of the dining area. She might just be the first person ever to get a positive ID and pertinent information on Cort. She couldn't wait to send the Section what she had so far. She could care less about what Garrison wanted, but she hoped Jonas would be impressed and forget the catastrophic outcome of her last mission.

She rounded the corner of the courtyard, preoccupied, and almost collided with two men walking in her path. *Shit!* It was the assholes from last night.

"Hey," said the blond named Cam. She tried to push past without acknowledging them.

"Hey, sweetheart, I'm talking to you," he insisted, reaching to grab her arm.

She twisted away, shrugging out from his grip, and fixed him with a stare filled with as much hate as she could muster.

"Sorry," he said, raising his hands up. "I thought you were someone else." He looked curiously at her as though she were familiar.

Elliot noticed her too. She saw recognition in his eyes but looked away and continued around the corner without a backward glance. She breathed a sigh of relief not to be facing another altercation with them, and looked behind just to be sure they weren't following her. Out of the corner of her eye she saw a tall, dark-haired man making his way towards the shrubs and the parking lot beyond. Cort had witnessed her encounter, she noted, as she climbed the stairs and unlocked her door.

Sitting on the bed with her phone she started writing her report. She wrote a complete description of Cort's face, making sure to include the small scar by his temple and the color of his eyes. For a second she sat stumped, as she tried to describe their exact shade; navy blue with a hint of violet. She remembered how transparent they had looked, like she could see through them and read what was hidden. She brushed the thought aside, settled for indigo and continued with the physical description.

She finished, hit send and then checked her texts. Still nothing from Adam. The clock on the bedside table read 11:07, which left her with almost an entire day to do what she wanted. And all she wanted was to swim and read by the pool but after her confrontation with Cam and Elliot, she thought better of it. She hated being trapped in her hotel room.

Then she remembered what Cort had said earlier about the local market. There wasn't a cloud in the sky and she could escape the resort and see some of the island. Decided, she grabbed her purse and phone and headed out the door.

The concierge at the entrance was a young, local woman. She gave Evera the name of the market for the cab driver but tried to steer her towards the tourist market, a short shuttle ride away.

"No thanks," she said politely. She was sure it was the attendant's job to keep the hotel's high profile and wealthy clientele away from the local riff raff.

As Evera left the resort the sun shone down on her, hot and dewy. She was suddenly excited to be out in the sunshine with a whole day stretching before her. She couldn't wait to wander around the tables and check out the different food and trinkets. Maybe she could find something for Adam, something unique to let him know how much she appreciated him.

There was a cab waiting for her the instant she exited the resort. Climbing into the stuffy backseat she told the driver where she wanted to go.

"No problem," he said, and pulled out through the resort gates. Evera opened her window letting the perfumed Maui breeze wash through the cab.

CHAPTER 10

Perceptions

The cab pulled off the main highway and onto a gravelly, dusty road about twenty minutes later. They followed the well-travelled path for another five minutes. Evera watched as the tall palm trees swayed from the light breeze, with nothing but hearty green outside her open window.

As the cab rounded a curve, the tropical forest opened up to a wide open space. They pulled into the parking area and Evera was immediately assaulted by the different sights, smells and sounds coming from the market.

Pulling over, the cab edged its way off the grass and came to a stop away from the heart of the chaos. The driver turned around to let her know the price of the fair and she handed him the cash as she climbed out. As she closed the car door she couldn't help but feel overwhelmed amidst the excitement.

The market was huge, possibly the equivalent of a city block made up of tables and small, tidy shops. The space itself was just a large sandy opening in the middle of a lush forest in the heart of Maui. The sound was just a constant din of voices all talking and shouting at the same time. Between the loud noises and the delicious smells of cooking food and local spices, Evera had to admit she loved it already. She walked immediately into the fray, looking forward to losing herself in the crowd.

As she neared a solid bank of tables she watched an elderly couple barter with a young Hawaiian girl over a pen. Evera headed over to take a closer look for herself.

The pens were handcrafted out of Hawaiian Koa wood. Adam would love it. She selected one and started the back and forth bartering process. Satisfied with the price after two minutes of haggling, she took her treasure from the young girl and tucked it in her purse. She wandered around, looking at trinkets and people watching. After only ten minutes, the feel of the sun beating down on her hair was too much so she decided to go in search of food and water and possibly a hat.

As she wandered among the food booths she saw a tamale stand near the end of the row right in front of her. She loved tamales. Looking around she saw another stand farther back but there were three times as many people in line. She was dying of thirst, so she got in line at the one closest to her with only two people waiting.

"I wouldn't if I were you," said a low, sexy voice in her ear.

She turned, startled, already knowing by the accent and the enticing smell of aftershave who it would be. She met his piercing blue eyes and again, was caught off guard and could think of nothing to say.

Cort was looking back at her, his eyes mischievous, a hint of a smile on his full lips. His ruggedly handsome face was so close she felt momentarily overwhelmed. Again, she felt the sweet warmth of his emotions tingle against her skin.

She opened her mouth, not sure what would come out but knowing she needed to say something or risk looking like an inarticulate idiot.

"Um, hi," she managed, inarticulate idiot indeed. His feelings and proximity were distracting and uncomfortable. She could feel herself blushing again.

"Miss Dark," his tongue caressed her name as he said it. He was looking at her sheepishly. "I'm not stalking you, I promise," he insisted, smiling and still holding her eyes with his. "I was in line at the other tamale stand when I recognized you." He was standing very close, his arm almost touching hers. "I was here a few months ago and made the mistake of eating at this vendor versus the other one," he pretended to shudder. "I didn't want you to make the same mistake."

She shifted her feet, putting some distance between their bodies; she couldn't seem to help it, his emotions were too intense for her to handle and still be able to keep a clear head.

"I appreciate the warning," she said honestly. "I noticed the difference in the lines, but I forgot to bring water with me and so I thought I'd chance it," she added.

"Water?" he asked. "That I can help you with." He looked down into a bag slung across his chest and started rummaging. She watched him, noticing his clothes for the first time since he spoke. He was wearing different clothes than when they met this morning, but he was dressed much too casually for a meeting. His torso was wrapped with a fitted grey, sleeveless T-shirt, hinting at his hard physique underneath. On the bottom he was wearing khaki shorts and flip flops.

The line suddenly moved up so Evera moved off to the side as he handed her a cold bottle of water.

"Thanks." She reached for it and ended up brushing fingers with him. Again, intense warm feelings ran through her at his touch, stronger this time than earlier.

She opened the bottle and tilted her head back, draining half of it instantly. She pulled the bottle away from her lips and saw Cort watching her with interest.

"Thanks," she repeated, her thirst momentarily quenched.

"Glad I could help," he said.

"Yes, offering me your help yet again." She shook her head in wonder. "You must think I'm a damsel in constant distress," that was the third time. She couldn't help but be impressed by his chivalry. She found it odd that a man with such a dark and brutal reputation could be so thoughtful.

"Not at all," he said chuckling. "On the contrary, I think you're more than capable of taking care of yourself. I'm just glad you're gracious enough to let me hang around and keep pestering you."

"Believe me, I appreciate you being around. I mean you've just saved me from what could have been an atrocious meal, not to mention staving off my dying of thirst." She really was grateful, especially for the water. She wondered if he had any more or if he'd given her his only bottle. "I hope you didn't give up your only water?" she asked.

"Not a problem," he said. "I can share."

She smiled, took another sip and then handed the bottle back. He glanced quickly at her, running his lip along the opening of the bottle before taking a drink himself.

"Now let's get us something to eat," he said, placing his hand, lightly on the small of her back, leading her towards the other food stand.

He passed the bottle back and forth between them as they made their way through the crowd. She could still feel his sweet intensity but there was more than that now. Every time she took a sip and then his lips followed she could feel passion smoldering in him. He seemed to like that their lips were touching the same space. She was surprised that he could find something erotic in such a simple exchange.

As they made their way to the back of the line, he finally released his touch on her back. Inwardly, she breathed a sigh of relief. He was still close enough that she could catch all his emotions but they were diluted by the lack of contact. She turned to face him and start the conversation for a change.

"I must say I was completely surprised to see you here." She hoped for some information she could use and send onward.

"Oh," he replied coolly.

"I just thought when you left this morning it was because you had somewhere else to be." She wondered if that was too prying and quickly redirected. "I'm glad that you ended up here, though," she added, smiling up at him. Definitely tall. She still had to look up at him even from her five feet nine inches.

"I had a change of heart which led to a change of plans," he said, not meeting her eyes. "Actually, this was supposed to be just a quick stop on my way back to the resort." He looked at her then, his eyes playful but his emotions intense. "I just couldn't drive by this place without stopping in for the tamales, the ones worth eating that is," his tone more lighthearted than the feelings coming off him.

"You're really pumping these up," she teased. "They better be worth the wait."

"I promise," he said, brushing her arm quickly with the back of his fingers. "You won't be disappointed."

"We'll see," she said, wanting the playful banter to continue. "You know I'm not some tamale tasting virgin. I've had my fair share of amazing, mind-blowing food in my travels." She wondered if her comment was too suggestive. He seemed so proper and polite; she wasn't exactly sure how to come across as demure and still let him know she was interested.

He laughed out loud, setting her mind at ease. "I'll be sure to keep that in mind," he replied.

"But," he added, raising a dark eyebrow, "sometimes it's the unexpected in something that makes it the best." His eyes were searching hers intensely but his grin kept his words from coming across too seriously.

"So I'm in for something I've never tasted before, am I?" she questioned.

"Perhaps," was his single word answer, his smile smug as he looked towards the front of the line. "Perhaps we both are." He said the words so softly she almost didn't catch them amidst the noise of the crowd. She pretended not to have heard his last comment, wanting to get the conversation moving in a less intimate direction.

"So, you were heading back to the resort? I imagine to enjoy the day by the pool or the beach." She wanted to keep the conversation light as well as try and find out what she could about his schedule for the day, he kept changing his plans and making it difficult for her to keep up.

As he touched her back to move her along with the line, whispers of heat diffused from his fingertips. "Well I was, but it seems as though I may have to change my plans again." He was looking at her, his eyes soft and teasing, and then he tilted his chin towards her and waited.

"And why is that?" she asked coyly.

"Well, I imagine you didn't drive yourself here," he stated. Again they moved forward in the line. Just a few people away from the front, his hand still warming her back.

"No," she answered, waiting for the punch line, "I came here in a cab."

"And did you arrange for the cab to come back and pick you up?" he asked, although he formed his question as if he already knew the answer.

"No, but aren't there cabs waiting to take people out of the market?" she asked.

"Nope, definitely not," he gestured to the outer perimeter of the market, not a cab in sight.

She thought about his words and grimaced. It hadn't occurred to her to make arrangements to get back to the resort. Her idea for the trip had been so spur of the moment.

"I'm sure I can just call a cab company and have them send a car to pick me up," she answered confidently. She hated that he had thought about her scenario before she had.

"Out here?" he said doubtfully. "I think you'll find most cab companies reluctant to send a car all the way to the market. They can get three fairs in the time it takes to make one trip out here," he assured.

"So, do you have a solution for me or are you just going to keep shooting down every suggestion I have?" she asked, tilting her chin up at him.

"Yes," he said, returning her gaze. "You can come back with me." His eyes were ambivalent, as though he wasn't certain if she would take him up on his offer.

They reached the front of the line before she could answer him and the man behind the counter asked them what they wanted. The man looked Evera over, rudely, from head to toe while he waited for them to place their order.

She could feel Cort's distaste for the man brush against her skin. "Evera?" he asked, turning and moving in front of her to shield her from the leering man's view.

"Umm," she hadn't had a chance to look at the chalkboard menu propped up on the long table. "Why don't you just pick something for us," she said. She saw his eyes flicker with interest when she said the word 'us.'

"Alright." He seemed surprised by her trust. "Would you like mild or spicy?"

"Spicy," she said, giving him a coy smile, "definitely."

He returned her smile and then turned his attention back to the man waiting for the order. "Four regular tamales with the spicy green Chile and tomatillo sauce," he said.

"Four regular," shouted the man to the cook behind him, "and spice it up." He took in Cort's harsh stare and averted his eyes. He handed Cort a ticket and they shuffled off to the side to wait for their food.

"So?" he asked, a questioning look on his face and a raised eyebrow. Evera was momentarily distracted from the question by the curve of his brow and the depthless blue of his eyes.

Dammit, Evera! She castigated herself, pull it together. What the hell was the matter with her? She encountered attractive men all the time in her job. This should be no different than any other mission. It was just his proximity and intensity, she was sure of it, that was throwing her off. She forcibly cleared her mind and was brought back to his question, which wasn't exactly a question.

"So?" she repeated back to him.

He smiled knowingly at her. "So, would you like a ride back to the resort with me?" Again, he seemed to be waiting with uncertainty for her answer.

She opened her mouth to respond when he interrupted her.

"I realize you barely know me and that taking a ride from a stranger is not the smartest thing for a young lady travelling alone to do. I assure you I'm harmless," he defended. How untrue they both knew that comment was. "You can call ahead and let the resort know you're coming back with me if that will make you feel more comfortable."

"Alright," she said, keeping her answer vague, forcing him to continue the chase.

"Alright you'll come with me or alright you'd like to call the resort first?" his eyes flashed with confusion.

"I'll come with you," she said smiling, hoping to reassure him. Then a thought occurred to her.

"Although, I suppose I could call the resort and have them send a cab for me," she said, looking innocently at him. "I'm sure they could get a car to come out here for me, after all, I'm a guest."

"True," he admitted, a sexy smirk on his lips. "But who knows how long you'll have to wait. Not to mention, the accommodations in my car would be preferable to a cab that's been driving around with various bodies in hundred degree heat."

The idea of making the thirty minute drive in a sweaty, body odor filled cab made her grimace. "You've got me there," she agreed.

"Besides," he continued, pleading his case, "if last night is any indication as to how you can handle yourself then perhaps it's me who should be wary." He grinned, looking down and shaking his head as he remembered their non-introduction from last night.

"Four spicy up!" yelled the cook, as he slid their order towards the edge of the counter.

Cort handed the man the ticket and then grabbed their food and looked at it chagrinned.

"Sorry, they put all four in one box. I should have asked for two separate orders," he said, showing her the four tamales lying side-by-side in the box. They were covered in a green sauce that smelled spicy and delicious. Evera's mouth started to water.

"We shared your water, I'm sure we can do the same with these." He was so unlike any other dirtbag mark she had ever encountered. His concern and manners again taking her by surprise.

"Water," he said, and hit the heel of his hand against his forehead. He handed her the box of food and started walking to the end of the line. He looked back at the long line, thought better of it, and headed to the pickup counter.

The same cook who had just brought their food out was bringing out another order, extending his arm to slide it across the counter; Cort reached for his arm before he pulled it back.

"Two bottles of water, please," he insisted, firmly gripping the man's arm.

The man looked down at his arm and then uncertainly at Cort. "You're supposed to order and pay in line," said the man, confused and pointing to the back of the still long line.

"No, thanks," his menacing tone leaving no room for argument. He reached into his pocket with his free hand and grabbed a twenty dollar bill, handing it to the man.

"As I said, two bottles of water," he repeated. Evera imagined by the frightened look on the other man's face that Cort's countenance was leaving no room for argument.

"Sure…" said the man, murmuring and stumbling in his haste to get away from Cort's fierce glare and grip. He practically ran to the cooler, grabbed two bottles of water and rushed back, holding out the water and pulling change from his pocket at the same time.

"Thank you," said Cort, smiling at the man, holding his hand up to refuse the change.

"You're welcome," he mumbled. He was looking at Cort with an awed and confused look on his face.

It was in that moment that Evera caught a glimpse of why Cort was so effective. Fierce was the perfect word to describe him. Fierce and gracious, an unexpected and enticing combination. She could see why his clientele dealt with him. He insisted on getting his way but then was sure to reward those who gave him what he wanted. She imagined there were very few people who were brave enough or stupid enough to cross him. The prospect of him being White was looking more and more likely.

Cort turned back to her, holding up the bottles of water and smiling.

"I think this will get us through the spicy tamales," he said, as he looked around for a place to sit.

"I don't see any free tables," said Evera, searching.

"Why don't we make our way over to the trees and some shade? I'm sure you'd like to get out of the sun as much as I would." He was looking at her with concern and she realized that yet again he was trying to take care of her. She couldn't help but feel charmed, which was surprising. She was never charmed.

"That sounds great," she agreed, as the sun beating down on her head was giving her a bit of a headache.

As soon as they left the market and hit the dirt road the welcoming shade covered them and the sounds of the crowd were muted by the trees and distance. Cort looked around for a grassy level spot for them to sit.

He started to pull the bag he was carrying over his head when it caught on his shirt and lifted it, revealing his hard stomach. Again, she was surprised by what she saw. For a man of almost forty he was impressively lean and cut. He looked at her, noticing that she noticed. She quickly looked away, feeling like she'd been caught in the act of something naughty. She peeked at his face and noticed a small smile on his lips; he seemed pleased by her appraisal of his body. *Good,* she thought. The demure but interested attitude she was going for was obviously working. A small voice in the back of her mind pointed out that she hadn't planned the sensual inspection. She looked at the ground, frowning to herself.

"Here," he said, gesturing for her to sit on his empty bag as he took the box of tamales from her. He grabbed her hand and pulled her down on to the canvas bag, as he knelt down on the bare ground beside her.

He handed her a fresh bottle of water, cracking open the seal. As she adjusted herself more comfortably to sit she put her hands on the ground. The earth was still damp from the rain last night. She was immediately grateful for his bag under her skirt, keeping the cold and wet away from her skin.

She noticed he was kneeling on his bare knees so as not to get his shorts wet. She couldn't imagine that he was comfortable, and although she didn't relish the idea of the intensity of his touch, her objective was to get close to him.

"Why don't you share my seat with me," she offered, scooting over. "The ground is still wet from last night, and there's room." Unfortunately, they would have to sit extremely close.

"Thanks." He shifted so he was beside her, their arms and legs touching.

She sucked in a sharp breath from the hot feelings that swirled around her at his light touch, and looked for a diversion.

"I'll hold that," she took the tamale box and balanced it on her knees. His feelings were so compelling that she felt almost panicky as they started digging into the food. She wasn't used to this. Before him, all her marks had actions and emotions that were so predictable. On very rare occasions a mark would start to feel something more for her, but not before something physical had happened. Never before that.

"So, what do you think?" he asked, looking her over.

"About what?" She wondered if she had been so preoccupied by his feelings and handsome face that she'd missed part of a conversation.

"The tamales," he reminded, gesturing with his fork towards the food.

She looked down at the half empty box and realized that in her haste to distract herself she had been wolfing down her food without tasting it. Scooping another forkful into her mouth, she paid attention to the flavor. He had been right about them being delicious and unique. There were small pieces of avocado tucked inside with the masa, completely unexpected.

"Amazing and definitely worth the wait," she agreed.

"I can tell you're enjoying them," he chuckled softly, looking into the half empty box.

She laughed too; she must have looked ravenous eating so much so quickly.

"The rest is yours," she relinquished, putting her fork down and handing the box over.

"Certainly not," but he accepted the box from her. He cut up the remaining pieces and took a bite, and then held a piece out for her on his fork. She leaned forward towards the morsel of food and he met her gaze. He shared the food between them back and forth, just like with the water bottle. And again, desire pulsed through him and against her bare arm, as her lips slid the food off his fork. As he held out the last bite for her, she felt overwhelmed and even a bit afraid. Again no sex, no touching and yet she felt cocooned in an air of eroticism.

"Had enough?" he asked, after she swallowed the last bite.

Yes, she thought, *more than enough.* What would happen when he really touched her? Or worse, when they were tangled naked together and this feeling intensified.

Fuck Evera! She screamed inwardly. She could handle this. She just had to keep reminding herself that he was just a mark, probably her most dangerous one.

"Yes, and that was delicious, thank you," she answered, looking at him, his face still so close. She shifted her gaze towards the market, needing a break from the intensity of him.

His look followed hers towards the masses several yards in front of them. He wrapped his arms around his knees, his hard forearm touching her leg as he did so. He seemed so content and relaxed next to her; the complete opposite of the uncertain, nervous mess she had become.

They sat in companionable silence, people watching as their food settled. She shivered once, her nerves and the cool shade making her feel chilled after the blistering rays of the sun.

"Let's get back in the sun," he suggested. After rising, he reached down to help her up. She grabbed his hand and let him pull her to standing. His hand was rough and strong but his grip was gentle.

He pulled her close as she stood, his hand still holding hers, their chests touching. She looked up at him, his eyes burning into hers, his passion wrapping around both of them. His face was so close. Too close. His lips parted and Evera had a horrible feeling he was going to kiss her. Kiss her here, in public, with no opportunity for her to use any of her other skills to run interference and stop him.

Without considering the consequences, she broke free from his eyes and looked down, pulling away from his body at the same time. He dropped her hand immediately and cleared his throat. She peered up at him to see how much damage her action had caused. He was running his hand through his dark hair and looking down. He started picking up their belongings and repacking his bag.

"I'll help you with that," she offered, reaching for the empty bottles in his hand. She made sure when she grabbed for them that she brushed her fingers against his.

"Oh, thanks," he said, his face a mixture of confusion and pleasure.

They walked out into the sunshine and dumped their empty containers into the garbage bin on their way back to the crowded market.

"Would you like to stay a while and shop or were you anxious to get back to the resort?" he asked, letting her decide.

"I'm good either way." She turned her face up to him and smiled. He smiled back and was walking close enough that she could feel his interest in her hadn't diminished in the least.

"I'll call for my car and we can get going shortly," he said, reaching in his pocket for his phone.

Her thoughts went ahead of her back to the resort, and the idea of running into the two men from last night and this morning, put a damper on the idea of going back. She frowned and wished she'd said she wanted to stay longer. Looking up she met his eyes. He was holding his phone but hadn't dialed yet.

"Evera?" he asked, his voice strained.

"Yes?" she questioned.

"Are you sure you want to come with me? You don't have to. I can arrange for another car to come and get you." He sounded disappointed but was trying to hide it.

"What?" she asked, confused by his question. "No, I'd like to go back with you. Why do you ask?"

"The look on your face just then." His eyes moved over her face. "You seemed displeased with the idea and I thought maybe you'd changed your mind."

The most dangerous, powerful man she had possibly ever met and he seemed so unsure of himself. She laughed softly, in spite of herself. He watched her, his eyebrows knitting together in a frown. She grabbed onto his arm immediately, hoping to show him she hadn't meant to offend.

"Believe me," she said, feeling the hard muscles of his arm beneath her hands, "my sour look had nothing to do with you. I was just remembering the two unpleasant characters from our first meeting last night," she said honestly.

"I saw them bothering you again this morning," he commented. His eyes looked suddenly angry. "I know who those men are," he confessed. "Most of the people who come to our resort fall into one of two categories. Famous or important. But not in those two idiots case...they fall under an entirely different category. Dangerous."

"So which category do you fall under, Cort?" she inquired, realizing it was the first time she had said his name out loud. "Famous or important?" But she knew he'd choose important. He was only famous as far as the underworld was concerned.

He looked down at her hand still wrapped around his arm and then into her eyes. "Neither," he rasped, trapping her eyes. She was shocked. He was letting her know he was dangerous too. She wasn't sure how to respond so she simply looked ahead, away from his probing gaze, but kept her hands tightly wrapped around his arm. Evera had been worried about revealing too much of herself and here he was, giving up secrets.

They walked close together towards the start of the tables, neither of them saying anything further. He still had his phone in his free hand, and she released his arm as he started texting.

"The car will be a half hour or so if you want to look around for a bit," he stated.

"Sure, that sounds great," she answered, truthfully. Now that she was full, hydrated, and distanced from his touch, she was happy to wander. It was fairly congested where they were walking. He stayed close by her, his strong arm brushing against hers as they passed through the crowd.

Cort spoke with several of the people at the different booths. She paid attention to the fact that he used different dialects. At one of the booths he spoke Hawaiian to a local looking gentleman. At a handmade jewelry table he spoke Japanese. It was run by a middle-aged woman in a red and gold sarong. She spoke animatedly to Cort while she gestured to Evera.

Cort turned to her smiling. "She wants to know if I would like to buy something for my lovely wife."

Evera smiled back at him, but felt uncomfortable at the harmless comment.

"Let me see." Looking coyly at him she tried to play along. There were bracelets and necklaces, all handmade with shells and beads. Some of them were quite beautiful. The Japanese woman looked at Evera quizzically and spoke again to Cort.

Cort moved close to her, their arms touching and whispered in her ear, "She says there isn't a piece of jewelry here as beautiful as you."

Evera felt his emotions brush against her skin as warmly as his breath against her neck. She turned to look at him and instantly wished she hadn't. His eyes were full of warmth and something mystifying.

She cleared her throat nervously and said, "You realize she's just trying to get you to buy something by flattering me."

He smiled. "Possibly," he agreed, "but her words couldn't be more true." She felt uncomfortable and helpless. Helpless because she wanted to look away but somehow his eyes held her captive.

Breathe, she commanded. She took a deep shaky breath and broke free. She looked back at the table, not really searching for anything but a distraction from the intensity of the moment.

Cort resumed talking to the woman in the red sarong while Evera continued looking at the jewelry. She picked up a bracelet, turning it in her hand, not really seeing the colors. What the hell was happening to her? Sure he was good-looking and sexy, so what? His looks were nothing she hadn't encountered before. But she knew it wasn't just that. He was also intelligent, thoughtful and sweet. She couldn't let the fact that she liked his personality get in the way of her mission. This could become a complicated disaster very quickly if she didn't get a hold of herself.

The woman pointed at the bracelet Evera was holding.

Cort turned to Evera. "You like that one?" he asked.

She looked down at the bracelet she had been fidgeting with. It was simple and pretty with blue and green inset shells.

"It's very nice," she said to both Cort and the woman.

"Great," he said, and then turned back to the woman, obviously haggling over the price. She watched as they argued back and forth in Japanese. He leaned in close to the women and smiled, pulling out his wallet. The woman couldn't help but smile at him as he handed her the cash. Evera could tell she too found him charming and hard to resist.

"It's yours," he declared, taking the bracelet and sliding it slowly on her, his hands lingering around her wrist as heat pulsed through his touch and up her arm.

"Thank you," she said, looking down at the new bracelet, so very different from the one wrapped around her other arm.

"Your other bracelet is very beautiful." His fingers reached to touch it. "I've never seen anything quite like it."

Her heart rate picked up instantly. Unique indeed, she thought. Suddenly a picture flashed in her mind, the bracelet apart, the garrote wrapped around Cort's throat and her pulling it tight. She couldn't help but wonder if it was more than just a thought. Maybe even a premonition. She looked up at him and felt a flicker of unease.

His phone rang just then and he turned away quickly to answer it, speaking quietly. He smiled, but moved farther from her so she couldn't hear his conversation.

While Cort was still talking she took the opportunity to move forward on her mission. Making sure her flash was off, she quickly took several discreet pictures of him. As he moved around and spoke she managed to get every angle of his face. Satisfied, she quickly changed to her text app in order to send the pictures to Garrison and wipe them from her phone. She knew he would be ecstatic when he saw them.

"Just take care of those loose ends," she heard Cort demand before he hung up and started back towards her.

"Sorry, I needed my driver to arrange a quick errand so he'll be a little bit longer," he explained. His face looked open and calm but he was standing close enough to her that she could feel his tension.

As they walked towards the parking area, the crowd got denser and they had to move almost single file. Cort was leading the way when he stopped suddenly and turned to the side, reaching his hand towards her. "Don't want to lose you in the crowd," he said. She held her hand out and his wrapped hers in a warm grasp.

He moved them slowly through the throng of bodies, the heat from his fingers and sentiments melting into her. Evera tried to block Cort's emotions and concentrate instead on the people passing by. After a while, it seemed an impossible draining battle so she caved and tried to accept and relax.

Once they made their way to the other side and away from the constant noise, they started talking. He asked her questions that, surprisingly, she could answer. His questions were careful, almost as if he knew not to dig too deep. He asked her things like places she'd travelled too, things she liked and didn't like. Never questions about any people in her life, where she came from or what she did for a living. She asked him the same questions back. She wondered if he had done that on purpose, only asking questions he would be willing to answer.

Conversation flowed easily between them, and she learned more about him with this line of questioning than the usual conversation between two virtual strangers. Unfortunately, because it was more personal, it was not at all helpful towards her mission's purpose.

She found out that he had travelled all over the world. His favorite place was South Africa. When he spoke of it she could hear the longing in his voice. He got a faraway look in his eyes the way someone thinking fondly of their home would. She imagined he had spent a lot of his life there, which would account for his accent.

His phone beeped but he ignored it and kept talking. He was describing the African countryside. They talked about the different wines that came from the different regions there. She was surprised to hear him say that at one point he had owned a vineyard just outside Kenya. He talked excitedly about how he had bought the failing land from a local man and nurtured it back to life. He'd done most of the work himself, which she assumed had contributed to the roughness and strength in his hands.

They walked and talked for what seemed like no time at all when Cort looked at his watch. "It's been about an hour since the driver beeped that the car is here. I guess I should let him know what our plans are. Are you ready to head back yet?" he asked her.

She was shocked that the time had flown by so quickly. She looked up at the sun in the sky and sure enough, it was already making its decent into late afternoon.

"Alright," she said, and noticed for the first time in a long time that they were still holding hands. She thought about that and decided that it was a good thing; it meant that she was getting accustomed to his touch and feelings. Hopefully, that would make things easier for her later if things got heated.

But the professional in her, the assassin side, disagreed. That side of her pointed out that maybe she was getting too accustomed, too comfortable with Cort and his touch. She pushed away the disconcerting thought. Certainly the mark was different and more intense than she was used to, but she was Jezebel. And Jezebel knew how to handle herself.

They rounded the end of the market and Evera noticed a black Audi sedan waiting, windows tinted dark, its engine running. Cort led her towards it and opened the door, keeping her hand as he helped her in.

Cort folded his long frame in close beside her. He put his arm along the back of the seat, which meant she was tucked in close beside his body. The hard muscles of his torso pressed against her bare arm. Without a word from Cort, the driver started pulling away from the market and towards the winding road she had come down earlier in the day.

As they started their trek down the forested path the driver opened the windows in the back. The sultry air permeated the cab but the air conditioning kept the temperature cool. She could smell the green of the passing trees and a hint of brine from the ocean, just beyond the woods.

She tried to relax against Cort's side, accepting the closeness as best as she could. His hand reached out to hers, resting on her lap. He gently twined his fingers with hers and she could feel his gaze upon her. She looked up at his face, shockingly close and attractive. He gave her a quick, almost shy smile, his eyes boring down into hers. She smiled back and then averted her gaze, looking out the window at the passing forest. His feelings of passion for her were so strong she could taste it in the air around them, the heat of it encompassing her, making her palms sweat and her head swim.

For thirty minutes she would have to tolerate this. As they sped through the steamy forest, his body so close to hers, she was sure it would feel like the longest thirty minutes of her life.

CHAPTER 11

Dinner and Secrets

They spent the thirty minute drive in relaxed silence. At least Cort seemed relaxed, other than his desire for her never subsiding. Evera, on the other hand, found she had to concentrate just to keep her body from tensing up the whole journey.

When they pulled up to the resort gate she sighed inwardly with relief. The driver spoke briefly with the guard manning the gate and then the arms of the barricade lifted as they drove through. As the driver pulled into a vacant spot not far from the hedge and the lap pool, Cort lifted his arm from around Evera. She could feel his disappointment in giving up the embrace of the last half hour.

They stood outside the car, her hand in his, inches between them.

"Are we still on for dinner or are you sick of me yet?" He looked down at her smiling and waited.

"We are definitely still on," she said, returning his smile.

"See you at 9:00 then," he said, not releasing her hand.

"See you then," she agreed, as he let her go. Turning to walk to her room, she could feel his eyes following her.

The second she rounded the hedge and was out of his sight she sucked in a mouthful of air. It wasn't so much a huge sigh of relief as it was her body trying to catch its breath. She needed space…distance between herself and Cort.

She made her way as quickly as she could to the stairs leading up to her room. Climbing them she could feel her discomfort turn to anger, at both herself and Cort. Pulling her room card out, she wrenched the door open and slammed it behind her, securely locking it.

She needed water and something to occupy her hands and her irritation. She was vacillating between anger at herself and fear. She took her purse off, flung it on the bed and started pacing. *What the hell!* She yelled in her head. She downed some water and went over the afternoon in her mind. She had made no missteps, no slipups. All in all, if she removed the emotion, it had been a successful afternoon. She'd made initial contact, had a plan for another meeting and an opportunity to get intel; not to mention the first official photograph of Cort's face. An accomplished afternoon and yet here she was practically unravelling in her hotel room.

A shower. She needed a hot shower to wash away the stress and regain her focus. That and to wash away Cort. The smell of him—his aftershave, his skin—was clinging to her making it harder for her to plan and concentrate.

She went straight to the bathroom, stripped off her clothes, turned the shower to hot and climbed in. The heat from the pelting spray unknotted her tense muscles. She shampooed her hair vigorously and then started to soap up. As she ran her hands over her body, Cort's face suddenly came to mind. Just as before when she went over the afternoon from a professional perspective, the emotions that played out through the afternoon came rushing back to her. His attentiveness and thoughtfulness, right from their first meeting. The piercing blue of his eyes. The gentle touch of his warm, rough hands. And most disconcerting, his desire for her, constant and hot against her skin the whole afternoon.

The muscles in the pit of her stomach tightened at the memory. She felt suddenly uncomfortable in her own skin. The water running over her naked body felt wrong, too intimate, as if she could feel every drop as it rained down upon her, making her skin tingle. She needed to get out. She rinsed off as quickly as she could, no longer feeling the relaxation of the water. She turned off the shower and got out, drying off her body harshly, taking great pains to ignore the feel of the towel rubbing against her bare flesh. She pulled a robe off the back of the door and wrapped it tightly around herself.

Her one relaxing solace, the shower, washing away the dirt from her mind and body, had now become an agitation. "For fuck's sake," she hissed out loud. She wrapped her arms tight around herself feeling lost and confused.

She looked towards the bed where she had thrown her purse and noticed that her phone had spilled out. Adam. She needed so desperately to hear his voice. She lay down on the bed and started dialing his number even though it was a direct breach of protocol. The line started ringing and she held her breath, waiting for him to answer. She was certain once she heard him that she would feel like herself again.

Six rings, then seven and finally a beep signaling voice mail. She hung up. She hadn't spoken with him since he'd left and she didn't want to leave an impersonal message. Besides, she had no idea what to say to him.

She opened her private reporting app on her phone and decided to get started on her day's activities. She hoped that by recording all the pertinent events of the afternoon that she would regain her focus on her assignment. She found it helped immensely, writing down everything from an impersonal and factual perspective. And she had been right, removing his feelings from the afternoon put her emotionally back on an even keel. She sent it and then contemplated how to fill the rest of her afternoon.

She looked over at the clock on the bedside table and it read 4:37. She rolled over onto her side, groaning. Four and a half hours until dinner and she was trapped in her room again. She could go for a run but she dreaded accidentally bumping into Cort. Not until she had a chance to talk to Adam and feel grounded again. She didn't want to chance running into her other unsavory friends from last night either, which reminded her of her conversation with Cort that afternoon. She couldn't help but wonder if he just knew about the two men or if he was actually acquainted with them.

In the end, she grabbed *Jane Eyre* from her bedside table and continued where she left off that morning.

Two minutes later her phone pinged. She reached for it and was rewarded with a text from Adam. He was in a meeting with Jonas and would be heading back, alone, on a mid-evening flight. He said he would call her once he was on his way to the airport, around 8:00 p.m. her time.

She was instantly relieved. She would have a chance to talk to Adam before her dinner with Cort. The idea calmed her and she got up to make some coffee.

The phone in her room rang at 6:04...Adam was early. As she reached for it she thought it odd that he would call her in her room instead of on her cell. Maybe they were keeping track of her phone and he didn't want to get caught making an unauthorized call.

"Hello," she said, breathless and happy.

"Miss Dark," said a sexy, accented voice. Cort...speechless again.

"I'm not catching you in the middle of anything am I?" he prompted.

"Um, no, not at all," she replied, stuffing the bookmark in between the pages. "I was just reading," she answered. He must be calling to cancel, she thought, waiting for him to say more.

"*Jane Eyre* was it?" he asked. She stiffened on the bed, feeling suspicious. How could he know that? Was he somehow watching her? She looked around the room and noticed the window shades were open. He didn't seem like the Peeping Tom type, though.

"Yes, how did you know?" she wondered.

He laughed softly on the other end. "This morning," he reminded her. "I noticed you reading it before your bookmark blew away and I went scurrying after it."

He'd been watching her this morning. And somehow she hadn't noticed him at all.

"So, how's the book?" he asked, politely making small talk. "I've never read it myself. I know it's a classic but I could just never warm up to the whole Elizabethan language."

She smiled to herself. He was so proper and chivalrous...she could actually picture him as a character in the book.

"It's wonderful," she said. "I've read it before, several times actually. It's my favorite book." Her honesty made her bite her lip. Here she was again, caught off guard and saying more than she should.

"Well, then I might just have to reconsider and give it a try," he said, pausing. Evera could tell he had something else he wanted to say but was stalling. Definitely cancelling. She was disappointed about not getting more information but a small part of her was relieved.

She waited for him to continue and when he didn't she asked, "Is everything still okay for dinner tonight?"

"No, actually," he sounded unsure again. She tried not to allow his vulnerability to draw her in.

"I was wondering how you'd feel about moving it to 7:00 instead of 9:00?" he asked. She hadn't been expecting that. He must have a meeting later tonight. Good, she could cut the night short and let Garrison know.

"That's fine." She'd already showered so she could be ready to meet him in under an hour but it would mean that she wouldn't be able to talk to Adam before she went. Or, she could avoid him altogether and get out of their arrangement now.

"Unless you have somewhere you need to be?" she questioned, hoping her fishing wouldn't be noticed. "We can always reschedule, if that would be easier for you."

"No, it's not that at all." Again he sounded reluctant. She wished she could get at his feelings through the phone.

"Honestly," he confessed, his voice soft and intense, "I just couldn't wait until 9:00 to see you again."

Her heart skipped a beat. All her confidence about the evening slowly drained away replaced by the fear she'd felt earlier.

"Oh." She wanted to say more but she didn't trust her voice.

"So, I'll see you at 7:00?" He formed it as a question.

"Yes," she answered, trying to sound enthusiastic through her panic.

"I'm looking forward to it. Good-bye, Evera," he finished quietly. The phone clicked as he hung up.

She sat there for several seconds, still holding the phone to her ear. *Fuck!* What was she going to do now?

The calculating Jezebel in her came to the rescue, giving her direction. She was going to stay calm, focus, and get the information the Section needed. And most imperatively, remember his bio; that of a cold-blooded killer. Her enemy.

The self-pep-talk helped and she began getting ready, talking herself through the way she thought the evening would play out. She would just need a few minutes to tag his phone, which would be her main focus. She purposely avoided thinking about the situation that would have to occur first, in order for her to be alone with his phone.

She finished her makeup, wearing more than she usually did during the day. She did a critical once over of herself in the mirror. Her hair had air dried so it was falling in long, soft waves down her back. She had done a deep brown smoky look with her shadow, playing up the green in her eyes. She added a sheer tinted lip-gloss which emphasized the fullness of her lips.

Taking off her robe, she slipped into her lacy black bra and panties; a matching set that she had picked up in the Paris airport the last time she was there. It felt as amazing as it looked. Then she pulled on her knee length, sheath dress. It was made out of a thin jersey material that clung to every curve. She went back to the bathroom and dabbed on her favorite oil blend perfume called 'If'. The scent diffused sensuous white flowers and citrus. Subtle yet alluring.

She grabbed her small Dior clutch off the counter and went through it one more time. Lip-gloss, phone, credit cards and condoms. She frowned as she took into account the last item. She reminded herself again to keep things in perspective...it was just business.

She checked herself over in the mirror one last time. Sexy and unassuming, perfect for Cort. She looked down and noticed her locket on the counter. She really didn't want to wear it. Here in Hawaii, she was Jezebel. She despised the thought of bringing a piece of Evera along tonight. Not being able to leave it behind, she put it over her head, letting the heart rest against her chest. It looked good; fitting perfectly into the cleavage of her dress's neckline.

Lastly, she took off her bracelet and double-checked it. She separated the arms and strung out the garrote. It ran smooth and clean just like it should. It retracted quickly back in when she released the pressure. She clipped it back on her arm, confident she wouldn't need to use it but grateful that it was in perfect working condition. Just in case.

She remembered to add the bracelet Cort had bought her and then stood ready to go...6:58, perfect timing.

She slung her slender clutch on her shoulder and strapped on her sandals. As she opened the door to leave she paused. Relax, she thought, it's just another assignment, just another man. She crossed the threshold, confident in her ability to meet whatever came her way tonight.

*****

Evera arrived at the empty hostess station at exactly 7:00. She waited patiently, seeing the girl in black and white busy seating another couple.

She scanned the elegant outdoor dining area. There were torches lit throughout, giving the area a soft, warm glow. She could glimpse the ocean at the end of the beach, the waves brushing softly against the shore.

Then she saw him. He must have already been seated because he was weaving his way through the dining tables towards her. His eyes met hers and her breath caught in her throat. He was dressed simply, in dark linen pants and jacket with a crisp white shirt. He looked incredible, but that wasn't what had started the blood pounding through her veins. It was the look in his eyes when he saw her. Hunger.

All the self-talk and confidence from moments ago started to fade. Her palms started sweating and fear weighed heavily in the pit of her stomach.

He stopped in front of her offering her his hand. "Evera," he said breathlessly, his eyes moving along her body.

"Hi, Cort," she replied, taking his hand, hoping he wouldn't notice the dampness of her palm.

"You look...." he hesitated, searching for words, "amazing."

She looked down, feigning shyness, but really she just needed to break the intensity of his eyes boring into hers.

"Thank you," she said quietly.

He led them back to the table he had been sitting at. They were on the periphery of the dining area closest to the ocean. The same table she had been sitting at for breakfast this morning when they'd first met. He pulled her seat out for her, only releasing her hand after she was seated. She was thankful for the break in contact.

He seated himself next to her, not across the table. His knee brushing her bare leg as he sat. He smiled at her, his eyes crinkling at the corners. A dark, sexy five o'clock shadow was running along his strong jawline. She caught the clean, musky smell of his aftershave. The top two buttons of his shirt were undone, showing a hint of his well-formed chest between.

"I apologize," he said, gesturing to his half full wine glass. "I arrived a few minutes early and ordered some white. I hope you don't mind a Riesling to start?"

"No, that sounds great," she said, thankful for an immediate glass of wine to calm her frayed nerves. He poured her some and she reached for it, also grateful for something to occupy her hands.

"So, how was the rest of your afternoon?" he asked.

She looked at him and smiled. "Nice and relaxing," she lied.

"How was yours?" she asked, hoping he would give her something she could use.

He leaned towards her, his arms on the table. "Long," he answered seductively, reading her face.

Thankfully, the server appeared, bringing down the temperature of the moment. The young man looked at Evera and did a double take.

"Can I get either of you anything to start?" he asked, only speaking to her. She caught his instant feeling of lust as he stood too close to her side.

She looked up at him. "I haven't decided yet." She returned her gaze to Cort. "Cort?" she asked. Evera could feel the waiter still looking inappropriately at her.

"Nothing at the moment, thanks," said Cort tersely.

"I'll be back shortly," he said, smiling knowingly at Evera. She imagined most women would fall for his over the top flirting. He was incredibly good-looking but Evera knew his type; arrogant and slick, a player. The type of man she despised.

She felt relieved when he left the table and took his lustful feelings with him. She hadn't noticed that she had subconsciously leaned closer to Cort in an attempt to get farther away from the waiter. When she turned back to look at him their faces where much closer together. His expression as he looked at her was one of longing and sadness. She was so surprised that her hand automatically reached to touch his arm.

"What?" she asked, searching his face. His feelings mirrored his eyes and she couldn't imagine what could have just transpired to change his mood so completely.

He shook his head, looking down at the table. "What the hell am I doing?" he asked aloud. His eyes were still down so she couldn't read them, but she could still feel him. He seemed mired in uncertainty.

"What's wrong, Cort?" she asked, genuinely curious at his sudden mood swing.

He looked at her, his eyes still unsure. She could feel his emotions at war with each other.

"You shouldn't be here with me," he answered. "Or more precisely, I shouldn't be here with you." He kept his eyes shielded from her as he spoke.

"Why would you say that?" she asked. She wanted to know the reason behind the words that contradicted his feelings.

His lips parted and then he hesitated. He seemed to change his mind partway through his thought. He smiled but it didn't reach his eyes. "I'm too old for you, for one thing," he admitted.

She almost laughed out loud. His response was so ridiculous and impotent compared to his expression. She smiled teasingly at him, hoping to lighten the moment. "First of all, you don't even know how old I am, nor I you." He shifted in his seat as his eyes came back to hers. "So that concern is definitely premature," she said. "And secondly," she leaned closer to him, hoping to reassure him with her actions, "if you feel you're too old for me, well, that would be more my issue than yours. Wouldn't you agree?"

He gave her a wry smile, looking only partially convinced. "I suppose," he answered, vaguely.

"Good, so let's just enjoy our dinner together," she added, searching for a safe change in topic when he started speaking again.

"I'm too dangerous for you," he said vehemently. These were the real words he was going to caution her with before he changed his mind. Eyes locked with hers, not letting go, he waited.

She stared back, unable to coax a response from her lips. Who was this man, really? And why was he being so honest with her? She tasted the air between them. He wanted her, badly, but he was also trying to warn her off, which meant he cared for her. The sentiment worried her.

She reached for a safe parallel to ease his mind. "You don't know me or who I am either," she said, keeping eye contact in the hopes of gaining his trust. "We all have skeletons in our closet, Cort."

He stared at her and shook his head in disbelief. "If only it were as simple as a few skeletons."

He moved his gaze towards the ocean. His eyes took on a faraway look and she waited for him to speak. When he met her patient stare again his eyes were softer, less tragic.

"I'm not used to feeling like this, it's confusing. I always play things close to the chest. But with you...I'm not sure why I'm saying more than I plan to. As I said, it's confusing." He averted his eyes again but she could see his face. And it looked achingly vulnerable.

His eyes returned suddenly, as he reached his hand towards her, brushing the back of it along her cheek. The trail from his skin was hot, his feelings so intimate she drew in a shaky breath. She wanted to move away, out from under his scorching hand, but she forced herself to remain while his bleakness dissipated.

"I guess we should order at some point," he said with a smile. The dark, intense moment behind them.

"Yes, good idea," she agreed, picking up her menu. She looked at the words on the page but couldn't seem to make sense of them. The strange confessions he just made had her mind spinning. He liked her. Very much. Which meant getting him to trust her might be simpler than she thought. And getting Jezebel what she needed could be even easier. She bit her lip as she reflected on the outcome. She felt Cort's eyes on her as she stared, without seeing, at the menu.

"What are thinking so hard about?" he inquired.

"Why would you assume I'm thinking hard about something?" she asked. He seemed so in tune with her it was unnerving.

"You're biting your lip again," he said, looking longingly at her mouth. "You seem to do that when you're contemplating something."

Damn, he was observant. Too much so.

"Just can't decide between the swordfish and the tenderloin," she misled.

She looked up at him, he was watching her and she could see he didn't quite believe her.

"The swordfish is quite good but the tenderloin is melt in your mouth delicious," he commented, letting it go.

The waiter appeared and took their orders. Evera leaned close to Cort as the man stood beside her, hoping to let both of them know where her interests lay. She could feel how the small shift in proximity between them made Cort's desire kickup a notch.

When the waiter left they continued their in-depth conversation from the afternoon. As before, their questions and answers were intimate and personal. The topics centered on them, books they'd read, hobbies and movies. Again, mostly information that was of no use to Evera's mission or the Section. As they finished dessert she could hear the music from the outdoor dance club starting up, just on the other side of the dense trees.

As she felt his eyes on her again, she turned to meet his gaze. Swallowing back her anxiety and fear, she smiled seductively at him.

"Would you like to go over to the club and have a drink?" he asked.

"That sounds great," she answered, hiding her surprise. She had been expecting an invitation back to his room. She couldn't decide which scenario she would have preferred, getting it over with or postponing it.

He rose from his seat and offered her his hand. When their hands met she was stung by the tension in him. Although, his tension was very different from hers, a sexual current snaking its way around her.

They made their way around the row of trees to the dance bar on the other side of the courtyard. He led her to a barstool where they both ordered drinks, him a cognac and her a martini. She rarely ever drank hard liquor but tonight she felt like she needed some liquid courage.

While they waited for their drinks she decided to use this opportunity to escape from him for a moment.

"I just need to head to the ladies' room," she said.

"Alright," he said, smiling warmly at her. She felt relief the moment he released her hand.

She headed to the bathroom beside the dance floor, all the while concentrating on not bursting into a run.

The room was filled with women talking excitedly and checking their makeup. Thankfully, one of the stalls was empty. Evera made her way straight to it, not bothering to check if she was butting in line. She latched the door and kicked the lid of the toilet down with her sandal so she could sit and collect her thoughts.

Fuck, but he was intense! She wasn't used to this from a virtual stranger. Her marks were usually so predictable and eager to get her in bed. She couldn't take much more of his courting and chivalry. This was going to get complicated...she could feel it.

She reached into her purse and grabbed her phone, checking for texts. The screen showed one missed call. Adam had called at 8:00 just like he said he would and she had missed him. She checked her text app. There was only one. Adam again and it said, "Sorry I missed u. I'll try u again at midnight when I land, if you're available. Adam."

She could almost taste the bitterness from his words in that last sentence. They rarely ever communicated while she was on mission for this exact reason. She knew how it hurt Adam to know she wasn't answering because she was seducing someone else. God, how she wished she could talk to him right now. She just needed to be reminded of who she was and what she was capable of.

She reached to fidget absentmindedly with her locket, and felt momentarily calmed by its familiar texture. She'd never mistakenly taken it with her on a job before and so she had never thought to use it as a source of focus and comfort. She opened it and took a quick look at the familiar pictures. One was of a young girl in her teens. She had sunny blonde hair and a big smile. The picture of happiness. Across, imbedded in the other side of the heart was a picture of a young couple; they had their heads close together, their faces content. The small photographs had faded a little over the years, but Evera could still make out all their features. Her heart ached as she looked at the face of the girl. A memory struggled to surface as she stared at the picture. She shoved it back down and quickly closed the locket. Reaching around her neck, she removed it and tucked it in her purse for safekeeping.

She felt a little better now, less scrambled. She used the stall and then fought her way to the sinks where she washed her hands and checked her makeup. The bustling bodies around her were pulsing with sexual excitement. She struggled to keep the atmosphere from interfering with her newfound focus as she dashed out the door.

She made her way towards the bar but could see no sign of Cort. She searched the dance floor and the surrounding tables. She spotted him over by the fire pit at the far end of the dance floor, backing on to the beach. He was talking to a familiar looking man and standing by an empty couch in front of the fire. The husky man had steel grey hair that looked almost black in the dim light of the fire. His shoulders were wide and imperceptibly bowed, as if time and gravity were hard for him to carry. As the man turned to gesture at Evera she recognized him as their driver from this afternoon. Cort turned and saw her. She noticed his jacket was off and he had the sleeves of his shirt rolled up, revealing the tanned muscles of his forearms.

She was still on the opposite end of the dance floor, and as he sauntered closer she could see several women eyeing him greedily. One of them reached out and grabbed his arm before he could pass her. She was with several other girls and it looked like she was trying to coax him into joining them. He smiled politely at the girl, leaned down to speak and then continued past her. Evera watched as the girl followed Cort's retreating back, her face crestfallen.

She studied him as he approached, a sexy smile on his lips and his eyes only for her. As he moved sensuously to close the last few feet between them, she could see why the girl would want him.

The forbidden thought almost made her choke. Immediately casting aside the intrusive notion, she explained it away as a moment of weakness and too much wine.

"Hello," he said, clear and soft, his eyes burning into hers with a fire she could feel. There was so much feeling and suggestion in his one word that it sounded like a thousand.

"Hi," she replied weakly. As he stood by her she was again aware of how tall he was.

"I've got your drink and a place to sit," he said, placing his hand gently on her back as they walked towards the couch. As the pulsing song ended, crowds of people shoved passed, pushing them together. He wrapped his arm around her, his hand sliding to her hip, pulling her closer. Passion and heat flared from his hand, sinking into her skin. It spread from her hip and across her stomach, making its way down her body. She drew in a calming breath and tried to block his desire.

The girl who'd been rejected by Cort, eyed Evera scornfully as they passed by together. She had to admit she felt a bit smug... she was with the man that every woman wanted.

They arrived at the empty couch, her drink on the table waiting for her. She looked around as she sat down, several people were watching for seats. She wondered how he had acquired the most preferred seat in the outdoor club.

"Great spot. How did you manage this? It looked so packed when we came over," she asked.

"Actually, this seat was taken," he grinned conspiratorially at her. "However, I can be quite persuasive when I want something."

"I believe you," she said, knowing full well that whether it was a man or a woman, Cort would find a way to bend them to do his bidding. She could see it even now as he leaned back against the couch, his arm stretching behind her. The power and confidence he exuded was unmistakable. Men would bend out of respect and fear, while women would take one look and give in just to please him.

Evera reached for her drink, adjusting herself nearer to him as she sat back, their legs touching. She couldn't decide what was putting out more heat, the fire burning in front of them or Cort's body.

He took a long drink from his glass and then set it in front of him. He moved his hand to brush the hair back from her neck and kept it there, cupping her neck and stroking her jaw with his thumb. She waited for him to pull her up and lead her to his room. But he didn't. Instead, he leaned into her, his other hand sliding up her knee, his eyes burning into hers. And she watched, lungs frozen, as his lips came inexorably closer.

Holy fuck! What was he doing? He was going to kiss her. Here. Now. In public. With no way to use her body as a diversion. His breath fanned across her face and he closed his eyes, his lips almost touching hers. She couldn't breathe. His converging emotions were making her feel as though she were suffocating. Without meaning to, without thinking of the consequences, she sucked in a sharp breath and pushed him away.

CHAPTER 12

A Kiss

Shit! Shit! Shit! She squeezed her eyes closed, afraid to witness his reaction. She had just blown her only chance to get close to the most important conquest of her career. She forced her eyes open, prepared for the anger and suspicion she was sure to witness on his stunning face.

He was staring at her, his eyes confused but patient. Surprisingly, she detected no animosity.

"I'm sorry, Evera," he murmured, shifting his gaze to the fire. He started to pull away.

"No, Cort," she said, struggling to find words that explained her actions. "It's me who should be sorry. Don't leave." Putting her hand firmly on his, she held him in place so he wouldn't move farther away.

"It's okay," he insisted, his hand brushing her cheek. "You don't have to explain yourself. I know there's someone else."

She was so surprised by his words that her jaw dropped. He was so completely wrong and yet so completely right at the same time.

"I can feel how hesitant you are when I touch you. I don't know if it's because of your guilt for the other man or not, but you're still here. I assume it's because you want to be with me." His voice was soft and sympathetic.

Evera didn't respond, hoping her fixed gaze was answer enough.

He edged closer, his emotions heating up. "I don't care," he confessed, his voice rough and fervid.

She stared back at him, confused. "You don't care if there's someone else?" she asked, her thoughts going straight to Adam. She was shocked by Cort's acceptance. He didn't seem like the kind of man who was willing to share.

"No," he said definitively. "You seem to be here to escape something or someone. I don't care about the why. If you want to be with me I'd be a fool to let the threat of someone else interfere."

This couldn't have worked out more perfectly if she had planned it.

"If you aren't ready to take this any further, I understand," he said. His words were sincere but his body contradicted them; the sexual tension he was struggling to rein in was pressing against her, weighing her down.

Suck it up Evera, the Jezebel in her head screamed. She needed to listen to the less emotional, grounded side of herself and capitalize on the situation.

"I'm ready," she assured, running her hand up his leg to let him know she meant it. His feelings of heat and passion ran up her arm as she touched him. The sensations making her insides quiver.

"You don't have to, you know," he said, as he grabbed her hand from his leg. "There's so much tension in your body every time I touch you," he continued, holding her gaze. "And yet, I have never wanted to put my hands on a woman so badly in my life," he whispered, his voice raw.

She felt suddenly afraid of what was coming. Instinctively, she put her palms on his chest, wanting to push him away. She hesitated, the feel of his hard muscles beneath her hands strangely appealing. And then it was too late. His hands came up to hold her face, his fingers tangling in her hair, desire wrapping them both so tight and hot she couldn't breathe.

And then his lips came down on hers.

Every feeling coming from him transformed to a sensuous need; his mouth moving with hers was holding nothing back. The intimacy of it, of his kiss, was unnerving. And then his tongue met hers, sending a shock through her, pooling fire low in her body. His hands started moving down her face to her neck, his thumbs caressing her collarbone.

She tried to relax her hands against his chest and will herself not to pull away. Instead, she grabbed his shirt hard, twisting it in her hand as she held on tight.

Her internal war continued through the kiss. Wanting to push him away and stop this before she lost control, and the knowledge that she should give in and let it happen. The heat from the fire pit competed with the heat coming from Cort's lips until she felt like she was going to burst into flames. She was fighting a losing battle.

Because, without warning, something inside her gave and she was kissing him back. Heat exploded through her, burning her lips and singeing her tongue. She had gone from acting the part to kissing him back with a hunger that matched his.

The kiss was getting too hot. It was becoming too much and yet not enough at the same time. He must have recognized it too as he suddenly pulled away from her, gasping. They sat like that for a minute, both of them trying to catch their breath.

"Well," he said breathlessly while searching her eyes, "that has to be one of the sexiest things I have ever done in public."

"Yes," was all she could manage. Her head was still spinning as she tried to sort out what had just happened. She realized she was still gripping his shirt in her fist and loosened her fingers to let go.

She was completely stunned, in utter disbelief that she had willingly kissed someone and it wasn't Adam. Not just a kiss, but an achingly deep embrace of lips and tongues and heat. She couldn't decide how she felt about it. Cort was too close, clouding her feelings with his own.

He smiled at her, brushing his hand across her forehead to push a strand of hair from her eyes. She waited for him to say something, to get up, but he made no move to go. Again, she felt stuck in limbo with him. She wanted to get this over with now. Go to his room, have sex and get whatever else she could. But he seemed content to just sit close to her even though his need had transformed into a wildfire.

His bodyguard appeared suddenly, behind the couch, holding a blanket and cooler. He set everything down in the sand and handed Cort the bag he had with him earlier in the day. Cort gave a quick nod and no other acknowledgement as the man quickly turned and walked away.

He looked at Evera mysteriously. "Every time I come here I sneak away on a little adventure. Would you like to join me?" he asked.

"Now?" certain he must mean tomorrow in the light of day. Mentally, her mouth had dropped open. He couldn't be serious.

"Yes," he said. "And just so you know, you will get wet." He had an eyebrow raised as he said the last part. She wondered if he was serious or meant for it to mean more.

"Alright," she dragged out the word, unsure even though she was in agreement.

"Great," he said, as he put his bag over his shoulder and grabbed the cooler and blanket in one arm.

He held her hand as they made their way towards the beach. She felt uneasy. The beach was dark and as they got closer to the water the only sound was the waves. The suspicious side of her cautioned that this was not a good idea. There was nowhere to go beyond the ocean. She was a good swimmer but she knew if it came down to a struggle in the water that Cort would have the advantage.

Nothing she could feel from him hinted at any change in his attitude towards her, though. He clicked on a flashlight as they came to the edge of the water and dropped her hand.

"You'll want to take off your sandals," he said. He was already removing his shoes and rolling up his pant legs.

She did so, noticing that they were at the edge of the resort's tree line which had a fence just inside it. During the day the beach would continue to stretch east for miles, but now that the tide was in, the water met up with the trees making the beach small and cozy.

"You might want to lift the bottom of your dress too, so it doesn't get wet." The hem of her dress came to her knees so she shifted it up to mid-thigh. It was then that she realized he was getting her to undress herself. She had to hand it to him, he was good.

"Alright," he said, reaching for her hand. "Do you trust me?" He smiled at her, excitement and passion radiating off of him.

Absolutely not, she thought, but smiled and said, "Definitely."

Holding her hand tightly, he started leading her out into the water, just down from the trees. The tree line and fence tapered into the water, which meant the water level was about two and a half feet deep before they could get around it. The thick forest continued along the shore for several yards as they waded through the ocean.

Evera felt surprisingly calm. The moon was bright and the sky was a clear midnight blue. She could see endless stars and hear nothing but the sound of the waves. The water was still warm from the heat of the day, keeping the crispness of the air from chilling her.

Cort shone his flashlight along the edge of the trees and Evera could see a break in the forest coming up a yard or so ahead of them. They made their way to the opening and a secluded crescent shaped beach. During the day it would just be part of the larger beach, but at night, with the tide in, it was like a private oasis. With the help of the moonlight she could just make out the different shades of orchids scattered throughout the trees.

"What do you think?" asked Cort, his voice low and soft in the quiet of the night.

"It's amazing," she said, and meant it. The view from where they were standing was cradled by trees and opened onto the ocean with the moon reflecting on its surface.

She shivered. Without the warmth of the ocean she felt cold and hugged herself to keep warm while taking in the beauty of the water.

Cort noticed, of course. "You're cold. I'll get a fire started right away."

He quickly spread the blanket on the ground so she could sit. Digging through the cooler he pulled out a bottle of wine. He poured a glass and handed it to her.

"Start on this. It should help warm you up."

"Thanks," she said, and sipped the wine. It was delicious, a bit heavier than a regular white but not as sweet as an ice wine. She wrapped her arms around her legs as Cort set the bottle down.

"I might have a towel," he said, grabbing his satchel.

"No," she said, "I'm fine, really. The wine is working. I feel warmer already." She couldn't get over his constant attentiveness. He seemed to know she was able to take care of herself and yet still treated her like she was fragile.

"Here," he said, and started unbuttoning his shirt. She couldn't help but stare at his chest as he opened his shirt and pulled his arms free. Even in the pale glow of the moonlight she could catch every ripple on his stomach. He draped his shirt around her shoulders, his bare chest so close she could feel the heat coming off of him.

"Thank you," she said timidly.

"Anytime," he offered, his voice hushed in the silence.

She watched as he worked and had a fire going within minutes. The heat felt good but she was already warming; Cort's shirt still held the heat from his body. She could smell him all around her, his shirt veiling her in his scent.

Finished, he grabbed himself a glass and filled it with wine, topping hers up at the same time.

"It's really good," she said, trying not to pay too much attention to the fact that his bare torso was now bathed in the light from the fire.

"I'm glad you like it," he said, as he sat down beside her. They were facing the ocean, the fire burning beside them. "It's one of my favorites. It's called a late harvest."

They sat like that for a while, sipping their wine and watching the waves roll against the shore in front of them. Evera waited for him to move on her. Again, his patience was dumbfounding. But hers was spent.

"So, you come here often?" she asked lightly.

He laughed softly and turned sideways to look at her. "Yes, I try to sneak out every time I'm here."

She wondered how many other women he'd brought here. For some reason the thought irked her but she brushed it aside.

"I don't just come here for the view. Although tonight, in particular, it really is quite spectacular," he confided, never taking his eyes off her.

She turned away from his intensity and back towards the ocean. Why was she letting his words affect her? Maybe it was because it wasn't just words in his case. Not some smoothly delivered line by some slick player. Everything he said to her was reflected back in the feelings he projected.

"So, what do you come here for then?" she asked, certain that he would finally show her. Pull her down on the blanket and give in to what he wanted.

"Well," he said, looking towards the ocean, "you can join me and find out, but you might want to take off your dress first." He turned, giving her a wry smile.

She raised an eyebrow but said nothing.

"I mean, so that you don't ruin it. I apologize, I should have told you to bring a swimsuit," he amended.

Wow, but he was fucking smooth. "Just so I'm clear," her tone suspect, "you want me to take my clothes off?"

He looked down and laughed softly. "Honestly, I've thought of little else the entire day," he admitted, his eyes fierce. "But that's beside the point. The reason we're here requires us going fairly deep into the water and I'm sure the salt water would destroy your dress."

Again, she was impressed with his candor and more than just a little curious. He was looking at her, obviously waiting to see if she was willing or not.

"Okay," she said confidently, not breaking eye contact. He smiled and then stood, giving her his hand to help her up.

How demure could she play this? Not very if she was going to strip in front of him.

"I'll go first, seeing as how it's my idea," he offered.

She was surprised by his suggestion, but then realized that he would have to get undressed too or ruin his clothes.

He undid his pants button and zipper and then slowly pulled them down. She looked but didn't want to look. He had them off and was folding them, setting them on the blanket.

His body was beautiful…strong and lean, his black briefs contouring around him snuggly. She tried hard not to look too closely at them.

He stood there, a patient smile on his full lips, waiting for her. She met his eyes and for the first time she could remember, felt shy and nervous. *Ridiculous!* She thought, considering she was used to taking her clothes off and being naked in front of complete strangers.

She grabbed the hem of her dress and slowly pulled it up. She watched him, his eyes filled with a raw hunger that burned into hers, as the dress came up first to reveal her panties and then her bra. She pulled it over her head and tossed it on the blanket beside his pants.

Her breathing had picked up, as if the action itself had exerted her. Undressing in front of each other had somehow affected her more than any touch in the entire day. The air surrounding them felt thick and heavy, a strange, unfamiliar feeling. His eyes took her in slowly, meticulously, from head-to-toe. She watched him draw in a shaky breath.

"Alright," he said, his voice raw. "Let's go get wet."

He reached for her hand and with the other grabbed a strange flashlight from the blanket. They walked close together towards the water. His hand was warm in hers but it was nothing compared to the inferno of desire she could feel he had become.

They waded into the ocean together, going deeper and deeper until the water was swirling just above Evera's waist. The sand was sugary and warm against her feet, the ocean a tepid bath. Cort let go of her hand and moved away so there was several feet between them.

"You're not afraid of fish, are you?" he asked as an afterthought.

She smiled at him. "No," she reassured, catching his excitement.

"Good," and then he dunked himself in the water. She watched as he positioned the flashlight between his feet so it was held in place and shining upwards with an odd blue glow. He came up and shook the water from his face, brushing the hair from his forehead. She couldn't help but follow the path of the water as it ran across his shoulders and down his chest.

"Okay, now just stay still and watch," he said, excitement in his voice.

Evera did as he asked. Within seconds there were several brightly colored fish swimming around them. Within a minute there were what appeared to be dozens, maybe hundreds.

She stared down in awe at the colorful, swirling wonderland around her body. The fish were every color of the rainbow, some so small they were like tiny twinkling lights below the water. Others were quite large, close to two feet across. They weaved their way in and out between her and Cort's bodies, sometimes brushing gently against her legs. She loved it. The light reflecting off their scales turned the water into a sparkling, colorful light show.

She laughed out loud in delight. The sound startled her in the silence and she put her hand over her mouth. Startled and shocked her. Moments of pure joy were so very few and far between in her life that it felt odd she would have one now. She looked up at Cort and he was smiling at her with the same childlike thrill she was feeling.

"Amazing, isn't it?" he murmured.

She shook her head in ascent. "Truly," she agreed. She was surprised, but she had a hard time tearing her gaze away from Cort in order to return to the colorful fish. They stayed like that for quite some time, neither of them tiring from watching the beautiful choir below.

Suddenly, half the fish disappeared, swimming away towards the deeper ocean. Cort was close enough that Evera detected a sudden burst of fear coming off him.

She looked up quickly and met his frightened eyes.

"Evera," he said ominously. "Don't move. There's a small shark swimming behind you."

She did as he asked, staying very still.

"Dammit!" he breathed. "I'm sorry, this has never happened before. The water's so shallow..." he trailed off, his voice filled with fear. "Just stay where you are. I'm going to come a bit closer and try and push it away from you."

"No," said Evera, quiet but firm. "It's fine. I'm sure it's just curious about the light. Just give it a minute."

She saw it as it circled around her and moved towards the light. Watching the dangerous shark she couldn't help but be mesmerized by it. She knew it wasn't large enough to kill her but it could definitely take a chunk or two out of her or Cort before they could stop it. She wasn't frightened though. They both watched it as it slowly followed the pattern of the remaining fish, swimming in between them back and forth.

"Should I let the flashlight drop to the side?" asked Cort. His cold fear had eased some but she still felt his apprehension.

Evera smiled gently at him. "It's fine," she said softly. "Besides, we don't want to startle it. It's just like the rest of the fish," she said. "Curious."

He was staring at her in wonder, his eyes searching hers. "Who are you, Evera?"

Her mouth opened but no words came out. She had no idea how to answer him.

"What I mean is," he clarified, "I want to know you. I've never met anyone like you before."

How strange...she had been thinking the same thing about him. The moment felt surreal. They were staring at each other in the middle of the ocean at night, a shark swimming between them, and she felt serene.

Just then, the wind started picking up and with it the waves.

"I'll slowly turn the light back to the open water," Cort decided.

"Okay," she agreed. "Just be careful." She was sure he would be fine but a part of her was worried about him getting hurt.

Why? She chided herself.

It should make no difference to her whether or not he got injured. He was a ruthless bastard, she reminded herself. It would just make her assignment over that much quicker if he was taken out of the game. A game she was starting to feel very uncomfortable playing.

He slowly let the flashlight tip to the side. The fish followed, heading farther out. He went under the water again to retrieve it.

Evera watched as the shark followed the rest of the fish out into the black of the ocean, the water finally calm and quiet below them. She turned to look at Cort, wondering what would happen next. Would he have another trick up his sleeve?

He was staring at her. A look of pure desire in his eyes.

He moved slowly forward, closing the distance between them until there was barely room to breathe. Everything in her locked down. Her muscles tensed and she held her breath. The feelings coming from him were a mixture of lust and need. The raw heat was so intense in the small space between their bodies that she was surprised the water wasn't boiling.

He was just another man, just another mark. Keep your wits and remember how dangerous he is, she warned herself. The Section, her mission, reality.

He turned off the flashlight and threw it towards the shore, never breaking from her eyes. His hands came up, warm and wet, and grabbed her face. She could feel the reined in tension in every fiber of his body, or maybe it was hers. Their feelings were so tangled she couldn't separate them.

And then he kissed her. A sweet, slow brushing of lips. Once, twice and then he pulled back to look at her. She felt so tense and nervous but her face must have reflected something different because his hands tightened on her face. And then he was kissing her, hard.

Again, she felt an overwhelming need to pull away. It was too much and too close. She tried to relax, to play along while still keeping her mental distance, but it was a struggle.

His lips were so very unrelenting; hot and demanding against hers. She tasted the wine and ocean on his mouth, a heady combination of sweet and salty.

He wrapped his arms around her, pulling her tight against him and closer to the shore. She moved her hands up his shoulders to his neck, trying hard not to notice the feel of his sculpted muscles beneath her palms.

His kiss was getting to her. Submerging her with its intensity as if he was pulling her under the water. His hands moved along her back, caressing every inch of it and leaving her flesh tingling. His fingers moved along her bra strap and deftly undid the clasp. His hands started pulling her bra off but still she couldn't separate from her body. It was vital that she stay centered but she couldn't seem to gather anything lucid while he was kissing her.

Thankfully, he had to move away from her and her lips in order to completely remove her bra. He threw it towards the shore like he had the flashlight and then stared down at her. He sucked in a sharp breath as he took in the view, his eyes so intense she could almost feel them brush against her breasts.

"You are so beautiful," he said, his voice breathless.

And then he met her eyes and she could read everything he felt for her. She was trapped there, staring back at him and trying hard to stay in character. Then his lips were crushing down on hers again, his body hot against her naked skin. His hands were everywhere, twisting in her hair, brushing her shoulders and making their way down the front of her body. She felt panicked and out of control. She needed a minute. Just one fucking minute to disconnect before she was lost to his touch.

But it was too late. He made his way down to her breasts and as he put his hands on her she gasped against his mouth. The feeling shocking and unknown. A million times she'd been touched. But not like this. Never like this, with the Evera in her so present. And never by a man like Cort.

His hands were awakening something deep below the surface; something until this moment she'd managed to keep at bay. His fingers caressing and tantalizing her breasts in ways she had never let herself experience before. An ache was starting inside her, delicious and painful. She had to stop him and stop him now. Distraction and manipulation was the key. She was still coherent enough to make her hands do what they did best.

She tried to ignore his touch and his lips as her fingers played down his back to the waistband of his underwear. She moved her hands just barely inside them and worked her fingers in seductive circles as she moved around closer to his hips. Once her fingers made their way to the front, she stopped just short of her desired target and gauged his reaction. His lips halted and he held his breath—anticipating—wired. She wrapped her hand around him slowly, his pleasure mounting as her pressure increased. He let out a low moan against her mouth.

His hands moved from her breasts to her panties as he started removing them slowly. His fingers trailing down her backside as he eased them off, sending a surprising shock of pleasure down her legs.

She tried to pay as little attention as possible to his hands. Now that the kiss was broken she could concentrate more thoroughly on what he wanted. Or so she thought, but his lips had found a new occupation. His mouth was making its way slowly down her neck, his tongue tracing her collarbone.

She took over, changing tactics as she started pulling off his briefs, and in doing so had to move down his body and away from his lips. She used her mouth; her lips and tongue making their way down his perfect chest to his stomach. Cort shuddered as she moved her lips below his waist. Her confidence was back, along with her control. She was all about his needs and pleasures. As long as she could keep his lips from hers she was sure she could handle him.

They were farther out of the water, but what she needed to get at was still submerged. She grabbed his hips and kissed the skin above his groin. A deep, voluptuous kiss, and then angled her lips to the water line. He moved both his hands so he was gently gripping her hair, his breathing erratic. Then she took a deep breath and went under.

Her mouth went to work on him, the salt water making everything slick and slippery. She paid attention to how he was responding to every stroke from her tongue, every gentle bite from her teeth. She pulled him in hard against the back of her throat, holding still while he gasped, and then slowly moved her mouth up and down the length of him, his pleasure heightening. She had to come up twice for air and realized if she was going to finish him off she would need to get to shallow water. As she came up one last time before pulling him towards the shore, he suddenly moved his hands from her hair to her shoulders. He gripped her arms, lifting her up onto her feet.

"No, Cort," she refused, putting her hand firmly against his chest. "Let me finish. I promise you won't be disappointed."

"I believe you," he said, his voice strained as she felt him try to regain some composure. He pulled her close against him, wrapping her in his arms. "But not now, not this time," his lips against her ear. "I need to be with you," he breathed, the words hot against her neck. "I need to be inside you," he insisted, his voice breaking on the last word.

And then he was kissing her again, this time with a hunger that was so overwhelming she felt claustrophobic. She couldn't concentrate to catch her breath. She could feel his sincere passion and need and it was breaking her down.

His hands moved down to her hips and then across her backside to her legs. He lifted her up and she wrapped her legs around his waist with a gasp. She could feel him hard and ready between her thighs. Heat pressed into heat. And then she couldn't take any more...her resolve fracturing, she started kissing him back.

His mouth tantalized hers as he walked them as one to the shoreline. She was lost in his kiss. Some part of her was screaming at her to stop and gain some control. She tried to listen, tried to remember her routine and her focus, but his hard body so enticing against hers was too distracting.

He fell to his knees on the blanket, still holding her. Slowly, he eased her down onto her back, keeping his body pressed to hers. And then his hands were brushing against every part of her, setting fire to her skin.

His mouth started moving down between her breasts and she shivered. Fear and anticipation battled back and forth, making her head spin. His tongue made its way up the side of her breast and then his mouth came down, sending shock waves through her. He tasted and teased, his lips and tongue going back and forth, driving her mad.

Her usual routine, her script, was forgotten. She moved and moaned, unrehearsed and unplanned. She needed her blue sky, her escape. She tried to find it in the throes of all the sensations bombarding her, but it was lost, and because of that the fear was winning out. Fear that she was losing herself to him. Falling.

Fuck that! She screamed in her head. She sucked in a mouthful of air in an attempt to empty her mind. She gripped the blanket on either side of her and tried to hold herself together; but his feelings of pleasure as he worked over her body were almost as hard to take as his mouth and hands.

His lips started making their way down her body, across her stomach. He grazed her hip with his teeth sending a different kind of sensation through her—a deep, primal ache that made her bite her lip to stop from groaning. His lips moved down to where her thighs met her body. *No!* She wanted to scream. She'd gone through this before but never while she was present. She'd always been disconnected and found it an annoyance she had to endure. But his lips moving to her inner thigh were anything but annoying.

And then his mouth was between her legs, his lips and tongue setting her on fire. She inhaled but couldn't catch her breath, her hands gripping the blanket so hard her fingers hurt.

She wanted to beg him to stop but her traitorous body wanted him to continue. She couldn't let this go on or she would jeopardize everything, herself included.

She reached down and roughly grabbed his hair, hoping he would get the hint and stop. But he mistook her action as pleasure, his tongue slipping deeper inside. Her lungs heaved, her back arching, threatening to drag her all the way into the midnight sky. Her body writhed beneath his mouth. She struggled pointlessly to keep still.

Mercifully, his lips started making their way back up her body. He stopped suddenly and grabbed the wine bottle, taking a quick pull. Then his mouth was back on her waist. He trickled the cool wine onto her and she sucked in a startled breath. After the heat from Cort's lips the wine felt extra cold. He drank the wine off her skin, warming her back up with each stroke of his tongue. He continued this all the way up her body, drinking the heavy wine off her flesh, slowly and sensuously. Making his way between her breasts and up to her neck. The heat and cool bringing the ache in her body to the point of pain.

He reached for another drink and then brought his lips to hers, lifting her head with his hand. He shared the wine with her, the cold liquid slaking her thirst after the salt from the ocean. She couldn't decide which tasted sweeter, the wine or Cort's lips.

He removed his hand from behind her head but continued kissing her. She could feel his need building as his free hand fumbled somewhere beside her.

He broke their kiss and she saw that he was holding a condom packet. He tore it open and started putting it on. She brushed his hand away and grabbed on, the motions of her usual routine finally resurfacing, as she took her time sliding it on him. Only this time, her hands were shaking. He groaned in pleasure and she hoped he hadn't noticed. He pressed her back down on the blanket, and moved so he was on his knees between her legs. And then he pushed inside her.

The effect was an instant overload, forcing all the air from her lungs. He buried his face against her neck and held still, waiting for her body to adjust to the size of him. He began moving slowly back and forth, his arms braced on either side of her shoulders, his dark blue eyes piercing hers. Desire wrapped them together, keeping her warm.

She attempted one last mental stretch towards her safe haven. Closing her eyes to block out his face, she tried to concentrate but his body moving inside hers was too much. It was too late, she couldn't escape now.

Every thrust inside felt new and foreign and amazing. He was moving faster now, his pleasure mounting and she could feel something inside her growing hotter.

Instinctively, she let go of the blanket and wrapped her arms around his back. Her hands moved restlessly, clutching at him, the muscles of his back and shoulders rippling beneath her hands. She tried to grab on as the feelings coursing through her threatened to undo her. Her legs wrapped around his hips pulling him closer, deeper. Her breath hitched as his tempo increased. His lips on her face, her hair, intoxicating her.

And then she felt it. The sensation she had always kept reigned in. Felt it building, gaining force with every thrust he made. She would have to stop it. She couldn't allow herself to orgasm. Not with Cort. Not for the first time with a mark.

She groaned at the force it took to hold it back. He moved even faster now, his pleasure peaking. She griped his back hard and bit her lip to almost bleeding, her breathing making her light-headed. A part of her was begging, aching so badly to the point of pain, for her to just give in.

And then he arched his back as he cried out. She could feel his release deep inside her. His feeling of ecstasy exploded around her, dragging her down with him into oblivion.

She lost her grip on her control but it made no difference…she had waited long enough that her moment had passed.

Cort came down on his elbows so as not to crush her as he tried to catch his breath. His forehead was resting tenderly between her breasts. She moved her hands restlessly in his hair as she tried to calm herself down. She was stuck trembling from the overwhelming ache of what she had denied herself.

His lips brushed gently against her skin and up to her neck. He kissed her softly, working his way up her chin as his breathing returned to normal. His eyes met hers and she felt stunned, pinned to the ground by his stare. His hand cradled her face, as he searched her eyes and then kissed her lips once, softly.

She shivered at his warm touch, her teeth chattering, not from the cold but the shock of what she had just put her mind and body through.

"You're cold," he said, concern coloring his words. "Come here," he offered. He shifted onto his side, staying inside her, and pulled her into his arms. He grabbed the blanket they were laying on and wrapped it around them.

She curled into his embrace but couldn't stop herself from thinking of Adam. And then the guilt of what had just happened crashed over her like a tidal wave.

Cort's arms held her tightly, his emotions that of joy and contentment, now that his passion was spent. But Evera felt nothing but guilt and exhaustion. The sheer will of holding herself back both physically and mentally had left her drained.

She gave in to the feeling of his arms protectively surrounding her. Would allow herself this one small comfort. She felt herself drifting towards sleep, her eyelids too heavy to lift any longer. Her last thought, before she melted into unconsciousness, was how quickly Cort had unwittingly turned the tables on her. Had become the threat, a danger to her mission and herself. More dangerous than any man had ever been.

And yet it was his arms keeping her safe and warm. The irony of the situation was not lost on her. She shuddered in fear and uncertainty as she drifted off. Cort tightened his arms around her, holding her closer.

CHAPTER 13

The Morning After

Evera watched as the sun made its slow, lazy climb from its bed in the ocean and into the sky, trying to figure out what had just happened. Not once but twice. She was sitting up, leaning against Cort's chest, her head resting on his neck. He had her tucked in between his legs and the blanket wrapped around them.

Her thoughts catapulted her back to little more than an hour ago when she had awakened in his arms. She remembered waking and feeling warm and disoriented. She knew immediately that the arms around her were not Adam's and then a second later she remembered the night.

Cort. All her senses suddenly came alive as she started assessing the situation. She carefully opened her eyes just enough to look up at him and see that he was still sleeping. She was cocooned against him in the same way she had been when they'd fallen asleep, neither of them barely moving through the entire night. And she hadn't dreamed. She was surprised as the thought occurred to her, but she brushed it aside, unwilling to analyze the 'why' of that too closely right now.

The Jezebel in her was back with a vengeance this morning. She wanted this whole interlude with Cort over as soon as possible. Her realization of the danger he represented had stuck with her through the night.

She took in her surroundings without raising her head and disturbing him. It was still dark, just a hint of light peeking out on the horizon. The fire had all but burned out, the remaining embers giving off a small amount of heat. She saw his bag sitting three feet away in the sand, certain that's where his phone would be.

She remembered the bodyguard. The one who had done all of Cort's bidding without a word passing between them. Was he close by? Was he watching them right now?

But of more immediate concern was how she was going to disentangle herself from Cort without waking him. She felt hot and sticky from the sex and the wine on her body. She pulled herself gently away leaving room for the cold air to make its way between them.

Cort's eyes flew open unexpectedly. He sat up in a rush, panic and fear blasting off of him like a winter storm. The tortuous look in his eyes froze her in her place. He was frightened. She recognized that look, that feeling. Recognized it personally.

"Cort," she hushed, trying to lead him away from his nightmare.

His eyes lost some of their terror as he recognized her. He quickly rearranged his features into a sweet, sexy smile. "Good morning," he commented, his voice even. Reaching for her hand, he kissed it and brushed the hair from her shoulder.

His facade was good but he couldn't hide his feelings from her. He was still struggling to get out from whatever thought or memory had disturbed him in the first place.

Something in her reached out to him. The scared, lonely little girl in her touched his face affectionately, hoping to soothe away the last of his dread.

His feelings shifted instantly at her touch, desire overtaking his darker feelings. She regretted her sympathy immediately. "Good morning," she returned, tearing her eyes away from the intensity of his stare and towards the water.

"I was just going to go for a swim and wash up," she said, looking back at him.

"Alright." He was eyeing her hungrily.

She smiled as she got up, feeling self-conscious while his eyes followed her naked body all the way to the waterline. Again her timid feelings made no sense to her. This situation was becoming more and more complicated.

As she swam in the cool water and rinsed the night from her body she couldn't stop the guilt from collapsing on top of her again. She stood in the water, neck deep and watched as the edge of the world got noticeably lighter. She touched her lips momentarily, remembering the many kisses from the night before. Adam's silver blue eyes hovered in her daydream, looking down on her with pain and betrayal. Shaking her head, she attempted to clear her thoughts.

She heard a splash behind her and turned to see Cort swimming towards her. He stopped beside her about five feet away, giving her space. He looked out towards the horizon as if he was somehow uncomfortable.

"Any regrets?" he asked, keeping his eyes forward, not meeting her stare. He was too far away for her to catch what he was feeling, but his voice was filled with uncertainty.

She thought about her actions; leaving quickly to wash up and then standing in the middle of the ocean staring off into space. He must have decided she was thinking about someone else. He was more right than he could possibly imagine.

"None," she admitted, her voice much more confident than she felt. She turned to look at him, hoping she sounded convincing.

"I'm glad," he said, still facing the wide open water. "You should know," he continued, determined, "I don't have one-night stands." He turned back to see her reaction, his eyes cautious as he waited.

"Oh," she answered, bewildered. His words seemed hard to believe after the way she'd seen women serve themselves up to him; he could have anyone he wanted anywhere he went. She was surprised, then, that he was willing to break his rule for her. "I guess there's a first time for everything," she said, her voice catching on the last word. It bothered her that it wasn't just a first for him as far as breaking the rules went.

"No," he said, and looked down at the water, smiling to himself and shaking his head. "I didn't mean it like that." He fixed her with a penetrating stare. "I never break my own rules and I never change my mind. I don't have one-night stands." His eyes looked into hers, as dark blue as the morning ocean. He moved slowly towards her, the hunger from earlier still there in his gaze.

No, she thought, not again. It was too soon. She searched for some way out of this, some words that would delay him without putting him off.

He waded close, putting his hands on her hips, his chest barely touching her breasts. The sensation of his body heat against her nipples after the cold of the water made her start to ache again. He stood like that with her, the two of them naked in the water, his eyes searching her face, hesitating.

She couldn't stop this. Not now or he would suspect something. She moved her hands to his waist and slowly ran them up. She could feel the shape of his hard chest muscles and couldn't seem to help paying attention to his body. Her hands kept moving over his torso, appreciating the feel of him. She felt his uncertainty disappear and the fire in him ignite.

And then his lips were crushing down on hers, his arms moving to pull her against him in the water. His kiss was so hot and close. She tried to figure out a way to deal with it and what would be coming next.

She would have to give in. If she just gave in to the kiss then maybe she could gain back her control during the sex. She didn't think her body could fight off another onslaught like the one last night. And so she did. She let herself go and kissed him back willingly, allowing her lips to move hungrily against his mouth, her tongue rushing to tangle with his. And then, without warning, heat was pulsing through her veins, making her ache to quench the fire. She wound her hands around his neck, holding on tight as his rough hands made their way past her hips, the pleasure and pain feeling from last night rocketing back.

He slid his hand slowly between her legs and paused while she held her breath, bracing herself. He dipped his strong fingers inside, running them deliciously along her seam, back and forth, right where she needed them. And exactly where she shouldn't want them.

The combination of his touch and his kiss was too much. She couldn't cope with both and still breathe so she pulled away from his lips, resting her forehead against his chin. She gasped and moaned uncontrollably as his hands worked their magic. Some part of her was aware that her legs had given out and that he was holding her around her waist so she didn't slip under the water.

His hand relented and then he lifted her in his arms and carried her to the beach.

His lips were back on hers, keeping the heat coursing through her body with not a second of relief. Her barely functioning mind tried to bring her back from the brink, reminding her to take offensive action the moment he put her down. She held onto that one thought as his kiss threatened to knock her senseless. He was leaning down to set her on the blanket and as soon as he did she turned onto her stomach to grab a condom from his pants pocket.

But her shift in position didn't deter his hands or lips in the least. He started caressing her backside as his lips trailed kisses across her shoulders and down her back. She somehow managed to find the condom packet in his pants, her head all but exploding from the sensations pummeling her body. He grabbed her hips hard and pulled her up so she was on her hands and knees in front of him.

No! Her thoughts screamed in frustration. She wanted it to be on her terms this time. Under her control. She would just have to flip the situation around and fast.

As she was trying to figure out how to twist herself around so she would end up on top, his hands reached around to touch her breasts. And then she forgot everything. His hands started working her over and she could think and feel nothing but Cort. Her taboo sensation was back, hard and fast. It seemed to have been there, seething below the surface the entire night. As if it were just waiting for his touch to bring it back to life.

He was still kissing down her back when he reached down and pulled the condom from her hand.

Evera realized too late that she had missed her chance to take back control. Not only that, but her blue sky, again, was nowhere to be found.

And then his hands grabbed her tight around the waist as he eased himself inside her, the size and heat of him making her suck in her breath. He held her hips as he slowly started to move. As he went faster his pleasure and desire twisted with hers so that she couldn't tell the difference between the two. A part of her was pleading with her again; the undeniable need for release and relief was all consuming. She could feel his pleasure peak at the same time that hers threatened to break through. She gritted her teeth and chocked back a sob at the effort it took to contain it.

"Just let go, Evera," he rasped, and then he came. His ecstasy took her down with him. But, once again, she managed to hold back just long enough to stop her climax.

They stayed like that, Cort holding her close, for a few minutes. Him trying to come down from his pleasure high and her trying to stop her body from trembling. His arms still wrapped tightly around her waist, he lifted her as he turned to sit on the blanket. He kept her pressed tight against his chest and wrapped the blanket around them.

He waited a few minutes and then started digging in the cooler that was within arm's reach. He passed her a bottle of water, which she downed without stopping. He chuckled softly against her back and then handed her another. She took a few sips and then set the bottle down beside her. Then he started in on the food he had brought along. He passed her small chunks of fresh, Hawaiian pineapple and strawberries.

"Would you like some bread and cheese?" he asked.

"Yes," she said. She hadn't realized until she started eating that she was famished.

He handed her chunks of bread topped with a smoky cheddar until the cooler was all but empty. Then he went back to holding her close in his embrace, as they watched the sunrise. And that's where she was now. Watching the sun slowly come up while she tried to make sense of what had happened and what she needed to do next.

Cort sighed contentedly and kissed her hair as the sun crested the edge of the water. His feelings surrounding her so unbearably sweet she wanted to bolt. Or stay in his arms indefinitely. Fear ran through Evera as she recognized how very, very dangerous that thought was. The intimacy of the night was wreaking havoc with her state of mind. It was just his arms and warmth that were confusing her.

She saw a movement out of the corner of her eye by the now enlarging beach. They both turned and Evera saw Cort's bodyguard raise a sheepish hand and then disappear back behind the trees. The same man from last night. And still no one else but him.

Cort breathed out loudly, the sound resigned.

"I guess we should start making our way back," he said, disappointed. "The tide is gone and the beach is back. I imagine if we don't move soon we'll have company," he said as he started untangling himself from her.

"Alright," she said, thankful to be released from the power of his body.

He reached to help her up and then pulled her close against his chest, his eyes burning down into hers.

"Thank you," he said softly, his hand brushing the hair back from her face, "for the most amazing night. And morning..." And then he leaned down and kissed her softly, the sweetness of it causing something deep inside her to waver.

He pulled back. The tender way he looked at her tightened her throat. He released her and said nothing else as he started gathering their belongings. He handed over her dress and underwear and then started pulling on his pants. After he did up the button he reached into his pocket and pulled out his phone. She had been wrong about it being in his bag. It had been right beside her all night.

She shimmied into her dress as he finished checking for messages. Watching her, he stalked closer. "I have to say," he paused, running his thumb along his bottom lip. "As beautiful as you look in that dress, I can't help but wish it was still laying on the sand."

His desire for her was back again. She wondered if he was always this insatiable. The space between them was getting electrically charged again as he continued staring her down.

Drawing a breath he looked away, releasing her from the allure of his eyes. He smiled to himself and then looked back at her.

"We better go now," he said, "or I'll be too far gone and have to keep you here the rest of the day...audience or not."

Unbelievable. How was it possible that his words could be as sensual as his touch?

He grabbed his pile of belongings off the sand and reached for her hand. The tide gone, they walked silently back along the beach past the trees and towards the resort. The sun was fully awake now and its heat was already warming the sand.

As they moved closer to the resort Evera picked up a hint of anxiety in Cort's touch. She glanced quickly at his face but it was composed. They walked up the empty beach and through the dining area. The kitchen staff were busy draping the tables and arranging the cutlery. Evera wondered what time it was...most likely around 6:00 as the kitchen didn't open until 6:30.

The staff were discreet as they all averted their eyes when she and Cort made their way towards the rooms. She was certain their disheveled attire and his naked chest left no doubt as to what they were doing beyond the beach.

His anxiety was escalating and she wondered if she should be on guard. Again, she was frustrated by her abilities; she could catch the feeling but had no idea of its cause.

They rounded the corner to their rooms and he walked straight to his door. He dropped everything he had been carrying at the threshold, then turned towards the stairs. He laced his fingers tighter with hers, his anxiety touched with worry. She couldn't imagine what could have happened on the walk back to cause such a shift in his mood.

He went straight to her door, turning swiftly to pull her into his arms. He kissed her and kissed her until her head was clouded and her breathing ragged. He pulled away slowly, looking down at her longingly, his feelings a mixture of anxiety and desire.

"I have to leave," he murmured, pain threading his words.

"Oh," was all she could think to say. Her mind was still reeling from his unexpected kiss.

"I'm not leaving, as in leaving the resort. But I'll be gone overnight at least," he said, and now she could feel the source of his anxiety.

"That's okay. I have no plans to leave anytime soon," she said, smiling hopefully at him. The Jezebel side of her was breathing a sigh of relief. She was hoping to get some distance and get her shit together. *Get more than that!* She reminded herself. She needed to get something for Garrison that would make all this turmoil worthwhile.

"Good," he said, smiling down at her. She could feel him settle as she reassured him. "I don't want to go, believe me. But I already changed the meeting time twice yesterday and I believe my colleagues are quite through with accommodating me," he said, looking mildly amused.

She was surprised and pleased that he was being so honest with her. "I hope I'm not interfering with your business trip?" she asked.

"Hmmm," he said and ran his bottom lip along her jaw. "Actually, you are," he admitted, "and I couldn't be happier about it."

His lips ended up making their way down her throat and across her neck. She knew there was more she wanted to ask but his mouth was too distracting. He groaned against her shoulder. "What have you done to me, Evera?" he asked, frustrated. He raised his head to look her in the eyes.

"I really do have to go," he whispered, his arms still tight around her.

"I hope you're not going too far. Maybe we could meet for a quick bite to eat later?" she suggested, winding her arms around his neck.

"I would if I could," he said, pulling her so close his lips were just seconds from hers. "Unfortunately, I have to fly to Kauai for a meeting early this afternoon. As well, an unexpected complication has been brought to my attention that I have to deal with immediately after."

She tried to hide her amazement at his giving up his itinerary so easily. "So, I'll see you tomorrow then?" she clarified.

He pulled her mouth against his, the kiss long and languid, before letting her go. "Tomorrow," he replied, looking at her pensively. He backed away, holding her hand until the last moment before he turned and went down the stairs.

*****

She locked the door firmly behind herself. Leaning against it she could feel her agitation escalating. Her initial reaction was to pace but she was too physically exhausted.

She needed sleep, badly, but first she had to check her phone. She fell onto the bed and rolled onto her stomach, digging her phone out of her purse. There was one missed call. It was from Adam at midnight. While she was in Cort's arms. She started dialing his number but waited before pressing send. What would she say to him? She had needed his reassurance last night but it was too late now.

Unwillingly, she flashed back through the night—Cort's lips, his touch, and the sex that was so much more than just sex. Worst of all was the fact that she had been unable to detach from everything happening to her. For the first time ever she'd been herself, present. But it was the idea of the kiss that bothered her the most.

She reached into her clutch and held up the locket. It felt like an omen, as if by bringing it she'd somehow brought Evera instead of Jezebel. She felt raw and exposed, afraid of exploring last night any further, and she was in no state of mind to talk to Adam just yet. She shut off the phone, chickening out.

Instead, she headed to the bathroom and a hot shower. Pulling her dress off, she looked herself over in the mirror. Her body had always been her beautiful, reliable weapon to get what she needed. But now, when she looked at herself, she saw Cort reflected on every part of her. His hands and lips moving over every inch of her. She tore her eyes from the mirror and got in the shower. The soap and hot water rinsed all the remnants of the night and this morning from her body. How she wished it could do the same for her memory.

She dried off and grabbed a plush robe, trying to hold on to the heat from the shower. Crossing her legs, phone in hand, she sat in the middle of the bed and tried to organize the night in her head.

Cort had left about fifteen minutes ago and she needed to let Garrison know his plans for the day and then send her results from last night. Unfortunately, there was little to no information that the Section could use from the evening, but she let Garrison know about the upcoming meeting in Kauai this morning. After sending the report she crawled under the covers and hoped to nap.

Her phone pinged a second later, letting her know she had a text. She reached for it and saw the words: *Phone call? G.* She responded with a yes. Her phone rang almost instantly. She could imagine Garrison salivating on the other end, anxious to find out what her next move would be.

She answered, "Jezebel," and waited.

"Starting the ninety seconds now," he said. They would have a maximum of two minutes to talk freely without someone being able to trace her location. Garrison was nothing if not paranoid.

"First of all, the pictures of Cort are clear and complete, great work. Second of all, do you have plans for another encounter? I need what's on that phone, Jezebel." he insisted.

"We have plans to meet sometime tomorrow when he gets back. I'm fairly confident I can get my hands on his phone then," she said. "He's starting to trust me," as she said the words she knew they were the truth. Some part of her felt like it was wrong to give that last bit of information to Garrison.

"Great," he said, sounding excited. "Use that, Jezebel, and I give you my word that I will protect your cover. I'll see to it myself."

She was surprised that he would involve himself so completely in her mission. The intel retrieval and tracking was usually left up to either Adam or Kent, depending who was around.

"Thanks," she said hesitantly, although she was grateful that he was so intent on protecting her.

"From this moment on you will report to me and me alone. Do you understand? No information on this mission passes to anyone else," he insisted.

"Of course," she said, assuming usual protocol, but something in his tone had her wondering if he meant something more than that. "But that doesn't include the intel team does it?" she questioned, knowing Adam would lose his mind if he came back and was told he was excluded from her mission.

"No," he interrupted, his voice terse. "No intel team this time. No one but me. You can trust me to get you through this mission unscathed, but I can only do that if I am in complete control. There's shit going on here that you can't possibly understand and I can't explain right now."

She felt panic at his words. What the hell was going on?

"I need your word on this. No one but me," he waited. "We have fifteen seconds."

"Yes," she said, although she didn't like being put on the spot. "You have my word." She bit her lip as she gave her promise and hoped she could actually follow through with it.

"Thank you, Jezebel," he said, and then the line went dead.

*****

She was exhausted and tried to sleep, but Garrison's words kept ringing in her head making it impossible to shut down.

What was with all the internal secrecy? She wondered what could possibly have happened in the forty-eight hours she had been gone to make Garrison trust no one. A part of her couldn't help but be suspicious that there was nothing more going on other than Garrison trying to take full credit for her mission. It was no secret he wanted Jonas's job.

And Evera was becoming more and more convinced that Cort was White. If that was true, Garrison would look like the mastermind behind putting all the pieces of the puzzle together.

She couldn't sleep and now when she really needed to talk to Adam she couldn't. She had no idea how she would handle that situation if he called.

Minutes later her phone pinged, signaling another text just as she finished ordering breakfast. She assumed it was Garrison, but when she read the screen, it was from Adam. Could he call her? She hesitated only for a second and then sent back a yes.

She picked it up on the first ring. "Hi," she answered, happy to hear the unrehearsed longing in her voice. She really did miss him.

"Evera," his voice relieved. "You're okay," he said, wording it as a statement and not a question.

"Of course, Adam." She was surprised at his level of concern. "Why wouldn't I be?" She wondered if his worry had something to do with Garrison and the shit he referred to that was going on.

"Sorry," he said, sounding agitated, "I know I'm coming across as an anxious ass but Garrison's being a dick about your mission and insisting on keeping all the details to himself."

"What's going on, Adam?" she asked, hoping he would give her more than Garrison. "And what about Jonas, what's he saying about all of this?"

"That's the problem," he said angrily, "Jonas is still in Arlington trying to get information from Santos. Anyways, it doesn't matter, I hacked in and got all the information on your mission," he admitted. "Not being able to get a hold of you last night made me a little crazy. I was sure you were..." he struggled to find the right words, "otherwise engaged," he said bitterly. "But when I found out who your target was I all but lost my mind. I had to make sure you were okay."

Even though she understood his concern, she didn't want him interfering, especially after Garrison's request. "He's just a target like any other, Adam. I'm being careful just like I always am, I promise." She bit her lip and was glad Adam wasn't there to read her face. Neither statement she just made was true.

"No, Evera," he said fiercely. "He's not just like any other mark. He's not some stupid dealer with an ego and too much money." He sounded afraid. "Cort is ruthless and brutal. He's also shrewd and incredibly well connected. We have almost no intel on the man even though we've been chasing him for three years. Not to mention, everyone thinks he's White. I'm not buying into that theory just yet but it doesn't matter, he's always one step ahead of us. His evasiveness makes me think he might have a connection somewhere inside the Section—which is why I don't like this. Garrison should know better than to put you in a situation like this if there's even the slightest chance your cover might be compromised."

"Then I'll be extra cautious," she assured him. "And thank you for watching out for me." She vowed from this point going forward that Cort was just another mark. A brutal, dangerous target that she couldn't allow herself to see in any other light.

"You don't have to thank me. I'd do anything for you," he promised.

"I know, Adam." She didn't know what else to add, the silence lengthening. This conversation was plummeting to the depths again, and she was uncomfortable, again.

"I'm an idiot," Adam breathed.

"Don't say that," she reprimanded, not sure where he was headed.

"I am," he insisted. "The other night...I fucked up. I keep thinking about what could have happened between us if I hadn't stopped you. If I'd just let the whole 'no kissing' thing go."

Guilt was a cold, icy rain pouring over her. What had she done?

She clamored, selfishly, for a change in topic. "But it wouldn't have changed what I do or who I am," she reminded. She could sense where this was leading...the usual merry-go-round that went nowhere. "And you want me under conditions, Adam. Only if I quit Jezebel and leave the Judith program." But after what had happened between her and Cort last night, she couldn't help but wonder if she shouldn't do exactly that.

"I know that's what I said the last time we argued, but..." he hesitated.

"I don't feel that way anymore. Not after the other night," he admitted. She was stunned. He was willing to have a physical relationship with her even though he knew she'd go away on a job and screw a complete stranger.

She couldn't put him through that. "Adam, I can't ask you to do that. I know you think we can make it work but how will you feel every time I go away on a mission?"

He laughed without humor. "The same way I feel now, I imagine."

True. She knew how much he hurt every time she walked out the door and onto her next operation.

"I want you, Evera, so badly, in every way—in my life, in my bed—I'll do whatever it takes. Whatever you need, it's yours," he promised. "Just think about it." He was offering her everything she wanted and giving up everything on his side. How could she not love him?

"Okay, Adam," she agreed, hoping to appease him. "Let's talk about it when I get back." She'd never told Adam she'd be willing to talk about anything. Maybe she could turn things around after all.

"Alright," her answer seemed to have pacified him for the time being.

She heard a knock at her door.

"I think my room service is here, can you give me a minute." She got up off the bed and made her way to the door.

"It's okay, I better be going. You go eat. I miss you, beautiful, and be careful," he added, his voice soft and then the line was dead.

The server wheeled her breakfast tray to the foot of the bed and then left without a word. She scooted under the makeshift table and pondered her conversation with Adam as she dug into her eggs.

As she weighed in on what Adam had said about Cort, his bio came rushing back to her; his involvement in all things treacherous and why she was here in the first place. Cort was dangerous and a threat. But so was she, she reminded herself. She glanced quickly at the gleaming metal snaked around her wrist.

Jezebel was back.

CHAPTER 14

Edge of the Knife

Evera finished her breakfast in silent contemplation, feeling more secure about her and Adam. After putting her near empty breakfast plate back on the tray she curled up under the covers. Her senses and body dull and weak from exhaustion. She guessed she slept maybe four hours last night. She went rigid for a second as her mind flashed back to waking up in Cort's arms.

Coincidence. She was sure she could have fallen asleep on a concrete floor, her body was so depleted by then. At that point it had been almost three days since she had gotten more than a few hours of broken sleep.

Putting aside all thoughts—Adam, her mission and anything else troublesome—she closed her eyes and welcomed the impending unconsciousness.

For a while she slept peacefully, her dreams harmless pictures of nonsensical moments and faces. But suddenly Cort's face was there, in her dream, his azure eyes matching the dark ocean water in the background. His lips were coming to meet hers, only this time she welcomed them. Her mouth rushing to taste his kiss, his hands everywhere, the water slick and hot surrounding them. She closed her eyes and gave in to him and the fire he started, unable to stop herself. But his lips were no longer moving with hers and she was suddenly cold. She opened her eyes and found herself alone in the ocean, no shore to be seen. She searched the horizon for any sign of land but there was nothing, nothing but the fire he had ignited before he left. The waves were heavy, pulling her under, drowning her while she burned for him.

Coughing herself awake she realized she was in her hotel room. She threw off the blanket, unhinged and infuriated. Her unconscious mind was fast becoming her new enemy. Sitting still on the comfort of the bed, she waited for her racing heart to return to normal. She ran her hand through her hair and realized she was sweating. The ache from the dream was still there, a constant whisper below the pounding of her heart and her ragged breathing. Pushing it aside as best as she could she tried to ignore how her limbs still felt weak in the aftermath.

She got up from the bed and headed straight for the coffee carafe. The heat of it did little to erase the dream and the effect it was still having on her body. She needed something more. Reaching for her bracelet, she snapped it open, checked the wire and breathed.

Glancing at the clock, she was surprised to see that it was 3:07 in the afternoon. She must have slept four hours, maybe more before waking. She stopped her thought right there, not wanting to venture back to the dream before she had awakened.

She turned on the TV as background noise and planned to occupy herself with researching emotional empaths and coping mechanisms until dinner time. As she flipped through the channels she saw that *The Little Mermaid* was playing on the

Disney channel. *Dammit!* First Cort had ruined her one respite of long relaxing showers and now her favorite childhood movie.

Good, she thought. Be pissed at him. It would make things easier when she saw him again. Besides, he was not the prince but the villain. Angry at herself for ever comparing the two characters, she drank her coffee, searched her favorite sites on her phone and tried hard not to pay attention to the movie playing. What was more of a distraction was her constant internal battle to deny Cort's likeness with the hero of the movie.

She was grateful when the show was finally over. At any time she could have changed the channel or turned it off, but somehow it felt like a personal challenge to her stability to make it through.

Having reached her usual dead ends in her research she decided it was time for a change in scenery. Digging through her suitcase, she dressed for dinner. Satisfied with a simple spaghetti strap white sundress, she grabbed her purse and book before heading out the door.

As she rounded the corner, she saw that the dining tables were mostly empty. It was still early, barely 5:00. The sun was just starting to make its way towards the water, but the air was still simmering with heat.

She went to the hostess station and let the girl know that she didn't have a reservation but would like to sit by the water. The hostess was happy to seat her at a table of her choice. She was instantly greeted with the cool ocean breeze as she sat at a table for two. Ordering a glass of white from the hostess, she opened her book, eager to occupy herself with the story.

Immersed and not paying attention, a glass of wine was placed in front of her. She looked up, surreptitiously, to say thanks and came face-to-face with the waiter from last night. Of course it would be him.

"Good evening," he said, looking her over appreciatively.

She sighed heavily, knowing he could hear her. "Good evening," she said back. She picked up her menu wanting to order something right away and get her meal over with. Keeping her eyes down and away from him, she hoped he would get the hint.

"I'll have the risotto and halibut," she ordered, handing the menu back, looking coolly at him.

"Good choice," he said hesitantly.

She smirked, picking up her book and ignored his presence as she started reading again. He was close enough that she could feel his disappointment and then he turned and walked to the next table. She tried to focus on her book but she found it hard tonight. So many thoughts were going around in her head. Issues with Adam she didn't want to think about and recollections of Cort she shouldn't have.

Putting her book face down on the table, she sipped her wine. She watched the sunset, the sky streaked with fiery red and orange reflecting on the water. Her mind automatically likened the colors to the sunrise from this morning. She clenched her jaw, remembering the morning with Cort. His lips, his hands and his body, the memory making her insides ache. The feel of his arms as he held her close against his hard chest, kissing her hair as the sun came up.

For some reason she couldn't seem to control her thoughts. She grabbed her wine glass and drained it. She looked over at the kitchen wishing the waiter would come back and fill her glass.

Finally, she saw what's-his-name reach for her meal in the pass-through window. She felt relief at the idea of food to soothe her foul mood.

He placed the steaming plate in front of her and she gave him the most cursory of looks saying, "Thank you."

"Can I get you anything else?" he hinted, his words much more suggestive than necessary.

"Yes," she answered. "Another glass of white would be nice." She started in on her food and went back to ignoring him. He left and returned quickly to fill her glass without another word.

She noticed when he left that he was off trying to charm another table of ladies. Typical of his personality type, self-centered and so completely absorbed by his own sexual prowess. She shook her head as she watched him work the table of two very attractive women. They seemed to be completely taken with him, hanging on his every word. She was always surprised that seemingly intelligent women could mistake arrogance for charm. She'd had to play the part of the dumb, vulnerable girl so often to get her marks that watching the two girls made her skin crawl. Again, she was dumbfounded at how very much the same all the men she had ever targeted were.

With one exception. How she hated that she recognized that exception.

Finished with her meal and wine, she waited for the server to come back with the dessert menu. He was still at the other table trying to be entertaining but Evera didn't feel like waiting any longer. Grabbing her purse and book she headed to the hostess station. She signed off on her meal and ordered a dessert to be sent to her room. As she was walking away the waiter gave her a quick wave as she passed by the kitchen. She averted her eyes and continued out of the dining area.

Evera couldn't believe that Cort could possibly find a man like him in any way competition. She remembered how he'd felt last night when this same waiter had flirted inappropriately with her. She disliked most men in general but some young, ridiculous idiot like what's-his-name was the worst. Cort was so much better than that, she thought as she walked up the stairs to her room. He was better looking, sexier and intelligent. Not to mention he was so completely unselfish when it came to her.

She shut the door and realized what she was doing. She had been thinking about how much she liked Cort. *What the fuck!* This was bad, really bad. He wasn't even around and, somehow, he was still getting to her.

She reached to fidget with her necklace. Again she felt like it was part of the problem. It was making her lose her focus on her job and the role she needed to play.

She grabbed her bracelet instead. *Fidget with that*, taunted the Jezebel in her. But that didn't help either. If anything, it made things worse.

There was a quiet knock on the door and she went to open it and get her dessert. Lying on her bed she propped up the pillows behind her head, and settled into another quiet evening alone.

The phone on her bedside table rang, startling her.

She reached for it, biting her lip and pondering who it could be when Adam would call her cell and Cort was on another island. She refused to allow her mind to delve into who she would rather it be.

"Evera," an accented voice greeted her on the other end.

"Cort," she replied, the sexy all too familiar sound making her uneasy. "Are you back already?" she wondered, curious that she hadn't heard anything from Garrison.

"No, I'm not back yet. Not until tomorrow evening." He sounded disappointed.

"Oh," was all she could come up with, his constant unpredictability throwing her off again.

"I just wanted to hear your voice. I haven't been able to stop thinking about you since I left. I feel bewitched," he admitted, laughing softly. "Did you put a spell on me during the night?"

She laughed too, to lighten the mood. And to buy herself a minute to get over his uncomfortable honesty.

"No, I forgot to bring my witches' brew with me," she played. "It's good to hear your voice too," she added. Keep to the script and the purpose, she reminded herself. "When do you think you'll make it back tomorrow night?" A timeline would be helpful in predicting when all the players, including Cort, would be finished with the meeting.

"I'd love to have dinner with you again," he hinted, although the way he said it made it sound like so much more than just dinner. "How about 8:00? I'll try and finish up by 5:30 and get to the airport by 6:00."

Useful information for once. Garrison would be pleased.

"Alright, 8:00 then," she said. She waited for him to say goodbye first.

"So how was the rest of your day?" he asked, sounding genuinely interested.

That launched them into a lengthy conversation that lasted for an hour. They talked about music and art. Finding out that they had both been to the Louvre steered the conversation towards the impressive building itself. Cort was speaking about the feeling of being surrounded by ageless pieces of art work when Evera felt lost for words. She could barely contribute to the conversation, unable to remember any of the specifics he was mentioning.

The more they talked, the more depressed she felt. She had been to beautiful cities, incredible museums and picturesque beaches all over the world, and she could barely recall any details about any of them. Every time she travelled it had been for a job, her mind consumed by the criminals she was hunting and the tasks she needed to complete.

"And the Mona Lisa," he continued, "I know it sounds so cliché to say I loved the painting but I truly did, not the woman herself as much as the barely noticeable smile on her face. It was almost as if she was sharing a hidden secret with everyone who looked her way."

She loved how he interpreted the painting, how he described it to her. It had been in the room adjoining the gala she had attended and she never had the opportunity to look at it. Cort moved onto explain the smell of the museum; dust and old paper and paint. She was suddenly transported back to the Louvre, only this time she experienced it through his senses. She remembered the smells, just the way he was describing them. And the beautiful pieces of art work. Even the ones she had barely glanced at, she could see more clearly in her memory because of his words. She was grateful to him for giving her the gift of clarity as they reminisced. She couldn't help but admire his knowledge of history and art.

"So very cultured and yet you've never read *Jane Eyre*," she teased.

"True, but I bet until last night you've never stood in the ocean watching a fish display by flashlight," he joked back.

"That was amazing," she said, trying to picture just that moment and not what had come after. "You must love scuba diving," she commented, changing the subject away from all the feelings of the night before.

He paused before answering. "Actually, I can't go scuba diving," he said, sounding as though he was admitting to a weakness.

"How come?" she asked, wondering about his hesitation.

"I was in a car accident a long time ago and had a severe head injury. When you dive there's so much pressure on your head and your body it would be too risky for me." He had a physical vulnerability. A weakness that could be exploited. She wanted to ask more about the accident but he seemed uncomfortable discussing it. Evera guessed that the scar on his temple was likely from his accident.

"Have you ever gone scuba diving?" he asked, his tone wistful.

"No, I haven't," she was grateful that she could honestly say no. Her sympathy for him was getting harder to counter.

"And the shark was a first for me too," said Evera, wanting to bring the conversation around to a less melancholy topic.

"Yes the shark! That almost gave me a heart attack," he said with a laugh. "I can't believe you stayed so calm and unafraid." His words had a strange tenor to them; she wished he was close enough for her to feel why.

"I was right, though," she added smugly. "It was just like the other curious fish, you just needed to be patient and give it a chance. It was incredible to be that close to danger and still see the beauty in it."

"Beauty, really?" he asked, sounding strange again. "So you have a dangerous predator in your midst and instead of feeling fear and running like the rest of the prey on the planet, you what? Reserve judgment until something happens. That's a very dangerous game to play." He sounded upset and she realized they were no longer talking about the shark.

He was warning her off again. She also got the sense that he felt just as alone and ostracized as she did most of the time, as though he didn't deserve anyone's affections. He had no idea how very much alike they really were.

"I'm not like everyone else on the planet," she assured. "And besides, I'm no one's prey." How ironic that the most dangerous mark she'd ever had was the one she felt most comfortable letting her guard down with.

He chuckled softly at her confession. "Yes, I know," he agreed. "On both accounts. You are one of a kind." His voice passionate on the last sentence.

She had to forcibly close her lips so that she didn't repeat the sentiment back to him.

You're losing yourself to him, the Jezebel in her warned. The realization terrified her and cleared her head.

"Evera," he said.

"Yes," she replied, sounding more breathless than expected.

"I apologize, but I have to go," he said, sounding conflicted. "They're waiting for me."

"Of course," she said, her voice coming back to normal. "Besides, you've kept me from my favorite dessert. Shame on you," she laughed, wanting to leave things on a lighter note.

"My apologies, again" he said, laughing along with her. "What's your favorite dessert, by the way?"

"Chocolate mousse," she said. His interest in everything about her was still so surprising.

"I'll see you tomorrow night then," he finished.

"Yes," she said, and then he hung up.

She sat quietly holding the phone for a minute while she tried to digest the conversation.

About five minutes later there was a light tap at her door. She went over to the peephole but saw no one standing there. She opened the door to look down the hall when she noticed something at her feet. There, on a tray, was a bottle of raspberry ice wine, a crystal glass and a single flower; a perfect red orchid. She looked around but saw no one. Picking up the tray, she brought it into her room. As she set it on the bed she noticed a note tucked under the flower. 'Some wine to compliment your favorite dessert. Can't wait to see you tomorrow night. Cort.'

She picked up the flower, remembering that the beach where they had spent the night had been filled with them. She couldn't help but wonder if he had noticed too.

Of course he'd noticed. He missed nothing. At least nothing when it came to her.

How could she stop thinking about him when at every turn there was a reminder? Even now, holding the seemingly benign flower, her mind travelled of its own volition back to last night and the beach. She tried to fight the memory of his hands and lips on her body, his face and the heated blue of his eyes as he moved above her. No, she couldn't let herself do this. He was her job and to let him become something more would put everything in her life at risk. In a day or two she would walk away and what happened to him after that would be out of her hands.

Besides, she was in love with Adam. Adam would always be there for her and Cort was just a ghost, a moment of passing in her life that would end the second she left.

Something in her ached, and not in a good way, at the thought of never seeing him again. She shook it off, reaching for the bottle of ice wine and poured herself a glass. She didn't need another reminder but she wanted the drink. The sweet rich mousse and the tart full-bodied drink complimented each other perfectly.

She quickly texted the latest information about Cort to Garrison. Feeling hesitant as she went to hit send, as if she wasn't sure she should send this intel. She sent it, cursing herself for even questioning it.

It was still early, only 9:00, but despite her afternoon nap, she still felt exhausted. Moving the tray off the bed, she stripped down to nothing, put her necklace on the bedside table but kept her bracelet on. She crawled under the crisp, cool sheets and stretched out on her side. Just before she closed her eyes she glanced inadvertently at the delicate red orchid, and had to push away the image of Cort's face one last time before the relief of unconsciousness finally pulled her under.

*****

She awakened the next morning feeling groggy. She'd had a fitful sleep featuring a slide show with images of both Adam and Cort. She'd also had another of her nightmares.

The latter reminded her of how Adam's arms always kept the evil dreams at bay. She couldn't wait to get back to him and the safe haven of his embrace.

She flashed back momentarily to the sweet comfort she felt yesterday morning, awaking from a dreamless sleep, entwined with Cort's body. This had to stop. Her new weak, unfamiliar side was really starting to piss her off.

Evera got ready, putting on her bikini under a sundress and packing her purse with her phone and her book, looking forward to a big breakfast and then working on her tan. Adding her locket, she headed out.

The day was already warm and sunny, a perfect beach day. While she walked it dawned on her that, since yesterday morning, she'd had no other run-ins with Tweedle Dee and Tweedle Dum. She thought it odd, considering the size of resort but hoped that Cam and Elliot had left for good. She headed straight to the restaurant and her now usual table, as close to the water as possible. She ordered immediately, getting eggs benedict, fruit and a big carafe of coffee.

She ate and drank her coffee, watching the waves as they crashed against the shore. The water was impressively rough this morning and she imagined there would be lots of surf boards out later. Maybe she would rent one and go out herself. She'd always wanted to try surfing. Contemplating whether or not she should give it a go, she saw a shadow of someone standing behind her.

She turned, expecting her server, and felt jolted into shock as, yet again, Cort was unexpectedly there.

"Good morning, Evera," his voice sounding pleased as he surprised her once more, and his eyes saying so much more than just good morning.

"Cort," she looked up, attempting to keep the shakiness of her insides from coming through in her voice. He really was tall and his face was even more chiseled and handsome than she remembered, dammit. But it was his eyes that she found the most unsettling. The piercing depths of them were leaving no question as to how he felt at seeing her.

"May I join you?" he asked after she continued to stare at him in silence.

"Of course," she mumbled. "I'm just so surprised to see you. Pleasantly so," she added, hoping he wouldn't pick up on her discomfort as she bit her lip.

He sat down and continued to gaze intensely at her. Leaning in close, his arm brushed against hers. "You look so beautiful this morning," he murmured, his desire a fiery background noise to his words.

"Um, thank you," she said, feeling self-conscious again. She was surprised by the fervor in his compliment. Her hair was still damp from her shower and she was wearing no makeup. Breathe and focus, she warned herself sternly. She wondered if he always changed his plans on the fly like this. That would explain why in three years they hadn't been able to track him.

"Have you eaten yet?" she asked, grasping for something to cool the heat picking up between them.

"Yes, I ate on the plane this morning," he said.

"I'm glad you decided to come back early," she said, smiling up at him. If only she could check her phone and see if Garrison was privy to the change in plans; if he wasn't, she needed to let him know ASAP.

"Yes, well, I decided to postpone what I had planned for today. Actually, I'm contemplating cancelling the rest of my business plans for the trip at this point," he confessed.

She could feel an underlying tension to his words. Searching his face she tried to find her answers there.

"Is everything okay, Cort?" she asked, reaching to touch his arm. She wondered how far she could push him to open up. She wouldn't let herself consider how much of her feelings were forced and how much were real.

His warm, rough hand turned to hold hers as he looked down at the table.

"No, actually, everything is not okay," he said, smiling without humor. He ran his free hand nervously through his dark hair.

She waited patiently for more, tightening her grip on his hand in encouragement.

He smiled sadly at the gentle squeeze and looked up at her. His emotions were still strained but now he seemed afraid too. She tried to search through his feelings but could feel no anger.

"I came back this morning, mostly because I couldn't wait to see you, but also because I don't think I can do this anymore," he said, keeping his eyes on her. "When I told you before that I was dangerous Evera, I meant it. I'm not someone you would want around if you knew what I really was." He was trying to protect her again, but this time it was with what seemed like desperation.

"I'm that shark we were talking about last night. And although you are not my prey, many others have been. Countless others," he said, his voice bleak. He watched carefully for her reaction, his eyes filled with pain.

There was nothing she could think to say. Worse than feeling shocked by his confession was her sympathy, like she wanted to help ease his conscience.

Without thinking about it, she moved nearer to him, their faces close together. "We are not so different, you and I," she said quietly. The truth was never black and white. She killed scum and villains. He killed injudiciously. Worse, but still murder no matter how you looked at it, the intentions grey.

"Believe me, Evera, we are nothing alike. At least not in our choice of profession. I admit I don't know what you do or what your situation is, but you are nothing compared to the monster I've become." He looked down, afraid to meet her eyes.

"You can talk to me," she said earnestly. She wanted to say he could trust her but she couldn't bring herself to lie to him like that. She really did want him to open up. Suddenly she felt a blurring of lines between her job and her feelings for him. His sadness and vulnerability were wearing her down.

"I'm a killer, Evera. And whether it's me who pulls the trigger or someone else it's still because I choose for it to happen. That's all you need to know. Believe me, you don't want all the gory details or the nightmares that go with them." She could see it in his eyes, the root of his fear...he was afraid she would walk away. He wanted to scare her off but he wanted her to stay.

"I'm not some fragile bird, in case you haven't figured that out yet," she insisted gently, hoping to reassure him. "I know what it means to have a dark side." *Be careful,* she cautioned herself. He was looking at her as if he couldn't believe her words after his black admission.

"I'll admit it's shocking what we as human beings will tell ourselves in order to justify our behavior," she continued. "We do what we have to in order to survive. No matter what we see that survival as." Something dark and vicious pounded inside her, reminding her of the truth of her words.

He was staring at her with an unfathomable look in his eyes. His sadness had dissipated, replaced by a rush of intense affection and wonder...it drifted around her making her feel cherished and wanted.

"I can't believe you can see it that simply," he contemplated, hope in his voice. "Don't you want to run from me and everything I represent? I wonder if you really grasp the level of corruption in the man you have sitting in front of you." Eyes cast down, he took a deep breath and faced her.

"Those two men from the other night who were harassing you, they haven't been around. Have you noticed?" His voice was severe but quiet, cautioning her.

She stared back at him calmly. So they hadn't finished their vacation and left. Although she was surprised, she couldn't help but feel avenged. Whatever he gave them she was sure they deserved it.

"I assure you it's not because their stay was over and they checked out. Do you want to know why you haven't seen them?" He gripped her hand tightly, as if she would disappear if he let go.

"No, Cort, I don't," she said, never breaking eye contact with him. "It doesn't matter, they are nothing to my life."

He stared at her and sat back, staggered. "You are so unbelievable to me," he said, his voice filled with awe.

He broke from her gaze and looked out towards the water and the pounding surf. His free hand reached to grip the hand he was already holding, cradling her hand in both of his.

When he looked back at her, his eyes were touched with regret. "I never meant to turn out this way. I never wanted to become the very monster I spent my whole life in fear of," his voice hoarse with emotion.

Pain rippled across her chest. They were so similar. She could see it in his eyes. His past tortured him like hers did. It was like looking in a mirror. All her sadness and pain was reflected in him. Evera reached to stroke his face without consciously choosing to. She could feel his rough cheek and the warmth of his skin beneath her fingers. Something around her heart cracked and she gasped inwardly.

"Why do I feel like you know me already?" His eyes searched hers for an answer.

"I told you," she confided, "we are more the same than you could possibly know."

His lips parted as though he were going to speak but he hesitated.

"Alike in our demons, you mean?" he ventured. She could tell he was unsure if he should question her. "The demons of our past...the ones we can't escape and continue to haunt us," he said, although it was a statement not a question.

Her breath caught, the air around her burdened with both of their pain and memories. He knew. He could see her secrets. The Jezebel in her was slipping away too fast leaving her disoriented, until it was just her...Evera, stripped bare, with Cort's strong hands holding her in place.

"It's alright, you don't have to talk about your past," he soothed, as he ran his thumb across her parted lips.

"If it's as bad as mine, I'm sure it's behind a door, secured under lock and key," he said, smiling in sympathy.

"And brick and mortar," she added, her voice breaking. She stared at him, astounded. How was it possible she was having this conversation with Cort?

"That bad, huh?" he asked, the pain he felt for her travelling through his hand and into her veins.

"That bad," she admitted in a whisper. There was a pulse flowing between them now, one she'd never felt before. It made her want to pull him closer, feel his warmth against her.

The sensation of something breaking around her heart was more pronounced as he stared into her eyes. Only she could feel that it wasn't something breaking as much as it was melting, as if she'd had ice surrounding her heart and it was finally falling away. The craving to draw nearer escalating.

Something in him changed again, as if his feelings of trust in her were growing.

"My demon is my father," he stated. He looked away towards the ocean, as if he could find courage there to continue.

She was hanging on his every word...needing him to speak and wanting him to stop at the same time.

"It seems foolish, even to me, that a man just years from forty could still fear his father. Fear him and yet still want his approval." He looked calmly at her as if his words didn't bother him but Evera could feel his pain.

"It's not foolish, not at all," she soothed, intimately aware of the fine line between love and hate.

"When I was a child, I used to take solace in the fact that if there was a heaven and a hell then surely my dad would burn for the things he'd done," he said, shaking his head. "Now I know that if there is a God, I'll have the same fate as him," he spat, angry at himself.

His words antagonized her. "There is no God," she said, "so don't worry."

He looked at her surprised, his emotions turning to concern. His eyes lost their look of anger and lightened as he stared back at her.

"Maybe you're right," he said, smiling in an attempt to alleviate her bitterness. "Still, I'd like to think there's something more than nothing waiting at the end of all this."

"Like what?" she demanded. It was impossible to keep the skepticism from coming through in her voice as she contemplated their turn in conversation, this contrary and delicate subject of God. She had given up on the idea of him long ago, waiting in her dark dungeon of a room as prayer after prayer remained unanswered.

"I don't know for certain. I guess I've always hoped that when you die you just relive all the best moments of your life over and over, like one unending blissful dream." She sensed the sincerity in his every word. But his belief left her with an overwhelming sadness. Any moments in her life worth reliving could be counted on one hand.

She smiled sardonically at him. "That seems like a good alternative unless your amazing moments couldn't fill more than a couple of days. The idea of watching the same few dreams over and over for all eternity...I'm not sure I wouldn't prefer nothing." She could hear the hopelessness in her voice.

He gave her a knowing smile. "It wouldn't be like that," he insisted, leaning closer to her. "Haven't you ever watched a really good movie and wished you could watch it again as if for the first time? Or read a really good book and wished that you could read it again as if you'd never read it before?" He watched expectantly for her reaction.

She couldn't help but smile back at him. His alternative to eternal darkness sounded beautiful.

"Yes," she said, still grinning and shaking her head. "I could find a few choice memories I would love to dream new forever."

She could feel his joy when she smiled back at him. He seemed so happy to have taken away her sadness.

"That's what I hope it's like. Every worthwhile moment relived as if it was the first time you've dreamt it," he said, looking intensely at her again.

"The jolt to your insides the first time you see her, a woman so stunningly beautiful that you know you'll never get her out of your head. Her hair is tied back away from her face and you can see the curve of her neck, fragile and seductive," he breathed, his eyes boring down into hers. "You catch glimpses of her time and again, every moment significant somehow. Her emerald green eyes staring down at you in the pool from up above, her hair moving softly across her shoulders in the breeze. The first time you hear her voice, sexy and irresistible even though it's filled with sarcasm," he teased.

She imagined how she must have seemed to him that first time they met, almost rude in her refusal of help. She couldn't believe how he saw her. He'd noticed every move she made since the second she arrived.

The feeling of wanting to have him closer, to feel him against her body, was raging. Desire and something more, something scarier, pulsed through her. Taking a deep breath, she stared back at him. Struggling to keep this new sensation at bay, while the weaker side of her longed to invite it in.

His eyes burning down into hers, he lowered his voice as he spoke. "A dream of wading into the ocean, the moon shattering light on the ripples of the water, as you stand across from the most beautiful creature you could've ever imagined," he uttered, his voice raw. "The way she feels beneath your hands as they move across her bare skin," he said as he let go of her hand. He trailed his fingers down her arm causing goose bumps to rise on her flesh. "Every kiss, every touch, the taste of her, a flavor that's infinitely sweeter than any wine that has ever crossed your lips."

She was holding her breath, afraid to breathe. The last ounce of her resistance inexorably melting away under his fingertips.

He gave her a slow sexy smile. "All those moments and every breath, every movement after," he intimated, his eyes turning a darker shade of blue. "And you, Evera, wrapped in my arms as the sun rises out of the ocean." His eyes were soft now and filled with an affection that made her want to drown in them. And just as she feared, she was falling. With no way to stop herself.

"So you see, I hope to just dream through eternity, God or not. That would be my very idea of heaven."

His words were killing her, killing anything she had left to fight against him with. And now all that was left was how very badly she wanted him. The pulse between them was drawing her in, making it feel like he was too far away. She twined her fingers with his harder, but it wasn't enough. She wanted to feel him against her. Her want twisting and changing until it surpassed just a want and became a need. A burning all-consuming need to let him in in every possible way.

He must have seen the desperation in her eyes because he rose from his seat, handing over her purse as he pulled out her chair. He clasped her hand tight, keeping her close by his side as they made their way around the table.

Her breathing picked up as she saw how very far away it was back to the rooms. She reached her other hand across and grasped his arm hoping that the extra contact would help her make it. He shrugged out of her grip and wrapped his arm around her waist, pulling her against him. He was emanating the same desperate desire to be closer that she was. Her arms clung to him as he maneuvered them through the crowded tables. The strange pulse between them gaining strength until it felt like an electric current binding them together.

She looked to the corner and the rooms beyond, still an impossible forty feet away. She concentrated on holding onto Cort, but all she could feel was his strong lean body, hidden beneath his clothes, making her craving worse.

They were almost at the corner of the building but Cort's room was still two doors down. As they came upon the edge of the building she realized she wasn't going to make it. They rounded the corner and without hesitation Evera pushed Cort up against the wall.

He must have been thinking the same thing because his hands and lips were waiting for her. He reached behind her to pull her tight against the length of him while his other hand tangled in her hair, keeping her urgent lips moving with his.

She felt her complete and total surrender as she kissed him back.

They somehow made their way to his door. He struggled to get his card in the slot and Evera reached to help steady his hand and unlock it. They shoved it open with a loud crash and then Cort kicked it closed.

And then it was just the two of them and too many clothes between them. She needed to feel his skin against hers in a desperate way that went beyond just the physical. She ripped and tore at his clothing, not bothering to undo the buttons. She freed his arms from his shirt and put her hands on his chest in thankful relief.

She felt the bed against the back of her legs having had no sense of moving towards it. And then they were on the bed, their bodies pressed as tight as they could while still trying to remove the last few items of clothing.

Cort's hands were everywhere. Tracing her face, caressing her breasts, moving between her legs. She groaned against his mouth as he continued to kiss her.

Her hands explored him as if for the first time, moving over every muscular inch of him...his shoulders, his back, learning the feel of his perfect chest. It wasn't enough though. There was no longer any relief in touching or being touched.

Her fingers demanding to hold him, she reached down, blazing hot granite filling her hand. Now it was his turn to gasp against her mouth.

He moved himself between her legs as she guided him inside her. She sucked in a breath at the raw sensation of him, no barrier separating them, just hot flesh against hot flesh. He moaned but continued to kiss her, his lips moving more desperately with hers. She gripped his arms, holding onto his biceps, indulging in every thrust inside her. The fervid sensations firing almost instantly again. As achingly delicious as they were it was the electricity between them that was gaining strength. Evera struggled under the force of the pleasure to try and sort out what the feeling was.

Suddenly Cort was moving faster and she didn't need to figure out what the charge between them was. It braided itself with her pleasure, enhancing every feeling. She could feel him building and let herself join him. He moved faster still, her sensations coming to a peak along with his until, finally, she gave in as they climaxed together. He called her name against her lips as she let the feelings overwhelm her.

As her body was being inundated she figured out what the electricity between them was...a connection. She had connected with Cort in a way that went beyond anything physical. She gasped hard at both the ecstasy and the realization. Her consciousness only aware of Cort, holding her so tight they had become one.

And the whole time, they never broke their kiss.

CHAPTER 15

Confessions

Evera woke to a familiar feeling surrounding her. She was cocooned in the sensation of love coming from the body pressed against her. The arms around her strong and comforting, keeping her close.

She went suddenly rigid as the morning came rushing back to her and she realized the arms around her weren't Adam's. They were Cort's. She could smell his familiar skin and aftershave. If they were Cort's arms then it was Cort's feelings she had awoken to.

He loved her.

She felt the world tilt and shudder on its axis as the truth hit her full force. This beautiful dangerous man who was supposed to be her enemy was in love with her.

As frightening as that was, what terrified her even more was how she felt about him. She knew she had feelings for him but how strong they were she couldn't tell. He was too close, his feelings clouding hers so that she couldn't separate them.

She thought back to what must have been just an hour or so ago. Everything that had happened between them had been because she wanted it. There had been nothing proprietary or calculating about it. No agenda. Her mission completely forgotten.

It was a first for her. The first time she had wanted to kiss someone so desperately, the first time she had wanted to touch someone everywhere. The first time she had wanted to what? Make love with someone. Was that what it had been? If that was true did that mean that she loved him too?

The most disturbing memory had been the connection that she had felt between them. As if they were somehow tethered together, an invisible string connecting them.

She could feel it, even now. More powerful than his arms holding her to him, was that sensation.

And then she recognized why she couldn't separate her feelings from his. They had become one. The connection between them, her passion for him, to be with him physically. It was all Cort. She'd been falling for him this whole time, she'd just refused to let herself see it.

She loved him.

And now all that was left was for her world to come crashing down around them.

*****

Cort woke shortly after she did, kissing her tenderly on the forehead and pulling back to see if she was awake. He met her eyes and the feeling of love he had for her amplified, his arms pulling her tighter against him.

As she stared back into his endless blue eyes she felt her heart turn over painfully in her chest. She wondered how it was possible to fall in love and feel your heart break all at the same time. She wanted to tear herself from him and run. Her pain she deserved but the thought of breaking his heart made her want to slit her own throat.

He said nothing, but his lips came down on hers and he kissed her softly, at first. But as the kiss continued the fire between them started to burn.

His hands were instantly moving over her body, making her forget her reasons to leave. The desire she felt for him now matched his consuming need for her. She should be worried about how much more pain and suffering this would cause them both but she couldn't find it in herself to care. His hands were making her forget everything but the burning ache to have him inside her once more. *Fuck it,* she thought, and gave in to him.

*****

She was laying in Cort's bed naked, watching him on the phone as he ordered them lunch. She felt undone and inside out.

He'd put on his underwear and his shirt from this morning. His shirt was open, his hard chest showing, because there were no buttons left from when she'd torn them off earlier. She wanted to reach between the fabric and run her hands along his skin. She'd gone from being afraid to be with him to not being able to get enough.

He hung up the phone, leaning towards her and kissing the top of her head.

Regardless of her feelings for him, she knew she needed to leave and soon. Even if she'd chosen to forget her mission, Garrison and Adam had not.

Adam...

Her heart pitched through the floor.

"Lunch should be here in about twenty minutes," he said. "I was going to have a quick shower and ask you to join me but something tells me that would take a lot longer than twenty minutes." He was looking at her as if they hadn't just had sex twice in the last couple hours.

Unbelievably, she felt the same. Her passion for him still so powerful it was surprising. And terrifying.

"You go ahead," she said, hoping her smile looked genuine. She needed to leave. She needed to leave now!

"Ladies first," he said. His chivalrous offer for her to shower first made her stomach turn. It reminded her too much of her ritual with Adam when she stayed with him.

That was her out, she grabbed at it like a life raft.

She smiled sexily at him, hoping to keep him from suspecting that her request was anything but ordinary. "No, you shower. I'll head back to my room and get cleaned up there, and grab some clothes that are still in one piece," she said with a raised eyebrow as she saw her torn dress by the side of the bed.

"Alright," he said, laughing as he picked up her tattered dress. He made his way to his suitcase at the end of the bed and pulled out a fresh white T-shirt. "Here," he said, handing it to her, "wear this."

He searched the floor for her bikini. He found the bottoms but when he located the top the strings were ripped apart.

"Oops," he said sheepishly. She was impressed by his strength. It wasn't an easy thing to rip a bathing suit in half.

"That's fine," she said, and pulled his T-shirt on, grabbing her bikini bottoms. "I believe we're even. Your shirt seems irreparable too."

She finished dressing and he reached to help her up from the bed. Her heart rate increased as he pulled her to his chest and wrapped his arms around her.

He kissed her once, passionately. "I don't know if I can let you go even for a few minutes," he whispered against her lips.

She ached inside at his words. She didn't want to let him go either. The very idea made her anxious and scared. All the more reason she needed to escape.

Could this be it? The last time she ever saw him.

She resisted the urge to wrap her arms around him and hold on.

Willing herself to relax her embrace, she released him. *Go!* She commanded her body. Her feet seemed unwilling to obey her, as if they were cemented to the floor.

"I'll be back as soon as I can." The lie left a bitter aftertaste on her tongue. She had no idea if she would ever return.

"I'll be waiting," he said, smiling seductively at her. Her insides clenched and her legs went weak at the thought of what would be waiting for her if she chose to come back.

"Bye," she whispered and grabbed her purse and what was left of her dress as she walked out the door.

The second the door closed behind her she could feel her breathing pick up; the familiar hitching and gasping of a panic attack. She couldn't afford to fall apart outside his door, she had no idea who was watching.

She ran quickly up the staircase to her room and struggled to open her door in the midst of her lightheadedness. She needed to get inside before she unraveled completely. She managed to open the door and slam it shut behind her before she came apart. She fell to her knees, choking, tearless sobs ripping from her chest.

Oh my God, he loved her. And she loved him. The sheer impossibility of it made her want to tear herself in half. She stayed on the cold tile floor of the hotel room waiting for her body to stop shaking. It was incomprehensible that she had allowed herself to fall for a mark. Her, Jezebel. What the hell had she done?

Slowly, very slowly, her body stopped trembling, her breath returning to almost normal. Almost. Something in her realized that nothing would ever be normal or the same again. She had crossed a line inside herself that there would be no coming back from. She picked her forehead up from the floor and tried to unscramble her thoughts enough to figure out what she should do.

But she knew what she should do. If she didn't get away from Cort immediately she feared she would change her mind and end up back in his bed. The knowledge that once she left here she would never see him again was agonizing.

Her purse was beside her on the floor. Reaching for it, she grabbed her phone. She turned it on and saw that there were two text messages waiting for her, both from Garrison.

The first, 'There's been a change to our itinerary and our company is coming back. Let me know if we can accommodate them or not.' Discreet and to the point.

The second was clipped and seemed to carry some urgency, 'Change in plans again. Call me ASAP.' It was sent half an hour ago.

She abruptly dialed Garrison's number.

He picked up on the second ring. "Yes," he answered expectantly.

"It's Jezebel," she said.

"Great, starting the ninety seconds now," he said. "Cort backed out on his meeting. I wanted to make sure you knew."

"Yes," she admitted, calmly. "He showed up at my breakfast table and then I spent the morning in his room," she said, as the Jezebel in her resurfaced, rattling off mission information like nothing earth shattering had just happened. Where the hell had she disappeared to when she needed her a couple of hours ago?

"Good," he said, sounding relieved. "But I'm going to need you to speed up your process. It looks as though Cort has bailed on his colleagues for all but the one meeting last night. His actions are making the rest of the crew nervous and we've picked up some intel that a few of the players are going to leave. I need something, anything from him, Jezebel, or the CIA is insisting we take them all out, Cort included."

Until she felt the pain in her palm, Evera didn't realize she'd been digging her nails in so hard they almost broke the skin. She could think of nothing to say to break the silence.

"Jezebel?" he questioned.

"I'm here, just surprised. I thought Cort wasn't a kill target." She kept her voice even but it took all her effort to pull air into her lungs and keep talking.

"He wasn't, not until the CIA found out that so many hot targets were grouped together in one spot. I want Cort alive. I'm almost certain he's White," he admonished, frustrated. "If I can get anything from him, it'll buy him a pass and keep him out of the take down. No one, myself included, wants White mistakenly obliterated before we can interrogate him."

She mentally scrambled. "I'll get you something." Her words came out too fast, too desperate. She hoped that Garrison wouldn't notice.

"You're sure?" he sounded relieved and excited. No suspicion.

"I'm heading back to his room shortly. I'll do everything I can. And he trusts me," she admitted. She closed her lips to stop her audible sigh of relief, certain Garrison would clamp onto any chance for information that could get Cort a temporary reprieve.

"Okay, great. Send me what you get as soon as you can and I'll pass it on to Adam to decipher."

She blanched. Garrison was working with Adam? She was surprised Garrison would cave and accept help, especially from Adam.

"So Adam's involved in the mission now?" she wondered. Before this morning she couldn't have been happier to hear about his involvement. Now she wasn't so sure.

"No," Garrison clarified. "He's helping me keep track of all the different players in Hawaii. I'm grateful but it in no way alters our interchanges, Jezebel," he said stoically. "Everything still runs solely through me and all decisions will be mine. Clear," he demanded, speaking quickly as the clock ticked down.

"Crystal," she agreed. The less Adam knew about her and Cort the better. They knew each other so well that she was afraid he'd pick up on something being amiss.

"And times up," he finished, as the line went dead.

Exhaling loudly she tossed the silent phone on the bed and followed it in dizzying relief. She could breathe again. Rolling onto her back she stared up at the ceiling, going over the promise she had just made to Garrison.

Intel. The only thing standing between Cort and a certain death sentence. She headed straight to the bathroom and the heat of a shower. As impossible as it seemed, she had to get her hands on something, anything. She couldn't believe how fast things had just changed.

She was going back to Cort.

*****

She got ready quickly, throwing on the white dress she'd worn to dinner last night. Her hands were shaky with anticipation, both fear and joy, as she zipped up the side. There was a war going on inside her. A war that couldn't possibly have a victor.

She had been gone a long time, but somehow, the way he felt about her seemed to be lingering. Its warmth a comforting presence even though he was rooms away. She repacked her purse with her phone and her book and headed out the door.

She was surprised to see that while she'd been in her hotel room it had started raining. Making her way quickly through the warm downpour, she raced down the stairs to avoid getting completely drenched. Arriving at Cort's door breathless, her hair was almost as wet as when she had gotten out of the shower. She knocked sharply.

The door opened and there he was. He was on his phone but he smiled at her, relief and happiness emanating from him.

He grabbed her hand and pulled her into his room. He quickly and silently kissed her on the temple while he listened to whoever was on the other end of the line.

Evera noticed his dark hair was still damp from his shower. He was wearing a fitted white T-shirt, which emphasized his muscular torso beneath, and worn blue jeans that fit him snuggly. Her eyes finished travelling over his body and then made their way back up to his ruggedly handsome face and met his eyes. He was looking at her as if he hadn't seen her for a year. His blue eyes mingling with hers, touched with fire. The love he felt for her impossibly, stronger than when she had left earlier.

She felt lost in the moment. Forgotten was her conversation with Garrison, the intel from his phone, even her hair dripping down her back. The connection between them was back and singing through her veins.

He led her to the bed and the tray on it waiting with her lunch. There was also a carafe of coffee with plenty of cream and sugar.

"Could you hold on just a minute?" he said into his phone and pressed a button.

Suddenly his free hand grabbed the back of her damp hair and he leaned down to kiss her hard.

He pulled away slowly, reluctantly. "Hi," he said breathlessly, smiling down at her. "Welcome back."

"I'm happy to be back," she said, staring up at him.

"I'm sorry but I'm in the middle of a couple of business transactions that I can't put off. Go ahead and eat, I'm going to be a while. Feel free to watch TV or whatever you want," he said, gesturing around the room. "Or, if you want to hit the spa instead of hanging out here, I can meet up with you later," although she could feel that he didn't want her to leave.

"Thanks, but I brought my book. That is, if you don't mind me lounging on your bed while you work?" she asked, raising a suggestive brow. She longed to run her hands along the front of his shirt and pull him onto the bed with her, her lunch forgotten.

He growled and moved closer, kissing her neck. "This is so wrong," he said against her skin.

"Why is this wrong?" she asked, surprised at his choice of words.

He pulled back and looked at her. The earlier flicker of fire in his eyes had turned to flames.

"Having you here, on my bed, and me being across the room on the phone...so very wrong," he smiled sexily at her and stood up.

He shook his head as if to clear it. "Where was I?" he asked. She looked at him, hiding her pout, disappointed that he had pulled away before she could get her hands on him.

"Oh right, client on hold," he grinned as he returned to his call.

She sighed, resigned to the fact that she would be eating her lunch after all.

They spent the next hour seemingly content on separate tasks. He had paperwork scattered on a small round dining table along with a laptop. She couldn't help but notice several blue memory sticks sitting beside his computer. And one red one.

What surprised her so completely was that he was being so candid about her seeing them. He continued his phone conversations and seemed more than comfortable having her hear his many exchanges. She read her book and internally struggled with her obligation. Retaining as much of the information as possible, she hoped to hear something that would be useful. Just enough to keep him safe.

"I don't have that information in front of me. I'll have to call you back, just give me fifteen minutes," he said and hung up, putting his phone on the table.

"Evera," he said, as he walked to the door, putting his shoes on. "I just have to run out to the car and grab my other laptop," he explained. "Be right back," and he walked out the door, closing it firmly behind himself.

She froze. He'd left his laptop open but more importantly was his phone. It was sitting there like a beacon, calling her over. She only had moments if she wanted to try and tag his phone. And then she was off the bed and grabbing her purse. Digging through it, she found the tag she was looking for.

She hesitated. If she tagged his phone the Section wouldn't just have access to all his information but they would be able to track him. Before she plugged the tag into Cort's phone she removed the plastic sheath that would be left behind as a tracer. The Section would get the information they desired and Cort would be safe from them tracking him. She waited impatiently for it to download all his information, the whole time listening intently for footsteps approaching the room.

When it was finished she ejected it and grabbed her microfiber cloth, wiping his phone down. She plugged the tag into her cell and uploaded all his information. She went back and sat on the bed, hoping to look as though she hadn't moved. She felt sick when the process was finished.

She hit the send button with trepidation and tucked her phone back in her purse, loathing that she had added one more betrayal to Cort's list. Her one consolation was that hopefully this would be enough to keep the Section's wolves from his door.

She breathed and picked up her book, taking up where she had left off.

Footsteps sounded outside the door only seconds later. She heard him insert his card and the click as the door unlocked. Glancing quickly at his phone, she mentally questioned whether or not she had put it back in the exact spot he had left it. She had been so anxious about what she was doing that she hadn't paid as much attention as she usually did.

He walked in smiling at her and carrying another computer bag. "Sorry, I wish our day could be more exciting," he said, as he cleared a spot on the cluttered table.

"I don't mind," she admitted. She watched as he moved his phone out of the way to make room for his other laptop. He didn't seem to pay any attention to where it had been sitting. She breathed an internal sigh of relief.

"Well good, because I'm going to be a bit longer than I thought. I had no idea that rearranging my life would become so complicated," he said. He was looking at her as though he wanted to tell her more.

"Rearranging your life?" she questioned. He was still looking pointedly at her. She wasn't sure if she wanted to know what he meant by that or not. "Rearranging how?" She recalled bits and pieces of his phone conversations. Some she could tell were to clients and some sounded like conversations with financial planners. Phrases like, 'liquidating assets' and 'foreign investments.'

"Not yet," he said, looking smug and a little uncertain. "We'll talk more about it later," he said as he opened his new laptop and started working again.

Her curiosity was piqued but he was back on the phone so she couldn't press him any further. She had an overwhelming urge to check her phone and see if Garrison had responded.

An hour or so later Cort leaned back and stretched. Getting up from the bed, she moved behind his chair and started massaging his neck.

"Hmmm, that feels so good, thank you," he said. She was surprised by how just touching his neck and shoulders could get her blood flowing. Her hands, having acquired a mind of their own, started making their way down the front of his shirt. She'd been right to be afraid of being close to him again. The feel of his hard chest beneath her fingers was giving her a rush. *Just one more time*, she pleaded.

She could feel that he was right there with her. He tilted his head back, his mouth so close and tempting. She brought her lips to his and the heat flared between them. She ran her hands more insistently along his shirt, frustrated with the fabric keeping her from his skin. She started pulling his shirt up as their kiss intensified.

And then his phone started ringing. His mouth stilled as he pulled unwillingly away from her and reached for his phone, checking the number before answering. As soon as he looked at the screen his entire countenance changed, his body going stiff. She could feel his passion transform to anxiety.

"Sorry, but I have to get this," he said, his voice even and his eyes calm. He was just as good at deception as she was. She wondered who could be on the other end to cause him such turmoil.

"Hello," he said, his voice ambivalent and cautious. He stood up quickly and reached for her hand, leading her back to the bed.

He left her there and walked towards the door. He turned to her and gestured with a tilt of his head that he needed to go outside, his eyes guarded. She nodded and gave him a small smile. He didn't return the smile, but instead looked concerned.

He closed the door with an ominous click. She felt uneasy. Not once in all his interchanges throughout the day had he felt the need to hide anything from her. She waited impatiently for him to return. Suddenly she could hear him outside, his voice loud and angry. She listened hard but couldn't make out any words. He was arguing heatedly with someone. She watched the door, waiting for him to come back through it.

Some part of her felt alarmed. What if right now she was being given away? Had he somehow caught her betrayal with his phone? Worse yet, what if he was White and had found out who she really was?

Stay calm, she reprimanded herself. She reached to stroke her bracelet. The feel of it giving her no comfort for a change. A vision of springing it open and having to use it to defend herself from him suddenly appeared in her mind. Bile rose in her throat and she swallowed hard, pushing the disturbing picture from her head.

The door rattled as Cort unlocked it and turned the handle. She waited expectantly to see his face.

He came through, his face smooth and unreadable. He averted his eyes from her and walked to the chair at the round table, setting his phone down. He sat down heavily, leaning forward to hold his head in his hands. His posture one of defeat.

Her heart went out to him, no longer concerned for herself or her safety. She rose from the bed and walked quietly over. Standing in front of him, she reached forward to run her hands through his hair in a consoling gesture.

He reached for her, clutching her hips and leaning his head against her stomach. She continued stroking his hair and testing his emotions. She could feel anger and despair, grim and cold. Inside she was panicking, still unsure if his feelings were directed at her. She wished he'd say something to set her mind at ease.

He ran his hands down her hips to her thighs, pulling her closer. Despite the confusion of the moment his hands were heating her up. She adjusted her dress, straddling his legs, and sat down on his lap facing him.

She tugged on his hair, trying to lift his face so she could read his eyes. As soon as she did she regretted it; they were burning ice and fire.

Instantly, his lips came crashing down on hers, so hard she could feel them bruising her. His hands grabbed at her waist, pulling her dress up and around her hips. He stood without warning, holding her legs around his waist. He slammed her against the wall almost knocking the wind out of her. His lips moving with anger and passion against hers. His hands were ripping at her underwear, his breathing ragged.

She caught his desperate fire and started roughly undoing his jeans. Their hands pulled and grabbed at each other trying to get at what they needed.

And then Cort was pushing inside her with an angry thrust, the force of it bordering on violence. He grabbed both her hands in his and pinned them on either side of her against the wall. He moved inside her, fast and unrelenting, his desire and anger the only emotions she could feel. She wrapped her legs tighter around him, and broke free from his grasp, gripping his back hard as her nails dug in to hold on.

And then she could feel their passion building as one. His anger burning up in the fire between them until all that was left was their blistering need for each other. The antidote to their pleasure and pain just breaths away. They came together, holding on so tight she could barely breathe. She let the waves of pleasure crash over her, welcoming the feeling of being dragged under. She fought to catch her breath as she could feel her arms and legs start to give out.

The wall suddenly disappeared from against her back replaced by Cort's arms. He walked them to the bed where he laid her down gently, his breathing still erratic. He moved to lay beside her and started kissing her face, his hand stroking her cheek.

"Are you okay, Evera?" he asked, his voice full of agony. "Did I hurt you?" His hands caressed her tenderly from head to toe as if to erase any pain he might have caused.

She wanted to say that she was fine but she wasn't sure. She was fine and high and confused.

He stared into her eyes, the emotions she read there surreal and overwhelming. His lips kissed hers, so achingly tender she felt her heart heave. Whatever was going on with him she still couldn't decipher if it had anything to do with her. And more than anything, she wished she knew who was on the other end of that phone call.

CHAPTER 16

Choices

They lay quietly next to each other, still trying to catch their breath. She could feel her silence causing his concern to turn to worry. But, thankfully there was no anger left in him; she didn't believe it had been directed at her but at the person on the other end of the phone call.

"I'm so sorry, please forgive me," he said, his eyes pleading with hers.

"There's nothing to forgive," she said absolutely.

"I was unnecessarily rough," he berated. She had experienced rough sex before and this was nothing in comparison.

"I didn't mind and please believe me when I tell you that I'm perfectly fine," she said, grabbing his face in her hands and forcing him to look at her. "Much, much better than just fine," she said, smiling knowingly at him.

He smiled back at her but it didn't reach his eyes. She could tell he was still concerned but she couldn't grasp why. The phone call must still be weighing on him. She knew him well enough by now to know if he wanted her to know he would just tell her. He grabbed her hand and held it against his face. He closed his eyes and she could feel his uncertainty and fear return.

"I want to ask you something. The timing couldn't be worse...I was hoping to wait until tonight but I can't," his voice sounded worried. "Before I ask you, though, there are some things you need to know," he said, looking her directly in the eyes.

"That phone call earlier," he said, pausing as though he didn't want to continue, "that was my father." He said it as though he was confessing to a murder and not just a relationship.

He seemed reluctant to continue. "It's okay," she said soothingly. "You don't have to talk about it if it's too hard."

"No, I want to. You need to know what I'm involved in. I want to be completely honest with you," he said, while she held back a guilt induced flinch.

"My father's been part of the underworld for most of his adult life. He forced me along with him and it's all I've known. There's never been anyone but him and me. I don't know of any other relatives. My family died when I was younger, in that car accident I told you about. I don't remember much before that, my head injuries affected my memory and I can only put together bits and pieces. The bits and pieces aren't worth having anyways. My father was a cruel man. Still, is a cruel man," he paused and took a deep breath. She gripped his hand, holding it tight, sharing in his distress.

"In any event," he continued, "I grew up and wanted my own part of the business. It was so easy for me what with all the technology at our fingertips now. Creating different aliases and staying out of direct contact with clients helped me keep my identity hidden. Even the killing side of it. Most of the time I could hire it out and never get my hands dirty. Most of the time," he said, looking at her honestly. She kept her face smooth and patient.

"But my father didn't like that I'd made a name for myself and become just as successful as him. He kept interfering in my business, always inserting himself wherever he could whether I liked it or not. And I was too weak to keep him out," he said, sounding ashamed of himself. "It's surprising still, that after all this time he somehow manages to control me," he said, sounding momentarily defeated.

Evera felt an overpowering loathing for his father. She wished she could have a few minutes alone with him in a locked room with no windows.

"But I'm not going to let him control me anymore." She could feel his confidence as he pulled her into his embrace.

"I want out," he stated. "That's what we were fighting about earlier. Of course he doesn't want me to leave but it's done. That's what I've been doing all morning. When I told you it was complicated rearranging your life, I meant because I'm finished. I'm orchestrating my escape. I've been moving money and investments around, liquidating anything that might link me to my past."

She was shocked and relieved. He was doing the one thing to ensure his safety and didn't even know it.

"I can't believe you're doing this," she said, admirably. "To change your life so completely. You should be so proud of yourself." She imagined his father was anything but, if the anger Cort had taken away from the conversation was any indication. She couldn't help but feel a smug satisfaction at the thought of his parasite of a father losing control of his host.

He smiled, contrite. "It's something I should have done a long time ago. I don't feel happy about my life, just relieved that I can leave it all behind me," he said. She could feel his anxiety mounting, no relief inherent. She wondered if it was still about his father.

"And your father?" she asked, leaving the question open ended.

"My father is angry and suspicious. He can't believe I would want something different. He didn't buy my explanation," he said. His voice was calm but she could feel the hesitation in him, as if he was withholding something from her.

"What explanation did you give him?" she asked, curious despite his discomfort.

"I told him that I had been doing this long enough and wanted a change. Seems logical to me. I'm going to be forty in a couple of years, a great time to change my evil ways," he said, smiling at her. She didn't buy it either. There was too much anxiety in him when he gave her his explanation.

"But my father called me a liar. That's when the arguing started." The tension in his arms surrounding her was tangible, as if he was battling with something. He looked in her eyes and when he did she could feel fresh fear in him.

"He thinks it's because of someone…a woman," he paused, watching for her reaction.

She felt tongue-tied. She stared back at him, wanting so badly to ask him if it was true but afraid to hear the answer. She wasn't sure whether the 'yes' or 'no' would frighten her more.

"I told him there was no one, which he didn't believe. It's bad enough he knows everything about my business, I certainly don't want him involved in my personal life," he said. She wondered if his answer was just to pacify his father or if it was the truth.

"I was in a relationship a while ago and it was the only other time I ever talked to him about getting out. I guess he just assumed it was for the same reason," he said. His ambiguity about the conversation made her want to shake him. And although she had no right, she couldn't deny that the idea of another woman intimately involved with Cort made jealousy boil in her blood.

"The relationship ended about a year ago and in the time I was with her I never took a single step to leave the business," he said. He was looking at her intensely, his fear and anticipation hinting at something pivotal. "Two years I spent with her. In those two years I never felt anything close to what I feel for you after only three days," he confessed, his voice quiet and raw with emotion.

Her heartbeat quickened. She wanted to say something but her emotions were caught in her throat. She wondered if he could read in her eyes how she felt about him.

"So, getting back to the beginning of our conversation and the question I want to ask you," he continued, his hand cupping her face. "I'm in love with you, Evera. I'm leaving Hawaii tomorrow," he paused while her heart dropped. "And I want you to come with me."

She stared at him as she mentally tried to process the words that had just left his tempting lips. What he was asking her was impossible, impossible for so many reasons. But the most important reason was that he was wrong about his feelings. He didn't love her. He loved Jezebel. If he knew the truth he would be disgusted by her.

"Cort," she said, and then her throat became too choked to continue.

His face was patient, expectant, as if the answer would not be one that would tear him apart.

For the first time in her life when she wanted to be completely honest with someone she couldn't. The love she felt for him was real and growing by the second, which was going to make telling him no and that they were over that much harder to witness. She tried again, her voice clear and resigned, "I want give you an answer, but—"

He interrupted her. "Don't say but. Don't even say yes, yet. Think about it before you give me an answer. I know it's no small thing to ask. I don't want a yes or a no now if it means you'll change your mind later. Think about it and we'll talk tonight," he insisted, leaning forward to kiss her on the forehead.

"Just know that I love you and I don't care about your past. I know you're keeping things from me and I know about the other man," he said, not breaking eye contact with her. "None of that matters to me. This is a chance for both of us to leave everything behind and start a new life...together," he offered, his unconditional acceptance of her filled her heart.

"That is," he added, "if you want me, the way that I want you." He didn't ask if she loved him and she wondered if he knew how hard it was for her to say the words.

"Cort, I do want you," desperately, she wanted to add. The Jezebel in her wanted to tell him it made no difference and that it was over, regardless. But the words were somehow lodged in her throat refusing to come out. His beautiful face and the warmth of his hard body holding her was making it impossible for her to continue. "I..." her tongue stumbled, her mind changing at the last second, "am horrible at talking about my feelings," she said, smiling to hide the frustration at her cowardice.

He laughed and hugged her close. The tension in him finally subsiding.

"I suspected as much," he said, pulling back to look at her.

"You do realize that if you come with me it won't be simple? We'll have to hide. You can't just walk away from this kind of life unscathed and without consequence. You'll have to give up all contact with your past," he said.

But Cort's request was pointless. She couldn't leave Adam and the Section. And she would never know for sure how much of Cort's love was for her or Jezebel.

Adam and Cort. She was completely dumbfounded as to how she could love two men so completely and in such different ways. And yet, deserve neither of them.

"I know this is hard," he sympathized, but she could feel that it was causing him pain to watch her. "That's why you need to think this through," he said, stroking her face.

She collected herself, hating that she was making him hurt. "I'll think it through," she lied, her voice even. She wanted to smile at him to ease his mind but she knew it would be cruel to give him false hope.

He left the bed and gathered her clothes from the floor, handing them to her. He sat on the edge of the bed watching her as she dressed.

"I meant to let you go, you know," he said quietly, as she pulled her dress over her head.

"What do you mean?" she asked.

"When I came back in from that phone call. I meant to tell you it was over." He seemed pained to confess to her.

She was shocked that he'd planned to end it with her. How she wished he had and spared her the excruciating burden of doing it herself.

"At first my father said I was being played and to open my eyes and stop thinking with my dick," he said. "His words not mine," he mentioned, looking at her apologetically. She felt a flutter of panic; his father seemed wise and dangerous.

"When he realized that strategy wouldn't work he tried playing on my guilt. And it worked but not in the way he intended. I came back in so angry at both him and myself. Him for interfering in my life again, but I didn't feel bad about walking away from him anymore. I was mad at myself for wanting to put you in a position of danger just so I wouldn't lose you. That's what I feel guilty about, even now." His mood when he passed through the door suddenly made perfect sense to her. Just like her, he was battling with what he should do and what he wanted.

"But then you touched me and I lost all sense of reason and could think of nothing but how much I wanted to keep you with me," he said.

"You're giving me a choice, not an ultimatum. You've also been honest with me about who you are. You have nothing to feel guilty about," she insisted.

He pulled her up from the bed, his eyes burning down into hers. "You're amazing," he professed, love and desire radiating from him.

Just one more time, she thought. She wound her arms around his neck aware of the fact that this would be her last chance to be with him. She had no idea how this was going to end but wanted his body to make her forget her circumstances for the next hour.

But he removed her hands gripping his neck. "I don't want to cloud your decision with the chemistry between us," he said breathlessly against her forehead. "Just think about everything I said. Once we're gone there's no turning back."

"Okay," she agreed.

She grabbed her purse and he wrapped his arms around her once in a tight embrace and then pulled away.

"I'll see you later." She could feel the unspoken 'hopefully' hanging in the air. "Seven o'clock at the bar?" he asked.

It was 3:00 now, another four hours. Four hours for her to figure out how to break both their hearts. She was sure no amount of time would be enough for her to come up with words she could live with.

"I'll see you at 7:00," and she walked out of his room. The sound of the door clicking shut behind her ominous in its finality.

She didn't want to go back to her room. The thought of the small space seemed too confining for all the thoughts diverging in her mind. She headed straight to the beach. She'd always found a certain comfort from the sights and sounds of the ocean.

She made her way past the sunbathers, which were sparse today because of the damp beach from the rain earlier. The water was filled with surfers though. The wind and rain had caused the surf to become rougher, perfect conditions for the boards.

She couldn't believe how quickly her life had gone off course. From sitting at the breakfast table this morning wondering if she should go surfing, to falling in love, and now facing unbelievable heartache.

She walked down the beach to where it was secluded and looked out at the water, hoping for some direction. But all she could see was the color of Cort's eyes reflected in the blue of the ocean. And then she thought about Adam. She didn't know what was worse of the two betrayals. Going back to Adam and trying to pretend that she was the same person. Or leaving Cort because, in the end, he was just her job; a mission to accomplish. How could she ever go back to the way things were?

She felt her phone vibrate against her hip. She had forgotten to check it in the midst of everything going on with her and Cort. She pulled it out of her purse and tapped it, going straight to her texts. It was from Garrison. She read the one and only line and her whole body went numb. She felt the phone slip through her fingers and watched as it fell to the sand.

*****

She stood, staring down at her phone as if it had become corrosive and poisonous. She was afraid to touch it. She didn't want to pick it up ever again.

Her hands went subconsciously to the locket at her throat, gripping it as though it were a talisman against what she had just read. This couldn't be, she reasoned. There had to be some mistake. She folded her legs and slowly eased herself down onto the sand, continuing to look at her phone in despair. That one sentence spinning around and around in her mind.

'Take our company out for dinner, G.' Her heart was palpating. Take him out, was all she saw in her head. Take out Cort. Her adrenaline was pumping from the panic, her despair turning to anger. This new turn could have come from the intel she had stolen from Cort's phone. She gritted her teeth, the information was supposed to slow down the process, not speed things up.

Whatever Garrison's reasons, CIA or otherwise, he didn't know about the new intel she had gathered about Cort's father and his involvement, nor about his confession of having different aliases. That would be even more reason for Garrison to believe Cort was White if he was having doubts.

She felt almost certain he was White. Too many coincidences and allusions. Either way, if she could use this information to lift the death order on Cort then she would bend the truth as hard as possible.

She grabbed her phone and hastily started sending him a report. She added everything he had divulged to her this afternoon. Anything that would give Garrison reason to pause and rethink his order. She sent it and then wiped it, waiting impatiently. She crossed her arms in front of her and instantly wished she hadn't. The cold steel of the bracelet grazed her opposite arm, making her flinch.

Garrison had to call this off! If he didn't she knew she wouldn't be able to carry out his orders. And then what? She could lie and say she didn't have an opportunity or that she suspected her cover was blown. They'd send a plane to get her out immediately. It would devastate her to leave him but at least she wouldn't have to kill him. But that didn't mean he'd be safe either. She knew that even if a mission was compromised, the orders still needed to be carried out. Which meant that on the plane to get her out would be another operative in line to do what she couldn't.

Her phone pinged, the sound startling her in her anxious state. She could feel the dread in her spreading as she lifted it to read the screen.

Her heart sank.

'Thanks for the additional information but we will need to continue with dinner as planned, G.'

Why was Garrison going ahead with this if he thought Cort was White? She felt helpless as she shoved her phone back in her purse.

Then a solution popped into her head. One she despised, because Cort would be repulsed by her. She had to warn him. It was the only way. She flashed ahead to how he would take her confession. As she imagined the look on his face she felt sickened. He would hate her. And she would be leaving her backup operative at the mercy of Cort. She remembered how easily he had ripped through her swimsuit. He was strong and ruthless. And he would have the advantage. He would know they were coming for him.

Fuck! This wasn't a solution, this was certain death for her backup. Cort was not the kind of man to run from a fight. Even if she tried to convince him to leave before someone came for him she knew he wouldn't. She recalled bits and pieces of the conversations he'd had; no loose ends.

She started pacing the empty beach, looking for another alternative but knowing this was the only answer.

Her phone rang, the noise muffled by her purse. She was beginning to hate the sound, it seemed to herald nothing but bad news. Digging around she grabbed it and answered, no longer bothering to check who it was.

"Jezebel," she answered exasperated, running her fingers nervously through her hair.

"Hey beautiful, it's me," he spoke quietly.

"Adam!" For some reason just hearing his voice eased her aggravation down a level.

"Look," his tone low and cautious, "I know we're not supposed to be in contact so I'll make this brief. We're moving things forward and we'll be landing in Maui tomorrow morning between 8:00 and 9:00 to setup before the big meeting."

She stopped pacing, her legs locked. "What? Why...and who is we?" This could not be happening. Her psyche couldn't handle one more wild card.

"The operative team. Myself, Darren and three more. I'm not exactly sure who yet but there'll be five of us coming," he continued. She could hear the din from the hub in the background. "We're coming to take out the party guests meeting in Kauai at 2:00 p.m."

This was worse than not good; Adam and Cort in the same place at the same time. And her in the middle.

"And don't worry about your dinner guest. You can leave that issue until the morning when we arrive." Evera caught the menacing edge in Adam's words.

"What do you mean?" she inquired. It took her mind a few seconds to connect the dots, and then she felt as if the beach was falling away beneath her. She'd been wrong about her opinion of the universe. There really was a God. And he was going to make sure she was punished.

"You're my backup operative, aren't you?" she asked, trying to hide the panic from coming through in her voice. But she didn't really need him to answer. She already knew.

"Yes," he confirmed, preoccupied by whatever he was doing back at the Section. "And I'm coming for Cort," he finished, his voice filled with malice.

She stood stone still, caged by the change of events. Words. She reached for any words that could alter the course of this derailing train of a mission.

"No, Adam," she admonished. "It's my operation, my target. I'll dispose of him by tonight and you and the team can take care of the rest." She felt weak from adrenaline and fear by the time she finished talking. She gave in to the feeling, her legs folding as she settled onto the damp sand. Please, let this be the one time Adam would listen to her.

"I'm not going to leave you in harm's way alone, no way! Don't make a move until I get there. There are way too many unknowns. Where are the rest of his bodyguards? And how many are there? What about the man in your report, always lurking in the shadows? It's too dangerous." She could hear the fear in his voice, an ocean away.

"But it's my job to finish this, Adam." She had to convince him of her abilities and get him to back off. "I've never failed at a mission. I can't just sit back and wait for you to do my job for me."

"The fuck you can't," he argued, sounding scared and angry. "You are not expendable Evera, at least not to me. The thought of something happening to you..." he said, searching for words. "I couldn't live through that," his voice raw and full of pain.

"But Garrison—" she continued.

"Forget Garrison!" he growled. "Garrison and his fucking ego are going to get you killed."

She sighed loudly when what she really wanted to do was cry. Adam was coming and there was nothing she could do to stop him.

"Please, Evera," he begged, his voice softer. "I'll even let you do it and stand outside the door. Just wait for me to get there."

She quickly blocked the image his words were conjuring in her head, feeling genuinely sick. Her only hope was to redirect him without giving him an answer.

"I'm just confused, why is this even happening? If Cort is White, this hit makes no sense." She was reaching. For anything that would get Cort out of this alive.

"We received new intel that clarified a few things about Cort and made it necessary for us to take him out," he informed.

"You mean from the intel I sent?" she questioned, defeated. It seems it would be his entanglement with her, and not his bad business practices, that would put him in the ground.

"No, actually, it was from another source. We intercepted an e-mail from one of the other men attending the meetings in Hawaii," he answered. The background noise from the hub had disappeared suddenly so she could hear him more clearly.

"What did you find out?" she asked.

There was a strange, leaded silence before Adam answered. "Why does it matter, Evera?" he asked. For just a second, she thought she detected something suspect in his voice. She brushed it aside, her guilt was making her paranoid.

"I'm just curious," she explained, carefully choosing her words. "And I can't understand why Garrison would authorize getting rid of someone he's wanted to get his hands on for so long, especially when it's obvious he's White. It just doesn't make sense to me." She worried her line of questioning had come out sounding like a desperate tirade. And she hoped against hope that Adam hadn't picked up on it.

"Cort isn't White, Evera." He said it with such vehemence she was completely taken aback. Cort wasn't White? That had to be a mistake.

"How is that possible?" She couldn't seem to stop herself from questioning him. "He told me he uses aliases and that's why he's stayed anonymous for so long." She couldn't believe what he was saying. "What exactly did the intel reveal about him?"

"That's classified," he answered warily. She felt her stomach drop at his words. What the hell was going on with Adam?

"Classified even to me?" she asked in disbelief.

"Yes, even to you," he admitted.

She didn't believe him. Not after Garrison had made it clear this mission was closed to everyone but the two of them. Why was he lying?

"Adam, what are you doing?" she asked softly.

"What am I doing?" She could hear the seething anger in his voice. "I'm doing my fucking job, that's what I'm doing. One of the phone conversations we eavesdropped on had to do with you. About how obsessed Cort has become with the woman he's been in bed with for the last three days."

Something cold and unpleasant curled in her stomach. Making her wonder if there really was any information in an e-mail regarding Cort or if Adam was fabricating intel so he could take matters into his own hands. She kept her tone composed as she answered him. "What does that have to do with the intel you can't give me?"

Adam breathed frustration into the phone. "Evera, did you just hear what I said? He's obsessed with you. He's never going to let you walk away. Between the threat to you and the e-mail, Cort is going down," he ended fiercely.

They were a world apart and somehow Evera could still feel him; and not just his fear for her, but his suspicion. She hated herself.

"Okay, Adam," she conceded. "I'll wait for you."

He exhaled loudly in relief. "Good," he added, as though her words were the remedy he needed. "We'll do it tomorrow, together."

"Together," she added. Her feelings of fear and powerlessness were poised, ready to pounce on her the second she hung up the phone.

"I miss you," he murmured. "So much..."

"I miss you too, Adam," she breathed, biting her lip. It was the truth, and it was a monumental lie.

"See you tomorrow," he added, before the line thankfully went silent.

She sat in the sand, holding the dead phone, numb to the world. Adam had sounded appeased but she'd known him too long to buy his calm disposition when he hung up. His suspicions were correct, and he knew it. Because of her, he was hurting. Badly.

Cort was next in line. She had no idea how to say good-bye. Or how to make sure he avoided the reaper that would be coming to his door in the morning. Or how to make sure Adam didn't somehow end up in the crossfire.

Looking down at her shaking hands and her folded legs she felt disconnected, as if this body and the terrible things it was capable of was no longer hers; transformed, somehow, over the last hours into a living monster, a succubus. Draining the life and sustenance from both the men she loved until they were empty and wasted.

Heaven she didn't buy, but for now she believed in hell. Because she had just damned them all.

CHAPTER 17

Leaving

She watched as the surf crashed against the shore not ten feet from where she sat. The sun was blazing into her face as it set but she barely noticed. Hours seemed to have passed her by in a catatonic haze. It was time to move. As she got up from the sand she noticed the stiffness in her knees from sitting cross-legged for so long. Making her way slowly back towards the resort, she tried not to let the despair weigh her down.

Walking towards the rooms she couldn't help but feel the unwelcome pull towards Cort's room. She tried hard not to slow her pace as she passed by, but she could still hear his muffled voice on the other side of the door. Sexy and low, his accent making it all the more appealing. Her heart burned painfully in her chest.

She rushed to her room, closing the door firmly and paced to the bed. She sat down stiffly, every muscle in her body coiled tight; a snake waiting unwillingly to strike. The clock read 6:37. Twenty minutes, twenty minutes until she faced him with her cruel intentions.

As seven o'clock ticked relentlessly closer she put on the only dress left in her bag, a silk organza strapless mini. It was close fitting, hiding nothing—the perfect lure, and completely the wrong dress to break someone in.

Looking herself over in the bathroom mirror she avoided her eyes as she mechanically applied her makeup. Smoothing her hands over the silky fabric of her dress, she concentrated on the shade; black, the color of mourning. It suited her mood. Throwing on her necklace and black sandals, she grabbed her purse and headed out the door.

She made her way around the building, her feet heavy as though she were back at the beach, wading with effort through the ocean. Her hands were sweaty and agitated by the time she rounded the corner of the resort and looked towards the bar. Her nerve slipping away like water through her fingers. She was just about to concede defeat and retreat to her room, when she spotted him, leaning invitingly against the bar.

Her heart pounded in her throat when she saw him. He hadn't seen her yet and was speaking with the bartender. He was wearing a crisp navy blue shirt, just a shade darker than his eyes. It was tailored to fit him perfectly so that even from this distance she could see the shape of his body. Again, he had that five o'clock sexy stubble lining his chin and jaw. But it was his hand that distracted her the most. He was running his finger along his bottom lip as he contemplated his drink and all she could think of was how badly she wanted it to be her lips, and not his finger, brushing against his mouth.

Making her way to the bar slowly, she never took her eyes off him. Then he turned suddenly to look in her direction, their eyes colliding.

In that moment, everything inside her came undone. And all her plans to tell him it was over and finally let him go, burned to ash in the fiery gaze between them.

He was walking towards her before she could convince her feet to move another step, his glance travelling over her seductively from head to toe. As he closed in on her it felt as though her heart had ceased beating, his eyes paralyzing her. He paused wordlessly in front of her, waiting for a reaction. But she was frozen, her mind polluted by the nearness of his face and body. Mercifully, his hand reached for hers and she looked down, surprised sparks weren't visible between their entwined fingers. She felt love and passion radiating off of him in a sultry wave that wrapped around her. She was lost to him; a foregone conclusion and she knew it.

He led her to a secluded table for two, far from the dance floor. At the same moment he pulled her chair out she felt her phone vibrate in her purse, as if to remind her who he really was. Still a mark. Forbidden fruit. But right now, watching as he sat across from her sexy and beautiful, she was willing to sell her soul for just one last bite.

He smiled tentatively at her. "I ordered us a bottle of white wine to start, I hope you don't mind?" he asked.

"Not at all," she smiled back, grateful that as usual he had anticipated her wants. The idea of a calming glass of wine was incredibly appealing to her racing heart and head. Her mind frantic with too many unknowns, she needed a diversion and a foolproof plan fast.

Cort leaned forward on his elbows, moving his face closer to hers. "So, how was the rest of your afternoon?" he asked.

She decided to steal his line from two days ago. "Long," she answered, and gave him a weak smile. How could she be expected to think about a new and calculating course of action with his face and mouth so close to her? He appeared calm as he watched her but she could feel his apprehension.

"And how was yours?" she asked in return.

"Distracting," he confessed. "I'm not sure of half the things I said or did this afternoon. All I could think about was you."

The waiter arrived with their bottle of wine, giving her a reprieve from having to add anything to what he'd just said. She had no clue how to organize her words into a good-bye. And she had to let him go. She just needed to make sure he would make it out alive after she did it.

As soon as the waiter left Cort pulled his chair around so they were sitting close together. Her heart rate kicked up at his nearness. He put his arm along the back of her chair, his fingers brushing her shoulder while he reached his other hand under the table to rest on her leg. She held her breath, the heat from his hand was burning through her dress as if there was no fabric between them.

"This is much more difficult than I thought it would be," he added, sounding frustrated with himself.

She looked at him inquisitively.

He smiled without humor. "I promised myself I wouldn't rush you and give you space. But here I am, already my patience beyond my limits and now I can't seem to keep my hands off you."

"I don't mind," she said provocatively, the words slipping out before she realized she had said them. How she wanted him to put his hands on her.

His eyes blue fire, he leaned in…and then her phone started to ring. The sound surprised her and made her unintentionally look down, stopping his lips from meeting hers.

She looked up at him apologetically, as he sat up straighter in his chair, the air between them chilled after the heat from their almost embrace. He looked unfazed, his eyes calm, but she could feel the tension emanating off him. A tension was also weaving its way through her, reminding her that she was running out of time, fast. She pushed aside the misfortune of her lips being deprived of one last kiss and steeled herself against what she was about to do.

"Cort...I can't put this off any longer," she bit her lip, unable to stop herself. "But before I give you my answer I want you to know that I never intended to fall—" and then her phone was ringing again. *Fuck!*

"I don't need to get that now," she redirected, hoping to continue her speech and not have to start over.

"No, please go ahead," he said, gesturing to the source of the ringing. She could feel a hint of jealousy lacing its way through his emotions. "That's the third time you've looked down at your purse, so by all means," he encouraged.

She was surprised and irritated with herself. He'd noticed her minor preoccupation with her phone even though she hadn't. The sound had stopped and she felt torn as to whether or not she should check it.

"No, its fine," she said, not wanting to cause more agitation between them.

"Evera, I insist," he said quietly. His words were genuine despite the distress she could feel in him. "I have to check some of my messages as well. I..." he paused, his teeth grazing his full bottom lip in contemplation and then continued. "I have a private plane departing tomorrow morning at 8:00. I should make sure all of the corresponding details are in place. Why don't I head over to the bar and join you back here in a few minutes." He was already rising out of his seat. Leaning down, he kissed her bare shoulder and then walked away.

White hot relief spilled down her limbs. He was ready to leave in the morning. She looked up at the tropical night sky and thanked her lucky stars. And so far the Section had no idea. If Adam and his team weren't arriving until sometime between 8:00 and 9:00, Cort would already be gone.

Her eyes followed his tall, lean body as he made his way smoothly to the bar, her shoulder still tingling from the touch of his lips. Now that she knew he was safe, she needed to finish her speech and let him go.

But first she had to deal with whatever was behind the persistent phone calls. The fact that there were two in a row left her stomach tight; fingers fumbling, she pulled her cell from her purse. The text and two missed phone calls were all from Adam. Her stomach went from tight to a strangling knot.

She took a quick peek at the bar where Cort was standing as she started to dial. Evera couldn't help but notice the voluptuous brunette standing next to him, eyeing him explicitly. Irritated, she tried to concentrate on her phone call.

She dialed and Adam picked up immediately.

"What's going on Adam?" She kept her voice low, wishing that just this once the news wouldn't be dire.

"We have a problem and I'm going to need you to do some digging for me," he hedged, sounding anxious.

"Okay, what do you need?" she asked, hoping she sounded willing despite her apprehension.

"I need you to find out if Cort has a flight booked out of Hawaii tomorrow. He cancelled his private plane for the afternoon to Kauai. Which means he's bailing on the two o'clock meeting tomorrow just like we suspected. I'd like to head out on a flight right now but Garrison doesn't want me jumping the gun and losing out on information from the other men waiting for the meeting. But we're cutting it close if his flight is early. And I'm still not okay with you taking him out without me to back you." He sounded desperate, afraid for her.

"I'm having dinner with him now. He's just stepped away to deal with some business," her tone conspiratorial. "I'll do some fishing when he gets back," she promised, keeping his early morning flight plan to herself.

"Great," he said, his voice sounding relieved at her willingness to help out. "I'll keep digging on my end as well. I'll text you the minute I find out anything and you'll need to do the same if we're going to make the timelines work."

"I'll get back to you if I learn anything," she insisted, taking a quick glance at the bar. The dark-haired woman was making her play for Cort and being less than discreet about it. Evera's hand clenched into a fist in her lap. "I have to go Adam," she said hurriedly, "he's coming." Her lie came effortlessly off her lips despite her unease.

"Watch your back, Evera," he warned, as he hung up.

She glared poison at the curvy brunette as she tossed her hair and shifted in front of Cort, blocking Evera's view. Her anger evaporated slowly into sorrow as the reality of their relationship sank in. What difference did it make? Once she left, there would eventually be someone else to take her place.

She needed to hold it together just a while longer for Cort's sake. If she could just keep Adam in the dark about the flight for another few hours then it would be too late for him to make it in time to get to Cort. But enough time for her to watch him walk away. She looked back at the bar and saw him graciously turn down the woman and push past her. He smiled at Evera, noticeably pleased that she was off the phone.

He walked towards her, his moves stealthy and powerful, and she realized how completely she was in love with him. Her connection to him throbbed in pain at the idea of being ripped from him. Reaching for her wine glass, she quickly drank half of it as he took his seat close beside her. He looked her over furtively and then reached for her hand.

"Are you alright?" he asked softly, worry lining his brow.

The selflessness of his touch and his voice made a lump grow in her throat. Even now, on the cusp of a broken heart, all he could think about was her.

She cleared her throat and forced a smile. "I'm fine," she said, the insincerity in her voice noticeable even to her.

He looked instantly distraught. "I'm so sorry, Evera," he lamented. He reached to tenderly stroke her hair. She felt suddenly contrite that she had allowed him to witness her sorrow. "I'm pushing you, asking too much of you in such a short time. Forgive me, there's no rush," he said, his smile gentle. How like him to blame himself for her self-inflicted feelings of misery.

"I can postpone the flight for another day if you want some more time. I assure you its fine, whatever you need," he said.

Acid flowed into her stomach at his words. "No," she fired, much too loudly for their quiet surroundings.

He looked startled at the fierceness of her reply. She breathed in and out consciously, trying to hide her distress. He had no idea how exactly *unfine* one more day would be to his existence.

"I mean, that's not necessary," she corrected, as calmly as she could force her words to remain.

Awareness seemed to pass across his features and for a moment she could see agony in his eyes. Then he rearranged his face into a calm mask, but the anguish he felt inside was still there, cutting into her. He had left her the perfect segue to continue, but already she was spiraling down from the pain she was about to cause him. Unable to stop herself she ripped her eyes from his, afraid he would read all the lies and deceit swimming in hers, and anchored herself for the delivering blow. But he grabbed her chin, compelling her to look at him.

"Whatever it is you're struggling with, Evera, don't make it about me," he began. "What I mean is, make the decision that's best for you. It's your life and your choice and whatever you decide it's you who has to live with the consequences. You can't worry about hurting me." He looked sad when he said the words, as though he already knew her answer. But despite his sadness, he radiated determination. Like her, he didn't want or need anyone's pity.

"And if it's in regards to your current relationship," he continued, his eyes going a darker shade of blue, "you know that doesn't matter to me. I don't even care if you're married. I want out of my life, and I want you with me. It took finding you to make me realize how much I want this," he said, unbending resolve in his fierce gaze. "But I will leave and disappear with or without you."

It would be without her. Her throat constricted painfully and she wondered if, for the first time in a decade, she would finally cry.

"But I don't want to talk about this anymore, not right now," he insisted, changing course as he moved in.

"Okay," she agreed, swallowing the lump in her throat. Her body falling weak now that his face and lips were back, so close to hers. "What should we talk about?" she asked, her mind going blank as his warm breath brushed across her face.

"Right now?" he asked, as he reached to hold her face. "Nothing..." And then he drove his fingers into her hair as his lips came down hot against hers. His kiss echoed down the length of her body, undermining any strength she had to resist him. He started pulling away much too soon. The kiss a few drops of rain against the heat of her burning desire for him.

"Alright," he said breathlessly, his lips still so close they brushed against hers as he spoke. "Now it's time for me to go," he surrendered, his eyes guarded as he rose from his seat. He left a room card on the table by her hand. "I'll wait up for you. Just stop by when you're ready," and then he was walking away from her and out of the courtyard, leaving her submerged in the memory of their last kiss.

She waited until he was out of sight, and then drained what was left in her wineglass in one swift drink. She could no longer put off the inevitable, it wasn't fair to either of them. She would wait ten more minutes and then bring back his room card along with her good-bye.

Her only consolation was her deception. This woman Cort thought he was in love with didn't exist. Jezebel, with all of her confidence, wit and beauty, was just a figment of both of their imaginations.

Absentmindedly, she rifled through her purse, looking for a distraction for the next ten minutes. She paused as she lifted her phone, a missed text showing from Garrison.

'I need confirmation on taking out our dinner guest ASAP. We just received information that he's departing at 8:00 a.m. If the other party guests in Hawaii catch wind of his early departure or of the entourage we have arriving in the morning, the consequences could be disastrous for everyone involved.'

She stared for a heartbeat at the screen, and then her insides turned weak and boneless as she fought the urge to rest her forehead on the table. "This can't be happening! This can't fucking be happening!" she hissed. Scanning around her, she noticed the dance floor was filling, and the noise from the pounding music and the crowd had drowned out her tirade.

It was a deadlock. No matter what she chose, someone would die. If she told Cort the truth, admitted who she was and begged him to leave, it wouldn't save the team that was due to arrive in the morning. There was no way Cort would leave his colleagues to be obliterated. He would alert them and they would ambush Adam and everyone else coming to take them out. And she knew Cort well enough to know it wouldn't come to that. He would never run from a fight he knew was coming. No loose ends.

And if she did nothing, told Cort nothing, Adam would be there in the morning to do what she couldn't. What she should be doing herself.

She straightened up against the chair, her shoulders still caving with the weight of her dilemma. This was all her fault. She had complicated a situation that was inherently simple. Simple until she had fallen for her mark.

But what if she hadn't fallen? She would already be finished and on a plane back to New York. More importantly, her feelings didn't matter, as she'd already reminded herself, none of this was real. She had no choice left. None. Her heart felt sliced down the middle.

None of this is real, she chanted. She knew what she had to do.

*****

She waited until she hit the edge of the shadows by the side of building. Then she paused and unclipped her bracelet, stringing out the wire, the imperceptible sound searing her insides. She ignored the pain, retracting the garrote and wrapping the bracelet back in place.

Closing her eyes she tried to breathe her heart rate back into a normal rhythm, keeping her adrenaline in check until she needed it. She could do this. She'd already smothered what she could of her feelings for him, sealed them away in her sad and broken memory bank.

It was time to move. She glanced behind her, most of the guests were dancing or drinking at the bar. No one was heading in her direction, but it didn't matter anyways; she would wait until he invited her inside.

Walking casually to the corner she hesitated, hearing voices around the other side. She picked out Cort's accent and lush voice immediately.

"I understand your concerns, Jack, but I promised them me and me alone. If they don't get what I promised things could get messy," she heard him explain.

"I just don't think the end result is worth the risk," his bodyguard countered.

"It is for me. She's worth it. Worth risking everything for," he rasped.

His words whipped around the corner, threatening her willpower. Her adrenaline was pumping now, making her desperate to move towards him, to what end she had no idea.

She pushed off the building and walked around the corner, hoping she had enough Jezebel left in her to reinforce what she needed to do. Both men spotted her at once, pausing in mid conversation.

Cort reached to pat his bodyguard on the shoulder, his eyes melting into hers. "As early as possible," he murmured, as the grey-haired man walked away leaving them alone. His eyes were fixated on her, questioning.

She resisted the pull to glance at her bracelet, the feather lightness of it a contradiction, because at this moment it had the weight of concrete.

Cort was standing with his back against the closed door to his room, his rugged face and hard body calling to her. She walked irresistibly towards him, her breathing shallow and her heart pounding.

The closer she got the more his feelings spiraled around her, drawing her into him like the pull of a hurricane. Love, sex, lust—needful and greedy—an insatiable storm. Her hands, with a will entirely of their own, reached up and grabbed onto his collar. His arms circled her waist, pulling her tight and spinning her, shoving her back against the door. Their eyes locked into a fevered battle as they breathed into each other, their lips only seconds apart. She yanked on his collar, crashing her mouth into his and molding her body around him. His arms strained her closer, making her ribs ache, but still she wanted him to hold her tighter.

His lips, hungry and devastating against hers, finally broke her. She gave one piercing sob against his mouth and then pushed him away, running for the beach. She could hear him calling her name behind her but she didn't stop. Not until she felt the sand break free beneath her feet.

Tossing her sandals aside she slung her purse over her neck and looked back to make sure Cort wasn't following her. She was alone...and she had failed.

Overcome, she waded out into the water as far as the hem of her dress. The surface water was warm but the deeper she went the colder it got. She welcomed the chill of it, letting it clear her mind from the heat between her and Cort.

For just a moment she wanted to keep walking. Escape everyone and everything. She felt like she'd spent her whole life running away from things; it had become her only way to survive, to stay in one piece. But she was tired of running.

Her lips were still burning from the heat and urgency of Cort's kiss. She could admit that his feelings for her weren't real, but that didn't change how she felt about him. She had to save him. And Adam. One way or another, she had to get them through this.

There had to be a way. A direction she hadn't considered. She stilled herself in the water and deliberated.

A design was suddenly forming itself. A horrible but logical idea. Thinking through every angle, she could see no flaw. It would work, she could feel it.

She would have to choose Cort.

Take him up on his offer and leave with him in the morning. If she asked him to leave early she knew he would accommodate her without question. Adam would never come for him if he thought there was any chance of her getting caught in the crossfire. It was a solid plan.

She felt suddenly sick and scared. Could she really leave behind the only life she knew? She tried to think through another solution but there was no other way. And no time left.

A sharp, stabbing pain tore its way through her heart. Her intention of using Adam's unconditional love against him made her feel villainous. With a heavy hand she reached into her purse and pulled out her phone. Before she could dial her entire body started to tremble, knowing it had nothing to do with the frigid water. It was the knowledge that giving up Adam would demolish her, leaving her scarred for the rest of her life.

But she couldn't think about herself now, she needed to act fast before he left. Her teeth started chattering as the phone rang, her body anticipating the pain that was about to come. He answered as the end of the first ring reverberated through her, the sound a prelude to the heartbreak he had no idea was coming.

"Evera," he breathed in relief. The sound of his sweet, familiar voice pierced through her like a thousand knives. She paused, seeming unable to force his name past her desiccated throat.

"Adam," she scratched out painfully. Even she could hear the finality and despair in her one word.

"What's wrong?" he asked, his concern making everything that much harder. "Are you alright?"

"Physically I'm fine, so don't worry about that," she said, biting her lip.

"Good," he sighed in relief. "You got Garrison's text, I assume. Cort's leaving tomorrow morning at 8:00, which means we're really cutting it close. I'm on my way to the airport now." She could hear the anxiety creeping into his words as he spoke, knowing he might not make it there in time to back her up.

She took a deep breath. "I know," she said with quiet detachment, hoping the tenor of her words would sink in before she had to explain.

There was a long silence before Adam spoke. "What do you mean you know? As in you read the text and know or are you trying to tell me something else, Evera?" His voice was starting to shake by the time he finished speaking.

God dammit! She wanted to scream as she looked towards the night sky, cursing whatever divinity was out there.

She didn't answer, giving herself away.

"You knew," he demanded harshly.

"Yes," she said, forcing her voice to come out stronger than she felt.

"Why didn't you tell me?" he asked, his voice incredulous. "You know what, you don't need to answer." He sounded beaten, as if he already knew the answer. "It's to protect him. You're going to try and make sure he gets away. You know I can't let that happen."

He was on the right track but it was just the tip of the iceberg, the words she was holding beneath the surface were waiting to crush him.

"Yes," she said, taking a breath of courage. "But he won't be going alone. I'm leaving with him," she finished, and closed her eyes against her own pain.

"No!" It was just one word but he delivered it savagely. "You are not going with him," his voice rising as he spoke.

"Adam—" she tried to plead with him, but he interrupted her.

"Don't," he murmured. She could hear his tortured breathing on the other end of the line. She waited impatiently for what seemed like an eternity, hoping he would say something—tell her he hated her, call her names—anything but this interminable silence. Just before she was sure she couldn't wait another second for him to speak, he drew in an unsteady breath.

"Why?" he pleaded, his voice anguish.

He deserved some kind of explanation. The one explanation that would hopefully make him let her go. In essence it was the truth. The only truth amongst a mountain of lies and deceit.

"I love him," she whispered, her words an apology. It was the first time in her life she had ever said the words out loud. The very words she had never spoken to him. The impact of them was solidifying.

"You love him?" he whispered in disbelief. "How, can you love him?" His pain and confusion reached through the phone and shook her.

It seemed unbelievable even to her. "I don't know how it happened, Adam, but it did. I can't let you hurt him."

"Hurt him!" he roared. "I don't want to hurt him. I want him dead. I want him shredded at my feet."

"Stop, Adam," she pleaded. Maybe her plan wasn't as foolproof as she thought. Not if it meant Adam would still come for Cort.

"How can you be so naive? This isn't love, Evera. It's been three days. It's infatuation and nothing more. He's playing you and I can't believe you're blind to it."

"That's not true," she returned.

"He's a vile murderer. He's ruthless and cruel, and he has no respect for life other than his own. He's the epitome of why we do what we do. He's our enemy. He's your enemy."

"We're all murderers, Adam," she reminded him.

"Do not justify him so lightly to me. I've been tracking his wake of bodies for three fucking years. Why am I telling you any of this? These are things you already know—know but don't matter to you anymore," he said dejectedly.

"We're more than what the Section has made us into. I'm not just Jezebel any more than you're just their weapon. And Cort is so much more than just his bio," she said, defending him. She instantly regretted it. Adam would not be interested in her making Cort appear in any good light.

It would be better if he hated her. Easier for him to get over her.

"Why him?" he begged. "If it was anyone else, someone good, someone I could trust to keep you safe and make you happy..." he couldn't finish.

She searched for something to say to get him to understand... but there was nothing left but good-bye.

"I have to go, Adam," she finished. She tried to make her voice sound sure and cold but she was too upset.

"Please, Evera," he said, sounding so distraught it made her sick to her stomach. "Don't do this."

His pain ripped through her. Her resolve wavered and her heart started questioning her decision. But it was too late, she reminded herself. She'd made her choice and now she had to play it out.

"You deserve so much more than what I can give you, Adam, and we both know it. It's been ten years and we haven't been able to make it work. It's time to face that we're just not meant to be together." Fire torched her heart as she said the words.

"I don't believe that," he said, speaking quickly. "For ten years I've been in love with you. Ten years of waiting for you and wanting you. I'd wait a thousand if I had too. My heart is yours," he promised, his voice overflowing with pain and desperation.

She had always thought the same thing. That he was meant for her. But if that was really true she never would have fallen for Cort. It was her that needed to let go.

"I doesn't matter, Adam, it's over," she answered, trying to infuse a chill into her words. She bit her lip against her *sorry*. Finally, when she could say it, she knew she shouldn't. He would take it as a sign of her uncertainty.

"But it's not over, Evera," he reminded. "Do you really think Garrison is just going to let this go? Or Jonas?" His words struck a chord.

"When he gets back and finds out what you've done he'll consider it a personal betrayal. Then it won't just be Cort he's hunting for but both of you," he said ominously.

She had expected there to be fallout from her decision but she hadn't considered how far the destruction would reach. She'd been so worried about Adam, the rest of the people she was betraying seemed inconsequential. Both Garrison and Jonas. And Garrison was even more of a worry than Jonas right now. Garrison had no love for anyone at the Section but himself. And she was about to ruin the biggest takedown of his career.

But this was the elusive Cort they were after. He had evaded them for three years, which meant he was good.

"Jonas won't find us," she said, assuredly.

"I could find you, Evera," he said, his words a warning. They made the blood boil beneath her skin.

"So what are you saying, Adam? Either I come back or you'll help Jonas find us? Do you really want me dead?" The idea pained her more than she could have ever imagined. She knew he'd be hurt and angry, but not once did the thought that he'd want her harmed come to mind.

"No," he said, sounding hurt. "That's not what I mean. I'm saying that if I could find you so could Jonas. If he chooses to focus all his efforts on both of you there's no way to be sure you can escape him."

She breathed a silent sigh of relief. She was sure that without Adam helping Jonas, she could disappear with Cort forever. She felt terrible accusing him of giving her up to the Section.

"Whatever happens between us, Evera, you have to know I'd never hurt you. I love you, no matter what," he said quietly, his voice full of an aching sadness she could feel through the phone. And there it was, the internal sound of her heart shattering along with his.

"Good-bye, Adam," she managed to choke out before her throat closed off from the pain.

"Please, Evera, don't go," he begged.

She slid the phone from her ear and hung up before he could say another word.

She stood in the frigid water gasping in sorrow and pain. Adam—she would never see him again.

Suddenly, the phone in her hand was ringing. The sound trampled her heart and echoed across the sea, breaking the silence. She stared out into the infinite blue where the ocean met the midnight horizon. She longed to answer just to hear his voice one last time.

Instead, she closed her eyes, pulled back her arm and flung the phone as far as she could into the dark night sky.

Somewhere in the distance she could hear a splash as the phone hit the water and sank into oblivion.

*****

Evera stood outside Cort's hotel room, still chilled from standing in the crisp ocean water for so long but the numb feeling in her limbs was finally gone.

Her mind kept trying to return to her emotional breakdown after she threw her phone away, but she was good at blocking out tragedy. Biting her lip, she swallowed her grief and slid the card into the door lock.

The room was quiet when she walked in. She could see Cort's body curled up on the bed, his back towards her. She peeked over his shoulder to look at his sleeping face. Even in sleep he looked unsettled. Sympathy cut through her insides as she remembered their last kiss…and then her bolting. He must have believed she was never coming back to him.

His hands were outstretched and she could see that he had fallen asleep while holding something. She recognized the cover of the book. Her *Jane Eyre* novel. She'd forgotten it earlier in the afternoon. She removed it slowly so as not to wake him. Keeping his page, she looked at where he was. He had read several chapters while waiting.

Warmth spread through her, easing some of the pain from her heart and her mind. She knew she could push past the last hour, the last decade, her entire past, and start anew with him. Even though she was a fraud. She bit back her self-hate and took comfort in the fact that both the men she loved would be safe. She would tell Cort she was coming with him but that they needed to leave a couple hours earlier. She knew he wouldn't press for an explanation. That is, if he still wanted her after the way she had left him in limbo.

She watched him as he slept. Even though she was in pain, a part of her was filled with joy and disbelief at how things had turned out. She would get to stay with him. Her hand reached automatically to touch his arm and he stirred.

"Evera," he breathed, his voice surprised and cautious. He turned towards her and she could feel his eyes move over her face, as if he was memorizing every line, every angle. "I wasn't sure if you were coming back." He forced a tired smile across his full lips. "I'm sorry I fell asleep, I meant to wait up for you, just in case," he said, propping himself up on his elbow.

"It's fine," she said quietly, moving to sit beside him on the bed, searching out his eyes. "About earlier, when I came to see you and then I...left." Ran, fled, freaked out.

"You don't have to explain, really." He looked down at her hands and the book she was holding. "Thanks for keeping my page," he said warily.

"You were reading this?" she questioned.

"It's your favorite book." He looked in her eyes, probing, waiting for her to say something more. Everything he felt for her was exposed, she didn't need her sixth sense to know exactly what he was feeling.

"It must have been pretty exciting reading," she lightly teased and waved the book at him.

He smiled back. A sleepy, sexy smile that made her insides ache. His hair was disheveled from his slumber and his shirt unbuttoned down the front.

"Actually," he said seriously, "it's much better than I thought it would be. I can't wait to see how it ends. Is it a happy ending?" he questioned, looking at her pointedly. His eyes were boring into hers as if he was trying to read the answer he was looking for in them.

She reached to touch his face and his hand came up to cover hers, holding it tight against his cheek. He closed his eyes and seemed to hold his breath in anticipation.

"It's a happy ending," she said softly.

His eyes opened, blue flames burning into hers.

"You're coming with me?" he asked, his voice incredulous.

"I am," she said, "That is, if you still want me and all my baggage. And we need to leave an hour earlier on the flight. I hope that's not a problem?"

He didn't reply. His hand reached swiftly behind her head as he pulled her lips to his, kissing her with a fervor that left her breathless. When he finally released her lips he touched her face, and affixed her with a forever look in his eyes.

Pulling her hastily onto the bed, he rolled her beneath him. "If I'm still asleep and dreaming I hope I never wake up," he said, his voice rough and raw. And then he kissed her again, this time with no sign of stopping.

For the first time in her life Evera could finally see a way out.

Cort's feelings of love for her were so strong they crashed over her like a wave pulling her under. She wrapped herself around him, body and soul, and welcomed the drowning.

CHAPTER 18

Unravelling

Evera finally relaxed against the soft leather of the backseat as the car pulled out onto the interstate and away from the city. She leaned her head more comfortably against Cort's shoulder and resisted the urge to breathe an audible sigh of relief. She'd been a jumble of nerves since they'd left the resort this morning.

They spent the night together followed by Cort waking her at five o'clock in the morning with a steaming cup of coffee in bed.

The whole time she packed she kept watching the clock and windows. When she walked back to her room to gather the rest of her belongings she resisted the urge to detour to the parking lot. She had wanted to scour the area just to be sure no one from the Section had miraculously made it there in time to ambush them. But she'd spotted Cort's ever-present bodyguard waiting just past the pool by the hedge, leaning against the black Audi she'd ridden in the other day.

When she'd finished gathering the last of her things from the bathroom she had stood and examined herself in the mirror. This would be the last time she would look upon herself as Jezebel. Her emotions were a myriad of fear and anticipation; fear at leaving behind everything familiar and anticipation of a new life with Cort.

She'd contemplated ridding herself of anything linking her to her past but she couldn't bear to part with her locket. It was a part of her.

Running her hand over the cold metal of her bracelet she reached to release the clasp and leave it behind. But her fingers wouldn't move to undo it. Something inside her fluttered sickly. Just a little bit longer, just in case, she reasoned.

When they arrived at the airport her anxiety had climbed as she picked through the crowds, looking for familiar faces, but they made it through without incident.

Once they were comfortably seated in his private plane and belted in for liftoff, Cort handed her a cell phone. "I noticed you didn't have yours anymore when we went through customs so I thought you could use a new one," he said smiling sympathetically. She smiled back, hiding any pain the memory of that last moment on her phone had caused. As usual, he seemed to know not to ask her anything further.

They spent most of the long flight sleeping, tucked close together under a blanket. Cort mentioned, after waking from their long nap, that they had another couple hours to go so they watched a movie. Near the end of the movie Cort let her know they would be landing in New York in about half an hour. Apprehension flowed through her veins at his revelation. Of all the places, why did it have to be New York? So close to the Section headquarters in Virginia and the source destination of so many operatives' missions. Not to mention, if either Jonas or Garrison caught wind of Cort's flight path now they would be close enough to intercept them at the airport.

But they landed without any trace of a not-so-welcoming party. Cort's driver was shrewd and knew all the back roads that afforded them escaping the city limits faster than Evera would have thought possible.

And now that they were speeding down the highway, away from New York City, Evera found her anxiety melting into real excitement.

Cort rubbed her shoulder as they looked out the windows and watched as the green trees of the boulevard passed them by.

"You're so quiet?" he questioned. "What, no curiosity as to where we're going?" She looked up at him and saw that he was smiling down at her, a teasing gleam in his eyes.

She laughed softly, releasing the last of the tension she had about being caught. She supposed she should have questioned him but she'd been so preoccupied about making it out untouched it hadn't really crossed her mind. Besides, she trusted him. She knew that whatever he had planned she would be fine with.

"I guess I just thought you'd let me know when it was time." She resisted saying when it was safe, but she was sure he understood what she meant.

"It's time and don't worry, Evera, we're safe now," he said gently. "No one knows where I am. I covered my tracks well," he replied, his confidence reassuring.

"Alright then," she said, her excitement building. "Where are we going?"

His eyes beamed as he registered the excitement in her voice. "Well, tonight is just a stopover before we leave tomorrow afternoon for Italy," he said, watching for her reaction to his words.

Italy! She was ecstatic. She could feel the smile break across her face as he grinned back at her, like two kids who'd just been told they were going to Disneyland.

She reached to hug him tight. "Italy, really? I can't wait," she said. She could feel his joy at how happy he'd just made her. He couldn't have chosen a better place and they both knew it. He was doing this for her, his selflessness endless. Starting over in Italy with Cort by her side. She couldn't believe her good fortune. Maybe the cosmos had decided she'd suffered enough and was finally going to give her a reprieve. She looked up at him, her gratitude an overwhelming warm feeling spreading through her. She felt hope for the first time in her pathetic, tumultuous life.

"Thank you," her voice breaking, and then she kissed him hard.

He kissed her back, the heat between them building instantly. She hoped their destination wasn't much farther. She couldn't wait to thank him properly.

The car started to slow as the driver made his way over to the side of the shoulder and an obscure side road in the middle of nowhere.

"We're almost there," he said, his words echoing her desperation to get to where they were going.

"Where are we?" she asked as they made their way down a paved path with trees growing close on either side.

"My home," he said softly. "At least my home when I'm here in New York."

She was surprised. She'd always pictured him among the sun-baked landscape of the African savanna. Although, she imagined he probably had several properties scattered throughout the world. She never had a place to call home and now, with the possibility so close, she longed for one.

The driver followed the winding drive through the jade green forest for about a minute, and then suddenly the trees thinned and she could see brilliant sunshine and a wide opening about a quarter of a mile ahead.

They drove under the last of the bowery overhang onto a circular driveway. There was a rustic fountain in the center made of huge stones. The driver circled around and stopped before the steps at the front entrance. She loved the house immediately.

It looked like an old ranch house that had been restored. Although it was only one story it seemed grand with all of its vaults and peaks. She imagined the ceiling inside would be tall and open. It had a massive wraparound porch, complete with a porch swing. Not at all what she had been expecting from Cort.

He scooted out of the backseat. "Just wait," he said excitedly. He walked swiftly around the car to her door, closest to the staircase. He opened her door and wrapped his hand around hers, helping her from the car. She stood staring up at the beautiful house wistfully. Already she didn't want to leave it. It was like being transported back in time to the site of a classic novel.

"What do you think?" he asked. "It's late nineteenth century. I had it restored a couple of years ago. I kept as much of the original interior as possible."

She continued to look up at it; the whitewashed exterior was weathered, which just added to its charm. "I love it," she said. She wanted to go over and sit on the porch swing to see if it was real.

Cort's driver slash bodyguard tried to quickly pass them by with an armful of luggage.

"Jack," Cort said, putting a hand on the guard's arm to stop him from getting away.

He turned to look at Cort, his face surprised.

"This is Evera." He said her name like a song. "Evera, this is Jack."

She didn't know if she should reach to shake his hand which was holding her suitcase. She settled for, "Nice to meet you, Jack," and a smile.

"Nice to meet you too," he said, a puzzled look on his face. "Officially, I mean," he added and a small smile appeared on his lips. And then without another word he turned and made his way up the steps to the front door.

"He's all business," said Cort, shaking his head and watching Jack affectionately as he hauled their bags through the entry.

"I don't mind," said Evera, and she didn't. She understood wanting to get things done and keeping to yourself.

"Speaking of business, I have to take something down to my safe," he said, patting his coat pocket. "Then I can take you on a tour. Do you want to start with the grounds or the house?"

"The grounds," she said excitedly. The day was warm and bright for a New York autumn.

"I'll be right back," he said. He leaned in and kissed her quickly on the temple and then pulled back. She could feel an aura of absolute peace and love surrounding him as he gazed back at her. He gave her a tempting smile and then turned and made his way up the steps and through the front door.

As she watched him go she could feel her own sense of contentment settling in. She breathed in the delicious scents of the warm, green countryside and closed her eyes, holding onto the perfection of the moment.

Cort returned minutes later and as she watched him descend the stairs, her heart felt full to overflowing.

He led her around the corner of the house, showing her the abandoned stables and relaying every piece of history about the house and its surrounding architecture. There were crumbling buildings that used to house the farm workers sleeping quarters and an old worn guesthouse that was somehow still standing.

They made their way to the back of the house and a large patio. It had an outdoor kitchen complete with a double barbecue, a fridge and a small dishwasher. There were two chairs set around a small round table with an umbrella right next to a stone fireplace. Cort led her over to one of the chairs and poured her a glass of wine from a waiting bottle.

"You must be starving, I know I am," he said. "Can I cook you up a steak? Medium rare, right?"

He was already making his way over to the outdoor kitchen area. She could smell something divine cooking on the grill.

"Yes, that sounds great," she said. His staff were discreet and efficient at anticipating Cort's every need. She watched as he grabbed two seasoned steaks from the fridge and lifted the lid of the barbecue. He placed the steaks on the grill beside some shrimp and a pan of potatoes. He removed the shrimp before closing the lid and placed them on a plate, bringing them to her.

They sat quietly, eating shrimp and sipping wine as they looked out over the vast landscape that was his home. She noticed a clearing just beyond the forest in front of them. It was hard to see between the trees but it looked odd, as though it was man-made.

"What's that opening in the trees for?" she asked, pointing about a quarter of a mile in front of where they were sitting.

"That's where they used to bring in the supplies to the house through the cellar," he said. He pointed to the far side of the clearing, closest to the house. "See that little hill. That's actually a dugout with access to the basement. There used to be a railroad track not far from here. Now it's a road, but this place used to be quite the gathering place for the area. That's why I bought it. Some of the locals wanted to tear it down and use it as farmland. I couldn't stand to let such an interesting part of local history go."

This was a new sentimental side of him she'd never seen before. She fell in love with him a little more.

They dined leisurely as they finished the bottle of wine and watched the sun set behind the hills. She noticed a movement behind her, in the house. She turned and saw that the house was lit with soft lighting and candles. She could see right into the kitchen and dining room from where they were sitting. She couldn't wait to see the rest of the house before they had to leave tomorrow afternoon.

With the sun having set, the chill of the early fall evening brought with it a biting wind that was steadily picking up. The weather was changing, a fall storm felt imminent. She shivered despite the heat coming from the fireplace.

"It's getting chilly, lets head in and I can show you the rest of the house."

He wrapped his arm around her as he led her to the open double doors leading to the kitchen. Swiftly he lifted her into his arms and carried her through the open doorway. His lips were moving with hers before she could gasp from the surprise of having her feet swept out from under her.

She'd been imagining kissing him like this since she first woke up this morning. She twined her arms tight around his neck and pulled her body as close as she could to his. But it wasn't close enough. She ached to feel more of him.

He pulled away from her lips quickly, leaving her breathless and deprived. "Do you want to tour the house now or later?" he asked, his breathing ragged.

"Later," she murmured, her sordid need for him shutting down her mind and taking over her body. "Much later," she said and pulled his mouth back to hers, silencing any further conversation.

*****

Evera stretched her legs, the silk of the sheets a sensual feeling against her bare skin. She was thirsty but she didn't want to move from her warm spot snuggled close against Cort's chest. Thirsty, exhausted and blissfully happy. They had spent the night making love over and over. They would fall asleep afterwards only to wake up close together and wanting more.

The only dark cloud hanging over her perfect morning was the meeting he had told her about halfway through the night. It was first thing this morning and he would not be taking her with him; too dangerous he'd said.

Too dangerous for her to come and yet he'd told her not to worry and that he'd be fine. She felt more than fear for him in the pit of her stomach. He'd insisted that he wouldn't chance leaving her if it wasn't absolutely necessary, but it still made her frightened. Now that she had him and a life together so close on her horizon she was terrified that something would go wrong.

She shifted so that she could look up at him. He was sleeping peacefully, his lips slightly parted, his breathing even. This beautiful man now belonged to her.

She wriggled her hand out from between their bodies and rested her palm against his face. She ran her fingers softly down his cheek and across his lips. She continued down his chin and neck to the hard muscles of his chest. Even now, after a night of continuous sex, she couldn't believe how she still wanted him.

He sighed softly in his sleep and began to stir. He opened his lids slowly and looked at her with his sleepy indigo eyes.

She smiled at him. "Good morning," she said seductively, lost in his depthless gaze.

He smiled back at her. "Good morning, indeed," he commented, his voice rough. "That would have to be the biggest understatement I've ever heard," and then he kissed her. A slow, meticulous kiss that set her pulse racing. He groaned against her lips and pulled away, putting space between their heated bodies. He peeked over her shoulder and looked at the clock on the bedside table.

"I have to get up and get going," he said wistfully. He twined his fingers with hers and pulled them to his lips. She could feel his unwillingness to leave the warm bed.

She looked in his eyes and her fear came back tenfold. She desperately did not want him to go to the meeting.

She moved her free hand lower down his body and then wrapped her fingers around him hard. He inhaled sharply. She rolled on top of him, hoping her body would be enough of an enticement to make him change his mind and stay. He opened his mouth to protest but her lips collided with his, stopping whatever words were coming next. She moved her hand up and down on him in the hopes that he would give in to her. He moaned and turned his face to the side breaking their kiss. He shifted his body so that her hand lost its grip on him.

"You're going to make this as difficult as possible, aren't you?" he asked, his breathing labored. She could feel him struggling to hold his ground.

"Absolutely," she said honestly.

He disentangled himself from her and climbed out of the bed. He leaned down and covered her, pinning her wandering hands beneath the quilt, and kissed her on the forehead.

Pulling back, he stared her down. "When we get where we're going I'm going to keep you in bed with me for a week," he threatened, sex in his eyes.

His words made her body ache and she couldn't help but sneak her arm out from under the covers and run her hand down his naked chest to his thighs.

He sucked in a quick breath. "Make it two weeks," he said, his willpower breaking under the touch of her hand.

She reached up, gripping his hair hard, and pulled his mouth back to hers. He gave in for a few seconds and then pulled away again.

"Make it a month," he warned, his voice raw. He backed up so that he was out of her tempting reach.

He looked seriously at her for a moment, the desire fading from his eyes.

"I really do have to go, Evera," he said tenderly. He knew she was afraid for him so he came back and softly brushed the hair from her forehead.

"I'll get through this unscathed, I promise you. And then I can drop the last of my black life at the courier before we board the plane and be done with it. Once I get through this morning it will all be over. But I have to do this for us. I have to get rid of this last bit of information so that it doesn't haunt us for the rest of our lives." She could feel how adamant he was and so she kept her hands to herself.

"Alright," she said, giving in because she didn't want his past hunting them down either. "If you let anything happen to you though, you'll have to deal with me." She laughed to try and lighten the mood but deep down her words terrified her.

"I'll be back in a few hours for you, I promise," he said. He bent to kiss her and then turned and made his way to the ensuite bathroom and adjoining closet. She could hear the water running right away. She knew he had lingered long enough that he would be in a hurry now.

She rolled onto her back, staring up at the ceiling. She let out an exasperated breath and tried to focus on the words he'd said. He had to do this and then everything from his past would be done with and they could both move on. He would be alright, she told herself. He had to. She couldn't imagine going on without him.

She tried to think past the next few hours and focus on the days and weeks and years to come. Those thoughts gave her a sense of impending peace and happiness. She held the thoughts close like the down comforter surrounding her, letting them warm her and keep her calm.

Cort came out about twenty minutes later dressed in a blue striped dress shirt and pressed black pants. He had his suit jacket slung over his arm and was carrying a small bag.

Fear came rushing back as she realized this was it. He was leaving and the next few hours would feel like an eternity until he was back with her, safe and unharmed.

She moved to get out of the bed but he raised a hand towards her. "Don't get up," he said, smiling wryly at her. "If you do I may not leave after all," he hinted, as his eyes lingered at the edge of the comforter barely covering her breasts.

He walked over quickly, dropping down to her level. He grabbed her face in his rough, warm hands. "I will see you..."

he paused and kissed her passionately, "in about two and a half hours." He looked at her tenderly and then released her face, leaving her feeling cold after the heat from his hands.

He turned quickly before passing through the doorway. "I love you," he said, meeting her anxious gaze. And then he walked away without waiting for her reply.

As soon as she heard his footsteps fade down the hall she looked at the clock on the bedside table. It was just before 7:00. He would be back around 9:30. She would hold him to that.

Her body was tired from lack of sleep but she felt much too on edge to go back to sleep. She decided to shower and repack so that she was ready before he came back.

Getting up from the bed she stretched, enjoying the feeling of her muscles and bones lengthening. After last night's activities she was admittedly a bit stiff and sore, like she'd had a really vigorous workout. Which in fact was the case, she thought, grinning to herself.

She walked into the large bathroom and straight to the marble tiled shower. She turned the water to hot and watched as all six jets started spraying water. She looked over at the vanity, wondering if she should quickly brush her teeth while the water heated up, and saw an envelope propped up against the mirror. It had her name on it.

She reached for it and ripped it open.

It was a note from Cort, reminding her that everything would be fine and that breakfast would be waiting for her in the kitchen at 8:00. He also welcomed her to tour the house and go wherever she liked. Lastly, he left her his cell number in case she needed to reach him. His parting line, 'I can't wait to spend the rest of my days....and nights, with you, Cort."

Her throat tightened at his last words. She tucked the letter into her bag and climbed into the shower. And then all she could think about was being with him again. A small part of her couldn't help but feel anxious. This entire time he had been honest with her about who he was. She tried to sort through how much of herself she had given away; it was a lot but she had also kept most of the fucked up side of herself from him.

She finished up in the shower after the jets had unknotted all her muscles. She dressed quickly, the smell of coffee beckoning to her from the kitchen.

Walking down the long hall she couldn't help but appreciate the history of the house. Lining the walls were pictures of the house ranging from the late nineteenth century up to the present. Cort really had tried to keep the original architecture of the house intact. The exterior, minus a few current amenities, was almost identical to the first photographs. She couldn't wait to eat and then wander around until Cort returned.

Entering the kitchen, she was pleasantly assaulted with the smell of coffee, bacon and waffles. There were two middle-aged women dressed in black and white, bustling around the kitchen and filling the dining table so full of platters it looked as though they were expecting company.

Evera suddenly felt shy, not sure if she should greet them.

"Good morning, Miss Dark," said the older of the two. "Please have a seat," she said, gesturing to the massive harvest table laden with the steaming food.

Evera seated herself at the single place setting and watched as the older woman set about filling her plate to overflowing. She resisted the urge to laugh, not wanting to offend her, but she had no idea how she was supposed to eat such a large serving of breakfast.

"Thank you," she said to the woman who was already busy pouring her coffee into a beautiful bone china cup. She set it in front of her beside matching cream and sugar servers.

"Can I get you anything else?" she asked politely.

"No, that's fine," Evera answered. She wasn't accustomed to being waited on in a house.

"Very good," she said, and walked back to the kitchen to join the other woman already tidying up.

Evera dug into her plate. She couldn't tell if it was because she was starving or the food was that good, but the waffles and bacon were some of the best she'd ever tasted. And she surprised herself by managing to get through most of the mountain of food. She had never had a night like last night before and had worked up an appetite.

She finished the last of the bacon on her plate, leaving only a bite of the delicious Belgian waffle, and drained the last of her third cup of coffee.

Taking the napkin from her lap and placing it on the table, she pushed her chair back to get up. Almost instantly the woman that had served her was back, clearing the table and asking if there was anything else she wanted.

"No thanks, I'm full and that was delicious," she said.

"Well then, enjoy your tour of the house. If you have any questions please feel free to ask me, I've been here for quite some time," she said, smiling shyly at Evera.

First she wandered through the vast living room with its rough-hewn stone fireplace, the focal point of the room. She ran her hand along the weathered stone and immediately noticed the ancient clock sitting on the wooden mantel, its hands pointing to just past 8:30.

One hour left. She regretted looking at the clock. An hour suddenly seemed like a lifetime. She reached to fidget with her locket while she made her way aimlessly from room to room. She tried to pay attention to the details in each new space she visited but found it hard to concentrate.

Somewhere, in the back of her mind she was mentally keeping track of the time passing. Unfortunately, she was quite skilled at it, which only made things worse as 9:30 crept closer and closer with still no sign of Cort.

Evera made her way back to Cort's bedroom and checked and rechecked her bag, making sure she hadn't forgot to pack anything. She struggled to stop herself from checking it unnecessarily a third time. Her stress mounting as the sound of the ticking clock on the bedside table seemed to get louder with each passing second. Not being able to help herself from venturing a quick look, she was disappointed to see that it was now 9:45. She sat down on the edge of the bed and shifted between fidgeting with her locket and her bracelet.

She grabbed her phone from her pocket and double-checked that the ringer was on. It was. Her phone also showed that the clock in his room was off by a few minutes and it was actually closer to 10:00.

Fear was setting in and in turn her lungs felt heavy. *Don't freak out,* she cautioned herself. It was only half an hour. In the grand scheme of things what was half an hour?

Her stomach dropped though, as she remembered their conversation from last night. He'd told her the drive was just over an hour each way and that he didn't expect the meeting to take more than twenty minutes at most. That meant that he should already be on his way back. If that was the case, why didn't he call or text to let her know that he was running behind? Especially when he knew how scared she was to have him go in the first place.

She latched and unlatched her bracelet over and over, hoping to distract herself before she had a full blown panic attack. She would give him five more minutes and then she would call him.

Taking her time, she slowly reached down to the outside pocket of her bag and retrieved the letter from this morning that contained Cort's cell number. She set the stopwatch on her phone for five minutes and watched as it counted down.

When the timer read one minute and thirty-three seconds left she couldn't take any more, her hands already starting to shake. She shut it off and switched to her phone, dialing frantically. She misdialed twice, as though in a bad dream, in her desperation to hear his voice. When she finally got the number right and the phone was ringing it was almost 10:05. Three rings. Then five. Then seven and the phone disconnected not going to voicemail.

She sat there holding the phone in her hand, the line dead and her fear beyond comprehension. Her stomach clenched violently and she ran for the toilet, making it just in time as her stomach heaved, giving up most of her breakfast. Her knees against the cold tile floor started shaking. *Get it together!* She berated. Wiping her mouth with the back of her hand, she stood up and went over to the sink. Splashing cold water on her face and down her neck, she toweled off. She searched under the cabinet and found some mouthwash to cleanse the sour taste from her mouth and throat.

Leaning against the counter, bracing herself with her hands, her mind was racing. What now? Something must have gone wrong. There was no other explanation. Or maybe he was just running late and she was overreacting. Or maybe he was in danger. What should she do? She couldn't even go to him, she had no idea where he was.

Jack!

She ran out of the room and down the hall back to the kitchen. The two women still cleaning and cooking turned simultaneously as Evera came bursting into the room.

"Jack," she sputtered. "Can you tell me where Jack is? I need to talk to him immediately."

The older woman, the one who had served her this morning, started walking towards her, picking up on her panic. "Jack's not here," she said as Evera's heart sank. "Is everything okay? Is there anything we can help you with?"

"Is there any way to get ahold of him?" she asked brusquely.

"Um, no," said the woman looking confused. "He left with Cort first thing this morning. I can give you Cort's cell number."

"Thanks, but I've already called it," she said, fear and defeat taking over again.

"Is everything alright?" she asked again, concerned.

"I don't know," she said, as she hurried out of the kitchen, making her way back to Cort's bedroom.

Sitting down on the edge of the bed she went over her options. She could stay here and wait for him, but the idea of staying still and not putting some form of action into play made her agitated just thinking about it. Regardless, she was trapped here waiting. Waiting and hoping he would show up or call. If he didn't, then... but she couldn't think about that. Not yet or she'd fall to pieces.

The bedside table read 10:37, well past an hour late.

Then her phone rang.

"Hello," she said, her voice cracking from the tension.

"Evera!" It was Cort, but the distress and fear in his voice made it barely recognizable.

"Cort," she choked out. "Are you okay? Where are you?" she asked, her words coming out in a rush.

"I'm fine. Just listen to me, we don't have much time," he said, his voice grave. "Things have gone horribly wrong. I'll explain later, but right now I need you to do something for me," he pleaded, frantic.

"Anything," she replied passionately.

"Take only what you can carry and go to the end of the hall, opposite the kitchen. That's the door to the cellar. Go through it and down the stairs. At the far end of the wine racks is another door. It'll be locked, but there's a keypad on the wall. The pass code is Pretoria. Key it in and then hit enter. Make sure you close the door behind you so it locks," he said.

She was already moving, slinging her bag over her shoulder and heading out the door and down the long hall.

"You'll be in the cold storage cellar. There's a safe on the wall, I need you to get me something from it. I'll text you the access codes, it's a three part process with three passwords. I'm texting them to you now," he said. While she waited she could hear highway noise in the background and hoped that meant he was on his way back to the house.

She was almost at the cellar door now.

"There'll be a red memory stick in the safe, take it with you and then close the safe back up. Head to the big metal door at the far end of the room. It's only locked from the outside so just go out and wait for me across the meadow in the trees. Do you remember the clearing you asked me about last night?"

"I remember," she said, focused and determined now that she knew he was okay.

"There's a road right beside the clearing," he said. She pictured the clearing and the road that would run along it.

"Wait for me in the trees beside the road. And Evera," he said vehemently.

"Yes," she answered, as she descended the cellar stairs.

"Do not under any circumstances come out of the trees until you see that it's me. Do you understand?" he demanded.

"I understand," she said, breathless and frightened.

"Only me, alone," he clarified.

But he wouldn't be alone. She would help him. He had no idea what she was capable of.

There was a short break in the connection and then she could hear again. "I have to go, someone's calling on the other line. I'll be there in five minutes. Don't forget what I said. And Evera?" he insisted, his voice like gravel.

"What?" she whispered in fear.

"Whatever happens, I love you," and then the line went dead.

*****

At the end of the cellar was a large medieval looking wooden door. The modern keypad beside it looked out of place in the archaic surroundings. She walked over to the keypad and punched in the word Pretoria. She remembered him talking about the beautiful, bustling city in South Africa.

The door clicked open and with it a rush of cold air came blasting into the room. She hurried through and remembered to pull the door closed behind her.

There was a motion light that went on as soon as she stepped into the cold storage cellar. She immediately spotted the safe on the far wall, not because it stood out and was easy to find. But because the safe door was wide open.

She froze. *Fuck!* Someone was already here.

Still and barely breathing, she tried to taste the air, feel for the emotions of another body in the room. She stayed anchored and silent for so long that the motion light went off. She waited in near darkness, the only light coming from the open safe at the end of the room.

Her mental clock was ticking. Cort could be waiting outside for her any minute. If he showed up and she wasn't there he'd come looking for her. And he couldn't get in from the outside which meant he'd waste time coming through the house. The way he was talking on the phone, whoever was after him was close. They wouldn't have a minute to spare.

She moved her arm and lit up the room. Pressing herself against the door of the cellar she quickly searched every nook and cranny visible from where she stood. The room was small, no closets or cupboards, just a small wooden table in front of the safe and the metal door leading out beside it.

The room was empty of any other bodies. Evera breathed out loudly, not realizing she'd been holding her breath. She moved quickly to the safe and looked inside. There was one item but it wasn't the red memory stick Cort asked for. It was a white business card. Dread twisted in the pit of her stomach. She turned it over. It was blank on both sides.

White's calling card. *Impossible!* Icy fear slithered through her veins.

She stuffed the card in her jeans pocket and searched the rest of the room, making sure she wasn't missing something. Her mind was reeling. Adam had been honest with her. Cort wasn't White. But White was here now, somewhere close by.

She needed to move and get to the meadow, now. Slinking quietly to the door, she paused before opening it. Could White being involved have anything to do with her or the Section? Or was it just an unfortunate coincidence? Either way, she was terrified of what could be waiting for her on the other side of the door.

Undoing her bracelet and gripping it in her hands gave her only a small comfort. She wouldn't be much of a threat against someone with a gun.

Pushing the door open quickly it slammed loudly against the outside of the building. She waited, pressed against the side of the wall, for any sound or movement from beyond the door. There was nothing but the sound of her breathing. She crouched low and peeked around the edge of the door, scanning the wide open meadow in front of her. Still no sign of anyone. The air was frigid. She could see the steam from her breath and worried it might give her away.

Scanning the grass, she saw no sign of footprints. The ground was icy and covered with dew. As she started to walk she could see the tracks she was leaving behind. She breathed a sigh of relief. Wherever the thief was, he was long gone from this location. He would have had to come late yesterday or in the middle of the night to avoid leaving his shoe prints on the wet ground.

Regardless, as she looked down the open meadow, the idea of running across it was more than daunting. She would be out in the open and vulnerable for a good twenty seconds before she could reach any cover at the edge of the trees. But she had no choice, Cort would be pulling up any second. She hoped.

That last thought had her running full tilt for the trees at the edge of the clearing. She sped erratically over the slippery grass, hoping that if anyone was tracking her she would be a hard target to get a bead on.

When she reached the safety of the trees she ducked down fast, rolling on the ground. She tucked herself into the grass and shrubs, trying to obscure herself as best as possible. From this vantage point she could survey the meadow and saw no movement or reflections, nothing that would indicate someone was watching her.

The forest was all but silent. There were only small sounds from the wildlife but even they were quieter than usual because of the unexpected cold. Her hands were getting stiffer by the second. She clipped her bracelet back on her wrist so that her fingers wouldn't freeze to the metal. There was a sweater in her bag but she didn't dare move just in case she was wrong about being watched and gave away her position.

Amidst the cold silence she thought she heard the distant sound of an engine. She listened carefully and after a few seconds the sound was louder. It came from behind her. Carefully, she turned from her spot on the forest floor. She was happy to see the dark wetness of a paved road not thirteen feet beyond the trees. This must be the road Cort was talking about. Which would hopefully mean that it was him driving up. She listened, making sure there was just the one vehicle engine. Yes, she was certain she could just hear the one.

It was close but the closer it came the slower it went. He was being cautious and she needed to as well. But it was a struggle not to burst through the trees and run to him.

She could only see the vehicle from the tires down as it slowed, making its way down the last stretch of paved road. It was a dark car, likely the car they had driven in yesterday. It pulled up parallel to the trees, the engine turning off immediately. There was absolute silence for what seemed like an eternity before the driver side door opened.

The open car door was opposite her so she still couldn't see whether or not it was Cort. There was the sound of a pair of shoes on the wet road, making their way to the back of the vehicle. A click by the back end indicated that whoever it was had opened the trunk.

Just as she felt an overwhelming urge to call out to him, a tightness in her gut stopped her. Survival instinct. All the times she had listened to it and it had saved her. Was she absolutely certain this was Cort?

She watched curiously, as a pair of black shoes and black dress pants walked past her hiding spot and opened the front passenger side door. As they were fiddling with something in the front seat she tried in vain to peek through the trees to see if it was Cort's striped shirt perched above the black pants. He'd been wearing dark pants and dark shoes when he'd left this morning but she couldn't be sure these belonged to him.

Suddenly, the person backed away from the passenger door with a grunt and the lower half of a man's body hit the blacktop. Evera stared in shock as the man in black lugged the body across the road towards the back of the car. The corpse dipped lower suddenly, so the man was dragging the body by the wrists. Evera lay staring into a pair of familiar dead eyes.

The eyes of Jack, Cort's bodyguard.

She stifled a gasp and continued watching as the man hauled the body, legs splayed, across the pavement. Jack's chest was covered in a gory, blood spatter that patterned a close encounter with a pistol. The man in black stopped by the back of the car and started pulling Jack's lifeless body up to the trunk. The shirt was still not visible because the man was wearing a dark sport coat. The weight of the body being pitched into the trunk made the back end of the car shudder. The trunk closed with an ominous slam.

Evera concentrated on keeping her breathing quiet and even, pushing back her fear. That couldn't be Cort. But if it wasn't Cort, then where was he? And who was coming for her?

Too many faces spun through her mind, too many possibilities. Garrison? Adam? Someone unknown to her? Or White?

She watched as the man walked slowly down the road in front of her. He was trudging along, his shoulders hunched as if he was injured. There was a small break in the trees about thirty feet ahead of where she was laying.

The black shoes walked through the small pass way and into the open meadow.

CHAPTER 19

Revelations

Evera watched with trepidation as the man in black surveyed the meadow. As he turned to look in her direction she caught his face.

His dark hair in disarray, his blue eyes wild. Cort.

A sob of relief escaped her throat as she rolled out from under the bushes, anxious to get to him. She paused. The look she saw in his eyes stopping her in her tracks. Anguish.

But he didn't see her. He turned his back as he checked the doorway to the dugout. She remembered when he had first walked through the trees, walking as if he had been wounded.

"Cort!" she screamed in terror, running to him. As he turned towards her she saw him holding his chest. Her legs felt like stone and she stumbled. Horrified, she searched his shirt. Her heart seemed to stop its intrinsic beat when she saw the patches of dried blood.

He noticed her in an almost disoriented haze. "Stop!" he choked out, the pain in his voice matching his eyes. "Just stay where you are."

She slowed, confused, her feet moving intuitively towards him.

"I said stop!" he yelled, his voice changing from pain to anger.

She was completely taken aback. "Cort," she soothed, searching around them and seeing no visible threat. "You're hurt, let me come and help you," she persisted, frightened for him.

"Hurt," she heard him mumble, looking down and shaking his head. She took another step towards him.

"I said, don't come any closer," he spoke calmly, his voice deadly. And out of nowhere he raised a gun, aiming it at her chest. "Stay where you are, Evera. Or should I say...Jezebel?" he demanded, his words ice.

She stopped midstride at his last words, the air leaving her lungs in a torrent.

"No," the sound a mournful plea that came from deep in her chest. She clenched her freezing hands, his words burning holes through her heart and lungs. This couldn't happen, not now. She stared as he held the gun on her, his hand steady. His lips were set in a hard, cruel line but the pain in his eyes he couldn't hide from her.

"Cort, it's not what you think," she begged.

"Don't bother," he spit back harshly. "Surely you can't think me such a fool as to believe anything you say ever again?" He glared as if he hated her. She raked her mind for an explanation that he would believe. But she could see by the look in his eyes that it would be too little and much too late.

She remembered the call coming in on the other line just minutes ago. Someone had given her up.

"Let's get this over with. Just give it to me and we can be done with each other." The bitterness in his voice was like teeth tearing through her as he slowly advanced. He never took his eyes off her. She didn't need to feel his emotions to know that he no longer trusted her.

"I said give it to me! Throw it on the ground by my feet," his voice so beyond anger it was shaking.

His ultimatum finally registered amidst her grief. "Give you what?" she asked in confusion. She searched her afflicted mind for what it was he wanted from her.

"You know exactly what!" he barked. "Give me the stick, now," he commanded, his thumb flicking to release the gun's safety. The polished Springfield caught the sun, glinting a foreboding ray of light in her direction.

"The memory stick..." she mouthed to herself. The one thing she could tame him with. Her eyes fluttered down to her cold, empty hands. "I don't have it," her voice small and frightened. Even as she said the words she knew he wouldn't believe her.

He froze her with a glare so vicious and black she could sense the heat from the rage burning out of him.

"Do not make the mistake of lying to me. I believe I'm the only one here with a gun," he reminded, closing in. "And I can search you just as easily when you're dead," he threatened. "And even then, I can choose to make it quick and easy or I can draw it out, believe me." And she did. From this distance she could see blood on the barrel of his gun. Her eyes wavered momentarily to the red patches on his shirt. He was the one who shot Jack.

"Honestly, I don't have it," she repeated, reaching her hand in a placating gesture. He moved a step closer and stretched out the arm holding the Croatian pistol. She was familiar with that gun. Knew its potential for accuracy and devastation.

"Please, believe me," she whispered. "I would give it to you if I did." She was talking quickly, trying to fit in her explanation before he lost it and pulled the trigger. "When I got to the cold storage cellar the safe door was already open. It was empty except for a blank business card." She started reaching towards her pocket with the paper in it, keeping her eyes on Cort the entire time.

It was unlikely he would believe her story. Not unless he knew anything about White.

She pulled the card slowly from her pocket and reached it towards him, keeping her feet firmly planted in place. He moved smoothly forward, roughly snatching the card from her shaking fingers and paced back.

She watched as the expression on his face changed from anger to one of fear. He flipped the card over several times before looking up at her. He recognized the calling card. He quickly rearranged his features, the anger back. But she had already seen his reaction to White's card.

He sneered at her then, a cold hateful look that doubled the sickness inside her.

"Looks as though you didn't get what you were after either," he said smugly, believing she'd been after information this whole time. "It hurts doesn't it," he insisted, his harsh facade cracking as pain bled into his voice. "Betrayal."

He misinterpreted the suffering in her eyes, it was all for him. It didn't matter which of her enemies had turned her in. The damage was terminal. Cords of thorns twisted around her heart.

"Cort," she pleaded, "I never meant to hurt you. I should have told you the truth when I realized my feelings for you had changed, I just—"

"Enough!" he shouted, taking a step closer. "Your business is deception. And you're really good at your job, I'll give you that." When he closed the distance between them she could feel his emotions, his torture was a searing fire against her skin. For her lack of foresight, she was burning in misery with him.

"You're doing exactly what they told me you would do. Lie and manipulate your way out of this," he said, his voice clear and quiet.

An electric chill traveled across her skin as his words sunk in. She couldn't keep the shock from transforming her face. He'd said betrayal, a second ago. That would have to mean it was someone close. Someone she knew.

"Oh yes, they told me all about you. Your script, your schemes, doing whatever you have to. Using your words, your body," he said, looking her over in revulsion. "Anything and everything to get the job done." His words were cutting but she could feel his emotions balancing on the edge of love and hate.

The person who gave her up hadn't just wanted her exposed. If they were giving Cort this kind of information then they knew all about her. It would have to be someone from the Section, and that someone wanted her dead.

He shook his head in disbelief. "I have to hand it to you," he continued, "you had me completely fooled. I actually believed..." his voice trailed off as he looked down at the ground, hiding his eyes from her. But she could still feel him. His suffering endless.

She longed to reach for him, to find some way to convince him that her feelings had been true all along.

He looked up at her suddenly, the steel back in his eyes. "This is what I get for being fool enough to trust. I end up bested by a murdering whore," he said bitterly.

Fire flashed down her spine at his words, melting the ice and making way for her anger. She loved him but she hated how he saw her.

He shook his head in disbelief. "I can't believe that my father was right all along. All this time I was being played and I never had a clue. Shame on me. So how were you going to do me, huh? Use your garrote after you got your prize and slay me while my back was turned?" he asked, gesturing towards her wrist and the bracelet wrapped securely around it. "I should have known right from the beginning not to mess with damaged goods," he concluded spitefully.

Her mouth dropped open at his hypocritical statement. "Last time I checked you were just as damaged and fucked up as I am, you self-righteous son of a bitch." She knew it was dangerous to taunt him but she couldn't stop herself despite the gun pointed at her chest.

He grinned coldly at her. "Perhaps," he said calmly. "But at least I'm not prostituting myself out and calling it justice. Although, I imagine it's not your fault," he said, leading, a darkness entering his eyes. "Once you've been forced to give it up in the first place, I imagine it's hard to turn it off."

His words lashed out at her like a whip, the sting of it cutting into her soul as she stared at him, annihilated. Nothing he said could have hurt her more. There was no room for words, her throat too choked with anger. She could do nothing but glare at him with a poison she was certain should burn him where he stood.

"Hit a nerve, did I?" he asked, taunting her cruelly. "Oh yes, they told me everything about you," he informed as he met her stare unflinchingly. And she knew, in that second their eyes connected, everything they'd shared was over. She said nothing, not wanting to give him the satisfaction of knowing how deeply he'd just cut her.

He smiled with his lips only, his eyes turning threatening. He'd moved closer to her during their conversation and she became terrifyingly aware of how close the muzzle of the gun was to her body.

"Not in the mood for conversation?" he paused, tilting his head. His caustic, obsidian eyes sizing her up. "What do I do with you now? Now that you've given me away and brought my enemies down on me," he asked coolly.

He waited, seemingly patient for her to answer. But Evera could feel the coiled tension in every cell of his body. She had no answer. No information in which to dilute his rage. She closed her eyes, breaking their visual showdown and took a deep breath.

Her head cleared even though the agony in her heart was asphyxiating. It was over. And suddenly she remembered everything she knew of Cort, the kind of ruthless man he was. The person she'd stopped seeing when she'd fallen for him. She kept those thoughts foremost in her mind and opened her eyes to his waiting glare. His demeanor was one of patient fury. It wouldn't matter what she said, she wouldn't be able to stop what was coming. Because they both knew what he was going to do with her.

But as she looked at him for the last time she couldn't help but see the person he'd become to her. She held her lips and said nothing, knowing that her feelings for him were plain on her face.

His gaze faltered as he looked at her. "You know I can't let you go. The second I walk away you'll take me down. And I never leave loose ends. Never." He seemed to want to justify his actions to himself. She could feel his reluctance to harm her surfacing amidst his anger.

She watched as his face suddenly changed and crumbled. He grabbed his head in his hands, taking the gun off her for the first time since their confrontation. "I loved you," he rasped weakly, staring down at the cold ground.

His face flashed back to her. "I loved you!" he seethed, his body trembling.

She stared back, helpless. "Cort," his name slipped between her lips before she could stop it.

He shook his head. "No more," he pleaded as he started backing away. The dead eyes looking into hers belonged to someone else. "Words can't save you now. I've already buried you."

The hand holding the gun started to shake as he continued backing away from her, the barrel aimed at her heart. Evera remained silent as she watched him retreat. She saw the outcome in the last glance of his beautiful face...he was a man of his word.

At that moment she knew who she really was. The constant voice that had helped her survive, the person who had been below the surface with her all along. She pulled in one final breath, bracing for the impact.

"Good-bye, Evera," his cold words traveled on the wind, ringing with finality. She returned his unrelenting gaze with a calm glance.

"That's Jezebel to you," she said flatly.

His eyes went dark as midnight, his jaw clenched.

And then he pulled the trigger.

CHAPTER 20

Already Over

Time had become meaningless. She had no idea how long she had been lying on the cold earth. The sun never showed itself behind the dreary clouds so she had no point of reference.

Her blood had slowly stopped seeping between her frozen fingers. She was unsure if the cold was helping clot her wounds or if she was running out of blood itself. She was so cold that she felt frozen to the ground, but the chill had helped alleviate the pain. But just the pain in her body. The fierce agony in her heart was an entirely different story.

When the gun went off she'd been so shocked that the fiery kiss of the bullets had barely registered. She'd counted three shots, and remembered falling to the ground, holding her side as blood spilled between her fingers. She'd glimpsed the look on Cort's face just as her body hit the earth; seen the horror and pain as he gazed back at her. He hadn't gone for the kill shot. She'd seen the conflict in his eyes. He wanted her dead but couldn't bear to witness her death. Or maybe she was wrong and he just wanted her to suffer.

She had been futilely hoping with every passing second that he would return. But he hadn't. He'd left her for dead.

Mired in heartache, the cold and fatigue seemed to be taking over. As hard as she tried to fight off sleep, she couldn't stop herself from drifting. She jerked herself awake in fear as pain ripped through her body. There was a bullet lodged just above her clavicle, one stuck just above her hip bone, and the third and final shot had been in her side. That one had gone through her cleanly, no bones to hinder its progress. It had entered just below her rib cage and had punched a hole out her back. Although the entry site wasn't far into her body she was concerned that the bullet had shredded through her liver. She hadn't been able to see the color of the blood seeping from the wound. Once she'd fallen, her hand had stayed pressed tight against her side hoping to hold in her blood as long as she could.

To what end? She was just prolonging the inevitable. Death would come long before anyone could rescue her. The only person who knew she was laying in this desolate field had put her here in the first place.

Her head foggy and her strength wasted, she was certain she was fading when she heard the voices. These weren't the soft, soothing voices of angels. But then she'd known there'd never be angels waiting to take her away.

The voices were quick and harsh and their direction was confusing. They didn't seem to be coming from up above but from across the field and through the thick trees that separated the field from the house.

Could it be Cort? Maybe he'd changed his mind and come back for her. The feeling of hope shot through her veins like a rush of adrenaline. But if it was him why didn't he come up the road beside her instead of from the direction of the house?

The hope turned to dread and the blood that remained ran icy cold through her veins. There would be no defending against whatever was coming. She watched the forest with terror and anticipation, waiting for someone to break through the trees and reveal her fate.

Then she saw him.

And again, she was proven wrong by the cosmos. It was an angel after all, coming to save her.

He parted the trees holding his gun, confident and ready, by his side. The sun broke free from the clouds in that moment and lit him up like an apparition. He wore a black bulletproof vest over a dark green, long sleeve shirt. His dark fitted pants disappearing into his army-issued combat boots. He strode into the field, searching frantically.

Evera couldn't help but notice every aspect of him in that moment. He moved his arm up swiftly, so both hands were holding the gun as he passed by the dugout door, training the muzzle on it. He was now only yards away from her and she could see that he had pushed the sleeves of his shirt up. She could see the strong muscles of his forearm standing out as he tensed, waiting to use the gun if he needed to. His chiseled jaw was clenched in expectation, his eyes intense and icy blue.

He looked impossibly dangerous and beautiful at the same time. She watched him, her voice lost. Because no image would ever be as profound as at that moment.

"Adam," his name was a breath of salvation between her lips. But her weakened state allowed her no volume. At the same time she said his name he shouted for the rest of the team to come forward, her words lost amongst his command.

She saw several familiar faces from the Section break through the trees, including Stella. Her relief was a heady thing that, along with the blood loss, left her head spinning. She tried in vain to suck in a deep breath and call to Adam, but the pain in her collarbone hindered her and she ended up coughing, sending wracking waves of pain through her body.

Adam turned in her direction, the sound alerting him and he was instantly running towards her.

"Evera!" he shouted, both in relief and acknowledgement.

He sped towards her, his gun by his side forgotten as he slid on his knees to close the final few feet between them.

The second he touched her she felt overwhelmed by his array of emotions; joy, fear, pain, anger, but most of all, love. She let that last sensation melt into her and give her some relief. Adam's hands were everywhere, caressing her face, brushing the hair from her neck to take her pulse, running down her body to check for injuries. His hands were filled with such sweet concern and care that with every touch she felt stronger.

His eyes bored into hers, relief and agony at war in them. "You're alive," he said, his voice breaking at the end.

He was here and it was impossible.

"How, Adam?" She struggled against the pain to speak. "How did you find me?"

"It doesn't matter," he said, stroking her face. "I found you."

"But why?" she choked out, all the pain and guilt for both Adam and Cort made her rescue unconscionable. "After everything I said and everything I did, why would you want to—?"

He interrupted her. "Don't you remember what I told you?" his voice insistent, barely a whisper. "I will always come for you, Evera. Always," and he kissed her tenderly on the forehead.

Suddenly the rest of the team was on top of them. Stella pushed her way through the throng and started to work on Evera. She asked where she'd been shot, how many times and how long she'd been laying there.

Evera managed to answer the first two questions as Stella checked her vital signs and then started rummaging in the first aid kit that she had brought along. The whole time she could feel

Adam's anger escalating, as he started barking orders to the rest of the team. There were four of them and he sent them to check the house now that the surrounding area was secure. He told them they had ten minutes. He stayed put, and she could feel that he had no intention of leaving her side to check for himself.

"I don't know how long I've been here," she answered Stella weakly. "What time is it?"

Stella pulled out several mud patches from the first aid kit and started prepping them. "It's 2:37," she replied.

"I've been here maybe two...two and a half hours," she answered.

She heard Adam suck in a breath. "You've been laying here bleeding for over two hours?" he asked, sounding appalled.

He gripped her face tenderly in his strong, warm hands. "I'm so sorry," he whispered, as he looked into her eyes. "I should have been here sooner. I should have come to Hawaii and finished him off myself before you ever got on that plane." His voice came out raw with pain and remorse.

She was stunned. How could he blame himself when they both knew this was entirely her fault?

"And you don't have to worry about...*him*," he said darkly. There was no mistaking where his anger was directed. "I will hunt Cort down no matter how long it takes. Hunt him down and take him apart piece by piece for what he did to you," he professed, his voice whisper quiet and deadly.

A pain that had nothing to do with her injuries tore through her at his words. The man she still loved—the man that had just tried to kill her—was gone. And now the only other person left that she loved was going to hunt him down and kill him. Or be killed himself.

"Adam, please don't—" she started to beg, her voice rough from the pain and terror of it all.

"I'm sorry," he stopped her. "I shouldn't have said that to you now. Just don't talk, you have to save your strength," he insisted, brushing his hand against her cheek.

"Okay," said Stella, her voice filled with trepidation. "I have the packs ready for the wounds but we're going to have to turn you on your back. I'm sorry, Evera, but this is going to hurt."

"I can handle it," she assured, and clenched her teeth. She wasn't afraid of the pain in her body anymore. It was the pain in her heart that she feared more than anything.

Adam kept his face close, gripping both her upper arms firmly and locked his silver blue eyes with hers. As soon as he started to turn her she felt a tearing sensation in her back and couldn't stop the scream from escaping her lips.

"I'm so sorry," he said hurriedly, his voice as tortured as his emotions.

She lay gasping, a sheen of sweat breaking out all over her body as she shook.

"Your wound was frozen to the ground with your blood," said Stella, as she worked feverishly over the open hole in her back.

"Jesus Christ, Evera," Adam breathed in horror and outrage.

He held her tight, stroking her hair and after a few seconds she could feel the anesthetizing effects of the patch, giving her some relief from the pain. Although the area had gone mostly numb, Evera could still feel it as Stella pressed the last piece of tape alongside the wound.

"Okay," said Stella, her voice all business. "Turn her over, carefully so I can get to the rest of them," she ordered. Her voice was calm but Evera could feel concern reflecting off her.

Adam turned her gently so she was facing up and Stella went to work on her clavicle. She was extremely grateful for the mud patches. They were thick piece of square, gauze-like fabric with small fibers attached and filled with antiseptic and antibiotics. As Stella moved from wound to wound, down the side of her body, she felt more and more numb. Unfortunately, the relief from the pain was clearing a path in her head and the last encounter with Cort was trying to break through. She couldn't afford to let that happen. It would crush her with its agonizing weight and there was no way Adam should have to witness that.

The entire time Stella worked over her body, Adam's eyes never left hers. He watched her desperately as if she would disappear if he looked away. He kept caressing her face and hair, his touch so filled with love for her it was like a balm to her heart. She stared back at him, unable to believe that after everything she'd done and everything she'd said to him, he still wanted her. Wanted her and loved her with a passion and certainty that was almost overwhelming.

Adam broke free from her gaze as the commotion of his team running back through the trees interrupted them. She recognized all of them but knew only one of them by name. Darren, one of the combat trainers who often sparred with Adam, came straight over to them while the rest of the team waited at a respectful distance.

"Searched the premises, took two bodies down, no one of consequence, just wait staff," he said mechanically. Evera felt a prickle of remorse at the thought of the kind women who waited on her this morning being shot down in cold blood. "No sign of any persons or vehicles in the surrounding area. Didn't have time to go through and salvage anything," said Darren regrettably. He'd been with the Section for several years and knew how important it was to not leave possible intel behind. "We might have to come back with more—"

"No," said Adam, cutting him off. "Soak it down and light it up," he finished, turning back to Evera.

"You want to torch it?" asked Darren incredulously.

"Yes," said Adam definitively, staring down into Evera's eyes.

"But we have no idea what kind of information could still be in there," said Darren, pleading his case. "We could be talking about an unbelievable amount of—"

"I said," Adam repeated, his voice going louder with annoyance and frustration, "burn it!"

Darren stood looking at Adam in disbelief as Stella finished dressing the last wound. Evera could see the muscles in Darren's jaw twitching as he mulled over Adam's orders. The crowd of men standing ten feet away watched the exchange with uncertainty.

"Look, I know you're running the show but I can't do this. If Garrison or Jonas finds out we burned down a target's house without searching for potential information my ass is done, man." He seemed uncomfortable defying Adam but more than a little afraid of the consequences from higher up.

"Do you not understand what I'm telling you?" Adam asked, rising to stand and face Darren. They weren't more than a foot apart. Evera could feel his anger even though he was three feet away from her.

"She's been in the house," he said bitterly, referring to Evera. "Her fingerprints, her hair, her DNA. It's everywhere. It needs to be destroyed," he said, glaring down Darren. "I take full responsibility for this mission. I will even light the match, just douse the area and I'll do the rest," he said, waiting for Darren to move.

Darren tried hard to hold Adam's harsh gaze as he folded his arms across his chest in defiance. He pursed his lips and then opened his mouth to protest.

"Do as I say," Adam interrupted, in a quiet, menacing voice, moving closer so their faces were inches apart. "Do as I say, or I will slit your fucking throat in your sleep."

Darren's eyes popped wide as Adam's threat sunk in. He knew enough about Adam, and how he felt about Evera, to know he meant it.

"Yes, sir," he said, his voice shaky. He turned then, "Alright, you heard him. Let's soak the place," he yelled to the rest of the nervous waiting men.

The unit turned and started making their way towards the trees. Darren looked back at Adam. "You got a match?" he asked him, the bitterness from their standoff still apparent in his voice.

"A lighter," Adam said. "You've got three minutes, and Darren?"

"Yeah," Darren said, turning back reluctantly.

"Just take comfort in the fact that I never gave you a choice," said Adam. Then he added, "You can take it out on me the next time we meet in the ring."

"I will," said Darren, as he ran towards the trees to join the rest of the group.

"Three minutes?" asked Stella. "That's not enough time to get back to the van, get the stretcher and take her out of here," she said, looking at Adam skeptically.

"It's fine," said Adam. "I'll carry her." He spoke assertively, leaving no room for argument as he removed his bulletproof vest and kneeled down beside her.

Stella looked at him confused, "But the van's a quarter mile down the drive."

Adam's warm hand brushed the cold sheen of sweat from Evera's forehead. "I said I'll carry her," he said softly, his eyes piercing down into hers. She could feel a sense of relief in him as though he believed she would be okay, his terror subsiding.

"Alright," said Stella in capitulation. "We better get moving then. I'll help you position her so you don't open any of the wounds."

Adam leaned over her as he slid his arms under her legs. His face so close that she could feel his breath against her lips. He paused for a second, the proximity of their mouths distracting him. She could feel how badly he wanted to close the distance between them. Kiss her.

He'd just saved her life. Again. And she loved him. She owed him this one small thing. But he turned his face to look at the ground and sucked in a shaky breath. And then he was lifting her into his arms. He stood carefully so as not to jostle her and waited to pull her close until Stella checked the position of the dressings.

Evera wrapped her arms around his neck, taking care with her injured shoulder, as he pulled her against his chest. His body felt solid and warm, thawing all the parts of her that touched him. They made their way to the path through the trees with Stella following close behind.

As they broke free from the trees she saw the house, looming ominously, bringing forth a rush of feelings that made her cringe.

"Am I hurting you?" Adam asked with concern, having felt her flinch.

"I'm okay," she said, looking up at him and forcing a small smile.

"It's not much farther, just another quarter mile. Can you handle it or do you need some morphine to get you through?" he asked tentatively. He knew how much she despised any drug that altered her mental state.

"I'll make it," she said with certainty. The last thing she needed, on top of everything else, would be to lose control over her mind.

The team was just exiting the house as they made their way to the circular drive. Adam kept walking past the fountain and to the paved pathway leading to the trees. Darren came running towards them, trailing a line of fuel from the container he was holding. The perfume of flowers and grass that filled the air yesterday had been replaced by the bitter, acrid smell of gasoline.

"Everyone's out, it's ready to go," said Darren as he led the line of fuel past Adam's feet.

"Good," said Adam. "Get going to the van, I'll light it," Adam insisted, making good on his promise to take responsibility for the destruction.

Darren nodded and started running down the driveway with the rest of the team.

Adam looked back quickly at Stella. "Go with them, Stella. This one's all on me," he said kindly.

"Alright," she said, affectionately patting Evera on the head and then running to catch up with the rest of the team.

Once the team had gone far enough down the road and through the trees, Adam shifted Evera carefully. He let go of her back, her arms around his neck holding on, and reached into his pocket to pull out a lighter. She recognized the special ops lighter; the kind that you could flick, let go and the flame would still stand.

Adam walked towards the end of the gasoline trail, his back towards the house and ignited the lighter. He tossed the lit flame behind him without ever looking back.

Evera watched over his shoulder as the flame fell and caught the line. A gentle *swoosh* sounding as it travelled across the pavement and up the front stairs. Her eyes stayed focused on the house, unable to look away as the front door caught and was swallowed up by flames. Adam kept walking to the entrance of the driveway. They were now several yards from the house, his pace the same, his arms never seeming to tire.

Then suddenly there was an explosion inside the house, so powerful that it shattered every window, the front door bursting off its hinges. There were several more small bursts of flames, one after another, punching through the roofline of the house. Turning it into an inferno.

A wave of heat and ash crashed into them, burning her eyes and singeing her skin. But still, she couldn't look away. Adam's stride never faltered and he never looked back.

She blinked to clear her vision from the smoke tearing up her eyes. The fire roared as the house became completely engulfed.

Consuming all traces of her...all traces of him.

She tightened her arms around Adam and watched it burn.

First Cut,
Book One of the
Evera Dark Trilogy

Book Two
Coming 2017...

everadark.com

ACKNOWLEDGEMENTS

This story has been a labour of love, anxiety, frustration, self-doubt and absolute bliss! And without the support and encouragement of all the people in my life I never would've come this far. Because I'm trying to stay anonymous, I will not be naming names, but you all know who you are and how much you mean to me.

My family; I love, love, love you all. You are my rocks and my greatest source of strength. Thanks for tolerating my ups and downs and my zoning out between reality and my fantasy world.

To my friends; you are all amazing, gorgeous, brilliant, honest and the best cheerleaders any girl could ask for, thank you so much.

To my editor, S. Khanna, thanks for sticking with me through all the texts, emails and phone calls at all hours. And for believing in my story and helping me turn out a finished product I can't wait to share.

To Marlow, thank you for the beautiful rendering of the bracelet, and for being able to take what was trapped in my mind and make it into reality.

I also want to thank *30 Seconds to Mars*, *Skylar Grey*, and *Red*. Your music pushed me, inspired me, haunted me, and kept me writing long into the night.

And a special pre-emptive thank you to *Ed Sheeran* and *Transviolet* for what's to come...

ABOUT THE AUTHOR

The author, writing as 'S.L. Reid', spent most of her childhood with a book tucked under her arm. These days it's her laptop, as she makes time for novel writing amongst the many other projects in her busy life. She also finds a way to squeeze in her favorite distractions; movies, running, reading (of course) and visits with family and friends. *Evera Dark, First Cut*, is her alias 'S.L. Reid's' debut novel, and book one in the trilogy.

CPSIA information can be obtained
at www.ICGtesting.com
Printed in the USA
LVOW12s1914041116
511709LV00001B/4/P

9 781773 022079